until forever falls

MICAH RILEY

For those who have run—whether from heartache, fear, or the weight of the world—may you one day find the courage to stand still and catch your breath.

This is for the survivors, the fighters, and the ones still searching for home.

Content Warning

Until Forever Falls contains mature themes and subject matter that may not be suitable for all audiences. While this is a work of fiction, it delves into real-life experiences that could be distressing for some readers. Every reader's journey is unique, and I encourage you to take breaks or skip sections if it helps protect your mental health.

Please prioritize your well-being.

If you would like to review potential triggers before reading, a full list—which may contain spoilers—is available on the last page of the book. Above all, I hope this book reminds you that healing is possible and that love—whether in the arms of another or in your own strength—can exist even in the darkest moments.

Locksmith - Sadie Jean

Chasing Shadows - Alex Warren

Silhouette - Caleb Hearn

Stargazing - Myles Smith

broken - Johan Kagen

leave me in the dark - Alexander Stewart

something to remember - Matt Hansen

Couple of Kids - Maggie Linderman

the grudge - Olivia Rodrigo

GRAVITY - Matt Hansen

see you later (ten years) - Jenna Raine

This Love (Taylor's Version) - Taylor Swift

Screw Paris - Chord Overstreet

Memories - Dean Lewis

blame's on me - Alexander Stewart

pieces - Dylan Conrique

Love Her Next - VIOLÀ
wish I loved you in the 90s - Tate McRae
phones in heaven - Sam Tompkins
Dead the Day Ur Gone - Matt Hansen
unbreak - Camylio
Feel Something - Clairo
I Lost Myself - Munn
when you love someone - Alexander Stewart
Hopeless Romantics - James TW
Better Off Without Me - Matt Hansen
The Last Bit Of Us - Dean Lewis
Break My Heart - Matt Hansen
Before You Leave Me - Alex Warren
Better Days - Dermont Kennedy
Carry You Home - Alex Warren
DECLINED - Britton
Little By Little - Myles Smith

ON OFF
Fn
8 15 30 60
4 125
2 250X
1 500
T 1000
B 2000
A 4000
8000
VIEW MODE
+3
+2
+1
0
-1
-2

PROLOGUE

Brooks

THEN

Every step I take away from her feels as though a knife is twisting deeper into my chest, each pounding heartbeat a cruel reminder of what I'm about to lose.

My old Nikes press into the gravel with each step, but I force my eyes to stay fixed ahead, desperately willing myself not to turn around and pull Dylan into my arms.

Time stretches painfully as I approach my truck, each second dragging longer than the last. The parking lot feels endless, mocking me, luring me closer to the moment I'll have to shatter everything I've ever wanted.

Dylan was the dream I never questioned, the forever I never doubted. But everything changed in the span of a few weeks. Now, I have to end it—end us—to protect her.

I can't pull her into the darkness closing in around me. She's barely holding on as it is, and this might be the thing that makes her let go. She deserves a life free from pain, without the grief that will now inevitably follow me wherever I go.

She calls my name, and my stomach immediately churns, bile rising as I brace myself for what I'm about to do. My whole world is collapsing, the future I pictured with her falling apart before my eyes. But this isn't about me—it's about Dylan. It has to be. She deserves more than I can give her now; she deserves someone who can truly stand by her side, through both the highs and the lows. And it's the lows that scare me most. I know what's coming, and I'll take the hit alone before she has to.

Every part of me aches to be selfish.

I want to hold on to her with everything I have and damn the consequences, but I can't.

I love her too much for that.

My hands tremble against the truck door, a desperate struggle to remain steady. The urge to turn back, to steal one last kiss, presses hard—almost impossible to resist. But another kiss would only weave another lie, another thread of false hope. Sometimes the greatest act of love is letting go, even when it tears you apart from the inside out.

Even if I have to break her heart to keep it whole.

1

Dylan

Now

No. No. No.

This isn't happening.

Ten years should've been long enough to bury the memories, to piece together what he shattered and finally move on. An entire decade to forget the boy who tore my heart apart. Familiar as ever, the need to vanish creeps in as I'm crouched behind a ridiculous umbrella, praying that Brooks Holland doesn't see me.

Every effort went into running from my past—from him. Yet, one glance, and I'm back to being that broken, vulnerable girl again—a harsh reminder that the wound he left behind never truly closed. Time didn't fix it. I'm just better at pretending. And now he's here—not the boy I knew, but a man lounging outside the Beauport Hotel in Ogunquit—

miles from the place I swore I'd left behind. *Rockport, Oregon.*

My grip tightens around my camera, knuckles white as I try to steady the tremor in my hands. I wish I could turn back, return to capturing the rocky cliffs and endless ocean, letting the world exist through my viewfinder—but now, the lens feels useless. The damn I built is giving way, and the pain I've kept hidden is breaking through the cracks.

The ocean breeze pulls at my hair, its salty touch a reminder of the last place that felt like home. My heart betrays me, pounding in protest as that old ache brutally resurfaces. I force a deep breath, willing myself to stay calm, to hold back the memories pressing in.

Hiding behind the shade of the umbrella, I steal a quick glance at Brooks—lounging by the water, completely oblivious to my gaze.

He is even more handsome than I remember, his chestnut-brown hair catching the light, hints of gold flickering through it like sparks. Thankfully, his eyes are closed, but I can picture the piercing emerald green hidden beneath his lids. Even his dimples, those *infuriatingly charming* dimples, mock me from afar.

Then there's Aaron, my boyfriend, sprawled out on the cabana just a few feet further, waiting for me. The urge to bolt, to escape back to our room and leave him behind at the pool, is more tempting than I care to admit. I could easily pack my things, come up with some urgent excuse, and disappear before nightfall. But guilt sinks its teeth into me, refusing to let go. Aaron planned this trip to whisk us away from the chaos of the city. I can't abandon him now—especially not because my past refuses to let me go.

With a shaky exhale, I force my legs to move, stepping away

from the safety of my hiding spot and toward the pool. Aaron is unsurprisingly absorbed in a thriller novel. His black hair, flecked with subtle hints of gray, falls across his forehead, and I can't help but smile as I watch him absentmindedly brush it back.

His warm hazel eyes light up as he smiles, the corners crinkling with an easy charm. "I was wondering when you'd come back," he says, marking his place and setting the book aside.

"I'm sorry," I murmur, easing into the chair beside him.

"Did you get a chance to capture any of the views?"

"Yeah." I reply with a smile, though it feels stiff. "It's beautiful here—easy to lose track of time."

Aaron hums in agreement, and my gaze drifts to our joined hands. His thumb glides in slow, soothing circles against my skin, steadying my pulse as I battle the overwhelming urge to turn and face the one man I swore I'd never see again.

"Hey, is everything okay? You seem a little off," he asks, concern seeping into every syllable.

"I'm fine." The lie slips out easily as I tighten my smile, trying to shake the tension clinging to my shoulders. My camera rests beside me, and I glance down at it, my gaze drifting over the edges as if it holds the answers I can't find.

Art has always been my escape, a way to make sense of the world when nothing else could. But after leaving Rockport, picking up a paintbrush felt like looking too closely at the things I wasn't ready to face—so I turned to photography instead. Through my camera, I could hold on to the good without facing the rest. But with Brooks within reach, even the lens feels as though it's exposing too much.

Aaron's fingers skim my cheek, anchoring me for a fleeting moment. "You sure?"

"Mm-hmm." I nod, meeting his gaze. "Just a little tired."

But as soon as he looks away, the undeniable awareness of Brooks' presence pins me in place. His shadow spills over me as he rises, pressing down from behind like a suffocating blanket. I suck in a breath, praying he'll walk away before he notices me, but his unmoving silhouette locks the air around us like cement.

I've made a habit of running…I know that. I've used my camera as both a shield and an excuse over the years. Photography was his passion, and somewhere along the way, I picked it up without even realizing. It was easier than facing who I left behind.

"Dylan?" Aaron prods, his hand squeezing mine.

I exhale sharply, only now realizing I'd been holding it in.

"Are you ready to go?" I ask, springing to my feet and grabbing my camera along with the bag I left on the chair earlier. Brooks' stare is unshakeable, and when he finally speaks, my pulse nearly stops.

"Dill?"

I halt mid-motion, clutching my things, desperate for them to somehow make me vanish. His voice is deeper now, causing an agonizing throb to pulse in my chest. He repeats my name—no nickname this time, just a hesitant, "Dylan Rivers?"

A slow pivot locks us into a gaze that sends a distinct, sharp twist of loss and betrayal through every one of my nerves, urging me to flee.

"Wow, it's really you," he murmurs, awe softening his voice.

Fingers sift through his now short hair, a subtle reminder that time hasn't stood still, and a flicker of disappointment tugs at me.

"It's so good to see you," he says, green eyes shining, unaltered, just as I knew they wouldn't be. I've lived this scene a thousand times in my mind, each time hoping I'd find the words to make him feel even a fraction of what he left me with. But now, with him standing here, close enough to touch, every planned thought dissolves into nothing.

"You too," I say, praying my knees don't buckle from the way he's looking at me.

Aaron stands, his attention shifting between the two of us in obvious confusion. "You two know each other?" Uncertainty tinges his voice, but his curiosity is evident.

"We went to high school together." It's a massive generalization, almost as if I'm denying the connection we once had, but now isn't the time or place to get into specifics.

"Oh," Aaron murmurs, his expression softening as he looks at me. He's never pressed for details about my past—it's something I love about him. But masking my emotions has never been my strong suit, and there's no doubt he notices something's off right now.

The silence stretches between the three of us, suspense building until Brooks ultimately clears his throat. Just as he's about to speak, I make a sharp turn, bolting in the opposite direction.

"Dylan, wait!" Brooks calls after me, but I pick up the pace, the need to distance myself pushing me forward. His voice is a tether I *refuse* to grab. Instead, I run, my pulse pounding in rhythm with the memories I refuse to face.

2

Dylan

"**D**ill, I get it. You'd rather be anywhere else," my twin brother, Beckett, groans from the other side of the truck. "But could you, for once, just help with the boxes?"

Leaning against the tailgate, I steal a quick glance his way, meeting his eyes for a second before returning to my phone. It's not him that's the problem. But I've learned the hard way—if Mom thinks I'm adjusting, she'll start pretending this move is permanent.

"Dylan!" his voice rises, exasperated. "I just busted my ass at football tryouts. If you don't stop standing there like a useless sack of shit, every box with your name on it is going straight in the trash."

Letting out an exaggerated groan, I all but slam my phone into the back pocket of my jeans. "Happy now, KitKat?" I huff, grabbing the one box with my name on it. "Wouldn't want you to strain yourself with *all* my stuff."

Trudging inside, the cardboard digs into my arms as I search for my so-called "new bedroom." All thanks to Mom and her impulsive romance with some random trucker she met at a Kum & Go. One look, a few corny texts, and suddenly we're packed up and dragged against our will to this godforsaken town in Oregon.

Resentment simmers, growing more intense with every second I'm here. Eight months—eight *torturous* months—stand between me and graduation, the only thing that will finally allow me to claw my way out of here. I'll take any escape route necessary to get away from her.

My footsteps echo down the narrow hallway, the sound amplifying the creak of the worn linoleum. Peeling wallpaper curls at the edges, sneering at my forced arrival. At the end, the door to my new room scrapes open, revealing a cramped, bare space with a mattress shoved against the far corner. I had low expectations, and somehow, it still disappoints.

The box lands with a thud as I instinctively grab my sketchbook out of it. Sprawled across the bed, I let my pencil carve out my frustration, anger bleeding into every jagged stroke.

Getting ripped away at the start of senior year would be my luck. I'm not exactly a social butterfly—flying under the radar has always been safer. The idea of being the new kid again sounds about as fun as a root canal.

The sudden clash of voices outside my door snaps me to attention, my ears straining to pick up the words.

"You've never cared about what we wanted!" Beckett's voice tears through the small house, each syllable hitting like a hammer. "You dragged us halfway across the country for your new boyfriend! It's always about you!"

"Don't you dare turn this on me!" Mom fires back. "We're here because I'm trying to build a better life for us! You and your sister never appreciate the sacrifices I make!"

"Sacrifices?" Beckett scoffs. "You call ditching everything for some guy you barely know and dragging us along a 'sacrifice'? Real noble of you, Mom. Bravo."

Oh, lovely. As if today wasn't bad enough. If there's one thing Beckett and I excel at, it's setting Mom off—though, to be fair, she usually deserves it. The problem is, no matter who starts it, I'm always the one who takes the worst of it—before, during, and long after the fight is over.

Slipping my sketchbook out of sight, I cross the room in a few quick strides and test the window latch—it's loose. With a shove, it drags open with a reluctant scrape, and thankfully, the lack of a screen makes slipping outside easy. Dropping down into the overgrown grass, my black high-tops sink into damp earth as my footsteps carry me briskly toward the cracked pavement.

Small, weather-worn houses line the street, their lawns surrendered to wild weeds. Time slips by as the subdued neighborhood gives way to bustling sidewalks, the scenery shifting from worn-out to charming, with quaint storefronts dotting the street—a surprisingly small reminder of what used to be home amid this rundown town.

Nearly everything is shut down for the night, but the glow of a diner ahead stands out. The neon *Ruby's* sign buzzes in bright red, casting a warm glow against the pavement. My stomach clenches, making the decision for me as I slip inside.

The scent of fresh coffee and hushed conversations fill the space as I enter. At a nearby booth, a boy with golden-brown hair and piercing green eyes glances up, his gaze meeting mine for a heartbeat before turning back to his friends. Ignoring the quick, erratic beat of my heart, I make my way to the counter.

"Well, hey there, sweetie. What can I get you?" the woman behind the counter asks, her smile as warm as the diner's glowing lights.

"Oh, um…" My eyes dart across the menu plastered to the wall, searching for something to settle on. "A milkshake sounds good. Any suggestions?"

"Well, if you're a chocolate lover, the brownie batter's a favorite," she replies, beaming happily.

"Yeah…that sounds good. I'll take it." Returning her smile, I reach into my jeans and hand over a couple of crumpled bills. "Thanks." There's a sincerity in her that suggests she's the kind of person everyone in this town probably adores.

Before long, the milkshake is handed over, and the first sip hits my tongue, calming me and pushing everything else to the back of my mind. Turning to go, I meet the same boy's stare once more, his friends falling silent. Their eyes follow as I step through the door, the evening air closing in around me.

"Where have you been?"

My mother's voice lashes out as soon as I enter the house, eyes narrowed with a look that could set me ablaze. Why didn't I think to use the damn window again?

"Out for a walk," I respond, casually drifting toward the hallway. I know where this conversation is headed, and if I move fast enough, I might slip away before it escalates.

"I asked you a fucking question. 'A walk' isn't an answer," she snaps, her footsteps closing in behind me.

I quicken my pace. "I went for a walk, found a diner, and grabbed a milkshake. Why are you so wound up, Denise? Jesus."

She scoffs, her tone dripping with disdain. "Excuse me? You wanna try that again?"

"Oh my God. What's your deal today? We just got here. You'd think you'd be in a happier mood."

I don't need to see her face to know she's livid. "My deal? You and your damn brother are 'my deal,' Dylan." Her voice shakes with rage, growing louder as I reach my room. "You two are going to put me into an early grave, I swear to fucking God."

Gripping the edge of my door, my knuckles turn white. "*Right*, it's totally our fault you're on a fast track to an early grave, not your own decisions," I retort, sarcasm dripping with the sting of acid, baiting her further.

The flash of shock in her eyes is immediately overtaken by rage. I probably should've kept my mouth shut—but honestly, I don't care anymore.

"What the hell did you just say to me?" she demands, stepping closer until her breath warms my face. She knows exactly what I'm implying, but denial is the lifeblood of addiction. The addict has to keep lying to themselves to maintain the cycle.

Her hand shoots up, aiming to slap me, but I catch her wrist just in time. I hold it for a split second before letting go and slamming my door shut with a resounding thud. I'll deal with the repercussions later.

"You know what? Greg's coming home soon." Her clipped tone leaves no room for debate. "So, you and your brother better get your fucking act together, or else you won't like the consequences." She throws out the threat, but I know it's just her way of deflecting—her alcoholism is the real issue, not me.

"Whatever you say, Your Majesty!" I shout back, leaning against the door and releasing a long, shaky breath. As her footsteps retreat down the hallway, I stare up at the ceiling, willing my heartbeat to slow.

I startle at the sound of my brother's voice outside my door. Slowly, I open it a sliver to face him.

"Dill, some of the guys from football tryouts invited me to a bonfire tonight. You should come along—get away from Mom," Beckett suggests, clearly hoping to convince me.

I absentmindedly twirl a curl, trying to seem uninterested. "Oh, I see. And what makes you think I'm free tonight, huh?"

Beckett's laughter is effortless, his grin widening as if he's enjoying some inside joke. "Quit being a brat, Dill. We just got here. I know you haven't met anyone yet. Come on, they seem cool. It could be fun."

"Oh, please. You've known them for, what, a day? Let's not get ahead of ourselves." I prop myself against the door frame, already uninterested in the thought of mingling with a bunch of athletes I don't care about.

"Whatever. Stay holed up alone in this dump, pouting," Becks says with a dismissive wave.

"Fine, I'll go." I give in. "But only to avoid being around when whatever his name is gets here." Neither choice is ideal, but tagging along with my brother beats being left alone with Mom.

Beckett snorts. "It's Greg, Dylan. You know that."

"KitKat, I couldn't care less what his name is. I'm not sticking around here longer than I have to. Greg and Denise can ride off into the sunset together and never speak to me again, for all I care."

"First off, don't call me that. Second, could you maybe dial down the drama for once?" Becks groans, frustration evident as he thumps his hand against the doorframe before turning to leave. "Be ready to go in ten minutes, or I'm leaving your ass here."

I smirk, knowing exactly how much he *loves* the nickname. It started back home, thanks to Miss Patty, the little old lady who ran the food bank. She had a habit of calling Beckett 'eye candy' whenever he stopped by. Naturally, I ran with it. He's been KitKat ever since.

I flip him off in response, but I'm too slow. My middle finger meets the back of his head as he strides away.

3

Brooks

Football practice is the usual grind: the sound of cleats hitting the turf, Coach Tyler's sharp whistle cutting through the air, the sting of sweat running down the back of my neck. Routine. But today feels different.

I jog into position as the new guy steps onto the field. Beckett Rivers. His name has been floating around the locker room, and some of the guys joke that he looks too "soft" to try out for the team. But the second I saw him throw, all those jokes disappeared.

I'd bet he's been playing his whole life—he has a natural talent. His grip on the ball is confident, his release smooth. Every pass spirals clean through the air, hitting his targets with pinpoint accuracy.

Coach Tyler calls for a few reps, and I line up as his receiver. The chemistry between us clicks immediately. Beckett drops back, eyes scanning the field before launching a perfect pass. I barely have to adjust before snatching the ball mid-stride and taking off toward the end zone.

Removing my helmet, I sling it under my arm and walk toward him, amusement flickering across my face.

"Not bad," I say, offering a quick nod. "You ever think about playing varsity? We could use a solid QB."

Beckett wipes the sweat from his forehead with the back of his hand, then shoots me a sly grin. "That's the plan, Holland."

"Coach Tyler would be insane not to put you on the team," I reply, chuckling as I give him a light push. "Hey, you know what? We're all heading to a bonfire later. You should come. Everyone's gonna be there."

Beckett raises an eyebrow, clearly weighing the offer. "You sure?"

"Why not?" I shrug, motioning toward the team. "It's a good way to meet everyone. Plus, you'll fit right in."

"Alright, I'll think about it," Beckett says, the subtle tip of his head giving me the impression that he's not about to pass up an invitation.

I jog over near the bench, grabbing my phone before heading back. Holding it out to him, I nod. "Here—put your number in. I'll text you where we're meeting."

He takes it, punching in his number before handing it back. "Dope, can't wait."

With practice wrapped up and a quick shower behind me, I grab my gear and nod toward Graham and Miles, signaling them to follow me to Ruby's—our usual post-practice spot.

The bell above the door jingles as we walk in, and the familiar smell of greasy food and fresh coffee hits me. The place isn't packed, but it's not empty either. A few locals are scattered around, either chatting or reading the paper.

We slide into our usual corner booth, order our burgers, and settle in. But then, the soft thud of the door pulls my attention, and I glance up.

That's when I see her.

The owner greets her warmly, and something tightens in my chest. She tilts her head slightly, eyes scanning the menu, and I can't look away from the way her dark curls sway with every subtle movement. I force my focus back to Graham and Miles, determined to stay present, but it's no use. My gaze slips back to her, catching fleeting glances when she's not looking.

Finally, she turns, milkshake in hand, and in an instant, our eyes meet. Time stutters, and for a split second, I'm paralyzed—words hover on the tip of my tongue, but they won't come. And before I can make a sound, she's gone, slipping away as if the moment never happened.

I distract myself with my fries, but the curiosity continues to gnaw at me, making it hard to focus. The guys talk, but their words fade into the background, my mind too preoccupied. There's an inexplicable pull toward her, one I can't get rid of, even without knowing who she is. It's like she's stamped herself onto my soul, a mark that won't fade, even if our paths never cross again.

Shoving the thought aside, I toss a few bucks on the table for a tip and push myself up from the booth, heading out with the rest of the guys.

When I arrive back home, the house is quiet, save for the low hum of the television in the living room. My dad is there, sprawled out in his usual chair, a half-empty beer resting on the armrest. He glances up as I walk in, turning the volume down, as if trying to make our conversation less awkward.

"Brooks," he queries with a head tilt, his gaze discerning, even beneath the relaxed expression. "Good practice?"

"Yeah, it was solid," I reply, setting my bag down by the door.

After sizing me up for a beat, he takes a swig of his beer. "Been thinkin'," he begins, leaning forward slightly, "you should come by the site with me tomorrow. Start learning a bit more of the ropes. Won't be long 'til you're out of school, y'know. Good time to get serious about your future."

This isn't the first time he's brought this up. My dad's construction business is his pride and joy, and he's always expected me to take it over someday. I know it means a lot to him, but the idea of settling into a job in construction—my whole life mapped out in this town, doing the same thing he did—makes everything around me feel smaller, as if there's no room left for me.

"I don't know, Dad," I say, aiming to keep my tone casual. "I mean, maybe…just not tomorrow. I've got a ton of homework."

He grunts, clearly not thrilled with my answer. "Football is fine, but it's not a career, Brooks. You've got a good head on your shoulders, but college ball? That's a long shot. College ain't for everyone. Just think about it, alright?"

Of course, that's all he thinks I'd want to go to college for—never mind my actual interests. I nod, though, hoping that'll be enough to end the conversation. "Alright. I'll think about it."

I head to my room and quickly pull off my shirt, the cool air hitting my skin as I slip into my favorite hoodie. It's the type of comfort I don't always realize I need until I'm wearing it. I grab a pair of jeans from the pile on the floor—nothing special, just the ones that fit right—and run a hand through my hair. Within minutes, I'm grabbing my keys and heading back out to my truck, pushing the conversation with my dad out of my mind.

By the time I arrive at the beach, the bonfire is already in full swing. Someone has set up a couple of speakers, and the music mixes with the sound of the waves hitting the shore. Groups of people are scattered around, laughing, talking, some with drinks in hand. A few guys are setting up makeshift seats out of driftwood and rocks.

"Brooks!" Colt's voice carries over the fire, calling me over with a firm grip on his red Solo cup. He brings the same infectious energy to practice as he does everywhere else. "'Bout time you showed up!"

"Couldn't miss it, could I?" I reply, clapping him on the back.

"Hell yeah," Colt smirks, tossing me a beer. "You see the new kid today? Man, we're gonna have to step up our game."

Popping the tab, I take a sip, casually glancing around the beach to check if Beckett has shown up yet. "Yeah, he's got some skill. I think the team could really use someone with his ability."

"We'll see. The team's solid this year, but Coach is a hardass. Hope he can keep up."

As we talk, I catch sight of Chloe Vance moving toward us through the swarm of people. She's dressed up more than usual for a beach party—an off-the-shoulder, flowy white blouse, paired with a denim skirt and wedges. Her blonde hair shimmers in the firelight, the loose waves bouncing as she walks. It's been a while since we broke up, but she still manages to turn up at every party I go to.

She beams when she reaches us, her mood clearly lifted. "Brooks, I was hoping you'd come."

"Didn't realize I was in such high demand," I tease, aiming for a lighthearted tone. The last thing I need is any misunderstandings tonight. I'm not here for her.

She inches forward, her smile never faltering. "Wanna go grab a drink? Just you and me?"

I stall just long enough for Colt's amusement to grow. Chloe is hard to shake sometimes, and I know she still holds on to the hope we'll get back together. "Uh, maybe in a bit," I say, sounding more nonchalant than I feel. "I just got here."

A frown shadows her expression, but with a reluctant nod, she acknowledges it. "Alright. Don't keep me waiting too long." She bites her lip, as if debating whether to stay, then finally gives me one last look before retreating to find her friends.

Colt bursts into laughter as soon as she's out of earshot. "Dude, she's still got it bad. You know she's not giving up anytime soon, right?"

I sigh, shaking my head. "Yeah, well, I learned my lesson the first time."

Colt claps me on the shoulder. "You dodged a bullet if you ask me," he says before spotting someone across the beach and jogging off without another word.

I barely acknowledge it, my focus drifting as Miles steps up beside me.

"Tell me that wasn't as painful as it looked," he mutters.

I huff out a laugh. "Trust me, it was worse."

Miles shakes his head, but before he can say anything else, my attention snags on two figures beyond the edge of the sand. Beckett has just shown up—and he's not alone. I zone in on the girl beside him. Even in the low light, I recognize her from the diner—black curls framing light blue eyes that make it impossible to tell what she's thinking. Then it clicks. The resemblance between her and Beckett is undeniable. Their shared features, the way they move—it's obvious. They're siblings.

I elbow Miles, signaling toward them. "Yo, Beckett is here—and he brought someone along."

Miles casts a quick glance, intrigue lighting up his expression. "Oh shit, didn't expect that."

"Yeah…she was at Ruby's earlier." I try to sound indifferent, but the longer I look, the harder it is to ignore the feeling creeping under my skin.

Graham steps up beside us, catching the tail end of the conversation. "Who are we talking about?"

I gesture subtly toward Beckett and his sister, and the three of us weave through the crowd, dodging groups of people sprawled out on blankets and huddled around coolers. Beckett spots us approaching and raises a hand in greeting, a grin spreading across his face. His sister, however, seems a little more reserved. She scans me, then the others, as if she's already sizing us up.

And I'd be lying if I said I wasn't hoping to pass the test.

4

Dylan

The bonfire crackles, sending flickering shadows over the beach as Beckett and I arrive. The soft glow highlights clusters of people, their laughter and easy conversation making it feel like everyone here has known each other forever. I trail after my brother, willing away the nerves that crept in the moment we hit the sand. Maybe enduring an evening with Mom and her new boyfriend would've been the easier choice.

Beckett catches my hesitation and nudges me forward, grinning. He knows me too well. I'd rather be alone, sketching or painting, than stuck making small talk with strangers.

"Yo, appreciate the invite," he calls out as a few guys approach. "Figured I'd bring my twin sister along. Hope that's cool."

I glance up just as one of the guys looks over, and my breath catches. It's him—the boy from the diner. He barely acknowledged me then, but somehow, it was enough to set my nerves alight.

His gaze locks onto mine, and for a moment, the noise, the fire, the entire beach fades away.

Beckett gestures loosely to the group. "Dylan, this is Graham and Miles," he says, but the names barely register. "And that's Brooks—"

There's an intensity in his stare, a natural self-assurance that sends my heart racing. He's tall, effortlessly magnetic, and the way he carries himself—laid-back yet commanding—sets him apart, even in a crowd.

Brooks narrows his eyes slightly, as if he's trying to place me, and suddenly, it feels like the whole world is watching us.

"Not a problem at all," he comments, a dimpled smile spreading slowly across his face—one that feels meant just for me. Rosy pink blooms across my cheeks, and I pray the blush isn't as obvious as it feels.

The moment unfortunately breaks when one of the other guys— Miles, I think Becks said—speaks up. "You two thirsty?"

"Hell yeah," Beckett drawls, pulling me in with a relaxed arm around my shoulder. "What do you have?"

"Not much—just beer, beer, and..." Miles snorts, rummaging through the cooler before tossing two cans our way with a chuckle. "More beer. But don't worry, it's good stuff."

"Thanks," I mumble, accepting the drink and forcing a smile. My eyes immediately flick up to Beckett. "Becks, promise me you won't overdo it tonight. You know I can't drive your truck home."

Beckett groans, tossing his head back. "I'll be fine, Dill. Relax." He gives my shoulder a reassuring squeeze before wandering off with his new teammates.

I watch them walk away, feeling a bit out of place amidst all the unfamiliar faces. I decide to drift down the beach, letting the soothing rhythm of the waves and distant laughter fade into the background as I approach the shoreline.

Lowering myself onto the untouched sand, my toes press into the soft grains and a slow breath slips free. The beer Miles handed over pops open with a soft hiss, releasing a cool bitterness that mixes with the warmth of the evening air—a small but welcome escape.

The stillness breaks as a low voice calls out, startling me. "Hey, why did you sneak off?" Brooks eases down beside me, his broad shoulders slightly hunched beneath a well-worn dark-gray hoodie.

"Parties aren't really my scene," I offer cautiously. "I came to keep an eye on my brother and to get a break from…everything."

"I'm glad you did. Saw you at Ruby's earlier and was hoping we'd run into each other again."

Bringing the can to my lips, I stall, eyes fixed on the rolling waves rather than his.

"Is that so?"

Brooks lets out a laugh, a rough, reluctant sound that feels like it's not something he gives away lightly. "Yeah. Plus the view's a lot more interesting over here."

Small talk has never felt so intimidating. Before moving, every interaction was predictable—there was never any need to second-guess myself or try to fit in. Being alone had been a choice, one that felt safe, unlike the whirlwind of Beckett's social life. That safety had been necessary, a layer of control after what happened—something I've kept hidden, even from my twin.

"So, what's there to do around here besides sit on the beach and drink?" I try to keep my question firm, but the nervousness still creeps in.

"Well, this isn't the most exciting place to live," He shoots me a crooked grin before looking back towards the fire, the movement effortlessly drawing my own eyes there too. "You're looking at the best of it, unfortunately."

I take in the flames, as if their crackling warmth could somehow dissipate the nerves building inside me. Back home, I'd never wanted to be a part of the parties, the crowds. But here, away from everything familiar, it's hard to tell if the distance I've always kept is out of choice…or fear.

I tuck my knees up slightly, brushing my hands over them as I reposition. "So I have to leave town for anything worthwhile, huh?"

"Not unless you enjoy the outdoors," he laughs.

"Hardly," I admit, my voice edged with a quiet exhale. "Guess I'm stuck between getting wasted on the beach or signing up for park ranger duty."

Another small town. Another place I didn't ask to be. I can almost hear my mom's voice, as if moving to these nowhere places is a solution to something. A fresh start, she always says. But all it ever feels like is a dead end. Just another boring town we've bounced through, where nothing changes but the people.

There's a flash of mischief in Brooks' eyes before he stands, his hand outstretched in front of me. "Ah. It's not that bad. Let's go…explore."

Against my better judgement my fingers reluctantly slip into his, and a spark—unexpected and electric—jolts up my arm, catching me off guard. The sand shifts and sinks under my weight as he lifts me up. For a second, I teeter, feeling gravity pull me forward, but his grip tightens around my hand, steadying me. He doesn't look away, his expression hovering between playful defiance and quiet curiosity, as if waiting for me to make the next move. A languid, insistent pulse builds beneath my ribs, like he's holding open a door I hadn't realized was there.

"Oh? Stealing me away already? I must be special. Where exactly are we going?" The question slips free before I can second-guess myself.

He leans in slightly, nudging me with his elbow. "To explore," he repeats, daring me forward. His hand grazes the small of my back, keeping me close as we step further away from the bonfire's glow. The distant laughter and crackling flames fade behind us as we leave the packed sand, weaving through the trees lining the beach. The air grows cooler, thick with the scent of salt and seaweed, and the night feels quieter here—untouched.

Our steps fall in sync, the proximity between us comfortable, until the trees thin, and a towering silhouette looms ahead—an old building, worn and crumbling, half-concealed by overgrown grass. It stands like a forgotten relic, eerie in the moonlight, as if time abandoned it long ago.

My interest piques, and I glance toward it. "What's this place?"

His brows knit together as he studies the building. "A vacant church, I think?"

"Think the door opens?"

The idea of going inside surprises me, but my pulse betrays the thrill starting to take root. Back home, I never would've imagined walking off with someone like him, let alone into a place like this. But here, it feels like I'm testing my limits.

Brooks lets out a laugh, glancing back over his shoulder as if considering an escape route. "You're kidding, right? Not a chance."

"Why not?" My teeth catch the inside of my cheek as I struggle to keep a straight face. "Are you scared?"

He lets out a breath, ruffling his hair anxiously, though I can tell he's trying not to smile. "No."

"Then what's stopping you?"

Brooks eyes me with an exasperated look, his voice flat. "Because it looks like it'll collapse if we so much as sneeze on it."

"Come on, Brooks. Live a little—you said we were here to explore."

He shakes his head, a reluctant half-smile finally breaking through. "Alright, fine. But if I die, I'm haunting you. *Forever.*"

I smother a laugh with my palm, doing my best to keep it contained. "Deal."

We tread lightly, broken bricks shifting beneath us, twisted weeds brushing against our legs. The closer we get, the more details emerge in the moonlight—cracked windows, faded paint, and a set of heavy double doors, worn from years of harsh weather. It's quiet—the kind of silence that feels ancient. As we reach the entrance, Brooks' eyes flicker in my direction, a wariness hidden beneath his curiosity.

"Still think this is a good idea?" he asks, the tease in his voice undercut by genuine hesitation.

Instead of answering, I reach for the rusted door handle, pulling with more confidence than I feel. The wood moans under the pressure, opening into the dim, cavernous space of the church's interior. A cold draft sweeps past us, stirring the scent of damp wood and dust. Brooks edges closer, his shoulder bumping mine as we continue walking.

"Wow," I breathe, taking in the broken pews lined up in neat, ominous rows, each shrouded in debris. Light filters through gaps in the roof, casting a silvery glow over the space. Part of me wonders how many people once gathered here, sitting in these very benches, finding solace in something bigger than themselves.

The two of us maneuver our way through the building, drawn deeper in. I can't help but notice how Brooks' hand hovers near mine, as if he's ready to catch me if I fall, even though the ground is firm beneath me. Trailing a finger along the edge of a seat, grime coats my fingertips. In another life, maybe I would've felt at home in a place like this—somewhere that would've felt like a foundation instead of a question. Whatever version of me that might've belonged here disappeared ages ago, taking any real sense of safety with it.

"So, what brought you to Rockport?"

His question lands unexpectedly, making me rethink what I'm willing to share. Some things are meant to be unpacked over time—not dumped onto someone you just met. "My mom thought change would be good for us." It's the simple version, one that doesn't invite follow-ups, so I go with it. "What about you? Have you always lived here?"

"Yup, born and raised. My whole family too."

"Cool," is all I can manage in response. I try to imagine what that would feel like—to be so deeply rooted, to belong. But the thought slips away just as quickly. That kind of security isn't something I've ever known.

"So, what do you think—worth the detour, or should we have stuck with the bonfire?"

My mouth betrays me, tugging into a smile that's too real to hide. "I'd say it was worth it. There's something kind of peaceful about this place—like we've stumbled onto a secret that belongs only to us."

He chuckles, crossing his arms as he leans against a broken pew. "Yeah, I guess it's got its own kind of charm—if you're into that whole haunted vibe."

I square my shoulders, mirroring his stance. "Really? Didn't think you'd be into it."

For a moment, his bravado thins—a tiny fracture in the confidence I assume he wears like armor. "Maybe I like having an excuse to get away."

"Was this your plan all along?" I tease.

"My plan?" he echoes, one eyebrow lifting. "You mean luring you into a creepy, abandoned church late at night?"

"If that was your goal, I'd say you nailed it."

A smirk threatens to form, but the clench of his jaw keeps it at bay. "Not everything is a plan. Sometimes you just find the right place, the right moment."

"And you thought this would be the right moment?"

"I wasn't expecting any of this, actually," he admits, though his voice is a little more serious now. "Maybe the most memorable moments are the ones we never see coming."

I bite my lip, studying him, then glance back toward the entrance, the weight of responsibility pressing down on me. "I should probably get back…make sure my brother hasn't gotten himself into trouble."

"Responsibilities don't stop, huh?" He lets out a quiet breath, clearly trying to mask his disappointment with a shrug.

"Yeah," I reply, my gaze drifting to the door, as if it might give me permission to stay. "I wish it were easier to just…forget about them."

Reluctantly I take a step back and, of course, my foot catches on a loose floorboard. I lose my balance, and suddenly, everything just… tilts, pitching me forward before I can react. Just before hitting the ground, firm hands grip my waist, halting my descent with unyielding strength. I gasp, the air catching in my throat as I'm pulled upright into Brooks' chest.

His sudden closeness is shocking, and I'm immediately hyper-aware of every inch of him behind me. There's a push and pull in his hold, a mix of settling in and staying alert, like a muscle stretched too far. Then, out of nowhere, an unexpected chill runs through me—the fragile thread of a hidden memory snapping free. Each breath feels like an invitation to the past, and I'm standing on the edge of something I'm not ready to face.

When Brooks finally lets go, the embarrassment hits me full force, and I let out a nervous laugh, doing my best to shake off the overwhelming sensation swirling inside me.

"I'm sorry," I mutter, my voice barely there, as if saying it will somehow make the moment less…awkward.

"Don't be. Are you okay?" He lets his words fall gently, like he's trying to reassure me without saying too much.

"Yeah…I'm fine."

Brooks shifts, his hands slipping into his pockets before stepping toward the door. "Should we head back and see what Beckett is up to?"

There's too much going on inside my head, and I'm unsure of how to act, so I simply nod, trying my best to keep it together.

The walk back to the beach passes in the blink of an eye. I wish I could have stayed, but my mind is still scrambling, desperately trying to regain the calm I've spent years building.

Thankfully, I spot Beckett sitting on the tailgate of a nearby pickup, legs swinging lazily as he watches the bonfire crackle in the distance. As we get closer, he hops down, his cheeks flushed, and I can't help but feel a little guilty for disappearing earlier.

"What the hell, Dylan? Where did you go?"

I open my mouth, but I don't have an answer. How do you explain to your twin the decision to step out of your comfort zone? To wander off with a stranger when you've never been one to care about making friends? It's not a conscious choice, really. It's more like a moment when the familiar starts to feel too small, like you're suffocating in the safety you've built for yourself. So, you take a breath and try something new.

"I just needed some air."

Beckett eyes me, then shifts to Brooks, skepticism written all over his face. "Air? On the beach, really?"

Brooks laughs softly, clearly not rattled by Beckett's question. "We just went for a walk," he says smoothly, his tone friendly despite my brother's accusing glare. "Checked out an old church."

"A church, huh? Sounds pretty sketchy."

Brooks grins, shrugging slightly as he steps back. "You know, it's better than sitting around and doing nothing, right?" He glances over at me. "I'm gonna go find Miles, make sure he's good. You two okay?"

"Yeah," I say quickly, though I'm not entirely sure if I mean it. Beckett's still watching me closely. He takes a step back, crossing his arms over his chest, and I can feel the judgement radiating off of him.

"You're going on walks with people? Did you have a stroke?

I stiffen, irritation creeping in. "I mean…we were just talking, Becks. It's fine. Let's just get home before you're too wasted to drive."

"I'm not wasted," Beckett grumbles, brushing off my concern with a quick wave. "I've only had a few drinks. We're talking about you right now."

"No. We're not," I snap, gripping his arm and steering him toward the truck. "And I'm not taking any chances."

Beckett lets out a breath, offering no resistance as I pull him away to leave. The drive home is somber, broken only by Beckett's half-hearted attempts at small talk, his words fading in and out as he struggles to keep his focus. Truthfully, neither of us is eager to head back, but until we hit eighteen, there's no avoiding it.

The house is a mere outline in the dark ahead of us, emerging lifelessly as we near the driveway. Beckett cuts the engine and leans back, his head resting against the glass as he stares out, lost. His shoulders sag, his posture wilting under the invisible burden of the past few days.

"Thanks for driving," I mutter, more to break the silence than anything else.

Beckett glances at me, his usual teasing expression gone, replaced by something unreadable. "I hate this place, Dill. I know it's only been a day…but we need to get out of here."

"I know. We will, Becks. I promise." My words are meant for him, but I'm secretly trying to convince myself, too. Growing up with Mom has been a blur of constant change—no permanence, no safe space. There's never a moment to stop, to breathe, to *stay*. We're both just waiting for the day we can escape.

Beckett doesn't wait, already halfway to the door before I even have a chance to catch up. I trail behind, the world around us silent, save for the rhythm of our steps on the gravel. He stumbles as he reaches the steps, nearly tripping, and I grab his arm to keep him from toppling over, frustration simmering as he leans his full weight into me.

"Jesus, KitKat, how much did you drink?" I scold. "You shouldn't have driven us home. Do you have a fucking death wish or something?"

"Shut up, Dylan," he snaps, just as I reach for the doorknob. "I told you not to call me that. I'm fine, it was a long day. We're fine. I told you, I've only had a few beers. I'm fine."

"Yeah…how many is a few?" I urge him forward, keeping my grip firm as we slip inside, silently hoping our mother is too lost in whatever bottle she's clinging to tonight to notice.

"I don't know, a couple before we left," he mumbles, swaying as he tries to steady himself.

"A couple? Right. Sounds like it's more than that."

"Fuck off, Dylan," he mutters, leaning heavily against the wall.

"You know…I could just let you faceplant right here. How you went from driving to barely standing is a mystery, but if you tell me to fuck off again, I'll solve it by walking away."

"I'm just tired, Dill."

I huff a laugh and guide him toward his bed. As soon as he lands, he's gone—like someone flipped a switch, his body going slack against the sheets.

"Sorry," he mumbles, his voice thick with sleep, barely lifting his head from the pillow. "Love you."

"I know, Becks," I say softly, tugging the blanket up over him. "Just sleep, okay? Love you too."

5

Dylan

Now

I stand at the ocean's edge, the tide creeping up the sand, inching closer with each pass. Tears threaten, and I swallow hard, forcing them back down, but the tidal wave of memories from Rockport rises, ready to pull me under.

I didn't mean to run—I wasn't trying to. But seeing Brooks hit like a shock to my system, stirring up everything I swore was settled.

Ten years I spent building walls around the past, convincing myself leaving was the right choice—yet here I am, breaking all over again.

Aaron appears beside me, his presence grounding as he pulls me into a hug. I press my face into his chest, the tears spilling freely now, soaking into his shirt while he holds me close.

"Do you want to talk about whatever that was?"

"I…don't think I can right now."

"That's okay. If you ever change your mind, I'm here." With a gentle sweep of his hand, he moves a strand of hair from my face, and a sense of calm begins to spread through me. The sound of the ocean, the distant cry of seagulls—it all fades into the background.

"Want to grab a bite? Maybe get your mind off of it? There's this place I want to take you to—best lobster roll in all of Maine, or so they say." Aaron pulls back slightly and offers me a half-smile. "We could drive up to the lighthouse, maybe rent some bikes. Whatever you want. I'm not picky. Well…except if you suggest skinny-dipping. I'm drawing the line there. The hotel might not appreciate that."

A reluctant laugh escapes me, the tension in my shoulders easing just a fraction. A distraction might be exactly what I need. "Something to eat sounds great, but I need to go back to the room first. I want to shower."

Aaron squeezes my hand. "Sounds like a plan. I'll handle the reservation after I change and meet you in the lobby."

"Okay." I manage a small smile. "Shouldn't take me long."

"Take your time," he says, pressing a quick kiss to my forehead before gently taking my hand in his.

We make our way back to the hotel, and once we're inside our suite, he disappears to quickly change while I head to the bathroom. The sound of the shower and the warmth of the water help ease the ache in my chest, though my mind continues to race. I rush through washing up, swiftly pulling on fresh clothes and battling with my damp hair, trying my best to make it presentable. As I head to the lobby to join Aaron, I stop dead in my tracks.

Near the elevators stands one man, leaning against the wall, his presence lighting up the space like it always does. A sharp sensation pierces my ribs, and I struggle to inhale. I'm certain I'm imagining things—imagining him—until he turns.

And then, like the world is slamming into place with a force I wasn't ready for, the air stills in my lungs.

It's Brooks *fucking* Holland.

Again.

He chuckles at something on his phone, but the sound dies instantly when his gaze flicks up, landing on me—tracing my features like I might disappear if he blinks.

"Dylan." He says my name like a question, like he's trying to convince himself I'm real, that I'm actually standing here after vanishing by the pool.

I freeze. It feels like an eternity before I can even breathe, before I can process the fact that he's here…that we're both in Maine. He shifts slightly, exhaling like he has a thousand things to say but no idea where to start.

"I didn't know if you'd recognize me," he admits. "Um, at the pool." But there's a sadness in his eyes, something that tells me he's speaking of more than the years or distance.

"It's been a long time," I say, finally regaining a little composure.

Brooks acknowledges that with a brief, thoughtful nod, his eyes wary, as if he's not sure how I'll react. "Ten years."

Those two words land between us like a fault line, splitting open the past we never truly buried.

The years have piled up, yet even a lifetime wouldn't be enough to outrun the aftermath of what happened. A decade has passed since I gave my heart to him, and though time has clearly changed us, the past still tugs at me, like it never left.

I stand there, speechless. What do I even say? After I left, I turned my back on love. I turned my back on everything that reminded me of the pain. The idea of letting anyone close again after what he did took longer than I care to admit. He didn't just break my heart; he destroyed the version of me who believed in love, in trust. I spent years guarding myself, afraid I wouldn't survive another betrayal.

Brooks' eyes sweep over me, pausing almost imperceptibly near my mouth. I feel it, even if he doesn't mean for me to.

I start to ask why he's here, but the question forms in my gaze before the words leave my lips.

"I'm staying here…at the Beauport Hotel."

I raise an eyebrow. "I assumed." I mean, the fact he's staying here doesn't surprise me; it's the most obvious explanation. What confuses me is why he's come so far. I can't imagine for a second that he's left Oregon permanently. However, I tuck the question into the back of my mind—some things, I realize, are best left alone.

The elevator dings, its doors sliding open. Brooks steps forward first and holds them for me, his presence surprisingly solid. "What floor?"

"Lobby," I murmur, still trying to find my footing in this strange moment.

He presses the button, and then, after a beat, turns back to look at me. "So, are you coming? To the reunion next weekend?"

The question is deceptively simple yet there's so much more behind it. In the faint sheen of the elevator doors, I catch his eyes on me—searching, waiting. Hope flickers there, or maybe just curiosity. I force my gaze to my own reflection, rooting myself in the present. I am here. No longer the girl who ran, but the woman who never looked back. I try to hold onto that truth, but the past presses in, threatening to close the distance I worked so hard to create.

And now, here he is, standing in front of me, asking if I'll return.

"To Rockport?" I spit out the words, disbelief lacing my tone. "God, no."

"Right," he says, his lips pressing together, trying to hide his reaction, though a shadow of hurt flickers his eyes. "That's too bad. You could visi—"

The elevator lurches to a stop, and as the doors slide open, I sprint forward, desperate for air. For space. A tightness grips me, as if there's not enough oxygen in the room to fill my lungs.

"Wait!" Brooks calls after me, and this time my feet stop moving. I brace myself against a nearby table, spinning around to confront him. I open my mouth, but the command to leave me alone evaporates, hovering on the tip of my tongue. It doesn't come out. His eyes— God, his eyes—are full of something that mirrors desperation, as though he's silently pleading for my attention. I'm immobilized by it.

"Can we talk? Please," he asks, his voice insistent as he inches closer. "Just for a second. There are so many things I need to say to you."

I want to walk away, but my legs won't obey, staying frozen in place for reasons I can't explain. "We're long past talking, Brooks."

"That's not true," he emphasizes, as if he can't bear to let this go. "If you could just hear me out—"

I glance at my watch, more out of habit than any real sense of time. "I can't. Not right now."

He steps closer again, his hands slightly outstretched, like he wants to touch me, but he stops himself.

"When?" he presses. "Just tell me when."

"Never," I snap, my voice rising. "This is crazy. Seeing you again, it's just…wild. I don't even know what to say to you." I try to take a deep breath, but my chest is too tight, too constricted to allow one.

"It's not crazy, Dylan. Crossing paths with you here, so far from home, feels like a sign—this moment was meant to happen."

I'm on the verge of either laughing or exploding. "Home? Rockport isn't my home, and running into you isn't a sign—it's a curse."

Brooks flinches, his eyes shifting downward as he combs a hand through his hair, visibly deflated. "You still hate me that much?"

I shake my head, but the movement feels like I'm trying to rid myself of more than just the question. "It's not hatred, Brooks. It's… it's something more than that."

"Then why are you so determined not to hear me out?" His voice cracks, just a little, like *this* is the one thing he can't seem to understand.

"Hear you out? Now?" A cold, cynical laugh spills out of me. "Ten *years* later? You've got to be kidding me. I begged you, Brooks. *Begged* you to tell me what happened—what changed after—" My voice falters, reluctant to speak the truth, but I force myself to get to the point. "But you were gone before I could even grasp what was happening." I shake my head, the skin bunching around my eyes, a deep crease forming between my brows. "You fucking left when I needed you most."

His expression hardens, but there's a softness in his eyes that doesn't match the way he's holding himself. It's like he's caught between wanting to fix everything and knowing he might never get the chance.

"I needed you too," Brooks says, his voice tight, almost defensive. "More than you even know."

My next words are cut short as Aaron rounds the corner, and instinctively, I take a step away from Brooks.

"Hey, didn't mean to make you wait."

"You're fine," I reply, breathless. "I just got down here. Um…you remember Brooks? From the pool?"

Aaron watches us silently, his face impassive, yet there's a strange energy building in the space around him.

"Of course." His voice is polite as he offers his hand. "Aaron Sinclair."

"Brooks Holland. Nice to meet you."

"Likewise."

There's an edge to the exchange. The handshake holds for just a fraction too long, the space brimming with unexpressed thoughts.

"Here for long?" Aaron asks casually.

"Just for the night," Brooks replies, still giving me his full attention. "I head out in the morning."

Aaron nods curtly and then turns to me. "We should get going. The reservation won't wait," he says, his look a little pointed, urging me to wrap things up.

"Of course." Brooks agrees but he doesn't move. His eyes hold me captive, and in them, I can see an ache that pierces through to my soul. "Dylan," he says with a softness that feels intimate, like he's afraid to push too hard. "Can I just have your number? Or…give you mine? So we can talk."

A sharpness seizes my throat. I don't know what to say. The last thing I want is to open this door again, to let him in after all these years of avoiding it. Even though my mind is screaming to say no, my heart refuses to let him slip away.

I notice a shift beside me and glance over. Aaron's eyes flicker to me, his lips pressed into a thin line, impatience written all over him. He doesn't say a word—just stands there expectantly, waiting for me to respond.

"Sure."

"Yeah?"

I nod, just once, as I try to make sense of what I'm doing.

Brooks pulls his phone from his pocket, and I rattle off my number without a second thought, speaking a little too fast. "I'm not promising anything," I add, just to make it clear this isn't some attempt at friendship.

"I wouldn't expect that," he says, not lifting his gaze from the screen. I'm half ready for a ping, for him to double check that I didn't hand him a bogus number, but instead, he tucks the phone away and turns his attention back to me.

I look off to the side, keeping the mess in my head hidden. I shouldn't feel a goddamn thing. His presence is rattling me, and it's infuriating that

I'm apparently unable to close that chapter and move on.

"I should get going. But, Dylan, I—"

"Brooks," I say sharply, raising my hand.

He pauses, eyes searching mine, then exhales like he's releasing something buried deep. "I owe you an apology. I don't expect you to accept it, but you need to hear it."

I lift my chin in acknowledgement, my gaze barely meeting his before I drop it away. What am I supposed to say to that? A decade of agony—of shoving it all down, forcing myself to forget until nothing was left to feel. And now he's here, tossing out an apology like it can undo the damage, like it's not a knife straight to the chest. I'm not ready for this—hell, I'm never going to be ready for this.

"Not now. We can talk later."

"Oh…um, okay. Have a good night, Dill," he says softly, and the nickname feels awkward, like it belongs to someone else. It doesn't fit anymore—not when it feels like we're two completely different people now.

I spin on my heel and head towards the door, not sparing him another word. Aaron grabs my hand, but it's not the comfort it should be—I should feel relieved, but instead it's just a reminder of how hollow everything's become. And it's not even his fault, but damn if it doesn't make it harder to breathe.

I keep moving forward, but his apology clings to me, like a futile attempt trying to fix what's irreparably broken.

It's too much.

It's not enough.

It's everything and nothing.

6

Dylan

Slipping into a desk at the back of the room, I try to stay out of sight in my first-period visual arts class. But it doesn't take long for a petite blonde near the front to notice me. While she's chatting with her friends, their eyes repeatedly flicker in my direction, and I hear soft giggles ripple through their group.

Great. Here we go again. Being the new kid feels like a broken record—same anxiety, different school, and the same snarky smiles from the same kind of girls.

Much to my irritation, she walks over, her tone laced with a curious edge. "What's your name?"

"Dylan," I reply, keeping my voice even. "Yours?"

"Chloe." She tilts her head, studying me. "Where are you from?"

"Wyoming."

She lets out a small laugh, swaying slightly as she glances back at her friends. "A mountain girl, huh? I should've guessed."

"Sure. Whatever."

"Well," she says, her grin growing a little too stiff, "welcome to Rockport."

"Thanks." I force a smile in response, but it feels just as fake as hers.

Brooks steps into the room, and like a magnet, my focus snaps to him. It's been days since the bonfire, and despite my best efforts, I can't stop replaying that night in my mind. He strides in like he owns the place, and it's ridiculous how his presence unconsciously commands everyone's attention.

He's even more striking in the daylight—maybe because the morning sun filters in just right, casting shadows along his jawline, making him look like he stepped out of a movie.

His medium-length hair, touched with auburn hues and effortlessly wavy, catches the light as he moves. A fitted navy-blue T-shirt peeks out from beneath a crisp flannel, the fine stitching and tailored fit making it clear it's expensive—without trying too hard. The deep blue intensifies the sharp green of his eyes, making them stand out more.

Dimples flash when he glances around, and I fight the urge to smile as he heads straight for the empty seat beside me, my heart picking up pace.

"Damn, look who it is!" The natural ease in Brooks' voice sparks a flutter of self-consciousness in me, like maybe I'm the only one who didn't get the memo on how to act normal in this situation.

Chloe's gaze bounces between the two of us, her surprise written all over her face. "Brooks, you know Dylan?" she asks, her voice slightly higher, like she's trying to figure out if this is just some weird coincidence or something more.

The look he gives her is telling—like he wasn't expecting the question, or didn't think she'd be bold enough to ask it. "Yeah," he says, with a small shrug, like it's nothing big. "We met at the bonfire."

Chloe's eyes darken with irritation, suspicion clouding her expression. "That's funny—I don't remember seeing you there," she says, her tone clipped as she zeroes in on me.

"I wasn't there long," I admit, a little defensive, suddenly feeling like I'm breaking some kind of unspoken social code.

Chloe's expression doesn't shift much, but there's something strangled in her voice. "Oh. Bummer. Well, next time, I'll make sure you meet everyone. We're a pretty tight group." The smile she gives me is like the edge of a blade wrapped in silk.

I force a polite one back. "Looking forward to it."

Just then, the teacher steps into the room, calling for everyone's attention, and I can't help but silently thank fate for putting an end to that painfully awkward moment. Brooks nudges my foot, a slight press against the side of my sneaker, but it's enough to send a jolt of awareness through me.

"She's a real sweetheart, huh?" he whispers.

I bite my lip, looking over at the girl who just left. "She's… something. Not the worst I've met, though."

There's a beat of silence before he presses further. "Oh yeah?

Then who takes that honor?"

It's a knee-jerk reaction, spat out like I can separate myself from it. "My mother."

Brooks' gaze is intense, full of questions, but before he can say anything more, the teacher begins the lesson, effectively ending the moment.

Eventually, Mr. Lyons directs us to pair up for a photography assignment centered on the play of light and shadow, and as various desks slide together, metal legs scuffing against tile, students instinctively form pairs. A familiar sense of isolation settles over me. Everyone gravitates toward their chosen partners, while I remain an afterthought—left behind in the shuffle.

I hear the soft drag of a chair beside me and glance up just as Brooks scoots over, his movement unhurried, measured. He stretches his arms overhead before letting them drop with a finality that feels almost reassuring.

"Guess that settles it."

I raise an eyebrow. "Did I miss the part where I actually agreed?"

"Hmm. No," he teases. I figured I'd save you the trouble."

"How considerate of you."

"Always," he quips, tilting his head toward the front of the room. "Come on, let's go pretend we know what we're doing."

"Fine." I roll my eyes, half-serious. "I guess I don't have a choice."

Brooks feigns offense. "And here I thought we had something special—you said so yourself at the bonfire."

My brows shoot up, and I blink several times. "I said *I* must be special, not that *we* have something special."

"Semantics, Rivers."

With a smirk, he guides me toward a quieter corner, his fingers moving over the camera with expertise. There's no doubt, just fluid motions as he tweaks the settings, tests the angles and adjusts the focus like it's second nature. I should be paying attention to what he's doing, but instead, I'm caught up in the way he makes something technical look so effortless.

"Have you done this before?" I ask. "You don't really seem like the artsy type."

He exhales a short, amused breath. "What's that supposed to mean?"

"Well," I say, fumbling for the right words, "you play football with my brother, so…"

"So you think I'm just a dumb hot jock?" he teases, giving me a quizzical smile as he looks down at me. Then, as if to drive to the point home, he winks.

"No! That's not what I meant."

"Hey, I'll take what I can get, Rivers," he says, smirking, and I swear my ears burn red.

Back home, I'd barely tolerated my brother's teammates. They were loud, obnoxious, and mostly interested in showing off. The idea that one of them could be genuinely talented with a camera is surprising, to say the least.

"Relax, Dylan." He leans in just enough to bump me, making sure I don't take it too seriously. "I'm just messing with you. I took a photography class last year. Turns out, I'm decent at it."

"Well, I'm impressed," I say, acutely aware of the brief brush of his shoulder against mine.

"Good. So, you'll be my subject today?"

"Your—" I narrow my eyes and wonder if this is some sort of test. "Subject?"

"Unless you have better plans?" he challenges, gesturing toward the room as if it holds endless possibilities.

"Nope, this was my dream," I deadpan, crossing my arms.

"You'll survive." His words land with perfect timing, and I bite back a smile, but it's a losing battle.

While we work, he's unexpectedly attentive, offering small but clear directions, guiding me with a natural fluidity that makes it easy to follow along. We start laughing at random little things—the shadow my hand casts when I try to cover the sun, the ridiculous angle he contorts into while lying on the floor to capture it just right.

The minutes slip by, and for a while, I almost forget we're in a classroom. It's rare, this kind of focus, the kind that makes time stretch and compress all at once. But then the bell cuts through it, snapping everything back into place.

I blink, momentarily disoriented, like I've surfaced too fast from deep water. The room rushes back in, and I reach for my bag just as my stomach twists in on itself—an uncomfortable reminder that I skipped breakfast this morning. I press a hand to my stomach, willing it to stay quiet, but Brooks glances over anyway.

I brace for a comment, for some teasing remark, but he just tilts his head, considering me.

"What class do you have next?"

"Uh…chemistry." I pull my schedule from my binder, falling into step next to him and double-checking the room number as if it might've changed in the last hour.

"Oh. Really? Me too." He tilts his head slightly, sneaking a glance at the paper. "Hey, maybe we'll be partners again."

"Or…maybe they'll split us up and make us meet new people," I counter.

"Who needs new people when you've got me?" he quips, one brow arching in a playful challenge.

I huff a laugh, sliding my schedule back into place. "Touché."

We walk in sync, and Brooks lifts a hand, exchanging a few waves with other students as we make our way to the other side of the building. Then he looks over, the humor slipping from his voice.

"So, you and your mom don't get along, huh?"

I feel myself retreat, instinct kicking in before I can stop it. That brief crack in my defenses seals itself shut. "It's complicated."

Brooks seems to catch on, and his expression grows regretful. "I'm sorry. I shouldn't have asked."

"No, it's fine. We just don't see eye to eye on a lot of things."

His face relaxes, his features gentler now. "Parents are so out of touch sometimes."

"Yeah. No kidding."

Just before we reach the classroom, Brooks angles toward me. "So, what's your plan for lunch?"

"Uh, I hadn't really thought about it. The cafeteria?"

"I've got a better idea."

"Oh yeah?" I counter. "And what's that?"

"You'll see," he flicks the edge of my notebook with his fingers, a casual que for me to follow. "I'll take you somewhere after class."

7

Brooks

Then

Chemistry drags. I should be paying attention, but the words on the board blur together, my mind stuck replaying last period. I don't know why, but taking pictures of Dylan was the most fun I've had in that class all year. It wasn't just the project—it was her. The way she moved without thinking, how the light caught in her hair, the way her eyes narrowed slightly in concentration, she made the whole thing easy. Natural. And the pictures? They turned out incredible. I don't say that lightly. I've taken plenty of portraits before, but there was something mesmerizing about these—about her.

I have to physically stop myself from glancing her way. It's impossible not to notice her. She sits a few rows over, scribbling notes, her black curls spilling past her shoulders—several strands slipping forward as she leans in, completely absorbed. Like she doesn't realize half the room is only pretending to pay attention, counting down the minutes until lunch. I wonder if she's always like that—lost in her own world.

Before I can stop myself, I shift in my seat, resting my elbow on the desk angling just enough to steal another glance.

A silver butterfly necklace rests against her collarbone, shifting subtly with each of her movements. Her maroon cardigan drapes off one shoulder, like it's in the middle of a dance with gravity. She tugs it up absentmindedly, but it finds its way back down a few minutes later—like it's meant to be there.

I force my eyes back to the front of the room, tapping my pen against my notebook, trying to ignore…whatever this is I'm feeling. She's just a girl. It's not that deep.

Once the bell finally rings, the room erupts into motion—book closing, chairs scraping, the usual chaos of everyone eager to leave. I tap the edge of Dylan's desk, catching her by surprise. "Come on, let's get out of here," I say, nodding toward the door. "We're going to walk."

She perks up, slinging her backpack over one shoulder with an adorable sort of eagerness. "We're walking?" she repeats, narrowing her eyes. "How far are we going?"

"Not far." I grin, raising my hands as if to show I'm harmless. "It's just a couple of blocks from the school. Promise."

She laughs, probably assuming I'm winging it, but every move I make is intentional. I fire off a quick text to Beckett, letting him know where we're headed—a formality more than anything. He'll be fine with it. Or maybe he won't, but honestly, I don't care.

It's only a few minutes before my place comes into view. It's nothing fancy. A modest house, a bit rough around the edges, but Mom's touch is evident, turning it into something warm and lived in rather than just another generic house. She's poured herself into making it look like a home, and even though I've spent my whole life here, I don't feel trapped—not always, anyway.

"This is your place?"

"Yup. Home sweet home."

She takes in the details: the yard, the porch, the charm Mom has worked so hard on. I see a flash of envy in her eyes, and an offhand comment from Becks at practice about moving around comes back to me. It stings a bit, knowing I have something she doesn't.

"Make yourself comfortable," I gesture for her to enter. "You're about to experience the best sandwich of your life."

The kitchen smells like Mom's vanilla candles and the pancakes she whipped up this morning. It's a little embarrassing, but I feel comfortable here, even with Dylan sitting at the table, watching as I pull out everything we need. Making sandwiches isn't a huge deal, but it feels like a piece of normalcy I get to share with her.

"Your house has a lot of personality," she comments, her smile playful.

"Yeah, that's all my mom," I admit with a chuckle. "She's got this thing for 'telling a story' with the stuff she collects." For a moment, Dylan seems engaged, but then her expression tightens, and she pulls back as if she's catching a mask slip.

I finish assembling the sandwiches, cutting them in half like I always do. The first bite hits me immediately—the crisp crunch of the bread, the creamy richness of the avocado, the slight zing of the mustard. It's perfect. I glance at Dylan as she takes her first bite, and the look on her face is priceless.

She stops for a second, eyes wide. "Okay, this *is* good," she admits, her voice muffled as she chews.

I grin, leaning back against the counter. "Told you. It's a game-changer. Way better than that week-old pizza they would have served you at school."

Dylan takes another bite, clearly impressed. "This might be the best sandwich I've ever had," she says, laughing with a hand covering her mouth.

The atmosphere feels lighter now, the tension from earlier slipping away. I push my empty plate aside and ease back, watching her for a beat before wiping my hands on a napkin. "There's something I want to show you."

She raises an eyebrow, her curiosity piqued. "Ominous," she teases, pushing her chair back with a squeak.

"Don't worry, nothing weird," I assure her. "It's not like I'm taking you to some creepy church."

She laughs, shaking her head. "I wouldn't put it past you."

I chuckle, the casual banter helping to break the last traces of awkwardness. Leading her down the hall, I barely glance at the framed pieces of my childhood—the birthdays, the holidays, the memories my parents have tried to hold onto. We reach my room, a makeshift studio of sorts. Blackout curtains, a cluttered table, and the usual chaos. It's nothing special, but I've started keeping my photography equipment here—out of Dad's line of sight, where it won't set him off.

"This is where the magic happens," I say, offering a small smile. Her face lights up with interest, and for some reason, my movements feel more noticeable now, like I'm suddenly too aware of my own body.

"Not wasting any time, I see," she muses.

I fake a gasp. "So suspicious. And here I was, just trying to enrich your life with my talent."

The two of us stop by the wall where I've pinned a series of photographs—mostly old, abandoned buildings around town, places that no one has noticed but me. The photos capture them in their last breath, giving life to something broken. Dylan's eyes trace over each frame, and I can tell she gets it.

"These are stunning. What inspired you to take them?"

"It was kind of an escape. Walking around town, finding these forgotten places…it felt like an act of rebellion against my dad. He thinks it's a waste, you know? Says I should be fixing them up, not photographing them."

She frowns, but there's an openness in the way she listens, like she genuinely cares.

"It sounds like you have different plans than he does," she says, casting a sideways glance my way.

"Yeah." I pause, gathering my thoughts. "My dad's whole world is construction. Always has been. He wants me to take over, keep the business going. I get it. I want to make him proud. But sometimes I feel like there's more out there. More than just fixing roofs and building walls in Rockport."

Holland Construction—Dad's pride and joy—is waiting for me. Everyone assumes it's set in stone, like I was born to lay bricks and manage crews. It's not what I want, but then again, it doesn't seem like anyone's paying attention.

"If expectation wasn't a factor, what would you do?" she asks, and her lashes flutter as she looks back at the photos, fingers grazing her necklace, like she's contemplating her own answer.

"I'd leave," I admit. "See what's out there beyond this little town. Take my camera and fill it with places most people here will never step foot in. Paris, maybe—I've always thought about photographing the light spilling over the Seine. Or somewhere like the Scottish Highlands, where the mist cloaks the hills."

I laugh a little, feeling awkward. "It's probably stupid."

She lights up, her entire demeanor shifting. "It's not. I've always wanted to see Paris," she says, her voice humming with excitement. "I mean, I'd love to wander through all the galleries, just let myself get lost in the art. Maybe even try painting something while I'm there—let the city's colors flow onto my own canvas. I don't know, it feels like everything I've ever wanted is just waiting for me there."

It's easy to get caught up in the way her words flow so freely, like she's already halfway there. I feel this sudden pang of something I can't quite name. Maybe it's envy, or maybe it's the realization that I've never really had a dream like that. Not in the same way. Not one that feels so solid, so sure.

"It sounds amazing," I say before I can overthink it. "Why don't you just go for it?"

She tucks her bottom lip between her teeth, thinking. "My mom doesn't think it's practical. To her, it's just a hobby, not something worth chasing across the world."

It's a sentiment I understand too well, but I don't let it settle. "Maybe our parents are right. Maybe it isn't practical. But I'd rather fail chasing something real than stay stuck in a life that isn't mine." I pause, not sure if I'm saying too much. "I mean, it's kind of brave, really, to have that kind of vision of yourself."

She tilts her head, studying me for a beat, as if she's reading something between the lines of what I said. Then she shrugs, offering an innocent smile. "I think we all have our own way of figuring out where we're supposed to be. It just takes time to figure out how to get there."

Neither of us rush to fill the silence that falls after. We're comfortable being two people balancing between obligation and ambition, trying to find something real in the middle. And suddenly, that makes all the tension and teasing feel like smoke over a fire neither of us wants to name.

Her fingers graze the opening of my flannel, tugging just slightly before she releases it. "We should head back," she says, biting down lightly on her bottom lip. "I don't want to be late for my next class."

Then, without another word, she turns and walks away.

For once, Rockport doesn't just feel like a place I'm trapped in—it feels like somewhere that might actually hold something worth staying for. Exhaling, I give a tight half-smile before shaking my head and following after her.

The bell rings as we return, signaling the end of our free time together. I catch the faintest flicker of disappointment in Dylan's eyes—a shade of blue so soft it reminds me of morning frost—the subtle crinkle at the corners giving her away. But then she blinks, smoothing her expression just as quickly.

"Thanks for the escape," she says, shifting her books from one arm to the other. "I can't remember the last time I felt that normal, to be honest."

"Glad I could help," I reply, stuffing my hands into my pockets, unsure what else to say. Funny how something as simple as lunch—as sandwiches—could feel like the start of a bigger story.

A subtle lift of her fingers, a barely-there goodbye, and then she's gone—pulled into the tide of bodies moving in every direction.

I square my shoulders, pressing my lips together as I refocus and head to AP History. Just outside the classroom, I spot my best friend, Miles Davenport, leaning against the lockers. His eyes flick between me and the hallway Dylan disappeared down. With a quick push of his glasses—something I almost never see since he refuses to wear them at practice—he tilts his head, a smirk creeping in.

Miles has a way of always being two steps ahead, and judging by the look on his face, I can tell he's already piecing something together.

"You gonna fill me in, or do I have to guess?" he asks, matching my pace.

"It was just lunch. The way I see it, she had two options, she could either trust my sandwich or whatever's been sitting under the cafeteria heat lamps all morning."

"Uh-huh," he says slowly, dragging out the sound. "Totally not because you wanted to spend more time with her?"

"Miles you're reading into this," I say, taking my seat. "She's new. I was just being friendly."

He grins like he's already got the end of this story figured out. "So you're just out here making friends now? With our new teammate's twin sister? Can't imagine how that might backfire."

I give him a pointed stare, daring him to keep going, but he holds his hands up in mock surrender. "I'm not judging—just surprised, is all. I can't remember the last time you put in this much effort for someone—actually, never mind."

I shake my head and flip open my binder as the teacher launches into a lecture about historical figures we're supposed to know for the exam. Something about Alexander Hamilton and his never-ending string of bad decisions. Fitting. I try to focus, but Miles isn't done yet. He leans in, dropping his voice to a whisper. "One more time and then I'll drop it. You're telling me there's *nothing* there?"

I don't take the bait, keeping my tone even. "Dude, I don't know. Okay? It's not like it means anything. Just drop it."

"Alright, B, keep pretending. If that helps you sleep at night. But I'm not blind."

I grip my pen, trying to keep up with the notes, but all I can think about is the way Dylan spoke about painting in Paris—the ache in her words, the way her aspirations reached far beyond one place. The girls I know are all about appearances, the latest gossip, and making sure everyone's watching. She's a world away from that. She doesn't let others' judgements define her, and her ambitions are a whole lot grander than the tiny, shallow goals most people chase.

The clock ticks on, but the rest of the day blurs together, until it all feels like one long stretch of time. I go through the motions; nodding when I need to, answering just enough to keep the teachers off my back. Each period signaling a countdown, moving me closer to the one place where I can block everything out.

The last bell vibrates through the air, and finally, I can breathe again. I head to the locker room, already peeling off the day as I pull on my practice gear. Football will be a good distraction, a way to let everything go, if only for a little while.

As soon as I step out on the field, I feel like I can finally reset. Coach has us running drills—simple stuff, but the kind that demands every ounce of focus. My feet move on autopilot, my mind shutting off. I don't need to think. I just need to move.

The pace is relentless. My muscles burn, and my lungs protest, but I don't stop. When we finally break into a scrimmage, Beckett' energy shifts. He throws himself into the game with this intensity I haven't seen yet, like he's trying to burn through something too. I can feel it in the air, the way he's pushing himself harder.

By the time Coach blows the whistle to call it, we're both drenched in sweat, barely standing. I'm not sure if it's the physical exhaustion or the fact that for a few minutes, I could forget everything, but I'm grateful for the release. It's not the answer to whatever I'm feeling, but it's enough for now.

The team filters into the locker room, the buzz of conversation filling the space as everyone sheds their sweaty gear. The steam hangs thick in the air, making it feel like it's holding onto every ounce of the day's tension. I pull off my pads, feeling the weight of practice slip off with each layer. After a quick rinse, I slip into a fresh T-shirt, the fabric feeling like a small comfort against the exhaustion that's setting in. The kind that makes your limbs feel like lead and your mind just wants to switch off.

But before I can really settle, Beckett's voice cuts through the haze.

"Brooks!" He's got that lopsided grin of his that somehow looks both frustrated and amused at the same time. "Need a favor, man."

I glance over at him, raising an eyebrow. "What's up?"

He rubs the bridge of his nose, squinting like he's trying to push the frustration out of his system. "My truck won't start—again." He lets out a long exasperated sigh. "You mind giving me a ride home?"

I nod, slinging my bag over my shoulder, and we make our way to the parking lot. Becks is already deep into a post-practice analysis, tearing apart his own performance and spiraling over whether Coach is about to knock him down a peg.

"Coach's whole personality is making us work twice as hard." I say, unlocking the truck and tossing my bag into the bed. "You're holding your own—better than a lot of the guys, to be honest."

"Thanks, man. I just feel like I'm slipping. Got a lot on my mind lately," he admits, slumping into the passenger seat.

"Yeah, I get it," I say, glancing over at him before starting my truck and pulling onto the road. "I don't know all the pressure you're dealing with, but I'm here if you need to talk. We're all just trying to figure it out, right?"

"You're not wrong," Beckett says, suddenly straightening up. "Turn left here, and follow it straight down until you hit that old gas station on the corner. You'll know it by the sign—half fallen down, like it's been through a war. After that, it's the third left, but don't blink or you'll miss it."

I follow the directions, feeling the age of the neighborhood press in as we drive past rows of houses with peeling paint, cracked windows, and fences barely holding it together.

His gaze drifts to the window for a split second, his muscles tense, jaw set behind his closed lips, like he's bracing for me to say something—maybe judge him. But I don't. I stay quiet, focusing on the route he gave me, letting the music take over the silence in the cab.

The calm we'd settled into doesn't make it past the driveway. As soon as I cut the engine, Dylan explodes through the front door, followed by her mom. Her fists flex at her sides, her stare piercing, and whatever just happened inside—it wasn't good. Beckett tenses, curses softly, then throws me a quick look before climbing out of the truck. "I swear, this never ends," he grumbles, striding toward the group.

I follow, a surge of protectiveness rising in me. Dylan freezes when she sees us, her expression morphing from anger to embarrassment, like she's been caught mid-escape. Their mom stops too, noticing us for the first time. She smooths her expression into something more composed, but her eyes remain steely. The switch is unsettling, and I want to jump in—to somehow break this weird friction radiating off everyone—but I know better.

Whatever's unfolding behind those walls isn't just an argument.

The storm in her eyes tells me this isn't new, and I get the sense that she's used to fighting a battle no one else sees. And maybe it's time someone did.

8

Dylan

I shove my books into my bag and make a beeline for the door, eager to get home. Bodies press forward in every direction, the rush to escape almost frantic. Lost in thought, I don't see him until we collide—one second I'm walking, the next I'm on the floor, papers scattering around us like fallen leaves.

"Wow, that was graceful," I mutter, already standing and reaching for his arm. "Sorry, I wasn't paying attention."

He grips my hand, brushing off his shorts as he stands. There's something rugged yet polished about him, his muscular build clearly defined beneath his navy-blue Rockport Titans T-shirt. "You've got one hell of a tackle. I'll give you that."

"I feel awful," I insist, grabbing his books and a few stray pens. "I swear, I'm not usually this clumsy."

He flexes his fingers like he's checking for injuries before squatting down to grab the rest of his things. "Dylan, it's fine. At least you're dedicated to the full-contact approach."

My lips part in surprise and I scan his face for any hint of familiarity, tousled blond hair falling across his forehead. His blue eyes meet mine briefly, smoldering with a confident intensity. "How do you know my name?"

"It's a small town," he says, rolling a stray pen between his fingers before tucking it behind his ear. "Word gets around. Plus, your brother's on the team. We share a locker room."

"Oh. Yeah, that makes sense." Heat creeps up my neck, a reluctant realization setting in. Of course, people already know who I am. I fidget with the sleeve of my cardigan, the fabric twisting between my fingers before I pause, recognition resurfacing. "Wait…you were at the bonfire last weekend, weren't you?"

"I was," he admits, rocking back on his heels, like he's enjoying making me work for it.

"And do I get to know your name, or are we keeping this whole mystery thing going?"

"Colt. Colton Hayes."

I tap a finger to my lips, pretending to think. "Colton Hayes… nope, doesn't ring a bell. Is this the part where you tell me you're kind of a big deal?"

"You know," he drawls, crossing his arms. "I was going to play it cool, but if you insist…yeah, I'm a legend. Hall of Fame, really."

"Wow," I deadpan. "And here I was, thinking you were just some guy I tackled in the hallway."

"Nope. You've *officially* run into greatness." He steps back, but not before giving me a once over like he's memorizing the moment. "If you want another chance to be starstruck, I'll be on the field later. Feel free to come and admire."

"Tempting, but I should probably head home."

"Rain check, then?"

I huff an amused laugh. "We'll see."

"Oh, we will," he says playfully, stepping away. "Later, Dylan."

I don't look back as I head home. The air sharpens as the afternoon fades, slipping from warm gold to dusky blue. Each step pulls me farther from the weight of attention, the outside world shrinking behind me as my thoughts settle back into their usual, restless hum.

By the time I reach the front door, my shoulders are tense, bracing for the usual onslaught of my mother's pointed remarks, coupled with Greg's unfamiliar presence taking over the house.

But as I step inside, I'm met with nothing but stillness. No prying eyes, no sharp words waiting to hit me. Just space. I kick off my shoes and let out a breath, finally letting my guard down.

My room still doesn't feel like mine, the packed boxes proof of it. But past them, tucked beneath a pile of clothes, a flash of color catches my eye—my paint palette. I haven't painted since we moved. I tell myself I don't have time. That I shouldn't. But my hands are already reaching.

Settling down, I pull out a canvas and begin. The brush moves instinctively, each stroke pulling something loose inside me. The longer I paint, the more the world outside disappears, leaving just me, the colors, and a blissful feeling I've missed.

I'm so lost in the moment that the shift in the air doesn't register until a shadow cuts across my canvas. I glance up, my stomach tightening as I meet my mother's pinched, irritated stare.

"What are you doing, Dylan?" She speaks through clenched teeth, the strain bleeding through despite her attempt at control.

"Just…painting."

"Painting." The word falls from her mouth like it's something vile. "You'd be better off putting your energy into something that actually matters. Trust me, life doesn't have time for distracting little hobbies. You'll learn that soon enough." Her fingers barely graze the air in the direction of my boxes, like acknowledging them is an inconvenience. "Clean this shit up before Greg gets back."

"Right, because who wouldn't want life advice from you?" I mumble under my breath, something I know I'll regret later.

"What did you say?"

"Nothing. I'll clean it up. Wouldn't want to ruin the facade you're putting on for him."

"Watch yourself," she warns. "Do you have any idea how lucky you are? You should be grateful, Dylan. And this?" She wrinkles her nose in the direction of my paints. "This is why you'll never get anywhere if you don't grow up."

Her words should've dulled by now, worn thin from the endless repetition, but they still rip through me like a fresh wound.

"If getting somewhere means ending up miserable like you, I think I'll pass."

She clicks her tongue, shaking her head like I'm a lost cause. "I have given you everything, and you can't show an ounce of appreciation."

A dry chuckle scrapes out of me. "Appreciation for what? For making me feel like a burden in my own home?"

She moves closer, shoulders squared, her voice a razor's edge. "Don't test me, Dylan. I'm not going to let you sabotage everything we're building here."

"Sabotage?" I echo, feeling the bitterness rise. "You mean exist in a way that doesn't fit your perfect little picture?"

She doesn't yell. Doesn't warn me. Just launches my palette across the room. The wall absorbs the impact with a dull crack as it shatters, spewing color in all directions. Some of it lands on me. Fitting, really.

"You missed a spot," I snap, shoving past her, the need to escape burning through me. But I don't get far. Her fingers clamp around my arm, nails biting in painfully. I whip around, meeting her glare with a flat stare. "You want to talk about growing up? How about you try acting like an actual parent for once?"

Her grip falters for a split second, and I don't wait for her to recover. I lunge for the door, shoving it open so hard it smacks against the wall. Her voice warps behind me, edges dulled by whatever she's been drinking, but I don't turn back. The evening air stings my skin as I stumble into the overgrown yard—just in time to see Beckett pull into the driveway, riding shotgun in a red pickup I don't recognize.

I see the alarm in my brother's face a second before the door crashes open behind me. Our mother storms out, fists clenched, her breath heaving like a fucking maniac. My heart sinks as I look past him and spot Brooks in the driver's seat, reaching across to turn down the radio.

She spits my name, venomous, but as soon as she registers we have company, her spine straightens, dragging in a sharp breath. Her hands smoothing over her shirt while her face rearranges itself into something resembling control. Almost. The fire in her eyes refuses to dim.

Beckett's concern flares in the tightness of his jaw, his eyes glued onto mine like he's trying to assess the damage. "What happened?"

Mortified doesn't even begin to cover what I'm feeling. My life is a total disaster, unraveling for Brooks to see firsthand, and I'm powerless to hide any of it.

My mother's expression doesn't flicker, her silence louder than any words. She turns with slow, deliberate precision, walking away as if I no longer exist. The door shuts behind her—not slammed, not rushed, just a final, measured punctuation mark to her anger.

Becks straightens, rolling his shoulders like he's preparing for battle. "Thanks for the ride, Brooks. Truck's a problem for tomorrow. Right now, I've got damage control to run." He jerks his chin toward the house, then at me. "Let's go."

"No," I choke out, my breath coming in uneven gasps. I can't go back in. I won't.

Beckett's grip is gentle as he pulls me in. "Come on, Dill. She probably went into her room. You're not staying out here. Let's go."

I can feel Brooks watching me, like a spotlight I can't escape. I feel seen in the worst way, like my ribs are cracked open and my humiliation is spilling onto the pavement for him to sift through. I cross my arms over my chest, gripping too tightly, my fingers digging in, but I don't let go. The pressure is the only thing keeping me from falling apart. If I could disappear, if I could sink into the ground and never climb back out, I would.

I apprehensively follow Beckett inside, my shoulders curled inward, every step heavy with exhaustion. The house is eerily quiet again, and I worry it's the kind that doesn't feel like peace but rather another storm biding its time. Mom's door stays shut, for now. In Beckett's room, I sink onto his bed, and he sits behind me. He's my only constant in a world where nothing else seems to stay in place.

"Did she hit you?"

I shake my head, trying but failing, to find the right words. "Not this time. She just threw my paints." I wipe my face, but it doesn't matter. My hands are shaking, my whole body trembling with the effort of keeping it all in. Beckett tugs me into his arms. I stiffen, resisting the comfort I don't feel like I deserve, but the moment his hands settle on my back, the fight drains from me. My breath shudders, my body folding in on itself as the reality of everything finally crashes down.

"Why is she like this?" I sob, my voice breaking.

"I don't know, Dill. I wish I did...but it's not her. It's the alcohol. You know that, don't you? We're almost out, okay? We can make it until graduation."

I know he's right, but time feels endless, stretching between now and the moment we can finally leave. Beckett and I have been planning our escape since we were kids—whispered schemes under blanket forts, fingers tracing imaginary routes on old maps. Colorado was always the dream, the place frozen in memory like a photograph. Snow-dusted sidewalks, jagged peaks in the distance, and the tiny park where we tried and failed to sled on patches of stubborn ice. Ever since we left, we've sworn we'd go back, rent a little place, and work whatever jobs we had to. It wasn't about money or success. It was about reclaiming something that once felt like home.

It's cruel how time drags when you're desperate for it to speed up. The closer we get to leaving, the heavier each day feels—like wading through quicksand, knowing I'll be pulled under if I let my guard slip. I've lost count of the nights I've listened to her scream, felt the agonizing pressure of her anger pressing into my skin. It never changes. It never stops. It's not like when Beckett and I were younger, back when she still cared—if she ever really did. Now, there's only this version of her, the one whose voice is always sharp, whose words always bruise. And somehow, I'm the one she targets the most, like punishing me might fix whatever's broken inside her.

There were nights I used to pray she'd change, that I'd wake up and find the mother I used to know waiting for me at the breakfast table. But that hope withered away a long time ago. This is who she is now. Maybe this is who she's always been, and I was just too young to see it.

I shrug off Beckett's arms, pressing my palms hard against my face before forcing a steady inhale and standing. "I should clean up," I murmur, as if wiping away the mess could somehow make the rest of my life feel less out of control.

"Let me help," he offers, pushing himself up.

"No, it's fine. I can handle it."

He doesn't move at first, watching me closely, like he's trying to figure out if I really mean it or if I'm just pushing him away. "Dill, you don't always have to do everything alone. I want to help you. I can't just stand here and let you push me away when I know you're struggling."

I swallow, avoiding his eyes. "I've got it, Becks. Really. Just let it go."

His posture softens, and I can see the hint of defeat in the way he lowers his shoulders. "Alright. But I'm still here. And I'm not going anywhere, even if you try to shut me out."

I take a slow breath, my eyes lingering on his face for a moment before I step back into my room. The door creaks slightly as it shuts behind me, and my gaze lands on the dried paint smeared across the wall. It's nothing new. I've scrubbed away her anger more times than I can count.

I used to think if I tried hard enough, I could fix things. That if I was careful, quiet, perfect, she'd love me the way she used to. The thought leaves a sour taste in my mouth. My phone buzzes in the back pocket of my jeans, pulling me back to the present.

Brooks: Hey, it's Brooks. Got ur # from Beckett. He wasn't too stoked, but I talked him into it. ;)

Brooks: Just checking if ur ok

I bite my lip, feeling my ears redden, and despite myself, I bounce slightly on the edge of my bed, the thought of him having my number making me a little too happy.

Dylan: I'm good. Thx tho.

I know better than to admit how I really feel. Letting someone in means giving them the power to hurt you. I learned that lesson young, and I'm not about to forget it now.

Brooks: Cool. Wanna hang tmr after practice?

Dylan: Idk…where?

Brooks: Surprise lol

My fingers hover over the keyboard. A simple yes would be easy, but easy doesn't mean safe. Not after what he saw today. It's probably just pity. A check-in disguised as an invitation. I shouldn't fall for it.

Dylan: ummm, why tho?

Brooks: Why not?

Dylan: cuz u just witnessed my origin story as a future therapy patient…

Brooks: And???

I press my fingers to my temples, hoping clarity will somehow seep in.

Dylan: AND?

Brooks: All I saw was how tough u r tbh

I shift, trying to ignore the heat blooming across my face, a flush spreading steadily from my neck up.

Dylan: U don't even rlly know me

Brooks: Not yet. I wanna fix that.

My brain short circuits for a second, then immediately kicks into overdrive. A thousand interpretations all elbowing for attention. I read it again, hoping for clarity. All I get is more confusion and a racing heart.

Brooks: Just say yes Dylan ;)

Dylan: Fiiiiine

Dylan: Yes. (:

I shouldn't let this mean anything, but it does—because people usually leave, and the fact that Brooks still wants to spend time with me after today feels significant.

Brooks: Let's goooo!! see u tmr

As soon as I set my phone down, my stomach gives an obnoxious growl, like it's reminding me I've ignored it for way too long. I'm barely halfway into the kitchen when the air shifts—thick with syrupy laughter that's too loud, too sweet, like it's trying to cover something up. Mom's pressed against the counter, Greg's hands tracing lazy paths along her back. I freeze just inside the doorway, my stomach twisting, hunger draining out of me like water down a sink.

Mom turns to me, flinching for a fraction of a second before turning it into a grin that feels as fake as a store mannequin. "Hi, baby! How was school?"

"Good," I reply, the word feeling clunky in my mouth as I try to match her fake cheerfulness.

"That's great! I'm making dinner if you're hungry. Mac and cheese with hot dogs—your favorite." She's still performing, putting on a show for Greg, as if that'll somehow smooth over everything. I haven't liked mac and cheese with hot dogs since I was eight, but I nod anyway.

"Thanks, Mom." My smile feels as artificial as the powdered cheese.

Beckett slides into the room, one hand drumming absently on the counter. His raised brow is subtle, but I catch it. I nod once, a barely-there movement, trusting him to get it.

"Dylan, sweetie, could you set the table for us?" Mom asks, her voice honeyed with too much charm. I can't remember the last time we did this—played pretend. But pushing back now would only make things worse.

"Sure," I answer, stacking plates in my arms.

We sit down, and without missing a beat, Mom starts dishing out food. She serves Greg first, of course, making sure his plate is just right before moving on. I don't know many adults who treat mac and cheese like a gourmet meal, but I figure it's better not to question it. We're just extras in the show she's putting on.

I chew mechanically. Each bite feels like swallowing cardboard, but I don't stop. Neither does Beckett. We eat like we're on a timer. No words. No glances. Just quiet endurance.

As soon as our plates are empty, we clear them without a word, slipping away before the fragile peace at the table has a chance to break. I lead the way to my room, Beckett following close behind, neither of us looking back.

"Well, that was a nightmare," he mumbles, collapsing onto my bed.

"Don't get comfortable. That was too easy. She's holding it in."

"Maybe she'll get laid, and we'll get a free pass tonight," he jokes, attempting optimism.

"Ew, Beckett. I hate you for that sentence."

"What?"

"If I have to picture them naked, I might actually vomit," I say, shuddering.

"Hey, you'll be grateful if it buys us a drama-free night!"

"Here's to hoping," I say, crossing my fingers for emphasis.

Beneath the sarcasm, dread coils in my stomach. Mom is a ticking time bomb, and deep down, I'm terrified. When she finally goes off, we won't have time to run. We'll just have to brace for impact and hope the blast doesn't take us down with her.

9

Dylan

Now

"We don't have to go. I can cancel." Aaron's voice is careful, like he's trying not to spook me.

I shake my head a little too quickly. "No—don't. We go home tomorrow. Let's have a nice evening."

"Home?" He latches onto the word like a splinter under his skin. "Does that mean you're finally going to move in?" The question lands like a misplaced step on an uneven sidewalk.

"Aaron." His name leaves my lips, empty of the reassurance I wish it held. "We've talked about this. I'm not ready to live together. I just mean we're going back to New York."

"I know." He cuts himself off, his gaze dropping as if he's not sure he wants to say the rest. "Every night, I reach for you, and you're not there. Every morning, I wake up, and the apartment feels too damn empty. Sometimes I wish—"

The low hum of an approaching engine drowns out whatever Aaron was about to say, and I pretend not to notice his unfinished thought. The valet attendant barely has time to shift into park before I slip into the passenger seat.

"You're really dodging this conversation, huh?"

"No." The word comes out too defensive. I rein it in, smoothing my expression. "You wish what?"

I really, really don't want to hear this. I was hoping I could avoid it, that maybe he wouldn't continue the conversation and let me off easy. I…should have known better. But here we are, and I'm doing everything I can to keep my face neutral even though my stomach flutters like a trapped bird.

Aaron exhales sharply, rubbing his palm over his jaw like he's debating whether to say it at all. "I just wish we could be more committed, you know?"

I chew on my lip, my mind racing to find a response that won't make things worse. "I get that, but moving in isn't something I'm ready for yet. It doesn't mean I'm not committed—I just…need more time."

A lump rises in my throat. I care about him—I do. But caring doesn't erase the way I keep parts of myself locked away. I wish I could explain it, the way it feels like I'm caught between wanting more and fearing what 'more' really means.

"Do you think maybe I'm just…broken?" The words feel serrated as they leave my mouth. Aaron's fingers flex against the wheel, his knuckles paling as his head jerks slightly in my direction.

"What? No. I mean…what are you even talking about?"

I rub my hands over my thighs, trying to dispel the restless energy. "I don't know. I just—sometimes I feel like I'm too broken to be anyone's…anything."

The car rolls to a stop, the faint thrum of the engine fading. Aaron doesn't get out right away. He just sits there, drumming his fingers against his knee, like he's trying to find the right thing to say.

"I don't think you're broken, Dylan." The streetlights outside cast a faint glow across his face, softening the lines of his features. "I'm not asking you to be perfect. I just want you. You get that don't you?"

I swallow, my fingers knotting in my lap. "I do."

"That's all I want. I don't want to ruin this time with you. Let's just enjoy tonight, and when we're back home, we can talk—if you're ready."

I force a smile. I want to argue. I want to tell him that it's not that simple, that I am broken, but something in the way he says it makes me pause. Makes me reconsider.

I'm still trying to figure out if I'll ever be ready to let him see the parts of me I've hidden away. The thought of going back to New York feels like a countdown, a ticking clock that will eventually hit zero. And when it does, I know the pressure will either break our fragile connection, or strengthen it. Maybe a trip to Rockport is what I need—to finally close the door on old wounds, to take the chance I've been avoiding and open up to Aaron.

I reach across the center console and trace the back of his hand with my thumb, a quiet attempt at connection. He doesn't let go.

Instead, he laces our fingers together, squeezing once gently.

"You know what I see?" he muses.

I shake my head, my lips parting to ask, but he beats me to it.

"Lobster rolls. In our very near future. Maybe some fries. *Definitely* extra butter."

A small laughter escapes me, barely there, but enough. I don't know how much longer I can hold onto this fragile illusion of normalcy, but for now, I'll let myself pretend. I'm good at that.

Less than a week back in New York, and already, the city feels as though it's pressing in on me from every angle. I've managed to steer clear of nearly every conversation Aaron tries to have about commitment. I feel out of place in my own life. Maine cracked something open inside me, something I can't seem to shove back down, no matter how hard I try. Leaving Rockport's unfinished business behind was supposed to bring relief, but all it's done since seeing Brooks is fester.

He texted once. I stared at the message, reread it more times than I'd admit, but never typed a response. I didn't know what to say. Or maybe I wasn't ready to let the past claw its way back in. But in the end, I've chosen to go to the reunion—not for anyone else. Just for me. For closure. Because running hasn't erased anything, so maybe facing it will.

Now, I stand at the gate, my boarding pass almost a foreign object in my hand, like it belongs to someone else. The reality of the trip is starting to sink in, too fast. Anxiety swirls in my stomach, and I look up at Aaron, his face set in concern. He's waiting for me to say something, to reassure him, but I don't know how.

"You're sure you want to do this?"

A pang of doubt prickles at the edge of my thoughts, but I force myself to stand firm. "I need to." The truth is, I've been avoiding the past for too long, and if I ever want to feel whole again, I need to face it. If I don't, I won't be able to move forward with anyone.

"If you want, I could come with you?"

I'm sure he already senses my reluctance, but he still needs the words to come from me. I'm not going to have anyone to lean on this time. Beckett can't come with me. So, I'm going to have to face this reunion alone. "No. I'll be okay," I tell him. And even though deep down it doesn't feel true, I add, "You've got your own things to worry about." I offer him a quick, almost imperceptible smile, hoping it doesn't appear as weak as it feels.

"I could rearrange things, take off a couple more days from the gallery."

Aaron's gallery is more than just a business to him; it's a reflection of his dedication. I've watched him pour everything into it—late nights, early mornings. Our first encounter wasn't anything extraordinary, just a few chance run-ins on the street. The city seemed to conspire to bring us together. Then one night, he asked me to grab a drink, and somehow, without either of us planning it, we've barely been apart since.

"You'd really blow off work for something as silly as my high school reunion?"

"For you? Yes. Absolutely." He beams, his eyes gentle and I can tell he means it.

"That's sweet of you, but really…I'll manage. You don't need to."

Aaron's breath hitches, and for a moment, he stands motionless, as though he's collecting his thoughts. His fingers graze the back of my neck, tracing the line of my spine before they anchor around me, pulling me close. "Just promise me you'll let me know when you get there," he murmurs, a quiet insistence underlining his words.

"I promise."

I hope he understands I'm doing this for us too—a way to clear out everything that remains trapped between the past and my future. He presses a soft kiss to the top of my head, and I squeeze his hand a little tighter before pulling away and heading down the boarding ramp.

Once the seatbelt is secured, I settle back, feeling the slight jolt of the plane rolling to the runway. I tap Beckett's name, the call connecting before the first ring is even done. His voicemail picks up, over the top and silly as always. I let the sound of it wash over me, his voice a brief escape from the white noise of the flight.

"Hey, KitKat, it's me. I'm en route back to Rockport. I don't know why I'm going back. I honestly might be spiraling a little bit, and I could really use someone to talk to right now. I–I'm nervous, Beckett. I miss you. And you know, this would be a hell of a lot easier if you were here with me. Anyway, the plane's about to take off, so I'll have to cut this short. I love you. Bye."

I hang up the phone, but the sting of emotion is still there, creeping up my throat. Facing the window, I try to focus on the horizon, searching for anything to convince me this trip won't end in disaster.

"Can I get you a drink, or a snack, ma'am?" the flight attendant asks with a tilt of her head.

"I know it's a lot to ask, but is there any chance you could make a margarita up here?"

She arches an eyebrow, amused. "On the plane? Not impossible, but we'll have to improvise."

"Improvise away, and keep 'em coming. I'm all for a challenge right now."

She gives a quick, understanding glance, then heads off to prepare my drink. When the plane descends into Portland six hours later, I'm five margaritas in, and a serene numbness wraps around me like a blanket.

"You look a little queasy, miss," the cabbie remarks as I step out of the terminal.

"I'm fine," I counter, bracing myself against the cab. The tequila might be behind the dizziness, but the thought of Rockport, and all that comes with it, is what's really making my stomach flip.

He eyes me closely, pausing a moment. "You sure? You're not about to hurl on my seats, are you?"

"I'm sure. Let's just get in the car. Please."

The driver hefts my bag into the trunk with a grunt, then closes it with a soft thud. "So, where are we headed?"

I press my forehead to the cool glass of the window, the faint remnants of the plane's buzz swirling in my head. "A hotel in Rockport. The Drift."

He glances at me in the rearview, his nostrils flaring slightly, lips pinched in disapproval. "The coast? I don't know, that's pretty far, miss."

I pull a wad of cash from my pocket and count out enough to

cover the inconvenience, handling it over with a small nod. His eyes flick to the money, and his expression softens. He doesn't argue. "Alright, The Drift. Sure thing," he mutters, lifting a brow with a hint of a grin. "Give me a shout if you need me to pull over."

The drive drags on for over an hour, but time refuses to move, stretching unbearably slow. With each turn of the wheel, the town I fled from pulls me back, and my resolve crumbles as we draw near.

The moment the sign marking the edge of town comes into view, a cold rush of panic floods through me. My hands tremble as I clutch the seat, heart hammering a million miles an hour against my chest. I blink rapidly, as if I can undo the decision to come back, but the landscape outside is undeniable.

We come to a stop, and I can't tear my eyes away from The Drift. It's been given new life, sure, but the structure—those towering arched windows, those massive double doors with their worn brass handles— it's unmistakable. I'm looking at the church.

I think of this place as the first true escape I ever found. Back when everything felt uncertain, it was here, with a paintbrush in hand, that I finally began to breathe again. Brooks brought me here because he understood—this church, now a hotel, was where I could confront the emotion I didn't have words for. The stillness of the place, the way the light filtered through the stained glass—it was my sanctuary.

"You good, miss?" The driver's voice interrupts my staring, his tone a little cautious. "Still feeling off?"

I force my gaze away from the building, my stomach turning in uneasy waves. "Just carsick, nothing serious," I reply, but my voice wavers, betraying the lie.

"Take your time," he offers, gesturing toward the entrance. But I don't want time—I want to turn back. The doors seem to beckon, and yet all I want to do is run.

The buzz of the alcohol might be clouding my mind, but the lobby takes my breath away. Every inch of the space is carefully curated. I pause to admire the intricate details, my eyes landing on a mural on the far wall. It's a large-scale portrait of a young girl, her face obscured by a tangle of black hair, but the butterflies woven into her curls are unmistakable. And the way she's sitting on the beach, toes in the water, is an image I remember all too well.

I painted it years ago. A sharp pang shoots through me, my body tensing involuntarily.

"Dylan? Dylan Rivers!"

The voice, so familiar, takes me by surprise. I turn and find Ruby Miller, the owner of the local diner and my former boss, rushing toward me. Her eyes are bright, and the curve of her lips mirror a memory I've held onto for years.

"Oh! It's really you!" Her arms envelop me, and for a moment, it feels like the last ten years melt away .

"Let me look at you, sunshine." She holds me at arm's length, her eyes scanning my face. "Gosh, this is just the best surprise! I had no idea you were coming to town. Oh, we must catch up, dear."

"I'd really love that," I reply, my voice cracking slightly. Ruby was one of the very few people who didn't flinch when I walked into her life, baggage and all. She took a chance on me my senior year, offering me a job. Her faith in me was something I didn't recognize as a gift until the moment I walked away.

The diner belongs to another lifetime now, and the thought of returning knots my insides. I'm sure Ruby's hasn't changed, but I have—and I'm not ready to face the version of myself I left there.

Ruby's eyes soften as she appraises me. "You look fantastic, honey," she says, her voice full of an affection I hadn't realized I'd missed. "Have you run into Brooks yet? He's bound to be around here somewhere. I'm going to give him an earful for keeping you a secret from me."

"Wait—what?" I whisper, caught off guard. "He's here? Why would he be here?"

I hadn't planned on telling him I was in town just yet. I was hoping to ease into it, maybe even at the reunion.

Ruby, completely unfazed, continues, "You don't know?"

"Know…what?"

"Well, Brooks owns The Drift, sweetie. His father helped him renovate the old church a few years ago. I figured you knew—since you're staying here, of all places."

My brain misfires, like a skipped frame in an old film reel. Brooks owns this hotel? My mind flails, trying to process. I didn't even handle the reservation—I let Aaron take care of it.

"Oh," I exhale. "No, I haven't seen him. But I, uh, should just check in and head to my room. Get settled." I say it too fast, like I'm trying to outrun my own thoughts. "It was good to see you, Ruby, truly," I add, but I can't quite look her in the eyes.

"Take care, sweetheart. Enjoy the rest of your night, and don't be shy—come visit whenever you can."

Her hand rests briefly on my sleeve, the touch light. She steps back, watching me go with an expression all too perceptive, she knows there's more I'm not saying.

I sweep my eyes across the lobby, and everything seems different. The exposed beams, the stained-glass windows overlooking the ocean—it's all so familiar, yet undeniably altered. Sleek, refined, nothing like the crumbling, forgotten place I once escaped to. A decade has passed, but standing here, it feels like nothing's changed.

He actually bought the church.

Am I really ready to stay here?

I'm not sure how long I stand at the front desk, the check-in slipping by unnoticed as my mind drifts in a fog. When I finally move, the hallway feels like it's closing in around me. The photographs on the wall are hard to ignore, their presence suffocating in their quiet grandeur. They document the church's revival, each frame unmistakably displaying Brooks' work.

One shows the church in its dilapidated state—peeling wallpaper and windows long shattered. Another holds the forgotten pews, stacked like disused relics, the same image that's burned into my mind. My fingers brush the edges of each frame. I've been in town less than an hour, and already, everything I thought I outran is waiting for me.

The Drift is small, only big enough for a handful of rooms, but the view from mine is something out of a dream—glass walls stretching from floor to ceiling, framing the ocean as if it were painted just for me. I set my bags down with a delicate thud, barely registering my movements before I step onto the patio. The sky blushes with shades of pink and purple, casting a delicate haze over the water. For a heartbeat's length, the world feels calm—as though time has paused, leaving me in this space where, just for now, I'm allowed to feel okay.

Almost.

The mural of the girl on the beach seems to call to me, and the memory of the day I painted her follows, creeping in softly, as if she's been waiting for me to return.

10

Dylan

THEN

The bleachers are warm beneath me, and the hard plastic digs into my thighs, but the view of the field makes it worth it.

I watch Brooks glide over the turf with undeniable agility, running the last of his drills with the football team. The afternoon sun glints off his sweat-dampened hair, and a jittery surge of anticipation courses through me.

With each step he makes toward the bleachers, his smile grows, and my pulse seems to follow suit, hammering faster with each beat.

He stops just shy of the railing, towel clutched in his hand as he wipes his face. "I'm going to hit the showers. Don't go anywhere."

My reply is lost somewhere in the air, his retreating wink enough to leave me speechless as he jogs away. I'm motionless for a fraction of a second. Then, I pull my gaze away with a deliberate effort, training my attention back on the field. The last thing I need is for anyone to see me caught in the act of ogling him. Instead, I try to drown out the buzz of nerves by watching the other players leave, but the flutter in my stomach refuses to dissipate.

"Dylan?"

I jump, almost slipping off the edge of the bleacher. Whirling around I find Beckett standing there, his lips curled in that maddening all too familiar grin.

"Sorry, didn't mean to scare you, Dilly."

"You're such an ass." I force my breath in, but my heart refuses to listen, pounding too loudly to be ignored.

"And yet, here I am, keeping you company," he shoots back, crossing his arms. "By the way, did I interrupt your creepy staring sesh? You were practically drooling."

"I was not!"

"Oh, sure," his smirk deepens, clearly finding the situation amusing. "Because zoning out so hard you didn't even notice me walking up? Totally normal."

"I was watching the drills," I stammer defensively, motioning toward the field in a half hearted gesture that doesn't quite land.

"Watching the drills? What are you, a scout now? Maybe take a picture next time—it'll last longer."

I give him a careless shove, trying to hide the irritation sneaking up on me. "Shut up, KitKat."

"You're so bad at this. No wonder you've always been single."

My response dies on my lips when I see Brooks stepping out of the locker room, his presence shifting everything in an instant.

He looks stupidly good in dark jeans and a spruce-green T-shirt, the sleeves straining just enough to hint at the muscle beneath. His damp hair is a little messy, and there's this clean, woodsy scent that hits me as he gets closer.

"Ready to go?" he asks, smiling like he hasn't the slightest clue of the thoughts he's causing inside my head.

"Do I get to know where we're going yet?"

"Nope. You'll just have to trust me."

"Cool. I *love* surprises," I mutter sarcastically, earning a laugh from both him and my brother.

"Relaaax," Beckett drawls, messing up my hair as if I'm some bratty little kid.

"Seriously?" I shove his hand away, narrowing my eyes at him in annoyance. "Stop!"

Brooks pinches his lips together, trying to hold in a laugh. "Cute." But the dimples that appear are all the confirmation I need to know he's amused.

"It's something," I say, shooting a glare at my brother and scrunching my nose. "I wouldn't exactly call it *cute*."

Thankfully, we leave Beckett's laughter behind as we make our way to his pickup. Brooks opens the passenger door, and I slide in, the seat shifting as I settle. He rounds the truck, climbs into the driver's side, and with a turn of the key, the engine roars to life. We pull out, driving through a canopy of towering trees, the sunlight flickering through the leaves like a strobe. As the sound of crashing waves grows louder, I lean closer to the window, captivated by the vibrant landscape unfolding outside.

Eventually, Brooks pulls us into a dirt parking lot tucked between dunes, the ocean a faint glimmer in the distance. The scene is familiar, every detail demanding to be understood but refusing to fall into place.

"Is this really the surprise?"

"Part of it," he answers, stepping around the truck and pulling my door open, waiting for me to join him.

I match his pace, the breeze whipping strands of hair into my face as we walk toward the abandoned church. In the daylight, the place radiates beauty—its exterior is cloaked in ivy, while the stained-glass windows shimmer, alive with color.

Brooks drops a bag from his shoulder, the zipper's coarse rip punctuating the air. "Are you going to tell me what we're doing here?"

"Painting." He says it without looking up, sorting through the colors as if he's done it a thousand times before.

"What?" I blink, inching closer, unable to hide my surprise. "Why?"

He pauses, the faintest touch of irony in his eyes. "You mentioned you've always had your heart set on Paris, painting the city's colors. I thought maybe we could bring that here, let this place hold a small piece of that dream."

I stare at him, my heart tugging unexpectedly. "Brooks, this is…"

"Too much?" He watches my face closely, as if trying to gauge my reaction.

I blink, biting on my nail as my mind scrambles for the right words. "No. Um, it's…"

"Unbelievable?" He lifts one shoulder, his body shifting slightly as he rolls onto the tips of his toes, shoving his hands into his jean pockets.

"Yeah…" I shake my head, processing, a pink flush creeping up my neck. "I don't know what to say."

"After the whole situation with your mom yesterday, I figured this might help."

I avert my eyes, suddenly self-conscious. "You really don't need to do anything for me."

"Well, too late," he says, holding the brush in a way that makes it feel as though it's a challenge only I can accept. "You in?"

The sincerity in his gaze wraps around me like a soft rope, pulling me in. "Guess I'm not getting out of this, am I?"

"Not a chance, Rivers."

The light streaming through the stained glass bathes the floor in an array of colors. Brooks leads the way to a blank section of the wall he prepared, and I lower myself onto the ground. Without a word, he eases himself next to me, stretching out.

"So…tell me. What's your story, Dylan?"

I let out an apathetic huff. "Yeah, I don't think there's enough time in the world for that."

"C'mon, SparkNotes version. Give me the highlights while we paint."

I glance at him from the corner of my eye, the bristles of my brush hovering mid-air as I consider his request. "Well, I fear I'm not very interesting. You know my mom is crazy." I start, brushing a fleck of paint off my sleeve. "My dad has been out of the picture for as long as I can remember, so it's been me and Beckett raising ourselves, pretty much. We moved around a lot as kids, never really staying in one place long enough to get comfortable. My mom is an alcoholic, and—" A sudden stillness overtakes me, and my words stumble out of reach. "And long story short, she's always been angry, but I'm usually the target. What you saw wasn't even close to her worst."

Brooks' brush halts mid-stroke. "What do you mean? Does she hit you?"

"No." I squint, avoiding his stare. "She's thrown stuff at me, but mostly she just…yells. *A lot.* Screams about how I ruined her life. You know, the fun stuff."

His muscles tighten, a quiet crackling energy forming between us. I drop my gaze to the wall, focusing on the black streaks blooming across the surface as the rush of everything I don't want to name crawls through my veins, scraping bone from the inside out.

Brooks remains silent, but I don't dare meet his eyes. I don't need his pity or his well-meaning sympathy. My brush glides over the wall, leaving bold, dark lines behind—an outlet for everything I can't say out loud.

Finally, his words slip through. "That's not okay."

"I didn't say it was." My throat feels too small to hold everything in. Talking about this is the last thing I want to do, not at this moment, not with him. I don't know what I was thinking.

"I can see it, Dylan. The way you keep everything inside. You're allowed to be angry, you know. You're allowed to admit that you deserve better."

My brush halts mid-sweep, as if even the paint is listening. It's not the pity I braced for but something closer to indignation. I look up then, the multicolored glass spilling soft light across his features, catching on the edges of his emotion.

"Better doesn't just appear because we say we deserve it," I say, forcing the words out. "You can want something your entire life, but it doesn't mean it's ever going to happen."

"Maybe it doesn't," he counters, the conviction in his tone unmistakable. "But you shouldn't have to settle for just surviving. You're worth more than pretending like things are fine when they clearly aren't."

I don't say anything. Deep down, I know he's probably right, but it's easier to believe the story I've told myself a million times—that this is just how things are, and hoping for anything better is pointless. With every swipe of the brush, I feel the waves begin to take shape, unsure whether they should touch the girl's feet yet. The way her toes just barely breach the water feels like she's cautiously approaching something she's been avoiding, watching for a sign that it's safe enough to let herself feel what she's been holding back.

I stand, straightening my shoulders, my eyes taking in the scene from a different angle. There's something about it that feels right, even though I didn't expect it to. It's in the way the colors flow together, the way the water carries an energy that defies explanation. It's not perfect, but it resonates in ways I didn't expect. For a split second, I'm not hiding from the truth. It's as if the fractured pieces of me are finally coming together, falling into place where they belong.

Brooks draws closer, his eyes tracing the mural like he's trying to read between the strokes. "You're really talented."

"Thanks," I mumble, my hand tightening around the brush as I try to focus on the minor details, hoping it will distract me from this proximity.

He leans in, his arm brushing mine, and for a moment, I lose all sense of time. Goosebumps rise along my arms, responding to the gentle shift in his voice.

"Dylan…"

I glance out of the periphery of my vision, caught in the motion between strokes. "Yeah?"

"I wanted to say…"

Heat blooms in my chest, and I'm acutely aware of the space shrinking between us. "What?"

His lips twitch ever so slightly when I turn to him, like he's amused by something only he understands. "I think you've got paint on your face."

"Wait, what?" My eyes widen, disoriented as his laugh takes me by surprise. My hand flies to my cheek, and sure enough, wet paint smears under my fingertips.

"You're a mess."

"Oh, thanks," I tease, and I let out a laugh before I even realize it. I reach for him with paint-covered fingers, and he steps back, hands raised in surrender.

"Hey, hey, let's not make this a war!"

"Too late," I fire back, lunging forward with a smear of paint aimed right at his cheek.

His hand catches mine midair, stopping me before I can reach him. My body locks up, thoughts stuttering as his hand encircles mine. The quiet takes over, and with it, I sense a shift beneath my feet, as though everything around me is subtly changing.

The stillness is a force now, folding in around us, as though it's an entity of its own. The flicker of light from outside nearly draws my attention, but it doesn't quite reach me. Something about him keeps me here, waiting for what comes next.

"We should probably clean up." Brooks murmurs, his eyes briefly tracing the path of my hand before meeting my gaze again. "And get you back home."

Home. The word strikes, pulling me back to a reality I'm not ready for. I retract my hand, spinning to the side, trying to bury the disappointment before it shows.

"Yeah. Um, Good idea." My voice comes out stilted, and I know he hears it.

Neither of us says anything as we start gathering the supplies, the lighthearted rhythm from earlier now replaced with an awkward energy.

By the time we're in his truck, the sense of dread that comes with returning is almost unbearable. The ride is tense, save for the muffled crash of waves as we leave the beach behind. I glance out the window, desperate for the right words, but nothing comes.

I don't want to go back. I want to stay in this little pocket of time, where the world feels lighter. But I can't. The tether to everything I'm trying to avoid is already tugging me back.

The truck slows to a stop in front of my house, the headlights cutting through the early evening shadows. Brooks shifts into park and glances over at me, his hand brushing mine in a quick squeeze.

"I'm glad you came today."

I glance over at him, my fingers tightening around the door handle. "Me too. It was nice."

A lazy smile works its way onto his face. "I'm glad. See you later, Dylan."

"See you," I echo, slipping out of the truck. I take a moment, watching as he drives away, the butterflies in my stomach still going wild.

When I head inside, the house is quiet—thankfully. I toe off my sneakers and head for the kitchen, spotting a note stuck to the fridge.

Dee,

Got a load out of town. Back in a few days.

– Greg

I crumple it and toss it into the trash without a second thought. Filling up my water bottle, I wander down the hall, catching sight of Beckett sprawled across the couch in the living room, his phone glued to his hand.

"Hey," I call out, leaning against the wall. "Where's Mom?"

He shrugs, barely looking up. "She was screaming about something earlier then left. Haven't seen her since."

"Figures. What's for dinner?"

He glances up, his expression mildly annoyed. "Why would I know? Pretty sure the only thing left in the fridge is ketchup."

I let out a groan and flop onto the couch beside him. "Do we have money for pizza?"

Beckett tosses his phone onto the cushion between us and stretches dramatically. "Yeah, maybe if we dig through the couch cushions for quarters."

I close my eyes, letting out a long sigh. "Things haven't changed much, have they?"

He doesn't answer, his jaw shifting as if he's chewing on the words before spitting them out. My stomach lets out a low, visceral groan, the kind of sound that can't be ignored. His stomach protests next, like an unplanned duet, and something about it feels absurd enough to make my chest tighten.

The two of us raid the fridge, but it's as bad as we suspected: a nearly empty bottle of ketchup, an unidentifiable jar of something green, and a block of cheese that looks like it could double as a science experiment.

"This is pathetic," Beckett mutters, holding up the cheese like it personally offended him.

"I didn't think I could even feel this hungry anymore," I admit, bracing my hands against the counter's cool surface. Most nights, hunger fades into the background, a familiar presence. But tonight, it's sinking its teeth into me, desperately waiting to be fed.

The worst part is how unsurprising it is—how we just carry on, treating it as something to be endured. My throat burns, but I keep it down, stepping into the bathroom and yanking the shower handle. Steam curls around me before the water even hits, blurring the mirror, blurring everything.

Beckett's voice cuts through the humid air as I step out of the bathroom, water trailing down my calves. "Hey, maybe you could get a job. Something part-time like you had back in Wyoming."

I tighten the towel around me and roll my eyes. "Oh yeah? Where am I supposed to work, genius? This town isn't exactly full of options."

He smirks without looking away from his phone, one leg hanging off the couch. "Ruby's had a 'Help Wanted' sign up last week—unless you're above slinging pancakes for tips."

I grab my sweatpants and a hoodie, tossing the towel into the laundry basket. "I doubt a place like Ruby's hires high schoolers."

"It's your best shot unless you want to babysit brats or stock shelves at Mr. Doyle's hardware store down the street."

"I guess I could check out Ruby's tomorrow after school," I say, yanking my hoodie over my head, the fabric catching on my damp hair.

Beckett kicks his feet off the couch, stretching like a cat. "Wow. Would you look at that? You're growing up."

I grab a throw pillow off the couch and chuck it at him. "Shut up, KitKat. You're older than me by three minutes. Don't act like it's three decades."

"I'm just saying, with your sparkling customer service skills, we might be able to eat dinner next week."

"You're right. Then I can buy all the fancy ketchup and edible cheese I want," I shoot back, collapsing onto the couch beside him.

Our laughter fades too quickly, subdued by the same burden we've carried since we were kids.

"Seriously, though," I say, picking at a loose button on my cardigan. "If I can start saving, maybe we can go to Colorado after graduation like we planned."

Beckett doesn't say anything at first, his gaze fixed on the TV, but then he nods. "Yeah…maybe."

11

Brooks

My cleats press into the turf, leaving shallow imprints as I taper off into a jog toward the sideline. Practice has become my second favorite part of the day—second only to the time I get to spend with Dylan after it's over.

She's here again, sitting in the bleachers, just as she's done every day for the past six weeks. I don't know how it happened, how we went from two strangers that night at the bonfire to…this. But she's woven herself into my life so seamlessly it feels like she's always been here.

Her legs are tucked beneath her, one hand gripping the sketchbook she always brings, the other holding a pencil she twirls absently between her fingers. She doesn't pay much attention to the drills; it's clear she's here for the atmosphere—for me.

It all started after that day we painted the mural in the church. At first, it was just me giving her rides home when I noticed her walking. Then it turned into late nights after her shifts at Ruby's Diner, sharing fries and milkshakes we could barely afford. On weekends, we traded it for early mornings—pancakes before her shift, both of us watching the clock, knowing it was never enough. Hours blurred, then days, until there wasn't a clear before or after.

As I unscrew the cap of my water bottle, my eyes catch on her. She's lost in whatever she's sketching, her expression momentarily unguarded. Soft around the edges, her breath coming easier for the first time all day.

Coach Tyler yells for us to huddle up, and I force myself to focus. Practice will end soon enough, and then it'll be just me and her again. Beckett and Miles flank me, their shirts sticking to their backs, but there's no sign of exhaustion—just that restless charge that keeps them moving, always ready for more.

Becks smacks the back of his hand against my arm. "You're gonna burn a hole through her with the way you keep staring," he says, just loud enough for the three of us to hear. Miles, ever the instigator, snickers. "Yeah, bro, it's giving obsessed. Reel it in."

I throw him a flat look. "Maybe worry about your own tragic love life before dissecting mine."

"Love life," Beckett snorts, cutting in before Miles can defend himself. "Tragic? Nah, tragic has potential. He wouldn't know what to do even if the girl lived in his house. Hell, even if she was family."

"Funny," Miles deadpans.

I risk another look. Dylan is hunched over lost in her sketch, her focus unshaken.

Beckett exhales, his usual teasing edge dulling. "You're not gonna be the reason she stops smiling, right?"

The question knocks me sideways. "What?"

"My sister," he responds, and the change in his tone is unmistakable. "You're not gonna fuck her over, right? Because if you do, I swear I'll make your life hell. I haven't seen her smile this much since we were kids."

"Take it easy, Beckett," I say, holding his stare. "I wouldn't do that to her."

Miles chuckles, nudging Becks with his elbow. "Look at that, Rivers. Your sister has him all domesticated."

Beckett laughs, though it seems to carry reservation—he's testing my resolve. "Alright. Just know that if you're bullshitting me, the smart choice would be to stay in the friendzone."

Coach Tyler claps, signaling us to fall into formation. Beckett takes off, but Miles hangs back, catching me in the ribs with his elbow.

I exhale sharply, heading for the line of scrimmage. "It's not like that," I mumble, even though I know it's a lie.

It's *exactly* like that.

After practice, Dylan hops into my truck, her sketchbook balanced on her lap as she flips through the pages. She's quiet today, but her presence fills the cab with an intoxicating warmth.

"So, what's your plan while I'm stuck serving burgers tonight? More football? Brooding? Staring dramatically into the distance?"

"Actually," I say, adjusting my grip on the steering wheel, "my dad wants me to meet him at a job site. Says it's time I 'get serious' about my future."

Her smile falters, the lightness dimming into concern. "And do you? Want to, I mean?"

I hesitate. "I don't know."

She rubs at a faint smudge of graphite on her palm, a tiny movement of acknowledgement without interrogation. That's one of the things I've come to appreciate most about Dylan—she doesn't need me to explain everything.

We pull up to Ruby's, and she grabs her bag, but something holds her in place. "Hey," her gaze hooks onto mine. "Don't let him pressure you into it. Whatever you decide, let it be your decision. Not his."

She doesn't wait for a response, just gives a small smile, sealing the words between us. Her door swings shut, cutting her off from me. I drum my fingers on the dash, the truck idling like it's waiting for me to change my mind. I don't. I throw it into gear and drive toward the future I've been avoiding.

Metal bites into wood, a rhythmic clash of hammer and nail underscored by the growl of machinery. A familiar backdrop I've heard a thousand times, but it doesn't make it any easier to walk into. The site is a mess—boards scattered everywhere, half-finished walls, dust in the air. It's the same every time I come, and each time, I feel myself suffocating. Dad has been at this my entire life. It's his thing. And he's always been sure it'd be *my* thing too. But the older I get, the more I feel it pressing down on me, and the more I want to push back.

I step out of the truck, my boots crunching against the gravel, and make my way toward the crew. I don't know what to expect today, but I know it won't be all that different than the last time. Just a lot of heavy lifting and grunt work.

I'm not two steps onto the site when I see her. Chloe. She's leaning against a beam, her eyes catching mine before she pushes off and walks toward me with that same confident stride I remember all too well—the one that used to make my heart race before I learned who she really was.

She stops just shy of me, tucking a stray strand of hair behind her ear with an easy flick of her fingers. "Hey, Brooks," she hums, like gravity never pulls too hard on her shoulders.

"Chloe." I acknowledge her without offering anything more, my voice flat, controlled. The last thing I need is to get pulled back into whatever game she's playing.

"So, big game on Friday, huh?" She glances over her shoulder, as if casually checking for her dad. Our parents have been friends for years, and every time my dad needs HVAC work done, he insists on hiring hers…unfortunately.

"Yeah," I say, rolling my shoulders, wishing I could brush off this conversation. "Should be a good game."

She studies me—too deliberately, as if she's mapping out the cracks, looking for a way back into my life. "I'll be there," she replies, her tone unnervingly upbeat. "You know, for the game. Knock 'em dead, Brooks."

"Uh, thanks…Montclair's been steamrolling teams all season. We'll need it."

"Well, I'll let you get to work," she says, her voice still coated in sugar, but there's a crack in the sweetness now. A fracture. She's frustrated. "I'll see you around, Brooks."

"Mm-hmm, see you," I mutter, dragging a hand down my face as she turns on her heel, hips swaying slightly with each step. I don't know what she's hoping I'll do—stop her? I won't.

I shake off the unease, stepping into the controlled chaos of the construction site. The scaffolded pathways twist and tighten around me, forming a maze. Somewhere ahead, my dad is deep in conversation with one of the crew, his posture firm, voice lost in the clang of metal.

For a second, I wonder what it would be like to just turn around, head back to the truck, and go find Dylan—to spend the day with her instead of being here, trying to please him. But I'm not a quitter, and that's exactly what my dad expects of me.

I press my tongue to the roof of my mouth, shoving the contempt before it can surface. No point spitting it out now. This isn't what I wanted, but it's what I'm unfortunately stuck with.

I clear my throat and close the distance between us. "Hey, Dad."

He turns, and his eyes light up with that familiar spark of pride. "You're here," he notes, wiping his hands on his shirt absentmindedly. "Figured you might've bailed on me."

I glance over at the men working, their hard hats on, heads down. It's just noise to me now—the sound of something that's supposed to represent success but only adds more pressure.

"I said I would." The words slip out flat, drained. I just want to get this over with.

His hand clasps against my back with enough force to make me straighten. "Good. You're not gonna learn by standing around."

I acknowledge his words without really absorbing them—they barely register. My mind is already elsewhere—Friday night, the game, the chance to look up and see Dylan there, cheering for me as if I'm worth something.

"Just tell me where you need me." The words taste like dust, settling with grit before I force them down. I tug my gloves on, my fingers stiff inside them, already itching to be anywhere but here.

A cloud drifts overhead, a lazy escape, and I track it, letting myself pretend for just a moment that I could float away too. But the second passes, and I'm still stuck here.

12

Dylan

THEN

The referee's whistle cuts through the air, signaling the start of the game. The kicker launches the ball high, spiraling end over end as Miles sprints into position. He catches it cleanly at the ten-yard line, tucking it under his arm and surging forward. The field comes alive as players collide, bodies jostling for position. He weaves through a gap, pushing past the twenty, the thirty—until a Montclair defender lunges, taking him down just past midfield.

The roar of the crowd swells as the offense takes the field. I hold my breath as Beckett jogs into position, Brooks and Miles flanking him. He's locked in, riding the momentum without a second thought, as if the field was made for him. He's not just playing—he's proving something, and it's impossible to look away.

The ball snaps, and the game explodes into motion. Voices boom around me, but all I hear is the rush of adrenaline, my own heartbeat thudding in time with the play. Beckett drops back, eyes scanning the field. A defender breaks through the line, but Beckett shifts his weight, sidesteps, and rifles the ball downfield.

"That's my brother!" I yell, the volume of it shocking even my own ears.

The whistle blows moments later, signaling a timeout. One last play remains, the tension thick as the players jog toward the sideline, some gulping down water, others catching their breath. I sink deeper into my seat, my eyes locking onto Brooks as he tugs off his helmet. The floodlights skim over his sweat-dampened golden brown hair, casting a gilded glow around him, sending a flurry of wings loose beneath my ribs.

I reach into my hoodie pocket, fingers curling around my phone. The moment Brooks' name flashes on the screen, I straighten as a flutter stirs deep in my chest, climbing higher while a delicate pink blush blooms across my cheeks.

Brooks: You at the game?

Dylan: Obvi. Where else would I be? :)

Brooks: No clue. ;) Glad tho. Wouldn't wanna play w/o my good luck charm.

My cheeks flush a deep pink, revealing me before I can mask it.

Dylan: If that's the case, you better show out lol

Brooks: You got it, boss!!

A new wave of cheers crashes over the stadium, pulling me back into the game. The scoreboard flashes—Rockport 21, Montclair 7—but my focus is locked on my brother. A white-hot thrill tears through my body like a live wire as he rifles a pass toward Brooks, who snatches it midair without breaking stride.

"C'mon," I whisper, holding my breath as he dodges a defender, sprinting toward the end zone. Montclair's safety closes in, but Brooks cuts right, then left, sending the defender stumbling.

"Go!" I scream, jumping to my feet. "Go, go, GO!"

He crosses the line, the ball secured in his hands, and the stadium erupts. The referee's arms shoot up, signaling the touchdown. The scoreboard flashes—final seconds drained, no time left. Game over.

"YES! Six more on the board!"

The stadium vibrates with a tidal wave of cheers, the sheer force shaking the ground. Brooks rips off his helmet, his chest rising with each breath as he scans the stands, his gaze jumping from face to face before locking onto mine. The noise dulls, the night sharpens. A shift, almost imperceptible, settles across his face.

The field warps, a mass of bodies crashing together in celebration. But Brooks doesn't move. His helmet slips from his grip, thudding against the turf. Sluggishly, his fingertips drag against his temple, as if he's trying to find the source of something unraveling inside him. His breath hitches, shoulders lifting like it's taking all his strength to stay upright.

One drawn-out blink. Another. Then, suddenly, he crumples to the ground, his body going limp as the color drains from his face.

My feet barely feel the ground as I push forward, my body moving before my mind catches up. The crowd is a blur, their voices nothing but white noise behind the single thought clawing through my skill.

Brooks.

He's still on the ground when I reach him. The people around are useless, shifting in place like they can't decide whether to step forward or back. His chest rises, falls—too slow. Too shallow.

"Somebody help him!" My voice rips from my throat, but no one reacts fast enough. "Is he okay? Did someone call for help?"

Graham, one of the other players, rubs the back of his neck. "I— uh—he just collapsed. I think he's…tired?" His words trail off, unsure, and something inside me snaps. What's with everyone dragging their fucking feet?

"Dill, breathe." Beckett's grip is firm on my arm, holding me in place before I can reach him. But it might as well be a brand, burning against my skin while Brooks is on the ground.

"Breathe? You've got to be kidding me!" I rip my arm free, shoving past him, but I barely make it a step before I'm yanked back to a stop.

"Clear a path!" A firm voice rises over the murmuring crowd. The shifting bodies finally give way as a man in uniform—EMT, maybe— pushes forward, Coach Tyler right on his heels.

"I'm fine," Brooks mutters, his voice so faint it barely reaches us— almost as if speaking is a battle.

No one buys it.

Not Miles, whose jaw locks tight. Not Colton, whose leg bounces with agitation. Not Beckett, whose stare pins Brooks in place, searching for the cracks. And definitely not me—because if he were fine, I wouldn't feel like my own lungs were shrinking with every passing second.

Brooks drags a shaky hand over his face. "Look, I just haven't drank any water today—" He moves to stand, but his body betrays him, his legs folding as though gravity itself just doubled.

"Hey, just stay down for a second kid. You're not fine," the medic says, kneeling beside him, a steady hand on his shoulder.

"I was just dizzy. It's nothing."

The medic doesn't look convinced. "Lightheaded? Nauseous? Headache?"

Brooks stalls, jaw tightening. "Just a little dizzy."

The medic studies him a second longer before pulling out a blood pressure cuff, securing it around Brooks' arm. The soft hiss of air fills the space as it inflates. Brooks doesn't react, but I catch the tension in his posture—the slight way his fingers curl into his palms.

A moment later, the medic releases the valve and checks the reading. "Your pressure's a little low. You're probably just dehydrated." He shifts back slightly but keeps his voice even. "You need fluids—water and electrolytes. Sip, don't chug. And you're done for the night."

Coach Tyler levels Brooks with a look. "I know your parents are out of town tonight. You got someone to keep an eye on you?"

Colt doesn't miss a beat. "Dylan's got him." He tips his head toward me, the implication clear and heat rises to my face as every pair of eyes turns in my direction.

Brooks' lips part as if he might argue, but instead, he simply mouths, "Please."

It lands like a loaded question, even though it isn't—a responsibility I hadn't expected but can't refuse.

"Yeah, we've got him," Beckett says, his voice composed as he glances down at me.

I steel myself with a quick nod, my heart pounding as I move forward. "Yeah…yeah, of course." The words leave my mouth before I even realize I've moved.

"Hydration and rest," the medic says, his eyes hardening. "If he gets worse, get him to a hospital."

"Got it." The words leave my mouth before I fully convinced myself I do. I school my expression into something passably confident, but in all reality, I'm cracking open. A wildfire of uncertainty ignites in my chest.

Dylan, it's just dehydration. Not life or death. Chill. But the what-ifs still consume my thoughts. Brooks pushes himself to his feet, offering me a wink that borders on cocky, as if this is all just some big misunderstanding. *What have I gotten myself into?*

Colt and Miles trade glances, and whatever passes between them sets my nerves on edge. They're seeing something I haven't caught up to yet.

Brooks stretches, his jersey clinging to his skin as he swipes a damp curl from his forehead. "I'm hitting the showers. I'm soaked, and I'm about five seconds from setting this uniform on fire." Then, he cuts his eyes toward me. "Seems you're stuck with me, Dylan. I'll meet you at my truck when I'm done."

My hands tighten into fists, then relax, as if my body can't decide what to do with itself. I should say something else—ask a question, make a joke—but all that comes out is, "Sounds good."

Beckett rubs his knuckles against his jaw, glancing between me and

Brooks before settling his focus on me. "He's fine, Dill," he says, eyes narrowing like he's cataloging every micro-expression. "Just pushed himself too hard. Now you've got the perfect excuse to spend more time with him." His smirk is infuriating, but there's an undercurrent of reassurance in his tone.

I huff out a breath, aiming for exasperation, but the blush creeping up my neck betrays me. "Shut up, KitKat."

He chuckles, giving my shoulder a quick squeeze before jogging off after the team.

The guys disappear into the locker room, leaving me on the field, my thoughts spiraling. I rub my arms, suddenly aware of the chill pressing in around me. I force my feet to move, slowly crossing the empty stretch of turf.

Brooks' truck sits where it always does, and I make my way over to it, pressing my hip against the cool metal of the passenger door. The medic's warning loops in my head—a song stuck on repeat. With a measured breath, I tip my head back, eyes tracing the stars for any sign that everything really is okay.

It doesn't take long for him to come out of the locker room, and the moment he steps into view, I can't stop myself from staring. He flashes a half-smile—the kind that makes the butterflies swarm a little faster. His damp hair falls across his forehead, a bit unruly but gracefully composed. The cotton of his shirt hugs his frame, highlighting the lean power beneath, each movement exuding control without effort. As he steps closer, my anxiety dissolves, pressing down on the nerves that had been thrumming moments before.

"How's my good luck charm doing?" Brooks asks, mimicking my stance and leaning casually against his truck.

I chew the edge of my bottom lip before replying, "Worried about you."

He shrugs, his laid-back demeanor unshaken. "Hey, I told you, I'm fine. Promise." He slings an arm around my neck, a steady certainty in his touch. "Now, let's go. Colt is throwing a party to celebrate the win, and I'm not about to miss out."

I eye him skeptically. "Oh. A party? You sure you're up for that?"

His fingers graze my collarbone as he leans into me just a little more. "Dill, I'm good, but if you're that worried, you're welcome to keep a close eye on me all night." He pats the side of the truck. "Now, c'mon. Let's go have a good time."

I hesitate, torn between curiosity and caution. "You know what? Sure. But how about I drive? Give you a break for a bit."

"Tempting, but I'd rather let you sit there and look pretty while I handle the road."

"So, you just like being in control, huh?"

He slides a hand behind me, fingers curling around the door handle as he leans in, his breath warm against my ear. "You can call it control, but she's a little temperamental. You're better off letting me wrestle with her."

The truck's frame is solid against my back as he swings the door open, the motion erasing the last sliver of space between us. His chest brushes mine, heat radiating from him and seeping through my clothes.

His retreat is slow, measured—like he's making sure I notice. The truck creaks beneath me as I settle in, the scent of worn leather and engine grease curling around me. Brooks hovers just outside, his grip curled loosely around the top of the door.

I bite the inside of my cheek before glancing his way. "You getting in, or are we just gonna stay here all night?"

"Just enjoying the scenery," he says with a tilt of his head, pushing the door shut with a soft, purposeful click before rounding the front of the truck.

As he settles into the driver's seat, the flirty glint in his eye deepens into something more genuine. "I'm glad you came tonight."

"Yeah, me too."

The truck rumbles softly as we pull away, one of Brooks' hands steady on the wheel, the other draped casually over the center console. My attention drifts to his fingers for a moment, a thought sparking in the back of my mind—what would it feel like to touch him, even just for a second? I push it away and settle my head against the window, letting out a long breath as I watch the streetlights zip past.

It's going to be a long night.

An hour later, we roll up to Colt's house, the scent of burgers and milkshakes clinging to our clothes. I shoot a glance at Brooks, who—despite his earlier complaints—begrudgingly downed the bottle of water I all but forced on him before we even left Ruby's.

The party is already in full swing. People are sprawled across the front lawn, red Solo cups in every hand, while music blasts loud enough for the bass to rattle the dash.

Brooks parks the truck with a quick maneuver and jumps out,

making his way to my side to open the door.

"After you. Let's see if that luck holds up, Rivers," he teases.

I step out, a breath of laughter slipping free. "Dangerous game you're playing, setting expectations like this, Holland."

The distant murmur of voices turns into a full-blown roar as we close in on the house, the music growing louder with every step. Miles appears in the doorway and wastes no time pushing past people, like he's been waiting for us all night.

"Dude, you seriously freaked me out back there," Miles says, thumping Brooks on the back a little too hard. "I thought we were about to lose our star player."

"'Star player' is a bit of a stretch, dude. We all know Beckett takes that title. I probably just needed water or some shit. It's no big deal."

"Yeah, well, maybe next time, don't give us all a heart attack," Miles says, his shoulders shaking with a silent laugh. He throws an awkward side hug around Brooks before his gaze shifts to me.

"Hey, Dylan."

"Hi, Miles," I reply, tugging my hand from the back pocket of my jeans and lifting it in a half-hearted wave.

The three of us step inside, the music crashing into us, each note shaking the windows. The air carries a sharp blend of cheap beer and overly sweet perfume, and someone is already yelling above the noise. In the living room, a guy is on the couch, arms raised in victory, holding a ping-pong ball like it's a trophy.

Brooks' hand finds the small of my back, guiding me toward the kitchen without a word. The counters are a chaotic spread of Solo cups, half-empty snack bags, and bottles of booze—some tipped over, pooling onto the sticky surface. By the refrigerator, Beckett leans casually, his attention fully on a girl with sleek red hair and a laugh that cuts through the noise.

When Beckett notices me, his entire face lights up. "Dill Pickle," he calls out, abandoning the girl by the fridge without a second thought. Before I can dodge, he catches the edge of my sleeve between his fingers, dragging me into him. "Look at you! Did hell freeze over, or did Brooks finally drag you out of your hermit hole?"

I skim my palm down my thigh, resisting the urge to fold into myself as voices blur together around me. Every instinct is screaming for me to bolt, but I force myself to hold my ground. "Blame your boy," I grumble, jerking my chin toward Brooks.

"I think you mean *thank* my boy," Beckett counters, giving my shoulder a playful shake. "Lighten up, Dilly. You might actually survive this and have a good time for once."

He shoots me a wink before striding back toward the girl, his attention already redirected, leaving me to wrestle with the noise, the perfume-clouded air, and my own creeping discomfort. *Too late for second-guessing now.*

Brooks is watching me, his expression relaxed, but carrying that undeniable charm that always seems to throw me off balance. I grab a water bottle from the counter and toss it his way. "Here. Hydrate, *star* player. We're not dragging you off the field twice in one night."

He catches it with an easy motion, twisting off the cap and taking a deliberate sip. "Anything for my personal medic." The bottle meets granite with a soft clink, forgotten the second his gaze latches onto me—unhurried, intentional, peeling me back layer by layer.

From the living room, the party erupts into a loud, drunken chant. "Shots! Shots! Shots!"

Miles lets out a sharp whistle, conversations halt, a few heads turning his way as he smirks, clearly pleased with himself. "Dylan," he shouts, trying to be heard over the music. "First party, first shot. You're not skipping this."

The moment snags, catching on my discomfort. This isn't my scene, and every instinct is telling me to stay on the sidelines. My focus shifts to Brooks, who tilts his head, a subtle challenge in his expression.

"Fine," I say, the word coming out uneven as I push myself to play along. It feels like stepping off a cliff, but at least I'm trying.

Miles grabs a bottle of vodka and a carton of orange juice, moving with the confidence of someone who's done this a hundred times. He pours shots into red Solo cups then raises his own triumphantly. "To crushing Montclair!"

Brooks lifts his cup in solidarity, his movements unshaken, and the others follow suit. I join in, stifling the urge to back out.

The alcohol scorches a path to my stomach, liquid fire curling in its wake. I press my tongue to the roof of my mouth, chasing away the acrid after shock that refuses to fade. Miles slaps me on the back, laughing at my reaction, but I can only hold my breath and wait. The hairs on my arms stand stiff as I fight the rising wave of nausea.

"Should you even be drinking if you're dehydrated?" I choke, crossing my arms in what I hope comes across as disapproval.

"They said fluids," Brooks counters. "Never specified which kind." His tone melts, slipping into something softer. "You're kind of adorable when you worry, you know that?"

Embers ignite under my skin, catching faster than my thoughts. Before I can grasp for a response Colt barrels into the kitchen like a human tornado. He grabs my wrist without hesitation, his energy pulling me into his orbit. "Dylan, you're up! Beer pong. I need a partner. Let's go!"

"Wait, I don't even know how to—" Before I can dig my heels in, Colton has already swept me along, his unshakeable momentum making my resistance pointless. I stumble after him, half-annoyed, half-intrigued, and entirely uncertain of what I've just been roped into.

The beer pong table is sticky with a layer of spilled beer, and my shoes make an annoying squelch every time I shift my weight. *Awesome.*

"We've got next!" Colt announces, draping his arm around me like we've been lifelong teammates.

"You're gonna regret this," I caution, letting my head drop with a knowing sigh. "I've never played before."

"Relax, rookie. It's just beer pong, not brain surgery," he fires back, lightly tapping my arm to reinforce his point.

To my surprise, he's right—it's not complicated. Somehow, I start landing more shots than I miss, and by the second game, we're on a roll. The crowd around the table grows louder with every win, their cheers blending with the steady hum of music.

"You're killing it!" Colt says, shoving another beer into my hand as if it's my trophy. "Didn't expect anything less from Beckett's sister."

His excitement feels contagious, but I offer a distracted response. My focus fractured, scanning the room for something—or someone—I haven't seen in a while.

"Have you seen Brooks?"

Colt downs a mouthful of beer, then tilts the bottom of his drink toward the stairs. "Pretty sure he went up with Chloe."

"Chloe?"

"Vance," he says, as if that makes it better. "His ex. He dated her last year. Things were messy for a while, but he tolerated her—well, until you showed up, anyway."

The realization hits, like stepping off a curb I didn't see coming. Chloe is his ex? *Of course, she is.* How did I miss that? The party hums around me, but it's meaningless. Every shared moment with Brooks plays back in my head, only now the colors feel different—faded. Was I only seeing what I wanted? Is she in the picture? Was she ever really gone?

"Oh." The syllable barely makes it past my lips, drowned out by the bass rattling the walls.

The bottle sweats in my grip, slick against my palm. I don't hesitate. I knock it back, the liquid rushing past my lips, my throat working fast to keep up. One down. I don't stop to think before grabbing another. The burn of alcohol doesn't dull the ache in my chest like I'd hoped— it only seems to stir it up more. Or maybe it's the buzz amplifying everything, turning a twinge into a full blown ache.

Colt's words flicker around me, and it's predictable enough to fake my part. I tilt my head just enough to feign presence, but my focus dissolves before it can land. Our winning streak finally breaks, but instead of celebrating or groaning with the rest of them, I slip away. The press of people, the noise…it's too much. I weave through the crowded house, my only goal to find the one person who feels real in the haze of uncertainty.

The next thing I know, I'm stepping onto the patio. The damp air bites at my skin, but it barely makes a dent in the uncertainty curling around me. KitKat and Miles sit by the fire pit, shadows shifting over their faces, their heads tipped toward each other—sharing a quiet joke or a secret I can't hear. My brother notices me first, his posture swaying slightly before he catches himself.

"Dilly, I saw you playing beer pong. The apocalypse must be near!" He drags a finger through the air, pointing at me as if I've just rewritten the laws of the universe.

I slump into a chair, shedding the last hour off my back. "Colt had the enthusiasm of a golden retriever. I never stood a chance."

Beckett's attempt at a nudge turns into more of a slow-motion lean, his balance questionable but his grin intact. "Regardless, you stuck it out and you didn't bail—real MVP move, sis."

"Uh-huh," I mutter, eyeing him wearily, as if he just tried to sell me a broken-down car. "On a scale of one to regretting this tomorrow, where are we at?"

He waves off the question, his movements uncoordinated. "Enough to regret all of it tomorrow." His tone carries the kind of certainty only a drunk person can manage.

The liquid in my beer shifts as I tip it to my lips, my attention settling on the yard. A football cuts a smooth arc under the dim glow of string lights, rising, falling, caught. I watch the easy repetition losing myself in the motion, something predictable when everything feels off kilter.

Miles pops up from his seat, as though someone randomly hit fast-forward on him. "Who's up for a game?"

I lift a palm. "Absolutely not. I've had enough games for one night."

But it doesn't matter. Beckett swoops in, hauling me up with a grip loose enough to escape but determined enough to make resistance pointless.

"You're playing."

I huff. "And you're exhausting."

My steps lag, half a step behind, but the momentum is inevitable, drawn into the loose perimeter forming near the pool's edge. The game kicks off quickly, and I'm instantly aware of one glaring problem—I have no idea what's going on. Flip, Sip, or Strip, apparently, isn't just a clever name. As the rules unfold, I realize I've walked straight into a minefield of potential embarrassment.

13

Dylan

Now

When I wake up, the room is shrouded in darkness, and the pounding in my head feels like a drumbeat I can't escape. Squinting at the clock, I notice the time on the nightstand—2 AM. I must've passed out shortly after calling Aaron. We didn't talk long. I was too drained to hold a conversation, and must've fallen asleep the second my head hit the mattress.

My hand sweeps across the bed until I find my phone, wedged between the pillows.

One tap, two, nothing. Perfect. Dead battery.

The room tilts, or maybe it's just me. The tequila hasn't worn off—it's settled in, making itself at home. Regret settles in alongside the hangover, both making it abundantly clear: I'm not as resilient as I once was.

Dragging myself upright, the pounding in my head intensifies with each reluctant step. Pressure building at the base of my skull. A vague mental map of the room leads me to stumble into the corner, where my suitcase waits like a cruel joke. After a few clumsy attempts, my hands finally land on the zipper.

Flipping it open, the realization dawns: no painkillers. Not even a single packet tossed in at the last minute. "Figures." The frustration clings to the single word, my sarcasm lost on the empty walls.

A slow spin distorts the edges of my vision before my balance catches back up. I rifle through my bag, brushing over something solid—my charger. I shove the cord into the port with more force than necessary, willing it to work quickly, the tiniest thread of control slipping back into my grasp.

Ultimately, I decide I can't just sit here and let the pain eat away at me. Pushing past the exhaustion, I head for the door. Hotels usually have a drawer of forgotten essentials or a clerk who might take pity on me. I just need something—though at this point, I'd settle for a distraction, or a lobotomy.

The fluorescent lights in the lobby glare down like a personal attack, pressing on an invisible bruise. Each step toward the front desk sends a fresh jolt of nausea surging up my spine, my body protesting every decision that has led to this moment.

I try to push through it, but my legs turn to jelly. My vision spins as I stumble over to a nearby couch and sink into it, putting my head between my legs, hoping the churning sickness will pass.

"Dylan?" The sound of my name cuts through the pain, and my head snaps up to see none other than Brooks Holland at the front desk, watching me with wide, concerned eyes. His gaze catches mine, and he's on his feet in an instant, stepping toward me. "What are you doing here? Is everything alright?"

"I just—" I part my lips to speak, but the words die in my throat as my insides constrict. My stomach clenches violently, and before I can think, I lurch forward, seizing the nearest vase and retching into it.

Brooks drops beside me in an instant, guiding me onto the couch with a careful grip. He doesn't rush, doesn't fumble, like an anchor keeping me from slipping under.

"Easy," he says, as though my body isn't actively betraying me. Spent and shaking, my muscles go slack, my weight tilting toward him. I don't mean to stay there, but moving feels like too much effort, and he doesn't push me away.

"Are you alright?"

"I—" The answer sticks for half a second before slipping loose. "No." A wave of fatigue surges through me, engulfing everything in its path, my lungs hitching around a breath that doesn't quite fill deep enough. "I feel like shit."

I ease back, each motion calculated in an attempt to regain my composure. Not because I actually feel better, but because looking like I do is the next best thing.

"What happened?"

"I'm just nauseated," I manage, though my voice betrays me. "My headache won't quit. No meds. No food. No sleep. And—" I stop, biting back the rest of the sentence with an inhale.

Brooks watches me, but doesn't pry.

I focus on his eyes, searching for the right words, but all that comes is an awkward pause.

His gaze stays steady, like he already knows I won't ask unless I have to. "What would help?"

The instinct to wave him off is there, but the pounding behind my eyes wins. "Tylenol. Ibuprofen. Anything, if it's not too much trouble." I breathe through another wave of discomfort. "I'll pay for it."

"Got it. Stay put, I'll find something. You're not paying for it, so don't argue."

The moment he steps away, I press my hands against my thighs, willing strength back into my limbs. It doesn't work. When he returns, he crouches back down beside me, dropping two pills into my palm before handing me a water bottle. I don't think. I just swallow.

"I should get back," I say, though I make no move to stand. My eyes drift to the vase, and I cringe. "I— God, I'll replace that. I promise."

Brooks huffs out something close to a laugh. "I'd be more worried about making it up to housekeeping." He leans against the couch, arms crossed. "What's the plan? Think you can make it, or am I coming with you?"

"I've got it."

"If you say so." Brooks steps back, but not far, his attention narrowed in like he's waiting for me to prove myself wrong.

I reach my door, grab the handle, and push. Nothing. A harder pull—still no give.

Brooks tilts his head, watching as I try again, but stays quiet.

A fourth attempt ends with me smacking the wood lightly, my patience running out. My head tips back in frustration before I spin on my heel and stalk toward him, expression flat.

"You didn't grab your key when you left, did you?"

"No." It's an automatic answer, but not a confident one. "I was too focused on getting rid of this headache. And maybe I had a bit too much to drink on the plane. Plus, jet lag—"

His voice interrupts my spiral. "Dylan."

I force my attention back to him. "Yeah?"

"Breathe. No need to explain. I'll get you a new key."

"I'm sorry, I just—" My throat works around the words. "I hate feeling like an inconvenience."

"Pretty sure you couldn't be one if you tried."

He leaves to grab a new key, and by the time I finally step inside, gravity pulls me straight to the bed. I drag a pillow over my face, like it might muffle the relentless pounding that refuses to let go. The cool pressure is a brief mercy but my mind is fevered, running itself ragged in the dark. The headache will fade. The ache in my chest won't—not until I stop running from it.

The sheets twist around me like restraints, trapping me in this restless purgatory. My limbs scream for rest, running circles around my exhaustion like a cruel game.

Sleep, fickle as ever, must have stolen me away for just a moment— long enough for the sharp ping of my phone to yank me back, sending a jolt through my half-conscious body.

Squinting against the invasive flow, I rub my face before reaching for my phone. I fumble for it, but the moment my eyes adjust to the words on the screen, the air in the room seems to thin.

Brooks: Hey, uh…would you maybe want to grab breakfast? No pressure, just thought I'd ask.

My gut reaction is to turn him down. I barely made it through last night, but the emptiness in my stomach tightens like a fist. Begrudgingly, I type out my response, surrendering to the fact that avoiding him won't fill the empty space in my heart—or my stomach.

Dragging myself out of bed feels like a monumental effort, but the promise of a hot shower wins out. Steam clouds the mirror as my dark jeans and a fitted white cardigan come together as the day's armor.

My reflection staring back is less than inspiring—pale, worn down, teetering on the edge of exhaustion. I rub at my cheeks, hoping to bring some life back into them, but it doesn't help. With an exasperated sigh, I make my way to the lobby. As it comes into view, so does last night's vase disaster, mortification trailing close behind.

"Morning," Brooks calls out as he rounds the corner, his voice carrying that familiar unruffled comfort, like an old sweatshirt, broken in just right. The dark jacket he's wearing fits him well, structured but not stiff, the sort of thing he probably threw on without a second thought. Beneath it, a white hoodie softens the sharp edges, fabric stretched slightly across his shoulders. He looks like the kind of warmth you want to sink into, the kind of trouble you know better than to chase—but do anyway.

Meanwhile, I feel like I'm holding my breath in a room with no oxygen.

"Ready to go?"

"Yeah," I say, smoothing a hand over my shirt like it might press the rest of me back into place. "Food sounds good." If nothing else, it's a distraction. One I desperately need.

He shifts, leaving just enough space for me to walk past. For a breath, I don't move.

Food. Just focus on that. One plate. A simple, forgettable thing.

At least, it should be simple—picking up a fork and chewing—but the whole thing feels like trying to breathe with my head underwater.

As we walk, the ink curling around one of his wrists pulls my attention. The intricate silhouettes of trees, dark and deliberate, seem almost alive against his skin, with tiny stars scattered between the branches like distant embers. Something about it stirs an allure I can't quite ignore. The urge to reach out and trace the lines, to ask about their meaning, rises before I can stop it.

A deep breath steadies me, but the thought remains. My fingers twitch at my side as I focus on the pavement beneath my feet, willing myself to stay grounded. It feels safer this way—safer not to act on the impulse, not to let him see just how much I'm still drawn to him.

Tracing the edge of my left collarbone through my shirt, I press down as if I could force the memory etched into my own skin deeper or maybe even erase it altogether. But the tattoo remains, heavy in ways ink shouldn't be.

When his truck comes into view, a faint sting of disappointment catches me off guard. I'd been bracing for the sight of his old pickup from high school—a relic of long drives and late-night conversations, its faded paint telling stories of its own. Instead, a cement-gray Toyota Tacoma gleams in the morning light, its polished edges and modern design a glaring reminder of how much time has passed. The shift feels jarring, like another piece of the past slipping further away.

Brooks swings the door open, and I step up quickly, tucking my hands beneath my thighs the moment I sit. My stomach gives a quiet growl, a not-so-gentle nudge that breakfast is overdue. Brooks settles in beside me, his fingers tapping once against the wheel before he shifts the truck into gear.

The tires crunch over pavement as we merge onto the road, Rockport spilling past the windows. It's like looking at an old photograph, the edges faded but the core still intact. Every mile seems to draw my anxiety deeper. This town is a time capsule I'm not sure I'm ready to open.

The second we stop, the past rushes up to meet me—Ruby's Diner. The name on the weathered sign feels like a punch to the gut, and for a moment, I consider walking back to The Drift. This used to be *our* place, where everything felt unshakable. Now, it's the last place I want to set foot in with him. Regret coils in my chest. Hindsight mocks me. It's a small town with limited options. I should've seen this coming.

I make no move to open the door. My fingers stay curled in my lap, my breath shallow, my pulse a steady drum against my throat. Maybe if I sit still long enough, I won't have to do this.

Then, the soft click of a handle.

Brooks rounds the truck, his footsteps sure against the pavement. The inside of the cab feels safe, distant—but when my door swings open, the barrier shatters. A rush of air spills in, taming the blaze spreading through me. I grip the seat, but his gaze holds me captive—expectant, patient. He's not letting me stay here.

My legs are stiff when I shift forward, muscles locked in quiet rebellion. The first step feels impossible—like the moment before cliff diving—but Brooks doesn't waver. His hand rests lightly on the doorframe—not pushing, not rushing, just waiting.

Inside, muted chatter fills the air, pressing in with the scent of fried bacon and fresh coffee. But the lights cut through it all, casting long shadows on the wood-paneled walls. Everything here feels like it's been paused in time, stubbornly resisting the years. The aging photos hung haphazardly along the walls catch my attention, their worn borders framing moments I can't forget, no matter how hard I try.

One photo stops me—a shot of Cape Mercy Lighthouse. A figure leans against the railing, silhouetted against the vast ocean, the sun glinting off the waves below. The familiarity doesn't settle—it writhes, like a trapped insect under glass. Air stalls in my throat as the reason clicks into place. The photographer captured not just the lighthouse, but a moment I never thought would be shared. Salt-laced air lifts my hair, the water stretching endlessly toward the horizon—like standing on the edge of a moment that no longer belongs solely to me.

Brooks had said photography could hold time still, that it could turn a fleeting feeling into something permanent. Looking at this photo now, I understand *exactly* what he meant.

"Let's grab a seat," Brooks says, pulling my attention from his photo on the wall.

I follow him, easing onto the stool as it wobbles beneath me. The menu stares back, its words bleeding together the longer I try to focus, my mind grasping for something—anything—solid.

Brooks lifts a hand in greeting, catching the attention of the woman behind the counter. "Morning, Brooks. Didn't expect to see you before Sunday."

"Dylan, this is Nadine," Brooks says, tipping his head slightly toward her—a motion that feels instinctive, like muscle memory. Like the two of them have shared a thousand conversations at this very counter.

"Now there's a name I've heard more than a few times."

"And here I thought I was flying under the radar."

She chuckles softly, her energy radiant in a way that makes it hard to hold onto my defenses. "Oh, you were. Until Ruby opened her mouth. Let me take a guess—coffee to start?"

I exhale quietly relieved by the shift to something mundane. "Yeah, that sounds perfect, thanks."

She steps away to grab a pot, and I let my gaze wander around the diner, taking in the worn booths and chipped checkered tiles, trying to find something new.

Ruby Miller appears from the kitchen, her copper-red hair perfectly styled in silky waves that match her presence. The remnants of yesterday's awkward encounter dissolves in an instant, replaced with a comfort that feels like home.

"Dylan! Sweetheart, Nadine just told me you wandered in," she says, her voice brimming with its natural sparkle. "And Brooks—well, there you are. I knew you two would end up back here together soon enough."

"Morning, Ms. Miller."

She waves a hand, dismissing any formality before planting herself in front of us with a no-nonsense look. "Okay, here's the deal. You two are ordering whatever you want this morning. It's on me, got it?"

"That's too much, Ruby. We can't let you do that."

Her playful tone carries over as she winks. "Oh, I'm not joking, babydoll. It's not every day we have a little reunion here. Consider it my treat. You both deserve it."

"Ruby, seriously. I'm the one who dragged Dylan out this morning. I've got it covered," Brooks counters.

Ruby flicks an imaginary speck of dust off her sleeve before sending a mock-accusatory point his way. "Oh no, sugar, this isn't for you. It's for her."

Nadine chuckles from her spot behind the counter as she brings over our coffee. "You'll lose this argument, Brooks. You know first hand Ruby is as stubborn as they come. Just let her have her way."

Brooks lets out a resigned groan, tilting his head slightly. "Fine, you win. But you know I'm ordering half the menu now, right?"

"I always win, babydoll. Go on ahead. I won't regret a thing. But let's not kid ourselves, you'll be ordering the same pancakes you always do."

True to form, Brooks orders the same pancakes he's sworn by since we were younger. I, on the other hand, opt for strawberry waffles, though my appetite flickers in and out like a faulty light. Ruby stays close, keeping the conversation light like a well-timed distraction from the tension that might take root once we're alone.

The conversation flows easily, like it always does when we're together. There's no rush to fill every pause, but somehow we're always talking. It's comforting, like slipping into a pair of shoes you've had forever. And then, New York comes up.

I start talking without even realizing it, telling them about my move there after finishing my art degree. I think I've said it a thousand times before, but it feels different now. I moved there because I craved invisibility—because the city had a way of blending people into the masses. I liked that. I liked being just another face in the crowd, where nobody cared if I was there or not. It was like I could finally be myself without anyone noticing.

Then, I start to tell them how I met Aaron—except I hesitate, his name catching in my throat. Brooks stays still, but his shoulders pull back, a barely-there shift that speaks volumes. I tread carefully, choosing my words like stepping stones across a river, mindful of every placement.

"We connected over art," I say, testing the waters, eyes flicking to his, tracking his reaction like a second heartbeat. "Eventually, he convinced me to come work for him." The words feel heavier now.

I push forward, filling the silence further before it can stretch too long, explaining how stepping into Chelsea Art Haus felt like entering a different world—a symphony of bold colors and kinetic art, everything demanding attention. It's not the quiet life I thought I wanted, but it's predictable. And these days, predictable feels like a win.

Brooks is quiet—not in an uncomfortable way, just listening as Ruby peppers me with questions, offering little of his own. Every now and then, he answers when prompted, but for the most part, he's content to sit back and let our conversation unfold around him.

I don't push him. We don't need to talk about everything. But there's starting to be a part of me that wants to, to bridge that gap and close the distance after everything that's happened.

The clink of dishes and the sizzle of the grill are familiar background noises, almost making everything feel normal. But then Ruby's sharp clap cuts through it all. She's smiling, her eyes bouncing between Brooks and me like she's trying to piece something together.

"Feels like just yesterday you two were sneaking out back during Dylan's breaks, thinking no one noticed," she says, a teasing note in her voice.

Her words hit me like a sudden wave, pulling me under before I can even brace myself. It's strange how something so casual, so innocent, can dredge up a memory I thought I'd forgotten. I'm back there in an instant—reliving those stolen moments with Brooks.

I remember how he'd lead me through the back door, the cold bite of the metal handle against my fingers as we slipped away, shutting us off from everyone else. How his laugh would echo in the alley as we passed old wooden crates and faded posters on the wall, the ones that had started peeling away years before. Then, he'd pull me close, and in that slip of time, the world would soften, as though we were the only two stars left in a sky emptied of everything else.

"That was a long time ago," I say, forcing a casual tone, though the edge in my voice betrays me. The last thing I need is for this conversation to wander further.

Ruby isn't deterred. She chuckles lightly, brushing off my attempt to redirect. "Long time or not, I've watched a lot of folks come and go over the years. Let me tell you, what you two had? That kind of connection doesn't just come along every day. Most people go their whole lives without finding it."

Beside me, Brooks shifts in his seat, and a soft sound escapes him—his throat clearing, maybe—but he doesn't say anything. It's impossible to tell if his lack of response carries agreement or discomfort.

"People change," I say, knowing she wont believe me.

Ruby's eyes hold mine, unfazed. "Maybe. But there are things you can't rewrite, no matter how much time passes."

The bell above the diner door jingles softly. It's a small sound, but it ripples through the restaurant, drawing my attention. The room grows unusually quiet, conversations faltering mid-sentence. Even Ruby pauses, her energy suddenly still as her eyes lock onto the door.

When I follow her stare, icy clarity hits me. I understand the reason for her reaction now, but there's no escaping it. No escaping her.

Denise Rivers.

My mother.

14

Brooks

The party downstairs is loud enough to shake the walls, but up here, the room feels charged in a more deliberate way. Chloe leans against Colt's dresser, arms crossed, and her lips curve in a way that might be seductive if it weren't so calculated. Every move she's made tonight has led to this—her relentless circling, her careful timing, all designed to corner me here, away from everyone else.

"I figured you would have come looking for me by now," she quips, her voice dripping with confidence as she pushes off the dresser and saunters toward me. "Guess I was wrong."

I remain by the window, pretending to be interested in the group of idiots playing football drunk on the lawn below. The string lights flicker like they're about to give out, casting weird shadows on their stumbling forms. One of them trips, sending a loud cheer through the group, but even that doesn't drown out my building irritation.

"Didn't know I was supposed to."

"Come on, Brooks," she teases, stepping further into my space. Chloe's hand brushes my arm like it's supposed to mean something. "You can't tell me you don't miss it…miss *us*."

I instinctively take a step back, putting space between us. "I think we both know that ship sailed a long time ago, Chloe."

Her eyes narrow, and for a second, her playful facade slips. "Because of her?"

"Her?" I feign ignorance, though we both know exactly who she means.

"Dylan," she spits her name like it's poison. "Ever since she showed up, you've been different. Distant. You used to actually have fun, Brooks. Remember that?"

I laugh, though there's no humor in it. "Oh, my distance is because of her now, not because of anything you did, right?"

Chloe's expression hardens, and she steps closer, blocking my view of the lawn. "I know you, Brooks. You're always wanting to save people, *fix* things. Is that not what she is? A project?"

"You don't know what you're talking about."

"Oh, I think I do," she snaps, her voice rising just enough to make the door seem too thin, too close to the party below. "I see the way you look at her. Like she's some broken puzzle you can't wait to piece together. Honestly, it's pathetic."

"Chloe," the warning in my tone barely disguises the frustration coming to peak beneath it.

She doesn't stop. "Let's not pretend we don't know how this ends. She's counting down the days until she can leave this town in her rearview mirror. And you?" A cold laugh follows. "You're going to stay right here in Rockport. You'll fall in line, like always, because disappointing your dad? Not an option for you. So, go ahead, keep hoping. It's not going to make a difference, B. It won't last, no matter how badly you want it to."

"Yeah, I've heard enough. My connection with Dylan isn't something you get to comment on. You forfeited that right a while ago. I've played nice, mostly to avoid drama, but don't mistake that for anything more. This isn't about me—it never was. If it were, your actions would have shown it. No, this is you dealing with your own insecurities by undermining her."

Chloe's posture tenses, and she takes a step back, her expression contorting with a mix of fury and disappointment. "Fine," she snaps, turning on her heel. "But when she's gone, and you're left here alone, don't think I'll pick up the pieces."

She whips around, the door slamming with a finality that makes the room feel smaller. I lean against the dresser, a long breath escaping me as my fingers tug at my hair, trying to pull my mind together. The door remains closed, motionless, offering me nothing. It might as well be the end of the world for all the answers it holds.

The thrum of life downstairs seeps back in—laughter, music thumping, and Colt's voice rising above the rest with that unmistakable confidence that draws attention like a magnet.

I end up back in the kitchen, my steps dragging as Colt lounges against the counter, beer in hand.

"There he is," Colt drawls, raising his drink in mock celebration. "Saw you hiding upstairs. How'd that work out for you?"

I swipe a bottle from the counter, popping the cap with a satisfying snap. "About as well as you'd expect."

"Did she tear you to pieces or try to crawl back?"

"Both, I think," I answer, tipping the bottle back. The beer is lacking the chill I'd prefer, but it slides down anyway, at least it's something. "She said I've changed, called Dylan a 'project,' and then rounded it out by telling me I'll end up alone."

Colt snorts, nearly choking on his drink. "Damn, Chloe really went for the trifecta. Guilt trip, jealousy, and trashing your love life all in one shot. Gotta respect the commitment."

"She acts like she doesn't remember how we got here, like the past reset just because she decided she wants something from me."

"Or maybe you didn't care enough to call her on it. Something tells me you've been a little…preoccupied. Not that I blame you."

"Yeah, you've got me there. There's no angle with Dylan, no second-guessing what she wants. It just works."

Colt lets out a low whistle, dragging it out for effect. "No way! You like her? Who would've guessed? Oh wait…literally everyone but you."

"Thanks for the insight, Dr. Phil."

"Can't help it, man. I only state the obvious. And you? You're a lost cause."

"Glad to know I'm entertaining you."

"More than you know."

Graham slides into the space beside Colt, spinning a bottle cap between his fingers like a coin. "What's going on over here? Did Brooks finally admit he's whipped?"

"Give it a minute." Colt smirks, raking a hand through his blond hair before letting it fall right back into his eyes. "We're nearly there."

"Damn, I was ready to start taking bets on how long it'd take."

Miles' voice cuts through like a firecracker popping off. "B! Colt! Grams! Haul it—Flip, Sip, or Strip is about to start."

Colt's posture straightens, like a gambler reading a promising hand. "Now that's my kind of game."

Graham gives the front of my shirt a quick tug before letting go, like I'm a dog on a loose leash. "Let's go, Romeo. I'm sure your girl is out there, don't leave her hanging."

The backyard is packed, a loose sprawl of people filling every step, railing, and patch of grass. A game of chicken is happening in the pool, and a girl vanishes beneath the water with a dramatic splash, leaving only ripples and gloating survivors behind. Near the fence, someone's turned over a cooler, using it as a makeshift DJ booth, with their phone hooked up to a speaker that's seen better days. The music crackles but no one seems to care.

It's the kind of night I've lived a hundred times over—except this time, she's part of it.

Dylan doesn't call me over or motion for me to come closer. Just tilts her cup ever so slightly, enough to prove she's seen me, but not enough to mean anything. She's not demanding my attention—and yet, she has it.

Colt walks by, ruffling my hair just to be annoying before heading straight for Beckett who's stretched out in a patio chair, half listening to whatever Miles is saying.

I run my tongue along the inside of my cheek, buying myself a second, a breath, but it's a useless attempt at control. There was a time, maybe even yesterday, when I could've convinced myself we were nothing more than friends. But that time is gone. And I give it willingly. Because love isn't a decision, it isn't a carefully plotted course. It's a quiet surrender. And somehow, without even realizing it, I've already given in. And I never stood a chance.

15

Dylan

THEN

The game has dragged on long enough for the stakes to blur, and as much as I excelled at beer pong, this one is proving to be my downfall. Guessing wrong has become a recurring theme, earning me more drinks than I can count—and, multiple times now, the removal of yet another layer of my clothing. I cling to what I have left—a crop top, a lace thong, and the hope that I don't lose again.

Colt leans back, his smirk just shy of wicked. "Dylan, I gotta say… this game is working in my favor."

"Should've known winning beer pong would cost me." I look back at my now empty cup, turning it in my hands. "Guess I was due for a shift in luck."

"Or," Brooks says, not missing a beat as he shrugs out of his hoodie like it's second nature, "maybe your luck's just changing hands."

I push my arms through the sleeves, rotating my shoulders to settle it into place. The dark-gray fabric is soft and oversized, the hem falling far past my thighs. It carries a warmth that isn't just from the material. It smells like him, and that simple detail lodges itself deep in my core.

A slow, deliberate once over from Chloe is all it takes to make something twist uncomfortably in my chest. She's daring me to react, to care. It's a reminder—one I don't need—that I still haven't talked to Brooks.

Shirts, socks, and sanity are tossed aside as the game escalates, the buzz in the air growing heady. My losing streak finally broke, though not before my top was added to the growing pile of discarded clothes. At least I still have the hoodie to keep me decent.

A few unfortunate souls have lost their remaining clothes completely. Among them is my brother—I know it without looking. I refuse to confirm it. Some things can't be unseen, and I have no desire to add that particular trauma to my night.

"Dylan, you should be out. Brooks saved you, and we all know it," Beckett slurs, arms spread wide like he's exposing some major scandal—far more of him on display than I ever need to see.

I keep my gaze anywhere but on him, drifting to Colt instead, widening my eyes in a silent plea for support. "KitKat, you've got about three inches of dignity left," I counter. "And it's hanging on by a prayer. No one cares about the hoodie."

Beckett scoffs, leaning in like he's prepared to argue. "First of all, you're only still in this game because Brooks took pity on your sorry ass."

Something soft sails through the air, and I hear the rustle of fabric as Colton tosses him something to cover himself. I don't look—won't look—but the shuffle of movement tells me he's at least making an effort. Small mercies.

"Second," Beckett continues, as though nothing happened. "I'm very dignified. Thank you."

"You just tried to shotgun a beer with the tab still on."

Beckett pauses, like he's trying to find a loophole in my logic. "That was strategy. You wouldn't get it."

"Sure. Just like this argument is a strategy to keep yourself from admitting you already lost."

"Details, details. You're focusing on the wrong—"

Brooks cracks his knuckles like we're about to enter a high-stakes poker match instead of a game fueled by bad decisions. "Alright Dill. Let's raise the stakes. One more round. Win, and I'm at your mercy. Lose? You ditch my hoodie, embrace the elements, and give the pool a show."

"Deal." I say instantly, accepting the challenge before he can rethink it.

Might as well push my last chip forward. What's there to risk? At this rate, my luck is either burning bright or burning out, and I'm hanging on by borrowed fabric. Brooks, on the other hand, still hasn't lost so much as a sock. Winning would change that. Losing? At least I'd be the one deciding what comes off next.

Brooks swipes the coin from Miles and flicks it skyward, letting gravity pull it down straight into his palm.

I don't wait—I know my choice. "Heads."

The smack of metal against his hand is sharp, final. He peeks at the result, lips pressing into a thin line. A beat passes—just long enough to make me wonder. Then, with a sigh that feels a little too forced, he shakes his head. "Unreal." His head drops forward briefly before he tosses the coin back to Miles. "It's heads."

The group explodes around us, the energy doubling back in waves, but my pulse trips for an entirely different reason—his stare. Brooks is looking at me like he's decided I'm what's worth the risk.

"What'll it be, Rivers?"

I shrug, the words slipping out with a confidence I don't completely feel. "A deal's a deal. You wanted a show? Then step up, Holland. The pool's that way, and the clothes are coming off—unless you're having second thoughts?"

He rises like gravity is an afterthought, the shift in his weight impossibly fluid. His fingers find the hem of his shirt, pulling it up and over his head in one clean motion. Shadows dance over the cut of his torso, the kind of definition that looks like it belongs on the cover of a sun faded magazine. I exhale through my nose while heat gathers low in my stomach, spreading like ink in water.

Brooks doesn't look away from me. Not once.

His thumbs hook under the waistband of his clothes, a flick of his wrist undoing the button. The zipper lowers. The denim slides down his legs, gathering at his feet before he steps out and kicks them aside. A chorus of cheers erupt, someone else bangs on the nearest table, but it's all background noise. Static compared to the way he's looking at me. Like there's no one else here.

Then, he moves.

Brooks takes two unhurried steps back, the muscles in his legs flexing beneath the glow of the patio's string lights. And then, without a second thought, he pushes off, cutting through the air in a sharp arc before colliding with the water below. The splash is instant, sending ripples fanning across the pool's surface.

A heartbeat passes, then another, before he finally resurfaces.

Water clings to every defined ridge of his body, streaming down his chest in slow rivulets. His soaked hair drips into his eyes until he shoves a hand through it, pushing it back. Overhead lights catch on the droplets tracing the sharp cut of his jaw and the broad slope of his shoulders. He tips his head, shaking off the excess water, his gaze locking onto mine as he moves toward the edge.

His hands find the concrete lip of the pool, fingers flexing before he hoists himself up in one fluid motion. The roll of his shoulders, the subtle rise of his chest, the way his stomach tenses as he lifts himself free from the water—it's unfair. Unholy, even.

I should tear my focus away before it's obvious that I can't. But my mind is stuck, circling the same thought over and over.

"Happy now?" His voice is smooth, like he's the one holding all the cards.

"Getting there."

"Your turn," he taunts, and his voice dips just enough to make it feel like a private challenge, meant for me and no one else.

"What do you mean, *my* tur—"

My fate is sealed before I can finish the thought. Brooks bends, sweeping me up in an instant. His arm locks around my legs, his sweatshirt bunched in his grip to cover my ass as I'm swung over his shoulder. I push against his back, protesting, but he doesn't break stride.

The plunge into the pool is unforgiving.

Water slams into me, pulling me under with the force of his momentum. The world goes silent for a moment, just a rush of bubbles and blurred faces from above.

The two of us break the surface gasping for air. I wipe my face, blinking through the sting of chlorine.

"I hate you," I manage.

Brooks shakes the water from his hair, completely unbothered. "You love me."

I reach for his shoulders without thinking, bracing myself against him in the water. His hands steady me, fingers pressing against my waist as I instinctively tighten my legs around him to keep myself afloat.

"I won," I argue. "I didn't have to skinny dip, remember?"

He barely moves, but I feel a shift in his focus as his attention dips. "You didn't. You still have my hoodie on."

I glance down, waterlogged fabric clinging to me. He's not wrong. I'm still *technically* covered.

The backs of his fingers brush my cheek as he smooths my hair away, taking his time like he's memorizing the feel of it. Then he pulls me closer, words spilling gently into the curve of my ear. "You can take it off if you want, but I think I'd rather keep you all to myself."

A sharp shrill cuts through the moment, coming from the

crumpled pile of his jeans. His head jerks toward it, a muscle ticking in his jaw. "Fuck, that's my dad." In one swift motion, he lifts me onto the pool's edge, then pulls himself up beside me. Before I can blink, he strides over, snatches his phone, shoots me one last look, and vanishes into the house.

Chloe slips into the space he left beside me, like she's been waiting for the opening since the game ended. "You know, Dylan," she purrs, her voice oozing with a twisted kind of sincerity. "Brooks is only nice because, well, someone has to be."

The air stills. "What?"

She lets out a short, humorless laugh. "You really don't get it, do you? He keeps you around because—let's face it—he feels bad. We all do."

"That's not true."

She angles her head, considering me like I'm an equation that doesn't quite add up. "Please, you can't honestly believe he sees you as anything but a charity case?" Her tone is unimpressed as she exhales sharply. "Whatever helps you sleep at night. Eventually, even saints get tired. Just don't say I didn't warn you."

Beckett steps in, his presence settling over the moment like an unspoken warning. "What's going on?" His tone is calm, but there's an edge to it, like a blade waiting to be unsheathed.

Chloe lifts her chin. "Just explaining something to Dylan."

"Yeah?" Beckett challenges, unmoved. "And what's that?"

"That she's wasting her time."

"Funny," Colt drawls, stepping in lazily. "You seem a little too invested for an ex-girlfriend. Sounds more like jealousy."

"Oh, please. Warning a girl that she's wasting her time on a guy? I'm just being honest."

"Right," Colt says. "You sure this isn't about you, though?" He tilts his head, letting the question settle before continuing. "Because if I recall, you weren't exactly faithful to Brooks."

Chloe's nails dig into her arms where they're crossed over her chest. "Screw you, Colt."

My skin prickles with heat, Chloe's words still biting. "Brooks and I are just friends," I blurt, desperate to shut this down before it spirals further.

Colt watches Chloe, not me, his smirk creeping into place. "Sure, and Chloe and Brooks were the perfect couple...wait, except for the part where she was crawling into Miles' bed when no one was looking."

The color drains from Chloe's face, her mask slipping for half a second before she catches it. But half a second is long enough. Her glare cuts to Miles like a knife as he approaches, her face burning an angry shade of crimson. With a sharp pivot she storms off like a villain exiting stage left.

"Well, that was dramatic," Colt mutters, rocking back on his heels with a satisfied expression.

I can barely process his words. My mind is stuck on the revelation he just unleashed. Chloe cheated on Brooks...with Miles?

My stomach lurches as I glance at Miles. He's unnervingly still, his fingers curled loosely at his sides, lips pressed into a flat, unreadable line.

"What. The. Fuck?" Beckett asks, his stare bouncing between them.

Miles sighs, rubbing the back of his neck. "It wasn't like that. I didn't know."

"You didn't know?" Beckett presses, confused. "Brooks is like your best friend."

Miles clears his throat, his jaw shifting as if he's trying to piece his words together carefully. "It was right after I got back from my dad's cabin last summer. There was a party, and—"

"She took his virginity," Colt interjects. "Hell of a first time, huh?"

"I didn't know they'd just started dating. I wouldn't have…touched her if I'd known."

Colt shifts closer, bracing both hands on Miles' shoulders, steadying him just enough to say don't stress it. "That girl has always known how to leave a mess behind."

Oblivious to the conversation, Brooks moves toward us, still half absorbed into whatever's on his phone. "Who does?"

The hush that follows is suffocating, pressing against my skin like a second layer. I scan their faces, but no one steps in to answer. My pulse kicks against my ribs as I finally speak. "Uh, Chloe."

Brooks raises an eyebrow, looking between us. "Chloe?" His eyes sharpen, suspicion flickering. "What'd she say this time?"

"Doesn't matter," I rush to say, though the words feel like a lie.

Colt snorts. "Oh, it matters. She's out here making Dylan feel like your personal pity project."

Brooks' jaw flexes, tension creeping into his voice. "She said that?"

"Yep. And then we had a lovely little trip down memory lane," Colt says, dragging out the words like he's savoring them.

"What memory lane?"

Miles exhales sharply, pinching the bridge of his nose. "Chloe and me. Last summer."

Brooks stills, his eyes darkening just enough to be noticeable. He crosses his arms, and I lean forward, searching his face for a reaction. "Brooks, I—"

"I really don't care enough to deep dive into Chloe's greatest hits. I'd rather talk about literally anything else. Like leaving. You in, Rivers?"

"Of course." I wring out a lock of hair, droplets hitting the concrete before I reach for a towel, pulling it closer like armor. "I should probably change first," I say, shifting toward the house. "Give me a sec."

"I'll wait."

Colt clicks his tongue. "How sweet."

The downstairs bathroom light hums overhead as I peel away the soaked hoodie, wringing out the excess water before draping it over the shower rod. I grab my dry clothes, shimming into my jeans before pulling the deep purple crop top over my head. The cotton provides a sense of warmth, hugging me like it belongs.

When I step back outside, Brooks is near his truck, absentmindedly tracing slow circles in the dirt with the toe of his shoe. He doesn't seem impatient, just caught up in whatever's running through his head.

I tug the shirt down, the fabric slightly clinging to my damp skin. "You ready?"

He lifts his gaze, a smile tugging at his lips as he unlocks the truck. "Yeah. Let's get out of here."

I climb in, and as we pull onto the road, the party shrinks behind us. The air slipping through the open window catching the ends of my still wet hair, twisting the curls against my cheek.

Brooks exhales, fingers flexing against the wheel. "Sorry about earlier."

"For what?"

He keeps his eyes on the road, but his right hand drifts from the steering wheel to the center console, hovering there—like he's debating reaching for mine. "Chloe. The whole situation." His fingers tap against the surface, restless. "She's wrong, you know. Whatever she said isn't true."

"She was drinking," I say, tracing a pattern on my jeans with the tip of my finger. "Alcohol and exes are a dangerous mix. I told you, parties aren't really my scene. I usually avoid them like the plague. But honestly? I still had a good time."

"You never went to any back in Wyoming?"

"Not a real one," I admit. "Maybe a birthday party in middle school, but nothing like that."

"And yet, you walked in there and won every game like it was nothing," Brooks says, a coy smile unfurling as he glances at me. His long lashes frame his eyes—dark and unfairly distracting.

"Let's not act like you didn't save me with that hoodie."

Brooks flicks the turn signal on, then shifts left, extending his arm behind me with an innocent stretch. "I don't know what you mean. I just thought you'd look good in it."

Absentmindedly, I trace the chain at my throat, my fingertips brushing over the pendant as my gaze lingers on him. In the dim glow of the radio, the freckles on his cheekbones stand out—tiny constellations I want to memorize. His words loop in my mind until I give in, biting the edge of my necklace and exhaling a calming breath against it.

The road bends, narrowing between towering trees, their branches a canopy that turns the night sky into shifting light. Brooks slows the truck before easing off the path, dust rising as tiny stones skitter aside while we break into a clearing. Without looking, he reaches behind him, his hand searching like muscle memory until it lands on what he wants—a heavy wool blanket, its edges frayed from years of use.

The door creaks as I push it open, the cold air slipping around me as I step onto solid ground. Above, the sky is vast, stars flung across it like someone tipped over a jar of glitter.

"Where are we?"

"Washburn Heights," he says, rounding the truck bed. He gives the blanket a quick shake before smoothing it over the tailgate. "Hop up."

I follow him, pressing my palms to the cool metal as I push myself up. My legs swing idly over the edge, the town below nothing but a soft glow against the dark.

Balancing on one arm, he inches closer, his pinky looping around mine in a way that feels intentional. "Not many people know about this place. When life feels like too much, this is where I go to remember how to breathe."

Our small connection is impossibly soft, but I feel it everywhere. "This feels like the kind of place you could sit and dream about anything."

"Alright, then. If you gave in to those dreams, where would they lead you?"

"Paris," I breathe, lifting my gaze to the stars. "That will never change. The art, the museums, the Eiffel Tower, it's timeless. It just feels like a place I'm at least meant to see."

"Then we'll go someday. I promise, eventually, I'll take you."

I bite my lip, dropping my gaze from the sky, suddenly feeling too small beneath it. "You don't have to promise me things like that."

"I don't say things I don't mean."

"People always mean things…until they don't."

The space between us tightens—not in distance, but in the quiet pull of something inevitable. His pinky slips away, only to be replaced by the deliberate intertwining of his fingers with mine. Just as the moment pulls me deeper, Brooks' free hand brushes against my jaw. He tilts my face up toward him, pulling my eyes to his.

"Then let me be the exception," he whispers, each word sinking into my skin, stirring a longing that fills every corner of me.

My bones feel liquid, my entire body melting from the importance of this single moment. His mouth inches closer, near enough that I can nearly taste his words as they form. "I've been waiting for this since the day I met you."

The way he looks at me feels like a spell—his emerald irises pulling me in, impossible to resist. The past and future disappear. There's only now. Only this. I tilt my chin, the tip of his nose brushing mine in the gentlest collision of need.

My lips part, and then his meet mine—tender, unhurried, like a fairytale unfolding in slow motion. I melt into him, my fingers curling into his shirt as I pull him closer. He deepens the kiss, threading a hand into my hair, cradling the back of my head while his other molds to the curve of my spine. Brooks holds me like he's afraid to let go. And I go to him willingly, drawn by a force older than time itself—like the stars carved this moment into the universe long before we ever existed. When he finally pulls away, our foreheads rest together, both of us breathless.

"You," he exhales. "If my dreams ever lead me somewhere, they would lead me to you, Dylan."

There's an ache, a longing, a fear I don't have a name for. The edge of the blanket becomes my focus, and my fingers press into the thick weave of the blanket, kneading the fabric as if the right words might be hidden in its threads. "I can't…" I gather the courage like fragile glass in my hands before lifting my eyes back to his. "I'm leaving, after graduation. Rockport was never supposed to be permanent."

His hand catches mine, stilling my nervous movements. "Rockport might not be permanent, but that doesn't mean we can't be. I meant what I said before—you're worth more than just surviving. If leaving is what you need, then go. But give me right now. Give me tomorrow— hell, give me forever if you'll have me. However long I get to be yours, I'll take it, no matter what it costs me in the end."

When I look at him this time, it's different. I don't just see him—I feel him in every sense. The way his hair falls in careless waves, a few strands nearly brushing the smallest white scar above his eyebrow. The freckles dusting his nose, fading as they reach his cheeks. I wonder how many stories are etched into his skin, ones I've never thought to ask about.

Yet, somehow, I already know the most important one.

I'm the rain that never stays, and he's the earth drawing me in like

I was always meant to fall for him.

"Okay," I say, the word slipping past my lips like a promise, a quiet yes to exploring whatever this is between us. "Let's see what happens."

16

Dylan

Now

My mother's once bottle blonde hair has been replaced by her natural mousy brown, but there's no mistaking her. She looks different—healthier. Her skin, once ashen and lined with depletion, now has a glow to it. Her dull, hollow eyes I remember now shine, a striking blue that mirrors my own. She looks... well, tired, but undeniably well.

Noticing the diner around me feels impossible—blurred faces, the clink of silverware, none of it matters. She's the only thing that feels real. Resentment curdles beneath my skin, guilt threading through it like smoke, but I smother them before they can take shape. She doesn't deserve anything from me—not my excuses, not my forgiveness, not a single piece of who I am now.

Denise moves like she's forgotten how to walk, uneven, her body jerking forward like instinct pulled her to me before her mind could catch up. She doesn't dare blink, as if expecting me to dissolve before her eyes.

Her arms hover before she finally pulls me in. I don't move at first—my arms just hang there because I don't know what else to do. It's awkward.

Then, just as quickly as it started, it's over. She steps back, searching my face like she's trying to etch the changes into her mind. Tears stream down her cheeks, but she doesn't wipe them away.

"Oh my God," she breathes. "It's you. You're really here!" Her voice shakes, and I can tell she doesn't know where to start. I wonder if maybe she won't. Perhaps we'll just stay here, staring at each other while she tries to silently bridge the years between us.

But to my dismay, she speaks again, and the moment shatters. "I didn't know if I'd ever see you again. I tried—I um, searched—prayed. And now..." She lets out a laugh, but it breaks halfway through, turning into something else entirely. "You're back."

She announces it like that changes anything between us. That my return fixes the past and erases all the reasons I left in the first place.

She wipes at her face, her breathing labored, but the tears don't relent. "You're all grown up now. Look at you. Oh, Dylan, my sweet girl."

Her hands reach for mine, and every muscle in my body screams to pull away, but I don't.

I can't.

It's too much. The diner, the way she's looking at me, saying my name like it's something sacred. My stomach twists so violently it's a wonder I don't get sick right here on the diner floor.

I glance past her, scanning the space for something—an excuse, a way out, a vase, anything. But there's nothing.

"I've thought of you every single day since you left. How are you? Are you in town long? Do you have time to talk?"

I should've expected this, but nothing could have prepared me for the way her words snag against old wounds, stirring up the very things I've spent years trying to bury.

"Um," my response stumbles, leaving my mouth in pieces. "I… don't know."

It's a lie, a weak patch over something splitting at the seams. I know it won't hold, but letting anything else show isn't an option.

Wet trails carve through her cheeks, tracing the hills and valleys that age has gently sculpted in my absence. Time has reshaped her in ways I wasn't around to witness. My eyes drop to her hands, searching for steadiness in the small details: the slight shake of her fingers, the fine lines etched into her palms. Feeble distractions. Anything to keep myself from breaking down in front of her.

She steps back, hands disappearing as if the contact now burns her. Another pass over her cheeks, her eyes scanning mine, hoping for something I can't give.

"Okay. I understand." Her voice falters, cracking with emotion. "You look…absolutely beautiful, Dylan."

It doesn't make sense. Beautiful? *She's* calling me beautiful? It feels absurd, a mistake in a narrative I don't recognize. Not after everything that's happened. Not from her.

"Thanks."

"I'd really love to talk…even just for a minute." She presses forward, insistent, needling her way through my defenses. My focus darts to Brooks, a wordless plea for him to intervene.

As if on cue, he stands, the slight shift of his weight making the stool creak beneath him. "We should get going," he says smoothly, offering me his hand. "Don't want to be late."

His palm presses against mine, his hold unwavering. He doesn't rush to pull away, offering Ruby and unspoken sentiment only she seems to catch.

She breathes out slowly, her eyes holding mine. "Dylan, honey, make sure to come back to the diner before you go."

I try to smile, but it falters before it fully forms. Relief hovers just beyond reach. The door is right there, an escape waiting to be taken. But just as I move, cold fingers catch my wrist, tugging me back. I swivel, unsteady, facing the one person I was sure would have no problem letting me go.

"I ne—" The sound she makes isn't quite a word, more a fractured attempt at one. "I need to say I'm sorry. I did…*said* things I can't justify, and I regret them all. If you never want to see me again, I get it. But I—" She squeezes her eyes shut, and when they open again, she looks like she's afraid of what I'll do with her words. "I love you. I always have, even when I could never show it."

It's a bomb to the part of me that still remembers, still aches— no matter how much I've tried to forget. Time folds in on itself, and suddenly I'm not here anymore. I'm years behind, small hands gripping the edge of a hope that always felt just out of reach. Love? After everything she put us through, the word feels like a cruel joke.

She clings to me for a moment before her grip weakens and falls away. "I'm still at the old house. If you decide you're open to talking, there's a lot I'd really like you to know."

I make my exit without another word. One foot in front of the other until I'm outside, the truck ahead of me. The click of the door unlocking is the only sound I focus on as I climb in and close myself off.

Brooks doesn't ask if I'm okay, and I'm grateful for it. I rub my palms against my legs, but no matter how much friction I create, I can still feel her there.

I thought I was stronger than this—that years away would've given me enough distance to make this bearable. But being here now, in Rockport, with the past pressing in from all angles, I realize how naïve that was. My mom's voice, her apology, the ghosts I've never invited back—they claw their way up, and suddenly, I can't stop it. And just like that, I lose the fight.

When the truck eases to a stop, I don't need to ask where we are. I know. Washburn Heights. As I take in the view that once felt like everything, I realize Brooks brought me here for a reason—it's the one place that might still hold the illusion of escape.

The view hasn't changed—the town still sprawls toward the ocean, the beach still sits where it always has—but the feeling is different. Depleted. The trees that used to shield this place, that made it feel like our own private world, have vanished. The last time Brooks and I were here it felt like a promise. Now, it feels like a reminder of everything we lost.

At seventeen, I hadn't been searching for a place to belong, but that night staring out at the endless sky from Brooks' truck, I found one. I didn't know it then, but he planted something deep—an all consuming feeling I wouldn't name until much later.

"Rockport was supposed to be a closed chapter," I say, more to the wind than to him. "But then I saw you, and it hit me—I've never really left any of it behind.. I ran as far as I could, pushed it down so deep I thought it was gone. Now I'm here, and I don't know how to put myself back together."

His fingers skim the truck's hood, tapping out in a slow, uneven rhythm. "Have you visited him?"

The question is a match to a room soaked in gasoline. "No. " My confession sears through me as I admit it out loud, a merciless fucking wildfire that leaves nothing untouched. It doesn't just wound, it annihilates, charring the truth into the marrow of my bones. My heart was never meant to hold on, only to burn itself to ash with the things it was stupid enough to want.

"Dylan." It's not a suggestion. It's not a plea. It's a verdict. "You can't pretend it didn't happen."

His statement unearths something feral, something gutted and left to rot in the ruins of a life I once hoped for. "Then tell me Brooks— what the hell am I supposed to do instead? Lay down and let the pain eat me alive? Pretending is the only reason I'm still fucking standing."

Brooks doesn't answer, letting me turn back to the cliffside, my fists curled so tight my nails could draw blood. The ocean sprawls below, all soft shimmer and open arms, like it hasn't swallowed far worse things than me. The storm isn't out there—it's inside, clawing up my ribs, gnashing its teeth against my throat, begging to be let loose.

"I'm sorry, Dylan."

"You're sorry? Yeah, well, I've had plenty of time to choke it down."

"Stop," Brooks says, voice taut with regret. "I don't mean just that. I'm sorry for leaving you alone in it. I should've been there. You were the most important person in my life, and I convinced myself that leaving was protecting you." His throat bobs, and when he speaks again, it's quieter. "That staying away was what you needed."

His words settle in, fueling the fire already licking at my insides. I'm burning alive, heat riots in my veins, an untamed, vicious thing that refuses to stay ignored. *Protecting me?*

I snap toward him. "Are you actually standing there saying that to me? Like it's supposed to mean something?"

Brooks recoils, momentary guilt flashing across his face, but it's not enough. Not nearly enough. I close the gap between us, every restrained, suffocated, gut wrenching emotion I've kept hidden flooding to the surface. "Do you have any idea what you fucking did to me? What you left me with?"

"I—"

"Don't," The word rips from my throat. "Spare me the bullshit. Do you even hear yourself? You're talking to a ghost, Brooks. I trusted you once. And it fucking ruined me. So don't stand there and pretend I owe you anything."

His eyes drag over me like he's trying to pick apart the damage. As if he doesn't already know, like he didn't fucking cause it. Maybe he sees the fury splintered beneath my skin, the way it's festered into something unforgiving. Or maybe he just feels it, the repercussions of his decisions looking back at him.

His hand lifts, hovering—because he knows I should rip away. But I don't. Not yet. His fingers graze my cheek, the touch a fucking contradiction—too cold against the inferno pulsing beneath my skin. It teeters on the edge of soothing. Then, it fucking sears like a cigarette crushed into bare skin.

I finally manage to pull away, the absence of him both a mercy and an open wound. My breath snags, throat tightens, and I'm shaking my head before I even realize. "You don't get to do that."

My words cut, deep enough that I can see the moment they sink into flesh. He clenches his teeth, stiffens, but doesn't give me the satisfaction of a response. He just bears it, lets it stew in his silence. And I should hate him—I want to—but all I see is the boy I once loved so catastrophically it shattered me. The truth doesn't bleed from my mouth—it pours.

"You looked me in the eyes and promised me you'd be there. You fucking promised." The break in him is quick but vicious, a glimpse of ruin before he locks it away.

"And then you left me alone in the wreckage," I say, my voice catching like a blade to the throat. "You didn't even have the fucking decency to look me in the eye when you decided I wasn't worth it. I had to crawl to you—beg for answers, only for you to cut me down where I stood, like I never fucking mattered."

"It nearly fucking killed me" he says, his voice stripped down to nothing. "I thought—" He pauses, like he can't bear to finish. "I thought you deserved more than what I could give you. It wasn't that simple."

I let out a dry, brittle laugh. "What I *needed* was you, Brooks. Not some fucked up version of nobility. Just you. But you didn't care enough to stay, did you?"

He doesn't argue. Just stands there, spine bowed under the weight of my words.

"Sure, I may have ran from Rockport. But you? You left me to fucking drown first. You let me break, let me bleed out *alone*. Not a call. Not a text. You knew, and you just fucking watched."

I spin on my heel, each step away a battle, dragging the corpse of what we were behind me. "I screamed for you, Brooks. Cried for you. You don't get to be sorry now."

When I glance over my shoulder, the sight nearly takes me to my knees. His face is streaked with tears, and for the first time, I see it. What's left of him. Something torn apart and haphazardly stitched back together. "If I could go back, Dylan, I would tear myself open before I ever let you go. But I can't. I can't fucking change any of it."

He doesn't reach for me this time. Just moves toward the truck with desperation. The passenger door creaks open. An invitation. A surrender. I climb in, my jaw clenched so hard my teeth ache, the taste of iron thick on my tongue. The stillness between us is suffocating. Choking. A gaping wound neither of us dares to touch.

Brooks doesn't meet my eyes when we arrive back at The Drift.

Doesn't speak when he steadies me, his hands caught between holding on and letting go. He already knows it's too late, but I'd be a liar if I said I didn't want him to do it anyway. To grip my waist, to drag me back into something that doesn't exist anymore, and feel anything other than this all consuming pain.

The door to my room clicks shut behind me, and the moment it does, my ribs splinter, my chest caves in, and I finally let myself break.

Because today, I let things slip free that I never thought I'd say. I cracked myself open and let the mess spill out. I meant every single word—every razor-sharp, venom-laced syllable. But now, I see the truth. The heat of my anger burned everything in its path—except the one thing that truly deserved to go up in flames.

Me.

17

Dylan

"*There's no point in fighting, Dylan. No one will give a damn what comes out of your mouth. Not a single soul. Why would they? Your mom's a worthless drunk, nothing but a used up whore who can't keep her shit together. You really think anyone's gonna waste their time listening to you? You're nothing to them. Just noise. A problem waiting to be ignored.*"

He crowds in behind me, pressing in until there's nowhere for me to go. My throat locks, my hands fisting into the sheets as I shove my face into the pillow. "*You really thought you were special, didn't you? I made you feel that way. Made you believe you were important. But you're not. You never were.*"

His voice doesn't die with the dream. It stains the waking world. I bolt upright, breath rattling, sweat dripping, but the silence does nothing to wash him away. Sleep presses in, disorienting, and for a ghost of a second, I'm unsure if I'm awake or trapped in some cruel continuation of the nightmare.

My phone blinks on the nightstand, a dim beacon against the dark. Its glow cuts through the room in splintered lines, but nothing feels real enough to trust. My grip tightens on the blanket, desperate for the scratch of fabric.

"It's not real," the words tumble out quietly, more a plea than a reassurance. "He's gone. He's not here."

I peel myself from the mattress, the air biting at my sweat damp skin as my legs drag free from the tangle of sheets. The floor is unforgivingly cold, a shock of reality against the ghost clinging to me.

The bathroom light sputters to life, carving deep shadows into my reflection as I shove the faucet on. Water crashes against the sink, and I plunge my hands into it, dragging the icy relief up to my face. It drips from my chin, slipping down my neck like sweat, like blood, like a stain I can't scrub off.

I grip the edge of the sink, knuckles bone-white. The nightmare hasn't loosened his grip—it festers in the cracks of my skull, pulsing behind my eyes, whispering from the corners of the room.

A glass of water might help—might wash it down, remind me I'm still here.

The hallway feels impossibly long, each step down feels like wading through tar, dragging me deeper into the murk of the childhood I swore I'd buried. The sensation of his hands resurfaces, slithering back uninvited, and I force myself to focus on the smooth floor beneath my bare feet. The only proof that I am here, and not back there.

My throat clenches with a dull ache, as if something is lodged there. When I step into the kitchen, Greg's figure by the sink materializes out of the half light, flickering hues of the TV casting shifting patterns across his skin.

His voice cuts through the static in my head.

"Oh. Sorry if I woke you."

I halt mid step, my pulse still skittering from the nightmares claws. "No, I—um, was just getting water."

"You okay?" He moves closer, the shift in space sending a cold shudder through me.

"Yeah." A blatant lie, but I cling to it. "It's just been a long night."

Greg barely exists in this house, slipping in and out, always on the road, barely leaving an imprint. My fingers press into the counter's edge, biting into my palm as he moves again—too close. I jerk back before I can stop myself.

He hesitates, his brows pulling together, but at least he stops. "Are you sure?"

"Sorry," I blurt, the apology tumbling out desperately. "I'm fine. Just jumpy. I'm heading back to bed." I leave before he can speak. The water doesn't matter. I abandon it, turning sharply, and retreat to my room, my pulse a war drum beneath my skin.

I drop onto the bed, but my body won't settle. The adrenaline fades, leaking from my limbs. Closing my eyes feels like an invitation, a door cracked open for the nightmare to crawl back through, and I'm not ready for that.

I grab my sketchbook and flip to a blank page, the lead carving harsh strokes as I press into the paper. His face threatens to drift back into focus, but the frantic movements of the pencil push it away.

Unruly, erratic lines fill the surface, growing harsher with every pass. The night stretches on, and the sun begins to rise, its light filtering weakly through the blinds. My burning eyes protest from lack of sleep, but the drawing isn't finished. Yet.

The portrait glares back at me, unsettling in its vulnerability. A specter of myself bled onto the page—eyes sunken beneath brutal strokes, lips split and bruised in shadows. Hair erupts in wild, frantic tangles, like it's trying to escape the body it belongs to. She looks hunted. Cornered. Like she knows there's no way out.

Scrawled words overlay the image, repeated over and over—*why me?*—cut deep into the paper. My fingers trace the grooves, feeling the heaviness of the graphite ground too hard. It's a reflection of everything I've bottled up all these years. It's the pain I've hidden, the rage of every buried scream, spilling out in lines that snarl and snare across the page.

A glance at my phone on the nightstand sends panic through the moment. Time's run out, and my shift at Ruby's starts in less than an hour. My clothes are thrown on hastily—jeans, an oversized cardigan, whatever's within reach. I'm dressed and out the door in a rush, and the short walk to the diner is a blur, but as I arrive the clock inside reads just before seven—I barely made it.

"Good morning, Sunshine!" Ruby's voice rings from the kitchen, brimming with unshaken enthusiasm.

"Morning, Ms. Miller," I reply, though it's an effort to match her energy.

"Oh, none of that!" She waves a hand, already rounding the bar. "I told you—call me Ruby. I won't say it again."

Her golden-brown eyes gleam, her red hair spilling from a loose braid, as if she's always moving too fast to fuss over the details.

The hours blur together, the unwavering rhythm of the diner pulling me along until late afternoon sneaks up. The lunch rush ends, leaving only the sound of a damp cloth against the counter as I wipe it down. The bell above the front door chimes, and I glance up.

Brooks saunters in, all casual arrogance, hands buried in his pockets, that damn smirk already in place.

"What are you doing here?"

He gasps, clutching his chest like I just mortally wounded him. "Wow. No, 'Hey Brooks, so great to see you'? No, 'My day just got infinitely better'?"

"Pretty sure my shift ending was already the highlight of my day," I deadpan. "Your timing though, is suspicious."

"Suspiciously perfect, you mean?" He steps closer and presses a quick kiss to my forehead. "I have a sixth sense for knowing when you're about to be free. I was planning on heading to Cape Mercy Lighthouse for some photos and thought maybe you'd want to come along."

"I'd love to. Let me grab my stuff."

I clock out and head to the back, ditching my coffee scented shirt for something fresher.

The road stretches ahead, an ocean-kissed breeze sneaking through the cracked window. Music vibrating through the car like a second heartbeat.

Brooks flicks his fingers against the wheel, offbeat and unbothered, while the coastline stretches endless beside us. I glance at him, catching the way his lips curve with a grin that hints at excitement. His dimples deepen as he keeps his attention on the road, and I can't help but smile.

"You're staring."

I wrinkle my nose, a soft giggle escaping. "Just…enjoying the scenery."

"Oh yeah?" He throws a quick glance in my direction, the corners of his mouth twitching upward. "And what makes it so special?"

"Hmm." I shrug, squinting my eyes and offering a playful smile. "It's something I could get lost in."

"I could get lost in you…" There's amusement in his voice, and when his gaze drifts back over to me, heat spreads through every inch of my body. "Though if you keep looking at me like that, we might have to pull the truck over right here."

Heat flares in my chest, and I yank my focus to the windshield, biting my lip as the corners of my mouth threaten treachery. As we reach the lighthouse, he throws the car in park, barely waiting a beat before hopping out and pulling my door open with an exaggerated bow.

"Chivalry isn't dead, I see," I tease, slipping my hand into his as he helps me down.

"Only for you," he murmurs, like it's an unshakeable truth. "Come on. Let's take some pictures."

The climb up the lighthouse's steep staircase is enough to leave my legs burning, but the view at the top makes it worth every step. Cool air whips past us, sharp with salt, while sunlight dances off the water in rippling shards of silver.

"It doesn't feel real up here," I admit, leaning against the railing. "It's like we're both insignificant and invincible all at once. As if the world stops just for this."

"That's why I love photography," Brooks says, stepping closer. "You can capture moments like this. Freeze them. Own them. It's like holding time in your hands."

His camera clicks, the sound pulling me from the view.

"Did you just take a picture of me?"

He lowers the camera, a hint of a challenge in his expression. "I wanted to *freeze* the moment."

"Oh, sure. A picture of me looking windblown and confused. So sentimental."

"Not confused," he states, his eyes never leaving mine. "Just you, as you are. No doubts, no second guessing—just this moment."

His words sink in like footsteps in wet sand—fleeting but deeply felt. What is it about him that makes the sharp edges of my life dull to something manageable? Like the broken pieces aren't as jagged when he's near.

The wind whips strands of hair across my face, catching on my lashes, his hand moves, brushing them back with careful fingers. He stays close, the space between us shrinking until it feels like the world is holding its breath.

"You're thinking too much," he says softly, voice low enough to blend with the wind.

His lips hover close, and I barely manage to breathe before they press against mine. The cold metal railing digging into my back, a sharp contrast to the warmth of his touch. Brooks' hand moves to my neck, his thumb tracing a soft line across my cheek.

The kiss deepens, unraveling something in me I didn't realize was so tightly wound. For the first time in forever, the weight of my past feels distant, like it doesn't belong to me anymore.

Then, the moment shatters. My phone vibrates in my pocket, the buzz reverberating against the metal railing pressed behind me.

"Crap," the word slips out as I pull away and reach for my phone.

"What's wrong?"

"It's my mom." A sigh escapes as I stare at the screen. "I forgot to text her that I wasn't coming straight home after work." It's not because she cares whether I'm around—she just thrives on having the upper hand. "I have to go."

Brooks' fingers curl around mine as he steers me toward the stairs. "Alright, then I'll get you home."

The truck feels like a barrier as we drive, safe, but the moment I step out, reality crashes in. I press my palms against my jeans, restless with bottled up anxiety.

"I can come," Brooks offers, like it's not even a question, just a fact.

"No, it's okay."

"Promise?"

"I promise." The reassurance feels thin, but I don't want him involved in this. The chance of mom not caring is a fantasy. If I walk in with him, she'll play nice until he's gone—but the second the door closes behind him, I'll pay for it twice over.

"Alright. But text me if you need anything—*anything*, Dylan. I can come back if you need me to."

"I will." I press a gentle kiss to his cheek before pulling away, the space between us stretching taut with every step I take toward home.

The short walk inside feels like a march toward the inevitable. Pushing open the door, the low hum of the television cuts through the tension, and there she is—on the couch, her hair a tangled mess, frustration practically radiating off her.

"Look who finally showed up. Where have you been?"

"My shift ran late," the words come out steady, a practiced calm I've had years to master wrapping around them.

"You couldn't bother to text me? Do you have any idea how worried I was?"

"Sorry. It slipped my mind."

"Bullshit," she spits, standing now. "You're always forgetting something. Always screwing up."

Her words strike like a whip, but I bite back my response. Anything else would be fuel for the fire. Turning away, it's like wading through deep water, every step slower as her voice hooks into me, pulling me back.

"I was gathering laundry today. Had to wade through that wreck you call a room. It's just as messed up as you are—but want to take a wild guess at what I dug up?"

"You…went through my room?"

"Sure did. And lucky for me—otherwise, I'd have never stumbled across this little sketchbook." She dangles it like it's diseased. "The page it was open to? Downright deranged. Seriously, what the hell is wrong with you? Why would you draw yourself like that?"

"It wasn't yours to touch." The words barely make it past the tightness choking my throat.

"Well, isn't that just convenient." Her sneer could make even the strongest man cower. "Poor Dylan. Always pretending to be the victim, like your life is so hard. You don't fool me."

"That's not—"

"Shut up," she snaps, voice cracking as it turns into a screech. "Just shut up. You're more trouble than you're worth most days. And I'm done with you playing this act, like anyone should feel sorry for you."

"Mom, pl—"

"I can't do this right now. Just get out of my face."

The walls close in, pressing against me like a living thing, watching, waiting, as I drag myself toward my room. The door clicks shut, sealing me in, and I sink to the floor, the wood biting into me as I fold in on myself. My breath stutters, scraping against my lungs like it doesn't belong inside me.

Her accusation wraps around me, squeezing, strangling. She never stops to think—never wonders what I bury so deep it seeps out in lines. She only sees what she wants to. And now, she's turned it into something shameful.

I curl tighter, willing myself to be small, invisible. But disappearing isn't an option. Not anymore.

I plant my hands against the ground, deep enough that my nails almost splinter. My body protests, everything leaden, heavy. But I move anyway, hauling myself up piece by piece, as if I'm something irrevocably broken trying to remember what it is to stand.

The bathroom offers refuge, a fragile kind of sanctuary. Stepping inside feels like slipping between worlds, bringing me back to being that little girl, hiding. Into a space where I can breathe. The lock clicks into place, a flimsy barrier, but one that's desperately needed.

The shower tap sputters before water streams, filling the room with warmth. I peel away my clothes with the same numb efficiency that carries me into the water. The heat stings at first but quickly becomes soothing, easing the shame gripping every inch of me.

Water pools around my feet, carrying away the remnants of everything clinging to me—the anger, the hurt, the helplessness. For a few minutes, it's just the sound of water and the sensation of it cascading over my skin.

As steam blankets the room, I grab a towel from the rack on the wall and wrap it around myself.

My fingers wipe a section of the mirror revealing a foggy outline of my reflection. I hover on the edge, torn between facing myself or letting the mirror win. The face staring back doesn't lie, and I lock eyes with a stranger wearing my skin.

The girl in the reflection isn't the same one who ran to this bathroom for solace. Something is different now—an absence of fear I don't fully understand yet but can't ignore.

Her words, no matter how sharp or cruel, can't break what's already been pieced back together. They don't define me. Not anymore.

The floor, the conversation, the tears—they stay behind as I step into the hallway. The girl in the mirror is still learning, still finding her way, but she's standing again. And that's enough for tonight.

18

Brooks

THEN

Long after I've left Dylan, the air in my truck still holds a trace of vanilla, like it's waiting for something. It's a reminder of the lighthouse, when, just for a little while, she let her guard down. I wanted to hold onto that version of her, to make sure nothing could reach her, nothing could hurt her. But even as I watched her walk inside, I could see the shift creeping back in—her defenses going up, brick by brick.

Something's wrong. Dylan's good at hiding, but I've learned how to see through the cracks. She said she'd be okay. She always does. But I know better. It's in the way she moved, slower than usual, like her thoughts were dragging her down. It's in the moments when she thinks no one's watching, her expression betrays more than she realizes. And

I see it. Always.

By the time I pull into my driveway, my temples are throbbing. My grip on the steering wheel hasn't eased since I left her.

The last few days have been relentless—school, football, helping Dad, and now trying to figure out what's weighing on Dylan. I feel stretched thin, like I'm running on borrowed energy and running out fast.

I shut off the engine and slip out of the truck, slamming the door harder than I meant to.

The world feels slightly off-kilter, like I'm standing on sand, sinking with every second. My hands find the edges of the truck's frame, stabilizing me until it passes. God, I'm tired.

Inside, the house feels too still, like it's holding its breath. I toss my keys onto the counter, the clatter cutting through the empty kitchen. The fridge buzzes as I grab a water bottle and take a long drink, but it does nothing to ease the pounding in my head or the unease twisting through me.

Dylan's face flashes in my mind—the way her lips parted, like she wanted to say something, but thought better of it. Whatever she's carrying, it's heavy, and I don't know if she'll ever let me take some of the load. But God, I hope she will. She doesn't have to do it alone, not if I have anything to say about it.

I press the cool bottle against my forehead, exhaling as I push the thought aside for now. Later, I'll check on her. Maybe I'll stop by the diner again tomorrow and find some excuse to see her.

But right now, I need to shut my eyes, just for a little while. My body aches and exhaustion threatens to pull me under. Five minutes.

That's all I need. Just five.

The sunlight streaming through the kitchen window does nothing to soften the mood in here. I'm leaning against the counter, arms crossed, trying to keep my temper in check while Dad stands across from me, sipping his coffee like he's got all the time in the world.

"I'm not asking for much, Brooks. Just a few hours," he grumbles, his tone already edging into irritation.

I let out a slow breath, trying not to snap. "I told you I've got plans."

"Plans?" He narrows his eyes, setting the mug down on the table a little harder than necessary. "What plans? Hanging out with that girlfriend of yours again?"

"Her name's Dylan. Not that it's any of your business."

"Everything under this roof is my business, and right now, I need you at the site this afternoon. I'm short on hands."

"Well, maybe if you'd planned better, you wouldn't be!" The words tear free against my better judgement, but I'm past the point of reeling them back. Dylan mentioned she had a blowup with her mom last night, and I need to check on her, make sure she's really okay. Not just pretending. "I'm not your backup worker, Dad. I'm not putting my life on hold every time you can't figure out your schedule."

Mom steps into the doorway, clutching a dish towel, her movements uncertain. "Let's not do this," she insists quietly, as though her words alone might settle things.

Dad's voice drops, and somehow that makes it worse. "You think you're too good to help? That camera of yours going to pay the bills? Or fund this big future you're dreaming about?"

My pulse kicks up as I push away from the counter, stepping closer. "I'm not asking anyone to pay for anything. I just want something different! What is wrong with that? I'm not going to take over the family business just because it's what you want."

His jaw tightens, and he mirrors me, closing the distance with a deliberate step forward, his frame casting a shadow that feels bigger than it should. "This isn't about what I want. It's about doing what needs to be done. You think photography is going to put food on the table? You're chasing some pipe dream while I'm out here trying to give you a future!"

"That's your choice!" My voice rises, but I can't stop it. "You want this life. Not me. I'm not going to stay in Rockport forever, running a business I don't fucking care about. I have plans, dreams, and I'm not giving them up just because you think I should!"

His dominance hangs between us, a beast crouched low waiting to strike. Mom shifts uncomfortably in the corner, her grip on the towel tightening as though it's the only thing keeping her stable.

"An adult doesn't get to pick and choose when they're responsible, Brooks," he snaps. "You'll be at the site in an hour. End of discussion."

I want to argue more, to tell him exactly where he can shove his demands, but Mom steps between us, her voice calmer than either of us deserve. "Brooks, why don't you just go help your dad for a few hours? You can see Dylan another day."

I glance at her, her eyes pleading for some sort of truce, and I realize I'm not going to win this. Not with him. I grab my truck keys off the counter and head for the door without another word.

I pull into Ruby's parking lot, the pressure hanging over me like a cloud. I don't even bother going inside. Instead, I park and head around the back, knowing Dylan will find me. She always does.

A few minutes later, she steps out the back door, wiping her hands on her apron. When she sees me, her expression softens. "Hey, you okay?"

"Not even close," I admit, dragging a hand through my hair, fingers snagging at the roots. "My dad's pulling the same old puppet strings, yanking harder this time."

She slouches against the wall, waiting for me to speak. Not pushing, just there. A tether I didn't know I needed. Light slashes through the open door, catching in her hair, setting fire to the strands. But it's the way she stands that pins me in place—strong but defensive, like she's already bracing for something to fall apart.

I step in, erasing the space between us. Words are pointless, flimsy against the crush of everything bearing down on me.

My hands cradle her face, tracing the heat spreading beneath my fingertips. Her breath hitches, and I feel it against my lips before I even press forward. Then we're lost in it, in the way her body sways into mine, in the need pooling between us. The world shrinks down to this—her— and the way she lets me have this moment, like it's mine to take.

Reality slams back in like a cold wind. The second I pull back, everything I tried to forget crashes over me. "I have to go," I say, the words unwelcome. My hands stay where they are, desperate to hold onto something real, but the moment is already slipping. "He's waiting at the site."

Her forehead dips against mine, a small gesture of understanding. "Do you want to meet up tonight then?" she asks quietly, her voice filled with a patience I don't take for granted.

"Yeah," I say, nodding slightly. "Sounds great."

She gives me a soft look, like she knows I'm holding back. We're both battling our own demons. I let my hands drop and take a step back, forcing a half-smile that feels forced even to me. "I'll text you," I say, turning toward my truck.

As I cross the parking lot, the dizziness from yesterday surges again, stronger this time. It's like reality careens sideways, twisting under me like the universe just snapped my spine. My vision blurs, colors and shapes bleeding together. I pause to brace myself, but the ground seems to tilt beneath me.

"Brooks?" Dylan's voice sounds from behind me, sharp with worry.

I try to turn, to let her know it's fine, but my legs give out before I can. The last thing I hear is the sound of her running toward me before everything goes dark.

19

Dylan

Ipace the hallway, wearing a path into the dull gray tile, the harsh fluorescent lights overhead cast an artificial glare that makes my eyes ache.

"Hey, sweetheart," Emily, Brooks' mom, says softly. "Why don't you sit down? It'll be a while before the doctor comes out."

This is not how I imagined meeting his parents—unkempt, wrung out, and on the edge of coming undone. His dad, Scott, is built like the houses he's spent his life constructing, hands rough and calloused from years of labor. His face is weathered, but there's kindness in his eyes that makes you feel like you've known him forever. His mom, on the other hand, is a living, breathing hug—constantly making sure I'm comfortable, her voice the soothing cadence of a well-loved song.

I can tell she's the heart of their home.

They're nothing like the family I come from. Nothing like my mom. When she speaks, the words come slurred, edged with bitterness, never quite reaching her lips. Her bleached blonde hair looks overgrown, too bright against the dark shadows under her eyes. There's no solid ground in her presence, no sense of stability. I'm honestly relieved she hasn't attempted to show up.

I can't get the sight of him crumpling to the ground out of my head—the way his knees buckled, the way time seemed to stretch as I ran toward him, powerless to stop it. The moment replays, over and over, each loop tightening something in my chest.

"I'm sorry," I murmur, sinking into the plastic chair next to her. "I'm just—" My words stumble, exposing my anxiety.

"There's nothing to apologize for," Emily insists, her expression gentle. "It's been a rough morning for all of us."

Her kindness only intensifies the guilt gnawing at me. The Hollands are not only anxious for their son but are also extending reassurance to me, the stranger in their family's crisis. I wipe at the streaks of mascara I know are smudged beneath my eyes, exhaustion pressing against every part of me.

"You know," Emily says, resting a hand lightly on my arm, "I've never seen my son so taken with someone. He's grown so much this year, and I think you've been a big part of that."

Her voice carves straight through my defenses before I even realize I need them. "Thank you, Mrs. Holland," I manage, my voice uneven. "Brooks means everything to me." The air turns frigid, slicing through the realization—he should've been the first person I said that too.

"Call me Emily," she corrects.

Before I can say more, a man in a white coat appears at the end of the hall. He consults the clipboard in his hands before approaching us. "Are you the family of Brooks Holland?"

Scott rises immediately. "I'm his father," he gestures toward Emily standing next to him. "And this is his mother."

"How is he?" Emily asks, her earlier composure now hesitant as she stands.

The doctor pulls up a chair, sitting beside us. "I'm Dr. Abrams. Brooks' condition is stable. There's no indication of anything serious, but I'd like to keep him overnight for observation, just to be cautious."

Emily's relief is palpable. "Can we see him?"

"We can allow immediate family only," the doctor replies. "We still have tests that need to be run."

The clarity of his words rip through the thin thread of hope I didn't realize I was holding onto. I won't get to see him.

Emily notices and leans closer. "Don't worry, sweetheart. I'll tell him you came." Her words slide over the raw edges of my chest, a balm too thin to soothe the ache. But the pressure inside doesn't crack, doesn't ease. My head dops in a silent nod—because if I try to speak, I might shatter.

As she and Scott disappear down the hallway, the space they leave behind twists in on itself. The quiet isn't still, it pulses, scraping against my skin like something restless. The waiting room suddenly feels too small. I lurch to my feet, muscles wound too tight. The walls press in, the air stagnant—I need to get out before it suffocates me.

I weave through the sterile corridors, the sound of my chucks scuffing against the linoleum is the only thing stabilizing me. When I find the restroom, I step inside, grateful for the familiar solitude. The fluorescent lights buzz faintly overhead, harsh against the cracked white tiles.

I don't need to be here—not for its purpose, anyway—but the bathroom has always been a refuge, a place where I can shut out the world. The faucet roars to life as I twist the handle hard, cold water slamming against the porcelain, drowning out the nerves that pulse through my veins.

I lightly pat water onto my face, the cool droplets trickling down my skin as I watch them vanish down the drain. The tremor in my hands has finally stopped, though the memory of Brooks collapsing still feels like it's burned into me. I roll my shoulders, as if I can shake it loose.

I drift back into the hallway, but the thought of returning to the waiting room makes my skin crawl. My steps turn restless, prowling through sterile corridors, past shut doors and nurses who barely spare me a glance. The various machines hum like gnats in my ears, the smell of antiseptic thick enough to choke on. I keep moving. The further I go, the looser the grip on my sternum feels—never gone, just stretched thin enough to relax. A soft ping from my pocket pulls me out of my thoughts. I fish out my phone and see a text notification lighting up the screen.

Beckett: Dilly, I'm here. Got something for you.

Me: Wait, wdym you're here?

Beckett: At the hospital. Just come see.

Letting out a breath, I retrace my steps back to the waiting room. The low murmur of voices reach me before I step inside, and when I do, I see Beckett sprawled in one of the plastic chairs, the other flanking him with two cups of coffee.

He notices me immediately and straightens, gesturing for me to sit next to him. I sink into the chair without a word, and he pulls his backpack into his lap, unzipping it to reveal a familiar object: my sketchbook.

My heart lifts as I see it. "You brought that?"

"Figured you'd want something to keep your hands busy," he challenges, pushing it into my lap. His tone remains casual, but there's an understanding expression that makes me look away.

I open the sketchbook, flipping it to a blank page. My pencil isn't in its usual slot, but Beckett hands it to me before I even have to ask.

"I knew you'd need it."

"Thanks," I rasp, my heart swelling with appreciation.

The pencil stalls against the paper, the first line uncertain. Then something shifts. Each stroke carves through my worry, reshaping it into something tangible. It's not full relief, but it's enough to distract me.

***

"Dylan," a soft voice cuts through the fog, pulling me out of my thoughts. I've been lost in drawing for hours, and despite my half hearted protests, Beckett stayed with me. Eventually, he dozed off in the chair, his Rockport Titans Football hoodie bunched up beneath his head like a makeshift pillow.

I glance up to see a tall woman dressed in pink polka-dot scrubs paired with spotless white sneakers. Her dark hair is swept back into a tight ponytail, and there's something calming about her kind brown eyes. She holds a tablet in one hand, the other resting lightly on the doorframe next to us.

"I'm Maisie, Brooks' nurse." Her gaze shifts briefly to my brother, noting the gentle rise and fall of his chest, a peaceful cadence in the silence. "Have you two been here all day?"

I nod quietly, pushing down the need to ask her a million questions.

Her expression softens, something shifting in her eyes before she jerks her chin toward the hallway behind her. "Do you want to come see him?"

My heart skips. "Really?" The word barely makes it past my lips, drenched in disbelief. My gaze flicks to the clock on the far wall. "I thought they weren't letting anyone in but family. Is he being released?"

Maisie's lips quirk up. "Oh, sweetheart, Brooks hasn't shut up about you since his mom mentioned you were waiting. Now his parents left earlier, so come on, before the doctors start making their rounds."

I consider for only a second before setting the sketchbook aside and standing, moving as quietly as I can to avoid waking Beckett. As Maisie leads me down the hall, my footsteps quicken, and I feel a restless energy start to swirl around me. The cold hospital air does little to settle my nerves, but the thought of seeing him is enough to keep me moving.

The moment Maisie pushes open the door, Brooks is already out of his bed. His movements are dragging just a fraction, but he's upright, and that's all I need to see before I rush forward.

His arms clamp around me, pulling me in like he's afraid I'll disappear. I crash against his chest, my fingers curling into the flimsy hospital gown, the fabric too thin to hold everything I've been carrying. His scent seeps through the sterile stench of chemicals. The knot inside me doesn't loosen, it frays, thread by thread as I let myself sink into him.

"You scared me."

"I know." He exhales against my hair, pressing his lips to the top of my head. "I'm sorry."

I ease back, searching his face for proof that he's okay. "What happened? Are you alright?"

"They ran a bunch of tests earlier. The doctor says I'm anemic. My iron levels are shot, which explains the dizzy spells. They're giving me an infusion, supplements—keeping an eye on me, but it's nothing serious. Just something I'll have to keep in check."

"That…" Relief crashes into me, like breaking to the surface after drowning. My knees almost give out. "That's better than I thought."

"Yeah," he admits, followed by a rough, uneven sound that might be a laugh. "And it means I'll be out of here soon. So, looks like you're stuck with me again, Dill."

I raise an eyebrow. "What about football?"

"Eh, I'll have to take it easy for now," he shrugs, clearly unbothered. "It's my last season anyway, and there are plenty of guys who are more invested than I am. I'm fine with it, honestly."

I can't help but smile. "What you're saying is I have you all to myself for the foreseeable future?"

"Exactly. Just us. No distractions."

A throat clears, and we turn to find Maisie still standing in the doorway, one brow arched, giving us a knowing look. "Hate to ruin the moment, but keep in mind the doctor's will be coming back soon."

Brooks tips his chin. "Thanks, Maisie."

She slips out without another word, the door clicking shut behind her. The second we're alone, he hooks a finger around my wrist and pulls me closer, a silent demand. He drops onto the edge of his bed, and I follow without thinking, settling beside him, our bodies aligning as if we've done this a thousand times. Our knees brush, and I turn toward him, our faces inches apart. My heart beats faster, my thoughts scattering, but I don't pull away. I can't.

The room is quiet except for the faint beeping of the monitor and the vibration of the air conditioning. Brooks shifts, the movement slight but seismic, dragging in the air between us. Our noses nearly brush, his breath centimeters from my lips, the world narrows to the green of his eyes—dark in the dim light, ragged in a way that strips him bare. The usual confidence wavers, something unguarded slipping through the cracks, and it sinks its teeth into me.

"I appreciate you staying." His voice scrapes against the quiet, like the words are pried from someplace tender. "I mean it. More than I know how to say."

"You're my boyfriend, B. Of course, I'd stay."

He exhales, something loosening in his frame, and shifts just enough to press his lips to my temple—soft, reverent, like a promise.

Then, with a dimpled grin, he pulls back slightly and raises an eyebrow.

"Ooh, you're officially calling me your boyfriend now?" he taunts, his tone light but laced with affection. "That's a big step, Rivers."

I laugh, a soft pink flush spreading across my cheeks. "You're more than that. You're my best friend. I don't know how to put it, but…you're everything, Brooks. Losing you? That's not something I could walk away from whole."

"Dylan?"

"Yeah?"

He takes a deep breath, his thumb moving softly over the back of my hand before continuing. "I love you."

20

Dylan

Now

"**Y**ou're devastating," Brooks murmurs, his lips trailing along the curve of my neck. "I've been starving for you. For us."

A part of me aches to believe this isn't just a spark destined to burn out. That pulling him back into my space, into my orbit, wasn't a reckless mistake. But the doubt sinks its teeth in deep, tearing at the edges of my resolve. I can't.

I edge back, the space between us too small to matter but I just enough to keep me from unraveling. My pulse thrums, my chest tightens. "Please," I rasp. "Just stop talking. I'm done talking."

For once, he listens without protest. His lips drag lower, searing a path across my skin, settling against my breast. I bite the inside of my cheek, fighting to maintain control as his lips close around me, drawing me into a rhythm I can't ignore. The sensation is overwhelming, the deliberate way his tongue traces circles around my nipple feels incredible.

I squeeze my eyes shut, but that only amplifies my awareness of him—his hands, his breath, the sheer pull of him against every one of my defenses. His hand slides down my stomach, the touch both familiar and electric. A single finger dips between my thighs, exploring, teasing. The pressure builds as he moves with an agonizing precision.

For a fleeting moment, I lose myself to the sensation. But the reprieve is brief. The shame seeps in almost instantly, sharp and unforgiving.

What am I doing?

What about Aaron?

My hands clench into fists at my sides, nails pressing into my palms like some feeble attempt to ground myself. I hate the way my body responds to him, betraying everything my mind knows to be true. I hate the way I let him pull me into this, as if I haven't spent years building walls strong enough to keep him out.

Because this isn't strength. It's weakness. It's the same vulnerability that let me fall for him in the first place—the fragility that still holds, no matter how much I try to convince myself I'm over it.

This moment isn't a reunion. It's not a second chance. It's the fucking end.

And yet, I still let him touch me.

I despise him for making me love him. For the way his presence digs into my soul and refuses to let go.

I resent myself more—for holding on all these years, for letting the memories of us haunt the hidden recesses of my mind.

I loathe how being with him feels so perfect now, like this is exactly where I'm meant to be, even though I know it shouldn't.

No matter how hard I try to fight it, I can't escape the pull he has over me. It's as though every piece of me is tuned to him, aching to fall back into what we once had.

And I hate it. I hate that part of me still aches for a future with him, a part that clings to a hope I thought I'd buried long ago.

But despite the storm brewing inside me, my body betrays me, responding to every touch, every brush of his fingers on my skin. My hands move to his shoulders, nails pressing into his flesh as if securing myself to reality. My toes curl, and I cry out his name as the currents of pleasure crash over me.

"God, you have no idea how long I've wanted this," he breathes. "How many years…"

"Don't," I plead, my voice breaking. I can't hear this. I don't want to.

But this time he doesn't stop. "No, you have to know," he insists, his words cutting through my resolve.

I turn my head away, continuing to squeeze my eyes shut as if I can block him out. As if refusing to look at him will somehow protect me.

When I finally turn back, my bed is empty. There's no trace of Brooks anywhere. Just the faint scent of rain seeping through the window and the soft patter of drops against the glass.

I roll onto my side, every inch of me thrumming with an ache I can't name, only feel. The sheets cling, chilled and stifling, twisting around me like they know I don't belong anywhere else.

Of course.

It was a dream.

I let my eyes trace the raindrops racing each other down the pane, tracking the erratic paths they take as my eyes adjust to the darkness. Maybe this is all we'll ever be— Brooks and I—fragments of dreams and memories. Pieces of something I can't quite let go of, no matter how much it hurts to hold on.

Last night, my anger overshadowed everything else, like a wall I wasn't ready to break through. But now, as I lie here staring at nothing, the sharp edges of it have dulled, leaving room for something else to creep in. Regret? Maybe. Or just the growing realization that I've been avoiding the full picture.

I haven't let Brooks explain. Not really. My pain and confusion have been louder than his voice, drowning out anything he might have tried to say. Maybe I wanted it that way. It's easier to hold onto my version of the story—to keep blaming him—than to risk hearing something that might prove I made the wrong decision.

But no matter how much I try to shove it aside, Brooks wasn't just a part of my past; he was one of the few people who ever made me feel seen. Loved. Safe in a way that no one else ever managed to. Aside from my brother, he's the only other person who ever slipped past the barricades I didn't even know I was fortifying.

And that's what makes it so much harder. The betrayal doesn't just hurt because he let me down. It hurts because I trusted him completely. I gave him a part of me I never let anyone else touch, and he demolished it.

Even now, I can't let that go.

The blanket falls to the floor as I grab my dress from my suitcase and lay it on the bed. It's simple but elegant—enough to look like I've got it together, even if I feel far from it. The reunion is in a few hours, and I'm still trying to convince myself I have the strength to show up.

As I plug in my phone, there's a sharp knock at the door. My pulse picks up slightly, the sound unexpected. For a moment, I think it might be housekeeping, but when I drag it open, Aaron stands there, drenched from the rain and holding a small brown duffle bag.

"Aaron?" My voice falters in surprise. He doesn't belong here, not in this place that exposes so much of my past.

"Hey," he exclaims, raking his fingers through his damp hair. "I figured you could use a little company tonight."

"What?" My words stumble out as I step aside to let him in. "How? How…did you?"

"I missed you," he insists, dropping the duffle bag near the door. "Figured if you're going to this thing, you might like having someone with you."

"You flew all the way here for this?" I cross my arms instinctively, a shield against the vulnerability I suddenly feel. His gesture is thoughtful—too thoughtful. It's like he's peeled back a layer I wasn't ready to share.

"Of course I did," he boasts, his tone steady, as if it's the most obvious thing in the world. "The reunion's irrelevant, honestly. What matters is you. I'd go anywhere to be with you, Dylan."

I exhale, leaning back against the wall. "You shouldn't have." I may sound ungrateful, but there's no denying the truth. A part of me wishes he hadn't. My life in New York feels so far removed from the person I am here, like it belongs to someone else entirely. And Aaron showing up feels like a reminder of the fractured line between the two.

"Maybe not," he says, undeterred, "but I wanted to be here. So, where's the reunion happening? What's the plan?"

My eyes drift toward my dress. "It's at the high school. In the gym. Nothing fancy."

He nods, scanning the room briefly before looking at me again. "How are you holding up?"

"Not great," I admit finally, shifting to the edge of the bed. "I thought I'd be ready for this, but now that I'm here, it's…harder than I thought it'd be."

"I'll be there, and if anyone gives you grief, I'll take care of it."

I press my lips together, looking down at my hands. He has no idea what he is talking about. "Aaron, this isn't some big dramatic scene. It's a bunch of people talking, mostly pretending their lives are perfect. I'll be fine."

"Maybe," he replies, pulling off his damp jacket and tossing it over the back of a chair. "But it doesn't hurt to have backup."

I don't respond. He's here because he cares, I know that, but his presence feels like a reminder of how far I *haven't* come. I came here thinking this was about closure, about finally confronting my past so I could go back to him with a clean slate. But now I'm starting to wonder if that was just a story I told myself to avoid admitting the truth—I'll always be stuck.

"Thanks," I say finally, though the words barely make a sound.

"For coming."

He gives a small smile, and I look away, focusing on the dress again. It feels like a costume now, part of some performance I've trapped myself in. I'd wanted to do this for me, to prove I could. But with Aaron here, it feels like I'm just trying to hold up the version of myself he's always seen, the one who's brave enough to move on.

"I'll get ready," I say after a long pause, pushing myself up from the bed. "Might as well get it over with."

Aaron's expression softens, but I don't wait for him to continue. Instead, I grab the dress and step toward the bathroom, closing the door behind me. Alone again, I press my hands to the sink and stare at my reflection. The plan had seemed so simple before—come back, face what happened, and leave it all behind. But now, I'm not so sure the past is something I'll ever really escape.

The gym doors tower ahead, framed by an arch of gold and teal balloons that shine under the bright lights.

Aaron walks at my side, the steady rhythm of his steps syncing with my own. I fiddle with the hem of my dress, questioning every inch of it. The deep red fabric clings just a little too tightly, its sleek lines and soft shimmer too polished, too perfect. The strapless design is elegant, accentuating my every move, and yet, the color feels wrong, like an old wound I can't cover up. The murmur of voices and faint strains of music seep through the walls, like a thin veil that prickles uncomfortably at my skin.

"Hope you're ready," Aaron says, his tone calm but pointed enough to make me hesitate.

The reasons I'd given for coming this weekend—closure, proving I could face this, showing I'd moved on—feel insane now, flimsy excuses I don't fully believe anymore.

Inside, I stop in my tracks. Round tables are scattered across the gym, draped in white cloth and surrounded by chairs tied with gold and teal bows. Fairy lights snake across the ceiling, casting a soft glimmer that makes the decorations sparkle. It's so similar to our prom it's eerie, though the energy is far more muted now.

Aaron lets out a low whistle. "They really went for it, huh?"

I manage a faint nod in acknowledgement, my thoughts slipping from the present. In a span of a heartbeat, I'm back in the past.

Beckett had insisted we make the most of it, grabbing my hand and spinning me right there in the middle of the dance floor. The memory stirs, unsettling me before it finds its place. That was then. Now, it's just me, Aaron, and the undeniable burden of what's missing.

At the check-in table, a woman in a tailored navy satin blouse and delicate gold jewelry beams at us. "Welcome back!" she chirps, pushing a clipboard toward me.

I sign my name quickly, ready to retreat when a familiar voice catches me by surprise.

"Dylan?"

I turn and see Miles Davenport, wearing a look of disbelief that I'm here. He's older now, more weathered in subtle ways, but still Miles. His surprise feels too bright against the murkiness inside me.

"Miles," I say, my voice thin and not at all convincing.

He strides toward me, pulling me into a kind hug like no time has passed. "I can't believe it! Holy shit. Look at you! You look incredible."

I step back, brushing an invisible strand of hair from my face, motioning vaguely toward Aaron. "This is Aaron, my boyfriend."

Aaron offers his hand, his usual ease diffusing the moment. "Aaron Sinclair. Nice to meet you."

Miles takes it warmly. "You too. I'm glad Dylan's got someone with her."

The moment his words start to register, a petite brunette I hadn't noticed steps forward. "This is my wife, Breigh," Miles says, the word "wife" catching like a splinter.

Breigh smiles at me, genuine and unassuming. "I've heard so much about you over the years," she cheers. "It's nice to finally meet you. I know Miles was hoping you'd be here."

"You too," I reply automatically, though the introduction feels surreal. Miles has a wife. A wife he's told about me? He built a life. I don't know why he wouldn't, but the thought that people have moved on, stings more than I expected. Pressing against a part of me that's been standing still for far too long.

Miles shifts slightly, like he's testing the air between us. "I'm really glad you came out," his words are almost tender. "I mean, I know how hard it must've been for you to even make the trip back here."

I offer a single, firm, bob of my head, keeping my response measured. His careful choice of words leave me to wonder if he's holding back for my sake, or his own. Either way, one thing is clear: Aaron doesn't know the full story, and tonight isn't the time to change that.

"It's not the same without…" He pauses, his expression clouding as his words falter. "Without…everyone here."

There it is. The shadow I knew would be waiting for me tonight. The name he didn't say, the presence no one else in this room could feel missing the way I could. I murmur something polite, though I don't register what I've said.

Aaron lightly touches my arm, drawing my attention back to him. "Want to grab a seat?"

I latch onto the suggestion. "Please." My farewell to Miles and Breigh is brief, clipped, and final.

"It's good to see you, Dylan," Miles calls after me. "Really. If you're around later tonight, I'd love to catch up."

Aaron steers me toward the seating area, his presence keeping me from completely falling apart. Around us, voices blur, laughter bubbles up in bursts, and music hums faintly through the gym. None of it feels real.

Miles' words burrow deep. They dismantle me, leaving nothing but exposed nerve endings and the biting reminder that I can't break free from them.

It's obvious now that I clung to the lie that coming back meant moving on because it was easier than admitting the truth—that I have no fucking clue how to let him go. And part of me doesn't ever want to.

21

Dylan

The brush glides over the canvas in slow, deliberate strokes, blues and grays merging into waves that still don't feel quite right. I sit back, cross-legged on the floor, tilting my head to study them. They're too harsh, awkwardly restless. Not at all what I'm going for, but I don't know how to fix it yet.

"You've been at that for hours," Brooks says from behind me. "Don't you ever get tired?"

"Not really," I reply, keeping my focus on the painting. "If I stop, I'll lose my vision."

He hums in response, and I feel his attention settle on me. I dip my brush into white and swipe a small streak across one of the waves, softening it. Better, but still not there.

"You make it look easy." Brooks' voice is closer now. He's sitting on my bed, leaning back on his hands like he's always belonged here.

"It's not, but…thanks for saying that."

The door creaks open, and Beckett sticks his head in. "Dill, Mom said she's making tacos. Don't hole up in here all night or she'll get pissy," he warns. His eyes drift to the canvas, his features relaxing as he takes it in. "That's really good."

I shift uncomfortably, brushing off the compliment with a shrug. "It's not finished."

"Doesn't matter," Beckett replies. "It's still amazing." He looks like he's about to say something else, but then jerks his chin toward Brooks. "Make sure she eats, yeah? You know she'll forget."

"On it," Brooks says, giving him a lazy salute. Beckett shakes his head and disappears down the hall, leaving the door cracked open.

Brooks stretches, unfolding himself from the bed as he stands. "He's right, you know. You're ridiculously talented."

I roll my eyes, setting my brush down. "It's just a hobby, stop it."

He smirks, crossing to my desk where my sketchbooks are stacked. Instinctively I move to stop him, but he picks up the one on top and flips it open before I can move. "Brooks," I snap. "Stop—"

He freezes mid-page, his brows drawing together as he turns slowly to face me. My throat tightens as I see it again—the self-portrait I drew after my nightmare weeks ago. My face, my eyes, my pain, all so obviously splayed out on paper.

He lowers his voice. "Is this you?" It's more of a statement than a question.

"I—" I look away, my hands balling into fists in my lap. I focus on the smudge of paint on my knuckle, a meaningless detail I can cling to rather than face the real question. "It's nothing."

"It doesn't look like nothing," he presses, his voice cautious now. Like he's trying his hardest not to scare me away. "What's this about?"

I want to say I don't know, but that feels too simple. I *do* know. I just don't know *how* to say it. No one has ever asked me before—not Beckett, not my mother, not anyone. They always just assume I'm fine. That if I needed help, I would ask for it. And maybe that's my fault—I made it too easy for them to believe that. But it still stings, the way my mother never questions it, never wonders. Even after she saw the portrait. Like the idea something might actually be wrong has never once crossed her mind.

I've molded silence into armor. Speaking it aloud would tear open something savage I buried too deep to reach, and I'm not sure I could ignore it again once it's out.

"It's about something that happened…a long time ago," I say, the confession slipping out in fragments I can't pull back. The words pull me down with them, dragging me into a place I've spent years trying to forget.

Brooks sets the sketchbook aside, steps closer, then sinks down beside me, pulling my gaze to his without a word. That look, his distress—it cracks open the memory, tearing it from the depths of my mind. I've buried it for so long, but now it feels inevitable, like letting it surface is the only way to move forward.

I squeeze my eyes shut, the floor beneath me feels unsteady—or maybe it's just my body, betraying me, barely holding me upright. I can feel the years of suffering pressing in—ready to spill over.

I'm on the edge now, teetering. Maybe it's time to let it all out. Stop pretending I'm fine.

My chest locks, each breath shallow, like I'm drowning in air. Panic surges through me in frantic spirals, too relentless to outrun.

"Hey, hey, Dylan, look at me." Brooks' voice is urgent, laced with worry, but it feels distant—like a sound that's barely there. "You're safe. I'm here. I promise."

When I finally open my eyes, Brooks hasn't moved.

"I—" My throat is a dry, empty space. The words won't come. They never have. I've never let them. Talking would mean letting someone see what I can't bear to expose—and I don't know how to let anyone see the wreck I've kept locked inside.

"I can't," I manage, tears slipping down my face despite my best efforts to stop them. His eyes are full of sincerity, a kind of care that cuts through my spiraling thoughts. The way he looks at me makes everything inside me feel exposed, vulnerable.

"It's just something I've never told anyone. I don't even know how," I finally admit, the words tumbling out in a shaky breath.

He pulls me into a hug, a steady presence that refuses to waver. His arms stay wrapped around me, his hold full of something I've never known—support, safety, a wordless reassurance that reminds me I don't have to carry this burden alone.

Time seems to blur. Seconds stretch into minutes, minutes into hours, yet Brooks never lets go. Somewhere along the way, we shifted, moved from the floor to the bed, his arms still wrapped around me, keeping me close. His embrace is something I didn't know I needed, but now realize I can't breathe without. It's a silent challenge to my walls, proving to me I don't have to carry every broken piece alone.

"When I was eight, my mom was dating this guy named Levi," I start, the words scraping their way out of my throat.

"You don't have to," Brooks says softly, his voice careful, like he's afraid I'll break.

"No, I do." I sit back slightly, just enough to see his face, though I can't hold his eyes for long. "Levi was her boyfriend, and at first, he was…different. Nice. The kind of nice I didn't trust, but Beckett and I hadn't seen much of that in a long time." My fingers tighten around the fabric of his hoodie, twisting it as I try to steady my breath. "I should've known better. I think I did know better."

Brooks doesn't say anything, and I force myself to keep going before I lose the nerve.

"One day, Beckett was at a friend's house, and Mom was working late. Levi and I were alone. It started normal—he made lunch, asked about school—but then he…" My throat tightens, and I stop.

Brooks shifts beside me, not closer, not further, just enough to let me know he's still there. "Take your time."

"He started saying things—calling me pretty, saying I was special. But it wasn't right. It didn't feel right at least. I tried to brush it off, but then he cornered me. He kissed me, and I—" My voice cracks. I can't look at Brooks. "I tried to pull away, but he wouldn't stop. He held me there, and I couldn't—I couldn't move. I couldn't even make a sound."

I never understood how much of it I'd been bearing on my own, how much it had worn on me until now. My hands curl in my lap, trembling with a rage I can't control. I hate it. I hate the way it strips me down.

"I've never told anyone," I admit, the words spilling out before I can stop them. "No one's ever asked. At least not the right questions, and I never…told? I didn't know how to bring it up." My voice wavers, the anger and shame bearing down on me.

Brooks shifts, and then his arms are around me again, pulling me close like he can shield me from everything, even the past. He doesn't say a word—no promises, no clichés about how it's not my fault. Just holds me like he's bracing me until I'm secure again.

"I didn't know what to do," I whisper, voice raw. "I couldn't even tell my mom. She wouldn't have believed me, and even if she did…" I trail off, the enmity rising up like bile.

"She should've protected you," Brooks says quietly. His voice is calm, but there's a steel edge beneath it like he's grinding his teeth to keep himself in check. "None of that was on you."

My shoulders sag, the discomfort bleeding out slowly. "She didn't. And after he left her, she just…drank more. Like if she stayed numb, she could trick herself into believing she wasn't alone again."

I keep talking—about how I'd buried it, how I'd convinced myself I could just forget everything, even when it haunted me in ways I couldn't explain. I mention how I kept to myself, avoiding friendships, thinking it was easier that way. Brooks listens, never interrupting, while all I want to do is crumble, and somehow, that resolve in him makes it feel like I can.

Eventually, the tears stop, draining me until nothing's left but emptiness. Fatigue sinks into my bones, crushing and unrelenting. Without thought, I collapse into him, and he doesn't shift, doesn't let me fall.

After all this time, the isolation loosens its grip, and the darkness cracks. Someone's standing in the storm with me.

I wake up to a quiet room, the kind of stillness that attempts to stifle the air in my chest. My body feels leaden, even though I haven't moved an inch. The curtains are drawn, leaving the room dim, and for a second, I consider rolling over and pulling the comforter over my head. Staying here, hiding, feels safer. Easier.

A soft knock at the door interrupts my thoughts, enough to draw my attention. I lift my head as Brooks steps inside. His brown hair tumbles in messy waves over his forehead, and his green eyes, hazy and half-lidded, blink slowly as though the morning hasn't caught up to him yet. There's a softness to him in this state, bathed in the gentle half-light of morning, that brings a sense of calm to my heart.

"You're awake." His voice carries a quiet assurance, and it's comforting, to not feel like I'm something that might fall apart.

"You're still here."

"Of course," he replies, sitting on the edge of the bed like it's the most natural thing in the world. "Beckett let me crash in his room."

For a heartbeat, a queasy feeling rises in my stomach. "Did you tell him anything?" The thought of Beckett knowing sets off a flare of anxiety deep in my gut.

Brooks shakes his head firmly. "God, no. I wouldn't do that."

I exhale, a wave of relief following, and I sink back against the pillow. "Thanks," I rasp, but the word tastes too feeble, too insignificant for what I'm feeling.

"How are you feeling?"

I stall, words slipping through my fingers like sand. "Numb," I mutter, the only thing that doesn't feel like a lie.

Brooks leans forward, his hand finding mine. He doesn't squeeze or pull—just leaves it there.

"You're not alone in this, Dylan. You've got me. And Beckett, if you ever want to tell him."

My throat constricts, my fingers tightening slightly around his without meaning to. There's no way Beckett could handle this, not without making it his problem to solve. But Brooks? He's different. He knows how to just be here, and that's enough.

Instead of saying anything, I shift forward and wrap my arms around his neck, pulling him in. It's not something I think about—it just happens. A silent thank you.

His scent is a solid comfort, like pine and earth after rainfall. It's primal, something I've now come to associate with safety. When I finally let go, he watches me with a tenderness that hurts, then his hand moves like it's been aching for this moment. He hooks his fingers into my hair, cupping the base of my neck, but it burns like it's stitching up the broken parts of me.

"You've got paint on your face," he chuckles, ending the silence.

I touch my cheek instinctively, feeling the dry, cracked texture of yesterday's mess.

"It suits you."

Sitting up, I brush at the spot halfheartedly. The comfort of staying in bed all day is tempting, but a different idea begins to form—one that feels less confining.

"Would you do me a favor?"

"Anything."

"I want to go back to the church. I think I'm ready to work on the mural again."

His eyes don't leave mine as he stands, holding out a hand. "Then let's go."

The morning sun is still climbing, casting the sky in soft shades of pink and orange. Our drive is peaceful, and as we park and step onto the brick path, I'm struck by an unexpected sense of happiness. The church looms ahead, its silhouette a quiet promise. My pulse quickens, not with anxiety, but with something more akin to eager expectation.

I pause at the door, my hand hovering just above the handle. There's a brief moment where I reconsider, where I wonder if entering will ruin the fantasy that my healing is nothing more than a facade. But then I look back at Brooks. My fear is still there, but it no longer holds me with the same grip. I've fought against every fucking thing that has tried to bury me. I've survived, even when I thought I wouldn't.

It only took one person—*him*—to crack through the walls I've stacked so high around myself. To show me that I'm worth more than the scraps I've been settling for, that I deserve better than the endless ache I've lived with for so long.

He's my better. The kind of better I never thought I deserved, never thought I'd see. But now, I do. I see it—he's the answer I never knew I was waiting for.

I take a breath and push the door open with vigor. The familiar scent of aged wood mingles with traces of paint, filling my senses as sunlight filters through the windows.

The moment my eyes land on the mural, a strange sort of calm settles over me. It's unfinished, imperfect, but it's mine.

Brooks walks further into the room, stopping near the center. He looks around for a second before lowering himself to the floor, leaning back against the wall. I drop my bag beside me and sit cross-legged near the mural.

"You're just going to sit there?" I ask, pulling out my paints.

He shrugs. "I'm here for moral support. And documentation." He raises the camera I hadn't seen him bring, a grin tugging at the corner of his mouth.

I roll my eyes. He's always got that damn camera on him—capturing me, random trees, or the way the clouds move like they've got something to say. It's one of the things I can't help but admire about him. He spots what everyone else misses, sees the world in ways that make it feel a little less ordinary.

As I begin painting, the room narrows to the colors on my palette and the strokes of my brush. Blues, purples, greens—they all blend together in a way that feels natural, like they were always meant to exist in this exact combination.

Time slips away. I lose track of how long I've been working, only pausing when Brooks' camera clicks or when he mutters something under his breath about "lighting." At one point, I look up and notice him lying flat on his back, aiming his camera at the ceiling.

"What are you even doing?"

"Finding the angles," he explains, as though it's self-evident.

The butterflies I've painted twist and shift in the light like they're about to break free. They aren't just paint. They're pieces of me—the fractured parts I can't undo. Each one captures something I can't say, pressed into color, leaving behind something that may never actually fly but still feels like it's trying.

By the time the sun begins to dip below the horizon, my arms ache, and my palms smeared with paint. I drop my brush and lean back, finally taking a moment to breathe.

Brooks scoots closer, settling beside me on the floor. Without a word, he slips his arm around my waist, and I lean into him.

The church is quiet except for the faint sound of birds outside and I feel…lighter.

His eyes search mine, and there's something hidden in his expression. "Can I tell you something?"

I raise an eyebrow, intrigued.

"That first day we met, when we came here? I knew I was done for. You walked in like a storm, completely out of place in this quiet town, and I was lost in you from the moment you stepped through the door. Even now, in this room full of your art, my eyes are drawn to only you."

His words knock the air from my lungs, stranded in a space between reaction and silence. It's strange how a point in time can feel like the end of one thing, yet hold a spark to the start of another.

My surroundings dissolve as he inches closer, his lips a breath away from mine, leaving behind the start of a memory that will somehow always feel like home.

22

Brooks

Now

I t's the same gym—the same sound of squeaking sneakers, the same scuffed floors, even the same people—but it feels smaller now. Or maybe that's just me. Like I don't quite fit the way I used to.

But the second she steps through the door, I see her.

Dylan's standing at the check-in table, pen in hand, her shoulders tight but squared, like she's bracing herself for whatever's coming. I don't think she's seen me yet. *Good.* That gives me a second to figure out what the hell I'm supposed to do.

Our breakfast was a wreck, but Dylan let go of everything she's been holding in since I left her. I didn't take it personally. We both had our demons to fight ten years ago, and now, we're doing our best to come back unscathed.

I notice Aaron's with her. Of course, he is. I don't know when he got in from New York, but it's just the cherry on top of an already shitty situation—seeing him standing so close to her, leaning in like he belongs there. It's just another fucking reminder. I had my chance to tell her everything, and I blew it. *Again.*

I should stay put. Just keep my distance and let her have this. But damn, it's hard.

Maybe it's better this way. She looks…settled. Like her life back east suits her. Meanwhile, I've been stuck here, holding onto something that slipped through my fingers a decade ago. Everyone knows it. Part of me thought maybe—just maybe—she missed me, missed this place, and coming back here would make her see things differently. But seeing her now, seeing her like this, I'm not so sure.

I guess that's the difference between us. I never figured out how to. Not really. This town hasn't felt right since the day she left, and honestly, neither have I.

Miles notices her too, his face lighting up as he crosses the room. Dylan shifts, tucking her hair behind her ear as Miles leans in to greet her, his hand gesturing toward the woman by his side. His wife. I've met her a few times over the years, always bright and full of energy. After graduation, Miles and I faded into different lives, both of us lost in our own hell, trying to outrun pain we had no idea how to face. It's obvious now—Breigh was the one that saved him.

They exchange a few words, Dylan's smile tightening as Miles says something else, his expression softening like he's trying to smooth over whatever disturbance he's just stirred. Her posture stiffens briefly before she nods, her eyes flicking toward the tables. Moments later, Aaron guides her away, the two of them weaving through the growing crowd to find a seat.

I tear my focus from them before I do something stupid—like follow.

Instead, I scan the room until I spot Colt leaning against the wall near the bleachers, arms crossed, his shoulders tight like he's ready to bolt. The guy looks like he's just seen a ghost, and I know exactly why—Dylan's the phantom that's been haunting him. Her being here wasn't exactly on anyone's bingo card.

"Did you know she'd show?" Colt asks as I walk up, his voice just loud enough to hear over the noise in the gym. He's keeping his eyes on the far side of the room, arms crossed tight like he's bracing for impact.

"Yeah, she's been in town a few days," I admit, but it doesn't feel that simple. Nothing about Dylan ever does. "You okay?"

Colt huffs, barely looking at me. "Not really. It's like everything I've been trying to forget just walked through the door and signed the fucking guest book."

I shift, following his focus to the tables. She's smiling at something Aaron's saying, but there's a nervousness in the way she holds herself, like she's trying to keep it together for appearances.

Colt exhales through his nose, shoulders slumping. "This wasn't how I saw tonight going, man. I…don't know if I should be here."

Since prom night, Colt's been the type to let things fester until they hit a breaking point, and I know better than to push him before he's ready. Still, part of me thinks I should say something comforting, help him get ahead of whatever guilt he's feeling.

But my focus keeps drifting. No matter how hard I try to stay present, it always circles back to her. To Dylan. It always has.

We settle into a comfortable silence, watching people mill around the gym. A group from the drama club is reenacting some inside joke by the old trophy case, their voices carrying over the noise of conversation. A few rows of folding chairs sit mostly empty in the back corner, reserved for people who need a break from acting like they don't still hate everyone.

"It's weird, isn't it?" Colt says after a while. "How some people still fit here like nothing's changed, and the rest of us feel like we're walking through a museum."

He doesn't have to explain. I know what he means. Some people move through life untouched, their worst moments nothing more than failed math tests or unrequited crushes. Then there are people like us, dragged under by things too big to process at seventeen, left to claw our way back up while everyone else keeps living their normal lives.

"Not everyone had to go through the kind of crap we did."

I think about the nights we'd sit in my truck after everything went down, both of us too messed up to say much, but too afraid to be alone. I'd always thought Colt was holding it together better than me, but maybe I was wrong.

The gym doors creak open, and a new wave of people filter in. I spot some old teammates, a couple of girls from visual arts, even the janitor who used to let us sneak onto the football field after hours. The familiarity is comforting, but it also feels like a reminder of what's missing.

"Crazy how many people showed," Colt says, his voice quieter now.

"Guess some people like nostalgia." I lean against the wall, shoving a hand into my pocket. "Maybe they want to prove something—to themselves, to everybody else. Show off their perfect lives or some shit."

"Not everybody's here to flex, man." Colt's tone is surprisingly sharper now. "Some of us are just trying to make peace with the past."

I glance over at him, realizing I've hit a nerve. "Fair enough," I say, letting the topic drop.

We fall silent again, the hum of voices filling the space between us. I want to say more, to dig into the things we don't actually talk about, but this isn't the time. Not here, surrounded by ghosts of who we used to be.

Chloe's voice comes through the speakers, still high-pitched and unchanged. The projector flickers to life on the wall, casting a bright square of light over the gym. A slideshow starts, looping through photos that feel oddly distant and too close at the same time. A few of these were mine—pictures I took when we still thought everything mattered more than it actually did.

There we all are. Six of us. Me, Dylan, Colt, Beckett, Miles, and Graham. A mess of arms and heads crammed together in a group shot, each of us leaning into the other, acting like we had everything figured out. I can almost remember the spring air in that picture, that weird, lighthearted feeling that everything would stay the same forever.

Colt lets out a short, humorless exhale. "Look at us. A bunch of idiots thinking we knew anything about life."

His phone buzzes in his pocket, and he pulls it out, his eyes narrowing as he scans the message. The words are brief but the change in him is instant. "Looks like I'm off the hook," he mutters, mostly to himself. "The hospital's short handed, I've gotta go."

He stands a little straighter, dusting off his shirt, his expression hardening into that no-nonsense look he always gets when duty calls. No time for distractions. Not now.

I agree, unsure of what to really say. Colt's been at the hospital for some time now, deep into his surgical residency. Something about seeing things firsthand pushed him to do more, to become more. But it's also left him worn down.

His eyes flick back to the slideshow, the group photo still displayed on the screen. "Remember those letters we had to write to ourselves senior year, to open today? We thought we had everything ahead of us, like the world was ours for the taking. I guess I wasn't ready for how hard life would hit. When you grab yours, just…throw mine out, okay?"

Without saying anything else, Colt turns and walks toward the exit. His silhouette disappearing into the crowd, leaving me alone with nothing but the image on the screen.

I stare at the six of us, full of life, hopeful, and completely unaware of how quickly things could fall apart. A wave of realization hits me. We've all made our mistakes, lost chances, and come out the other side with scars we never saw coming.

Maybe it's time to figure out how to stop running from things *I've* been avoiding. Not just for myself, but for the people I still care about—people like Dylan and Colt. To try and make things right, not because I owe it to myself but because it feels like something I owe them—and maybe everyone else who's still here, still fighting, still trying to piece what we lost back together.

23

Dylan

A little more than a month ago, Brooks did something that left me dumbstruck. He led me back to the old church, the one we'd always seek out when we wanted to vanish from everything else. But he didn't stop at the usual. This time, he bent reality around it, making it something strange and beautiful.

When we stepped inside, everything felt the same—the familiar dusty smell, the faint traces of dried paint. But then I saw the walls. They were covered in photos. Pictures of us laughing, talking, and just being together. Among the collection, one photo pulled me in. It was from a night after practice, when the guys were all around me, but my gaze never fully left him. It was as though everyone else was invisible, and he became the only thing in focus.

And then, just like it was the most casual thing in the world, he asked me to prom. No big speech. Just him, showing up for me exactly as he always does. I don't think I even let him finish before I said yes.

Now, I'm in Beckett's room, standing in front of his full-length mirror while we get ready. He's fiddling with his bowtie like it's actively plotting against him, and I'm trying to figure out if my dress is too much.

The burgundy fabric hugs me in a way I'm not used to. The back dips low, leaving a lot more skin exposed than I'd normally be comfortable with. It's definitely a bolder choice than anything I'd usually go for, but lately, I've been trying to step out of my comfort zone.

Brooks has a way of making me feel like I can pull anything off.

Beckett finally gives up on the tie and looks over at me. "Stop overthinking. You look amazing. Brooks is gonna lose his mind when he sees you."

I laugh under my breath but don't argue. Brooks has a natural way of making me feel like I don't have to keep my guard up all the time, like I can just go for it. The dress, saying yes to prom, all of it—it's because of him.

"Thanks," I say, smoothing the fabric one last time. "You're not looking too bad yourself, KitKat."

Beckett grins, holding out his arms like he's showing off. His navy suit fits him perfectly, but there's something off about the energy in the room. "Speaking of looking good, who's the lucky date tonight?" I bait, trying to lighten the mood.

"Just some girl. Emma Reynolds. We've been hanging out a bit."

Emma. I've noticed her before, a junior with long brown hair who always seems to be around. I've never seen Beckett act particularly close to her though. At least he's never mentioned her in the way he talks about things that matter to him.

"Oh," I say, keeping my tone neutral. "She seems nice."

"She is," he confirms, shifting his attention back to the mirror as he adjusts his cufflinks. "It's not serious, Dilly. We're just going as friends."

My head moves slightly in confirmation, even though his attention is elsewhere. Beckett's never been one to get attached, and this feels no different. Still, there's a small part of me that wonders what it would be like if he ever did. If he let someone in the way I've let Brooks in.

Beckett shifts, grabbing his keys off the desk. "You good?"

"Yeah," I say, adjusting my dress one last time.

When I step outside, Brooks is waiting in the driveway, leaning casually against his truck. The late sun casts a soft glow, but it's not the light that makes me pause—it's him. He's dressed in a crisp white button-up, the sleeves rolled up just enough to reveal the sharp lines of his forearms. His green eyes catch mine as I approach, like I'm the only thing he's focused on.

He straightens when I reach him, handing me a small, clear box. Inside, I find a dried flower corsage in soft, muted colors—gomphrena blooms, pampas grass, and baby's breath tied together in a way that's both simple and thoughtful.

I glance at it, then back at him. "You picked this?"

Brooks rubs the back of his neck, his confidence faltering just enough to make me giggle. "Well, my mom helped. But yeah. I thought it would match your dress."

It does—perfectly. I reach for it, but before I can slip it onto my wrist, Brooks steps closer, gently taking it from my hand. His fingers brush against my skin as he moves to fasten it for me, his touch hovering just long enough to make my heart skip a beat.

"It's beautiful. Thank you," I whisper, watching him with a soft smile.

His expression relaxes, his usual confidence returning. "I'm glad you like it."

He holds out his hand, and I take it, letting him help me into the truck. As we buckle in, the sound of another car draws our attention. Beckett and Colt cruise past us, the thrum of music and buzz of energy radiating from their car as they speed off to pick up their dates.

We step into the gym as a group, the noise and lights hitting us all at once. Gold and teal bows are tied neatly to every chair, round tables draped in white cloth, and strings of fairy lights crisscrossing the ceiling like stars caught in a net.

Emma spins slowly, taking in every detail. "Wow," she exclaims, dragging the word out like it deserves to be savored. "This actually looks amazing."

Beckett snorts. "Yeah, because teal bows are the height of sophistication." He elbows me lightly, grinning like he's in on some private joke. "What about you, Dylan? Is it living up to the hype?"

I shrug. "It's nice," I say, though the word feels too small. The room is buzzing, everyone dressed up, talking in clusters, breaking into laughter, or testing the edge of the dance floor like they're daring each other to go first. For a moment, I let it pull me in. It's mesmerizing.

Beckett pulls me toward the dance floor, not giving me a chance to protest. "*This* is happening," he insists and I laugh as he twirls me under his arm like we're at some ballroom gala, instead of the gym we've spent the last year in.

The music shifts to something fast, the bass pounding through the room, and Beckett keeps going. He spins me again, dipping me dramatically just to get a reaction.

"Beckett!" I exclaim, swatting at him, but I can't stop laughing.

"Come on, you're supposed to be having fun!" he taunts, pulling me upright with an easy grin. "Stop overthinking and just dance. I couldn't convince you to go last year—at least let me enjoy this."

I let him lead me in a few more spins, the hem of my dress flaring out with every turn.

Around us, Colt and his date are trying out moves that could've come straight from an '80s workout video, while Emma's doubled over, laughing so hard she can barely breathe. Miles, surprisingly paired with Graham's date, is attempting something that might be the Macarena, all while Graham hides by the punch table, sipping his drink like it's the only thing keeping him centered.

Then, Brooks appears, like he's been waiting for the exact moment. He reaches out, his fingers wrapping around mine, drawing me toward him eagerly. It feels like a rhythm we've always known.

Beckett backs off with a little salute, heading over to his date. "She's all yours."

Brooks rests his hand on my waist, the other holding mine loosely as the music slows. "You having fun?" he asks, leaning just close enough that I can hear him over the music.

I nod my head, the words catching in my throat for a second before finally coming out. "Yeah. I am actually."

And I mean it. It's not the kind of fun I thought I'd have. It's better. This is me, here, surrounded by people I care about, feeling like I'm a part of something, instead of watching from the outside. The kind of night that doesn't need overthinking or second-guessing, just this moment.

The mass of people grinding in sync to the music for hours is surprisingly exhilarating. The lights are low, and the DJ spins a remix of a song that sounds vaguely familiar, but the bass is too loud to distinguish it.

Brooks stands so close I can feel the heat of his body. His hands roam over my waist, and instinctively, I lean into him, my hands tangling in his hair as he pulls me closer. His grip is firm, fingers pressing into the soft fabric of my dress, making everything else fade.

He shifts just enough to let his words slip through, his lips grazing the curve of my neck, breath stirring the air against my collarbone. "We could sneak out the back," he murmurs, sending a thrill through me. "Go for a drive, just the two of us."

"I'm gonna need a minute," I say, trying to keep it light as I step back, fanning myself with my hand. "As much as I'd love to take you up on that, I think we should at least swing by Graham's bonfire first."

"I'm down for anything as long as I'm with you." His voice is laced with something dark, yanking me through the crowd like we can't get away fast enough.

We navigate through the dance floor, the bodies around us pressing close, everyone moving with the music. Graham suddenly appears beside us, his arm around his date—a cute brunette with a shy smile.

"Hey, man," Brooks says, jerking his chin toward Graham, then turning to the girl. "Hey, Jules. Have you guys seen Beckett?"

Graham tilts his head toward the exit. "He just stepped outside with Colt. I think everyone's about to head out."

"Great, thanks."

Before I can turn away, Jules steps in, her presence effortlessly drawing my attention. "Your dress is beautiful," she says with an easy smile.

"Oh! Thank you." I glance at her deep purple gown, the lace and sequins catching the light in a way that makes her glow. "Yours is stunning."

A soft blush dusts her cheeks as she tucks a strand of hair behind her ear. Graham wraps an arm around her, pulling her close as they turn to leave. "We'll see y'all out there soon. Get ready to party!" he calls back.

I watch them disappear before turning back, only to find Brooks watching me, his expression intent, like he's barely holding back.

"What?"

"Nothing. Just come on, let's go find your brother and let him know we're heading out too."

It's a short walk to the parking lot, and I spot Beckett almost immediately. Even with his back to us, that familiar mop of black hair makes him impossible to miss. Colt stands beside him, hands stuffed into his pockets, his whole posture tight, like he's holding something back. They haven't noticed us yet, but from the way Beckett's talking, I can tell it's serious. Colt's voice is a low growl as we near. "I'm telling you man, she deserves to know," he reprimands. "You can't keep it from her. You're running out of time."

Wait. Who? Me? What is it that I deserve to know? My anxiety flares as I glance at Brooks, who has stopped in his tracks, watching them with the same unease I suddenly feel.

Beckett turns, glancing over his shoulder, and when he sees me, his face falls. He's not fast enough to hide the guilt, and it hits me all at once—they were talking about me. His shoulders sag like he already knows he's lost whatever fight he was putting up.

"Dilly."

"What is it that I deserve to know?" I ask, crossing my arms and narrowing the distance between us. The air feels heavier around me, and I prepare for news I'm afraid to hear.

Beckett steps closer, hands raised slightly, like he's trying to calm me down before I even react. "You have to understand, I just didn't want to hurt you."

"Hurt me?" My voice shakes despite myself. "What secret are you keeping that would hurt me, Beckett?"

He hesitates, and the pause stretches unbearably long. "Earlier this year, I was approached about a scholarship opportunity to play for Western," he finally admits, the words rushing out. "I didn't tell you because, honestly, I didn't think I'd get it. I know how badly you've wanted us to leave together—to get away from Mom and go back to Colorado—and I didn't want to mess that up over something that felt like a fucking long shot. Then, when I found out I got it, I didn't know how to bring it up. Especially after you started saving all your money from Ruby's for us. And—" he pauses, looking almost desperate "—when you and Brooks got closer, I thought maybe…maybe you were starting to find your own way out. Your own future. Without me. And that meant I could have my own too. So…I accepted the scholarship."

I stare at him, the admission hitting me like blows I never saw coming—each one digging deeper, leaving me bruised. "And you thought hiding it from me was the answer?"

"It was never supposed to be like this," he reassures quickly. "I promise, Dill. It wasn't."

"You thought I'd be so wrapped up in what *I* wanted that I couldn't—wouldn't—be happy for you?" My voice cracks, but I don't care. "That I wouldn't support you in having your own future? Do you think that little of me?"

"That's not what I meant," he groans, his frustration bubbling over. "You know that's not it!"

"Then what?" I demand. "Why lie to me?"

"Because I didn't want to fucking disappoint you!" he roars, fists gripping his hair, yanking at it like he's trying to tear his own frustration out. "You've always been the one with the plan, the one who's focused on getting us out. I didn't want to mess that up. Before Rockport, all we ever talked about was leaving. That was the dream, Dylan. That was it for us. But now…" His words stumble, momentarily lost, before he regains them in a softer tone. "I was just scared. I know that doesn't excuse anything, but it's the truth. I wasn't just afraid of not getting the scholarship—I was terrified of telling you if I did. Because it would mean leaving you behind."

My vision blurs, and I blink violently, fighting to keep the shards of my broken heart from spilling out. I'm staring at the person I thought I knew like the back of my hand—the other half of my soul. Now, suddenly, he's a stranger, pieces of him exposed that I never even knew were there.

Beckett reaches for me, but I jolt back. "I would've fucking cheered for you, Becks—like I always have!" I snarl, my words coming out in a rough hiss. "We're twins! We're supposed to have each other's backs. I would've screamed for you to take that scholarship, to chase your goddamn dreams. You should know that! I'd have figured it out—hell, I might've even stayed here. But if you honestly think I'm the kind of person who'd hold you back, who'd be disappointed in you and your accomplishments, then you don't know a single fucking thing about me."

He flinches, his body caving under the impact of my words like he's fucking crushed. Shame blooms across his face, but I don't regret it for a second. He *needs* to hear it. His mouth opens, but nothing spills out at first—like he's too ashamed to even breathe, let alone speak.

"Dill, I don't thi—"

I cut him off, the wound bursting through my chest like a dam breaking loose. "No, you *do*." I choke on the truth, my voice breaking. "Maybe you won't own it, but you lied to me Beckett—because you thought you had to. And that? That's what cuts the deepest."

I don't give him the chance to speak. Can't. My chest is fucking splintering, and if I stand here a second longer, I'll crack wide open for everyone to see. I spin around, storming off, fists balled so tightly my knuckles pop. Brooks follows behind me, but I can feel his concern—he's waiting for me to break.

I don't stop until we make it to his truck. I glance over to him and let out a frustrated sigh. "Can we just get the hell out of here? I'm not up for a bonfire anymore."

"Yeah. Of course."

I'm grateful he doesn't try to change my mind. I slip into my side of the cab and sink against the door, exhaustion settling deep in my bones. Words sit heavy on my tongue, but I'm not ready to speak—not yet.

How could Beckett lie to me like that? And for what? Did he really think I'd flip just because he wanted something for himself? A damn scholarship, of all things? A rage I can't control rises up in me. Does he really think I'm that selfish?

I should go back, fix this mess, force the words out before they twist into something worse, like resentment. But I can't. Not tonight. Not when my bones feel like they're cracking with anger, not when the hurt is so raw I can barely breathe. He'll have to wait. Tomorrow, maybe, when the fire inside me isn't ready to burn everything down. Right now, I just need a minute to be, to figure out how the hell the one person I've always trusted just…didn't trust me at all.

24

Brooks

Then

I park the truck on the shoulder of the road, killing the engine. The headlights cut out, leaving only the moonlight to guide us. The trailhead isn't much—just a gap in the trees and a sign so faded you can barely make out the words, but it's one of my favorite spots. Quiet. Out of the way. Exactly what Dylan needs right now.

She steps out of the truck, wobbling slightly on the uneven ground, and looks around, her expression skeptical. "Okay, and where exactly are we?" She tugs at the hem of her dress, glancing down at her heels. "Because I'm not exactly dressed for a nature documentary."

Her voice has that teasing edge, but I can tell she's still holding onto everything that happened back there with Beckett. She's trying, though, and that's something.

I gesture toward the faint sound of running water. "Just trust me."

She huffs, crossing her arms. "Famous last words."

I smirk, taking her hand before she can argue. "Come on, it's not a hike. The path is mostly paved, you'll survive, Rivers."

She lets me lead her, albeit with a dramatic sigh. "If I break an ankle, you're carrying me back."

"I'd expect nothing less."

I've been working on this for a while now—showing her all the reasons Rockport isn't as bad as she thinks it is. When she first moved here, she said she wasn't the outdoorsy type, and yeah, maybe that was true then, but I've seen her soften to it. Little by little, she's letting herself see it, feel it.

The trail opens up after a bit, the night's glow spilling through the trees in patches. It's enough to see where we're going, just barely. I glance at her again, catching that little shift in her expression. She doesn't say anything, but it's there—a reluctant kind of appreciation.

"You like it," I say, nudging her lightly.

She rolls her eyes but doesn't deny it. "It's…not terrible."

I chuckle. "I'll take it."

The swimming hole comes into view, the water catching the light just enough to look silver. I motion toward it. "Better than some crowded bonfire, though, don't you think?"

Her fingers find mine, fitting perfectly as I lead her closer to the bank. The water is so clear it mirrors the night sky, the trees rippling across the surface like they've been painted on glass.

After a quiet moment, she looks at me. "So, what's the real reason we're here?"

I tilt my chin upward. "The stars."

Her eyes drift skyward, mirroring my movement. Through the break in the trees, the sky feels bigger somehow, like it's stretching on forever. She stares, her silence speaking volumes.

"I thought maybe this would help," I add after a beat. "It's not just a pretty view, but something for you to keep. Another place you can tuck away when you need to think. A pocket in the sky where you can remember you're not alone, even in the darkest moments."

She drops her gaze back to me, her lips tugging into a faint smirk. "And here I thought you were bringing me somewhere secluded for a completely different reason."

"If that's what you want, all you gotta do is ask, Rivers."

She shoots me a glare, but there's no real heat behind it. She's deflecting.

I tug lightly on her hand, and after a second, she sits beside me at the water's edge, knees tucked to her chest. The fabric of her dress gathers around her legs, pooling softly at her feet, blending into the darkened earth. The stream tumbles over smooth stones, its gentle rhythm carrying a sense of calm. It's the kind of peace that feels earned, like the world is giving you a minute to just be.

She's still staring up at the sky a few minutes later, her expression softer than it was at the school, like some of the hurt she's been stewing on has started to lift. That's what I wanted for her, to give her a second to forget everything.

"Do you think he's right?" she asks suddenly, her voice tentative.

I know she's talking about Beckett without her saying it, and I answer honestly. "I think he's your brother, and that means he's trying to figure out how to protect you. Even if he gets it wrong."

She pulls at a flower, its delicate petals forcing their way through the rocks. "It just sucks, you know? That he thought I couldn't handle it. That I'd be so self absorbed that I wouldn't want him to have something good in his life because it didn't include me."

"He doesn't think that." I look at her, trying to catch her eye, but she keeps staring out at the water. "Fear makes people do stupid things. He was just scared of letting you down."

The water trickles in the background, a comforting rhythm while crickets echo from somewhere far off. The stars feel closer out here, like you could reach out and grab one if you tried to. I want to tell her that everything will work out, that Beckett was just trying to do what he thought was best, but it's not what she needs right now.

What she needs is to feel like someone's here, that she doesn't have to figure all of this out on her own.

"You know," I say after a while, "whatever happens with Beckett, you're still going to be okay. You've got this, Dylan. You always do."

She kicks off her heels, one after the other, shedding the night with them. Her bare toes press into the dirt as if daring the earth to pull her in.

Her voice is soft when she thanks me, sliding a ring off and rolling it between her fingers before tucking it back into place. I stay, letting the stars blaze overhead, the water ripple in the distance, as if the world itself is listening.

The drive back to my place is quick, Dylan's got her feet tucked beneath her on the seat, head resting against the window like she's somewhere else entirely. I don't try to pull her back. If she needs space, she can have it.

My dad's out of town again—some job two states over that probably has him holed up in a motel with my mom. He's always gone, always working. When I was younger, I used to wonder if he'd ever just stay. If maybe one day, work wouldn't come first. Now, I don't waste time thinking about it. It is what it is. Mom left after we stopped by to let her take pictures, then decided to spend the weekend with Dad since he'd been gone the last week or so. The house always feels emptier when they're gone, but at this point, it doesn't make much of a difference.

The porch light I left on earlier casts a dull glow as we pull into the driveway. Everything else is dark, but neither of us moves after I cut the engine.

"You good?" I ask eventually. "I can take you home if you'd prefer, Dill."

Dylan shifts, stretching her legs out before reaching for the handle. "Yeah, I'm good."

She doesn't sound convincing, but I know that if she wants to talk, she will.

We step inside, and I flip on a couple of lights to make the place feel less empty. My keys hit the table with an abrupt clatter. Behind me, Dylan hovers in the doorway, arms pulled tight around herself like she's still deciding whether she wants to be here at all. If I didn't know what she was dealing with at home, I might've asked her again.

It's not uncomfortable, just uncertain. Her eyes move around the room, like she's looking for something solid to hold onto.

"You hungry?" I ask, heading for the kitchen. The fridge hums as I pull it open. A couple of sodas, some leftovers, nothing worth eating.

"Um. Not really."

"Okay. Same." I shut the fridge, and lean against it. She looks drained, but not in a way that sleep can fix. I can tell what happened tonight is still on her mind, and I just want to help her forget about it, even if it's only for a little while. She holds onto things too easily, lets them take up space in her head until there's no room for anything else.

"You can wear some of my clothes if you want," I offer. "You don't have to, but if you want to get out of that dress, I can grab something. I'll probably change too, so we can just hang out."

She nods. "Yeah, I'd like that. Thanks."

I rummage through my dresser, pulling out an old hoodie and some well-worn sweats. She doesn't comment when I hand them to her, just smiles before disappearing into the bathroom.

Quickly, I return to my room, slip off my dress shirt, and change into a Rockport Titans T-shirt and joggers, doing it as fast as I can— just enough time for a brief glance at the TV in the living room before she's done.

When she returns, my clothes hang on her frame in a way that makes her seem smaller, but not fragile—like they were always meant for her. She tugs the sleeves over her hands, crosses the room, and drops onto the couch next to me, her knee bumping mine.

We put on *She's the Man*, but it's just background noise. After a few minutes, she leans against my shoulder. It's careful, almost as if she expects I'll pull away. But I don't. Of course, I don't. She exhales, and I feel her start to relax, like she's letting go—maybe not entirely, but for now, she lets herself rest.

"This is nice. Thanks for inviting me to stay tonight."

"Yeah," I murmur, but the word doesn't come close to capturing the way she makes the night feel endless.

The screen fades to black, and I glance down, memorizing the way she fits against me. Wishing time worked differently. "You want my bed?"

"I'm fine here."

"Humor me. It's better than the couch."

She breathes in like she's about to argue, but then lets it go. "Okay. If you're sure."

I guide her into my room, grabbing an extra blanket from the linen closet and spreading it across my bed. She sits beside me, her fingers slowly removing her rings, each one swirling between her fingertips before she places them gently on my nightstand.

"I just need a break from thinking," she says, pulling at a loose thread on my duvet.

"Then take one."

The next breath she takes is different—deeper, like she's choosing to let it go. And then she moves, climbing over my lap, her hands in my hair as she kisses me. She tastes like cinnamon, and I don't think, just pull her in. She exhales against my mouth, nails dragging slightly down my neck, and everything else—everything that brought her here—unravels.

My grip tightens at her waist, dragging her flush against me. She doesn't just take it, she meets me there, wild and unafraid. The kiss turns feverish, all tongues and teeth, and when I pull back to catch my breath, she follows, chasing me like she can't stand the distance.

"Say the word," I murmur, my fingers slipping beneath the hem of her shirt. "And I'll stop."

Her answer comes in the form of pulling my hair, her lips against mine as she whispers. "I don't want you to."

That's all it takes.

I roll us back, and she follows me down, her body pressing me into the mattress like a force I never want to fight.

Her touch is an ache, a need that spreads inside me, relentless. When she kisses me again, I swear I taste devotion on her lips.

Her fingertips graze my cheek, and I snatch them, pressing them against my racing pulse, needing her to feel what she does to me. "I love you."

Something in her breaks free, something feral. She tilts her head, her breath shaky, her pupils blown. I feel the second she gives in.

"I love you too."

The world ceases to exist. I flip us over, pinning her beneath me, and the moment spirals into heat, into surrender, into something neither one of us will walk away from unchanged. If she's mine, then I am hers—entirely, recklessly, without end.

25

Dylan

THEN

The worst part about tragedy is that it blindsides you. There's no warning, no slow buildup to let you know it's coming. One second, you've got the world by the throat, drunk on the illusion you're in control. The next, it's torn from your grasp, ruined. You're left gasping for air, but there's nothing but the brutal freefall, and the taste of your own goddamn carnage.

I step out of the bathroom, still floating, tasting Brooks on my lips from the night before—and then I see him. He's on the bed, gripping his phone like he's seconds from putting it through the wall, face blank in that terrifying way that tells you everything is already over.

"Brooks?" His name tastes like blood in my mouth. He looks up, and I know. I fucking know. The way he looks at me—like I'm glass about to hit the floor. It's a warning, a fucking eulogy.

"Dylan…" My name breaks in his throat, and his hands are fucking shaking when they reach for me, like he already knows he's about to rip my entire world apart. But he's not close enough to catch me before I fall.

He fights for air, his breath ragged, and then he fucking chokes on the word. "Beckett…"

"Beckett *what?*" My throat's on fire, and I'm screaming now, every inch of me shaking. "Tell me, what the hell is going on?"

"Beckett…died last night."

Something cold and rotten knots itself in my chest. "No." It's not a word, it's a plea, a denial, a scream I can't quite get out. "No, that's not—that's not fucking true!"

Brooks closes his eyes, breathing out like it physically hurts him. "There was an accident last night."

The sound I make is inhuman, ripped from some place inside me I didn't know existed. It's like being kicked in the ribs, the pain spreading before I even register what's happening.

"No." I backpedal, shaking my head so hard my vision swims, hitting my chest because I can't breathe, I can't fucking breathe, why can't I breathe—

"NO."

"NO!"

"FUCKING—NO!"

I spit it out like it'll reverse time, like I can fucking undo it. "He was just here. He just—" I still can't get enough air, can't make sense of the words.

Beckett. Died.

It doesn't fucking compute. A strangled sob rips free, but I swallow it back, turning it to rage. "Bullshit! You're fucking lying to me." My chest heaves, my whole body shaking. "Why? Why would you lie to me? Take it back! Please, take it back!"

His next words hit like a car crash.

Metal twisting. Glass snaping. Brakes screeching too late.

I hear Brooks say it again—Beckett died—but it gets lost in the roar in my head. Colt. Miles. *Survived.*

My throat makes some awful sound—choked, wet, broken. My knees give out. My hands slap the floor. I don't even feel it. I don't *feel* anything except this burning, this breaking, this goddamn undoing inside me.

"No." I rasp. "That's not—he wouldn't—he always called shotgun. He never sat in the back. You're WRONG, Brooks."

He always—

He always called shotgun.

I whip toward Brooks, like a marionette with its strings cut, I go slack—then stiff—then fucking feral. "Why? WHY WAS HE IN THE BACK?"

My feet carry me to the bathroom, and I slam the door shut like I can trap this *fucking agony* inside with me. The lock clicks. I hit the floor hard, but it doesn't matter. Nothing fucking matters.

Beckett should be here.

Beckett. My twin. My best friend. *Gone.*

I press my palms into my eyes, trying to squeeze the grief out of my fucking skull, but it just keeps growing. Spreading. Crushing.

My hands claw at my face, my ribs, my hair because it feels like something inside me is trying to get out, to escape this fucking nightmare.

But I can't.

I can't escape this.

Colt and Miles made it. They're in the hospital, breathing. And all I can think is—

Why not him?

Why the fuck did Beckett get erased from the world while they get to wake up tomorrow?

He should have fucking lived. I hate myself for thinking it, but— I'd trade them both for him.

They'll get better.

They'll walk out of that hospital, go home, *keep living*.

But Beckett—*Beckett won't*.

The rage is too big for my body. It burns under my skin, desperate to escape, desperate to break something.

So I let it.

A brush, a candle, my own fucking fists against the floor.

None of it helps.

The door rattles. A voice yelling my name.

Let them come in. Let them see what's left of me.

I drop my forehead to my knees, and when the door finally breaks open, I don't even have the strength to lift my head.

Brooks doesn't kneel. He collapses, landing hard, hands clutching my face like I might disappear if he doesn't hold on tight enough.

His whole face is a wreck—tear streaked, eyes swollen, mouth trembling like he too is seconds from imploding.

There's blood smeared across his fingers, his wrists.

I don't know if it's his. If he had to break down the door. I don't ask.

"I'm here," Brooks chokes, yanking me into him, and I submit. Like a fucking coward, because I'm not strong enough to hold my own grief.

I'm floating, or sinking, weightless in a way that makes no real sense. Brooks' arms are a tight cage around my ribs. The steady rise and fall of his chest lulling me into a haze.

It smells like pine. Like snowmelt. Like every Colorado memory we have together, laughing too loud on the playground that made us feel invincible.

And then it hits. *Beckett died.*

"I can't," I whisper, my hands clenching Brooks' shirt, knuckles going white. "I can't do this—"

He doesn't answer. Doesn't tell me I can.

"I won't survive this. I won't survive without him." The words come out so quietly I barely recognize them as my own.

He squeezes me so hard my ribs threaten to break, but I don't care. I wish he'd crush me. I wish I could disappear.

"You're not alone, Dylan. You hear me? On everything I have, everything I am—I promise I'm not leaving."

But Beckett left. And if he could leave, what the fuck is stopping the rest of the world from falling apart too?

A week feels like a lifetime. My mind keeps circling the same thought…there has to be a way to undo this. To bring him back. But no, this is final. The casket sits in the distance, a dark, cruel thing that feels like it's mocking me. It's there, holding the person I loved most in the world. It shouldn't be him.

It should be me.

The grass beneath my feet is perfectly trimmed, and the faint smell of wildflowers drifts through the air. It's the kind of day Beckett would've loved—blue skies, just warm enough to be outside. But all of it feels wrong. Too pretty, too calm. Like the world has no idea what it's done.

I look around, hoping to see a familiar face. Not for comfort, exactly, but just to feel a little less lost. Brooks isn't here. I haven't seen him once since that day, and the emptiness he leaves behind feels like one more thing I can't put back together.

I've tried. I've called. I've texted. I've pleaded with the fucking universe for some kind of answer, for *anything*—just a fucking reason why. But I get nothing. Every time, I'm met with silence. Not a goddamn word. I don't know if my mom has somehow kept him away, or if he's just chosen this—chosen to abandon me. But it doesn't matter. *Today, nothing matters.*

The pastor speaks about faith and glory and trusting God's plan, but the words don't register. My ears buzz with static. This isn't how today was supposed to go. It's our birthday. We were supposed to celebrate, to spend the day together laughing and planning our futures. Beckett would've made a joke about how we should get matching tattoos, and I would've pretended to hate the idea but secretly thought about saying yes. That's how it should've been.

Instead, I'm standing here, alone, tethered to this desolate place because Beckett's body is in that box, and I can't leave him. Not today. Not ever.

My mom is next to me, gripping my arm so tight it almost hurts. Her face is unreadable, her lips pressed into a line like she's trying to hold everything together through sheer willpower. I can feel her blame in the way she holds on to me. She doesn't have to say it. I already know.

Greg stands rigid on her other side, like he's bracing for the detonation. It hasn't hit yet, but it will. I can feel the charge in the air, the warning buzz in my body. And when she finally looks at me, it's sharper, like she's already carved me out of her world. The worst part? I don't fucking blame her.

I've heard the stories. I know how it happened. Beckett was pissed off, drowning in enough booze to make stupid choices feel like good ones. If I had been there, he wouldn't have set foot in that fucking car. Wouldn't have left to stay over at Colt's house. We would have talked, probably fought, and then I would've dragged his ass home. That was my job. That was my fucking job. And I wasn't there to do it.

No. I was with Brooks, letting myself sink into the easy way out. Avoiding. Now, Beckett's gone, and the thought won't leave me—the sick, gnawing certainty that it's my fault. I let this happen. I should have gone to that bonfire. I should've done something, anything. But I didn't. And now he's dead.

As the pastor finishes and the crowd starts to thin, my mom lets go of my arm but I stay rooted to the ground. My body won't move. Leaving means accepting this, and I can't. I *won't*. He's here, six feet under, and I can't abandon him again.

I glare at the casket in the ground, like I can change this fucked up reality just by refusing it. We were supposed to grow old, supposed to have years, decades. Now he's nothing but a box in the ground, and I never fucking told him I loved him. He needs to know I loved him.

The wind kicks up, rattling the branches above, and for a second, I swear I hear his voice in the rustling leaves. But then it slips away, drawn into the rift between one reality and the next. My fingers curl into fists, nails biting into my palms. I hold my breath, until the sound of footsteps crunching against the gravel shatters what's left of the moment.

"Are you done making this all about you?"

I turn, my pulse spiking. My mom stands there, arms cinched across her chest, knuckles white, like she's one breath away from breaking.

"What?"

"Are you done?" she snaps, her voice cracking like a whip, louder this time. "We just buried your brother, *my son*, and you're standing here like the goddamn center of the universe, like your grief is the only thing that fucking matters." She shakes her head, eyes wild, wet, furious. "You don't get to play the fucking victim today, Dylan. *Not here*."

I'm too numb to feel the sting of her words. The guilt is already eating me alive, tearing chunks out of me since the second I found out. She doesn't need to say it—I already fucking know.

"I'm sorry."

"Sorry? You don't get to be sorry. You've never cared about anyone but yourself, and now Beckett's dead because of it." Her voice chokes on his name, but her gaze remains unwavering. She just glares at me like I'm something vile, something she wouldn't scrape off her shoe.

I don't fight back. I just stand there. There's no point in arguing. She's not wrong.

Fingers clamp down on my shoulder with enough pressure to cut through the numbness. When I turn, Emily Holland is there. She doesn't look at me, just past me, locking eyes with my mom like she's about to drive a stake straight through her heart.

"That's enough, Denise," she interrupts, her voice calm but carrying the weight of a sledgehammer.

My mom's face hardens immediately. "Enough?" she spits. "You don't know what I'm feeling. You have no fucking idea what it's like to bury your own child."

Emily doesn't flinch. Doesn't so much as blink. But I swear, the air between them could ignite. "Don't tell me what I can or can't understand. And don't you dare use your grief like a weapon to rip Dylan apart. You want to scream, break shit, burn the whole world down? Fine. But not here. Not like this. As a mother, you should know better."

I swear my mother is about to detonate—veins tight, chest heaving like she's barely keeping the rage from splitting her in half. Her jaw locks, teeth grinding so hard I swear I hear it. Then, without another word, she spins on her heel and stalks off.

Emily's breath quivers as she lets it out, her chin tilting up as if she's searching for the right thing to say. But it doesn't matter. I know that look—the one that says, *you fragile, broken thing*. It causes every nerve in my body to flare.

Her arms spread wide, like she already knows I won't resist. "Come here, sweetheart." I try—to resist, to stand on my own. But it's useless. The second I step into her embrace, I realize how desperately I needed someone to hold me.

"Your mom is lashing out because she's grieving," she explains gently. "But that doesn't mean she's right. You didn't cause this."

She's wrong.

I did.

Not with my hands, but with my absence. With my choices. Beckett died because I wasn't there.

***

The days after the funeral blur together, one long, suffocating stretch of nothing. I don't feel like myself, don't feel much of anything, really. Everything about life feels wrong now, like there's a piece missing, and no matter how much I replay it in my head, I can't fix it.

Brooks hasn't returned my calls, my texts, nothing. Emily's kindness feels like a thin veil over the questions she won't answer. Ruby tries to distract me with extra shifts or small talk about customers, but I see the way she watches me, when she thinks I'm not paying attention. Worry is etched all over her face, but I can't bring myself to reassure her. It takes too much energy just to exist right now. Breathing is the hardest thing I do these days.

Greg has been hauling out of town every day since the funeral, which is probably his way of avoiding my mom. I can't say I blame him. Her silence isn't just a lack of sound; it's a noose, tightening every time we're in the same room. We haven't spoken since the funeral, and I know we never will. She doesn't need words. Her stare is enough. It says everything—*nothing.*

I want out. Out of this house, out of Rockport, out of the misery that's settled in my bones. But I have no plan, nowhere to go, no one waiting on the other side. And even if I did, there's still that stupid, desperate part of me clinging to the idea that Brooks will come back. That he'll pick up the phone, swear I'm not as alone as I feel, and say my name like it still means something.

Because without him? I have no one.

I didn't plan on coming back to school after losing Beckett, but I figured I should at least try to think about the future. I'm not even sure if part of me came back hoping to see Brooks here, but of course, he's gone. I've stopped by his house a couple of times, but it's always empty. No sign of his parents in weeks, no sign of him. The windows are dark, and I just…I don't know where he went.

Miles has stuck around, finding ways to keep me occupied at school, like he thinks if I stay busy enough, I won't notice the gaping wound inside me. I do. And I know he means well, but it doesn't change anything. I see the way he stiffens at passing cars, how the accident rewired something in him. We're both just ghosts of who we used to be, circling each other, pretending it helps.

The final bell rings, and I walk out of my last class. The hushed conversations have thinned, but their eyes still find me, still settle like an unwanted touch. Their pity is poison, seeping into the cracks I'm desperately trying to hold together. I don't want their careful words. I don't want their practiced grief. They don't know what it's like to carry this, and I wish they'd stop acting like they do.

The cold rain nips at my skin as I step outside, but it does little to douse the fire still burning inside me. My steps are quick, each one meant to outrun the thoughts eating me alive.

Then I see them—white Nikes. I follow the line of them upward, and suddenly, I'm looking at him.

Brooks.

Rain lashes against my face, soaking through my clothes, but I barely acknowledge it. My grip tightens around my textbooks, the edges stabbing into my palms. "Brooks!" I call, the sound of my voice cutting through the storm.

He doesn't stop. Doesn't even flinch. Just keeps moving, like I don't exist.

"B, wait!" Desperation pitches my voice higher.

His back stiffens, muscles coiled tight between his damp hoodie. I know he hears me—*I know*—but he keeps walking, as if I'm not even worth a second of his time.

A vicious panic surges up my spine. My chest constricts as I lunge forward.

I don't think. I run.

The pavement is slick, my shoes skidding through puddles as I chase him down. The wind steals my voice, but I don't stop. He's right there—

right there—but I might as well be a thousand miles away. When he finally turns, it's not with the fire I expect. It's exhaustion, grief carved into his face. "Dylan," he murmurs, as if my name tastes like regret.

"Say something," I demand, stepping closer. "Where the hell have you been? You disappeared after Beckett died, and now you're…what? Avoiding me?"

His shoulders go rigid. "I can't," he whispers. "I can't keep doing this, Rivers."

"Doing what?"

"Us."

My vision tunnels. "No. That's not—you don't mean that."

But he won't look at me, won't fight, won't even defend himself. He just stares at the ground, like he's already let me go.

"What changed?" The question is a wound splitting open, bleeding out between us. "What changed between when you held me on your bathroom floor and swore you wouldn't leave…to now?"

His eyes flick up, just for a second. A flash of something—guilt? But then his demeanor changes, and when he finally speaks, it's worse than anything I could've imagined.

"We just shouldn't be together. I'm sorry."

Everything inside me collapses at once. My ribs cave. My lungs forget how to work. How in my eighteen years of life have I lost every single thing important to me? I step closer, reaching for him like a drowning person clawing for a raft, but he doesn't move, doesn't meet my eyes, doesn't *save me*.

"You don't get to do this," I choke out. "You don't get to walk away, not after everything. Not after—" My voice breaks. "You promised."

His throat works like he's swallowing glass, voice barely holding. "It's not fair to you. I can't do it."

"What's not fair? That you just decided this for the both of us? Tell me! Where is this coming from?"

But he doesn't. I can feel his pain, see the war waging behind his eyes, but he won't let me in. He's shutting me out, brick by brick, and I can't break through.

"Dylan," he repeats my name, and this time it feels like a death sentence. "We were fooling ourselves."

My blood runs hot, frustration building with every passing second. "You're lying. Something happened. What happened?"

"Nothing. We should've ended things sooner. I just didn't know how. I thought I could make it work. But I can't."

"Can't or won't?" I'm shaking now, not sure if it's from the rain or the way the rest of my world is dissolving in front of me. "You're not making sense, B. I need you to explain!"

"There's nothing more to say. I'm ending things."

I blink, but the world doesn't right itself. He wasn't supposed to leave me.

A brutal weight slams into my chest, an avalanche of something dark. My pulse is a thunderstorm, and I try to fight against it, against him, against what he's doing.

"So that's it? You're just done? Just like that?"

His eyes meet mine, and it's already over. I see it. I feel it. He's not fighting for this. For me. I lost.

And it sets something violent and hopeless ablaze inside me.

"Fuck you, Brooks." It spills from my lips, something venomous like love turned to ruin.

His face slackens, like I've done what he was too much of a coward to do—destroyed us completely.

"I guess Chloe was right after all." My voice is detached now, broken without redemption. "I *was* wasting my time."

He doesn't argue. Doesn't flinch. Doesn't even have the fucking decency to look ashamed. Just stands there like this was the plan, and I was always meant to be left picking up the pieces alone.

My legs carry me forward, like I can slip out of my own skin.

Tears burn hot down my face, but I don't wipe them away. I let them sear this moment into me so I never forget what it feels like to be this fucking stupid.

To trust. To want.

To believe, even for a second, that *I* was worth fighting for.

26

Dylan

Now

The gym is packed, but I've never felt lonelier. I try not to look around the gym much, refusing to search for him—Brooks. But my body doesn't listen. My eyes betray me, drawn to him like a bad habit I can't break. And there he is, standing near the edge of the room, with Colton Hayes.

I tell myself it's not a big deal. They're just two guys. That's it. Nothing more. But my body doesn't quite believe it. I knew tonight would be hard, that the past would find a way to sneak in, but I won't let it take me under. So I take a breath, square my shoulders, and settle into the act. Calm. Unbothered. Like I'm ready to let it all go.

"Babe?" Aaron's voice startles me, but there's no impatience in his tone, just curiosity.

I plaster on a smile, but it feels flimsy, like a sticker peeling at the edges. His gaze narrows, catching the mask I hoped he wouldn't see. But he doesn't ask. He never does. Aaron is the kind of person who waits, who stays, who lets me come to him when I'm ready—even when I never quite am.

The crowd's chatter fades into the background as Chloe's voice momentarily blares through the speakers, the same high-pitched tone I remember all too well, and I feel a twinge of irritation. The projector flickers on the wall, casting a bright light that makes the whole gym feel even more surreal. The slideshow starts, looping through photos that seem both like a lifetime ago and like they happened only yesterday.

Then I see it.

A photo of Brooks, Colt, Beckett, Miles, Graham, and me. Each movement feels suspended, every detail stretching into painful clarity.

There he is. My brother.

His smile rips through scar tissue I was stupid enough to think had healed. Suddenly, I'm seventeen again—heart in my throat—watching him laugh like he belonged to forever.

"Who's that guy next to you?" Aaron asks.

I don't answer. My eyes stay locked on the photo—on Beckett's face. We look so carefree, so unaware. We had no idea what was coming, or how little time we all had left.

Aaron studies the photo, then me, his brows drawing together in confusion. "He looks a lot like you, D."

"That was, um…that was my twin brother," I answer, the words flat, like they no longer belong to me. *Was* my twin brother.

Aaron doesn't seem to fully get it. "Your brother?" He squints at the screen, trying to piece it together.

"Yeah." It comes out too brittle, my voice splintering. I grit my teeth against it, but it's already out there, exposing everything I swore I wouldn't. I hate that. Hate how easily it still sinks its teeth into me. It's like I never really left. Like some part of me has been rotting in this place, waiting for me to come back and tear the scab off.

Aaron watches me closely, searching for a crack to pry open. Hoping if he stares hard enough, he might find a way in. I don't blame him. I've never told him about Beckett, never let him close enough to see the parts of me that still bleed. Denial was easier. I know he has questions—probably a hundred of them—but I don't have the patience to answer any right now. This part of my life was never meant to be shared.

The slideshow moves on, but I don't. I stay locked in place, my eyes burning into the screen like I can will him back through sheer desperation. If I refuse to breathe, the universe might undo itself and put him back here where he belongs.

It never does. He's gone, and I'm here, clinging to a ghost that doesn't even have the decency to haunt me.

I snatch my purse, hands shaking as I put as much distance between me and Aaron as fast as I can without outright running. I need air, space, anything but this. The bathroom will do. At least there, I can regain some semblance of control over myself, even if it's a lie.

But the second I step inside, I feel it—her. Chloe Vance. I don't have to see her, I don't have to hear her voice. Her unchanging perfume has gone rancid, demanding my attention just by existing.

"Wow, I thought you'd never step foot in Rockport again after you *dramatically* ran away, leaving Brooks high and dry," she hums, her voice smooth with that all-too-familiar bite.

The fluorescent buzz of the overhead lights drills into my skull. I don't bother speaking—what's the point? Chloe and I were never friends, not even a little, and I'm not about to let her drag me into whatever game she's playing tonight. Instead, I turn to the mirror, my eyes locking onto my reflection, but it feels distant—like I'm looking at a stranger. A ghost of a girl who thought she could come back here and not drown in everything she tried to leave behind.

I can feel Chloe getting closer, the click of her heels echoing off the tiles. I know she's waiting for a reaction, for me to snap back, to engage. But I don't. Not this time.

Drawing in a breath, I finally turn toward her, though I don't meet her gaze. "Why wouldn't I come, Chloe?" My voice stays steady, even though I feel a little too wired inside. She's not worth the energy.

Her lips curl into that practiced smile she's always worn—the one she used in high school when she knew she had the upper hand.

"I thought you'd be too busy. You know, since you haven't found the time in, what, ten years? Not even to visit your little sister."

Classic Chloe.

She's always had a way of pushing buttons. But I'm not about to give her that satisfaction. Not tonight, and especially not over something as absurd as me having a so-called little sister.

"My little sister?" I repeat, confusion knotting in my chest. "What are you talking about? I don't have a little sister."

Chloe doesn't even flinch. Her eyes meet mine, smugness radiating off her. She knows she's got me, and she's not letting go.

"Blake," she sneers, leaning in a little, her voice lower now. "She's in fifth grade now. She was in my class last year—super sweet kid, by the way. Even asked if we went to school together. But I guess you wouldn't know much about that, since you didn't stick around after you—" She trails off, letting the implication settle between us, savoring it like it's her favorite part.

The name floats between us, one I'll now never be able to escape. *Blake*. It doesn't click, doesn't land in a way that feels real. My mouth goes dry, and I take a step back, hoping that some distance from Chloe might somehow bring clarity. "You're lying," I say, the words betraying more of my own doubt than anything aimed at her. My hands are suddenly cold, and I tighten my grip on my purse, willing it to calm me.

Chloe doesn't seem to be lying. There's no playful gleam in her eyes, no hint of the usual mockery. This is something different, more intense. She's serious.

"I'm not lying, Dylan," she urges, muted now, more controlled. She's finally getting what she wants, but it's obvious it's not in the way she expected.

Something snaps inside me...a frantic feeling I can't pin down. My thoughts are racing, trying to connect dots that don't even exist. My mom had another kid? When? How could I not know? Why didn't Brooks tell me? Why didn't my mother?

"I just saw my mom at Ruby's," I manage, my voice unsteady.

"She…she didn't say anything about someone named Blake." I tell myself it doesn't matter, that I had my reasons to turn her away at the diner. But the guilt seeps in anyway. She asked if I had time, and *I* couldn't get away fast enough. No matter how hard I try to twist it, the truth sticks—I don't really know my mom anymore. Know who she is now, not who she's been for years. She's a stranger.

"I didn't know," I say, as much to myself as to Chloe.

"You didn't want to. You left, Dylan. You disappeared. What did you think was going to happen? That Rockport was just gonna pause and wait for you to come back?"

Her words split me open, and I blink repeatedly, caught off guard. I wasn't expecting the hit, even though I should have. She's right in ways I don't want to admit. I thought leaving meant cutting myself free, severing every last thread. But now I see the loose ends I never even knew were there—things I abandoned before I realized they belonged to me.

Chloe shrugs, a little too pleased with herself. "Well, sorry. I just assumed you knew. My bad." Her apology isn't remotely sincere, but that's not the point. She's already gotten what she came for.

I shove the door open and step back into the gym. I don't stop. I don't second-guess. I barely acknowledge Aaron at the table before pinpointing Brooks. He's laughing at the bar, seemingly untroubled, and my control burns out. He doesn't even see me coming—not until I plant myself directly in front of him and demand his attention.

"Did you know?" The question erupts before I have time to reel it in. My voice is louder than I intended, drawing the attention of others, but I don't care.

He frowns, his drink paused halfway to his mouth. "Know what?"

"About Blake," I say, disbelief coating each word. "Did you know about her? My—my *sister*. Did you know and not tell me?"

His expression falls, and I can see the guilt flicker across his face. That's all I need.

"You did," I accuse, my voice rising. "You knew. Brooks, I've been here for days, and you never said a word. You let me walk around this town, completely clueless, and you didn't think I deserved to know?"

He sets his drink down, his shoulders tensing as he straightens up. "I was going to tell you," he cautions. "I just…didn't think it was the right time. I didn't want to throw that at you when you were already—"

I cut him off. "When I was already what? Dealing with being back here? Seeing my mom? Grieving my brother? Feeling like my entire past is staring me in the face?" My voice hardens. "You don't get to decide when the 'right time' is, Brooks. You should've told me."

"I was trying to protect you," he protests, but it only infuriates me more.

"Oh, please! Try a new excuse, Brooks. Hell, maybe try the truth for once! You think you're protecting me? Tell me, when has that *ever* worked? When has keeping me in the dark ever made shit better?"

I don't give him the satisfaction of offering me another lie. I spin on my heel and walk away, my thoughts a fucking cyclone. A sister. I have a sister. And somehow, the whole damn town knew except me. As if I'm some delicate little thing they have to protect.

But that's not who I am anymore. Not even close.

My footsteps echo in the empty parking lot, each step faster than the last as I try to outrun everything—Chloe's words, Brooks' silence, the sudden reality that nothing in my life is what I thought it was.

"Dylan, wait!" Aaron's voice carries from behind me, quick and panicked. I don't turn around. I don't have the patience for this.

"Dylan, come on!" That voice isn't Aaron's. It's Brooks'. It's deeper, rougher, with just enough edge to stop me in my tracks for just a moment. "Don't do this again. Don't run away!"

Run away? He has no right to say that to me, not after everything he's done. I force myself to keep moving, heading toward Aaron's rental car.

Aaron reaches me first. "Dylan, what the hell is going on? Are you okay?" He grabs my arm gently, but the irritation it sparks shoots straight through me, rattles me like a goddamn earthquake.

I shake him off. "I just need to go."

"Go where? What happened back there?" His voice rises, and I know he deserves an explanation. But I don't have it in me right now.

"Can we not do this here, Aaron? Please," I beg, hoping he'll let it drop.

But of course, now he doesn't. "No, we're not just glossing over this. Not this time. First, you ditch me without a word, and now this guy is chasing you down like his life depends on it. So tell me—what the fuck is going on between you two?"

"Nothing!" The word bursts out of me, too forceful to sound convincing.

"You expect me to believe that? Because it doesn't feel like nothing,

Dylan. It hasn't felt like nothing since we ran into him back in Maine."

I wrap my arms around myself, trying to steady my nerves. "I told you, Aaron. Brooks was a friend from high school, and that's all there is to it. Can we just leave it alone? Can we just go back to the hotel?"

"No, we can't," he snaps. "Because every time I see him, every time his name comes up, this fucking shadow falls over you. And now this?" He gestures back toward the school, frustration radiating off him. "There's something you're not telling me. Fuck, I didn't even know you had a brother until tonight! What else haven't you told me?"

I turn away, hoping to end this, but his voice stops me.

"Is the 'B' tattooed under your collarbone for him?"

I whip around, disbelief coloring my voice. "Are you serious right now?"

"I am." he insists, his gaze digging into mine. "Is it for him, Dylan? Because, damn it, it sure as hell doesn't feel like you've fucking let him go."

"Oh my God! It's not for Brooks!" I shout, my throat raw from the intensity. "It's for Beckett. My twin brother, Aaron! Who died when we were seventeen."

The admission lands between us like a grenade, and I watch the impact crack through him in real time. His expression slipped from anger to something shaken, as if he's realizing how much of me exists outside what he thought he knew.

"The one in the photo."

"Yes, Aaron. Beckett. *My twin brother.*" My voice trembles, and I don't bother hiding it. I clutch my chest, simply speaking his name is enough to make it feel as though I can't breathe.

My fingers dig into my ribs, pressing hard, as if I can hold myself together just by the force of my grip. "He died right before I left this fucking town." My head drops, my breath shallow as I struggle to loosen the painful knot in my chest. "*That's* why I have the tattoo. *That's* why I don't talk about it…because it hurts." I wrestle down the instinct to choke, my throat burning, and I pull my arms in tight, as if holding myself together will make the pain stop. "It *still* fucking hurts."

"You're telling me all of this now?" Aaron stumbles back, my words slamming into him like a punch to the gut. "How did I not know this? How could you never tell me something so important?"

"Because I don't talk about him," I snap, my emotions bubbling over. "I can barely even *think* about him without falling apart. And maybe that makes me a terrible person, or maybe it makes me weak, but it's the truth, Aaron. I don't talk about Beckett. Not to anyone."

"Not to anyone," Aaron repeats, his tone flat. "And I'm supposed to be the person who you want to spend your life with."

"Aaron—"

"No, Dylan." He holds up a hand, cutting me off. "This isn't about Beckett. This is about us. How am I supposed to feel like I really know you when you keep entire pieces of your life hidden? You say Brooks is just a friend from high school—your past—but it feels like you're still stuck there, and I'm on the outside, looking in."

"That's not fair," I argue, my voice wavering. "You have no idea what it's like to live with this—to wake up every damn day feeling like a piece of your soul was ripped away, and no matter how hard you try, it's never coming back!"

"You're right, I don't!" he yells, his voice hoarse from pent-up frustration. "Because you've never let me! I tried, Dylan. I *tried* to be what you needed, but every time I thought you might let me in, you pulled away. You've always kept me at arm's length! And I told myself it didn't matter…that as long as you were with *me*, it would be enough. But now I'm starting to think I was wrong. Maybe I can't give you what you need. May—" He cuts himself off, his voice faltering as if the confession is too much to bear. "Maybe…I was never meant to have you."

The words cut deep, and no matter how much I try to convince myself I don't have the energy to fight with him—not right now—the sting is excruciating. It feels like everything I've been holding in is about to explode, but I'm too fucking exhausted to even scream.

I hear Brooks before I see him, but it's Aaron I feel first. His body locks up, and the air around us suddenly turns to stone. His shoulders tense, a telltale sign this is about to get worse. He doesn't turn immediately, but I can sense it—the weight of his anger cracks, and something colder, more detached settles in.

It's not just resignation. It's the crushing realization that nothing either of us says or does will fix this. And he knows it. The second he knows…the fire drains from him, and all that's left is defeat.

Aaron lets out a bitter laugh, the sound slicing through me like a dull knife. "Right on cue." He gives Brooks a look that could cut glass. "She's all yours man, I'm done."

I should call after him. Do something. But he's already turned his back and walked away, leaving me standing there, my pulse thrumming against my skin.

Brooks steps closer, his hands now shoved into his pockets. "Are you okay?"

I shake my head, pressing my lips together. If I try to speak, I might break.

"Dylan, can we go somewhere? Somewhere quiet, where we can talk?"

"Why? So you can *protect* me more? Keep more secrets?"

"No," he pleads. "So I can explain…tell you what happened after Beckett died, why I pushed you away."

I stand there for what feels like forever, my body can't decide whether to fight or flee. I meet his gaze, and briefly, I swear he thinks I might stay.

"No," The word is barely an exhale, but it guts me on the way out. My hands tremble, empty of fight, empty of anything else but pure exhaustion. "I can't do this anymore."

27

Dylan

Now

I've been wandering aimlessly for hours. Tonight everything I've built the last ten years has completely unraveled, abandoning me in the middle of a life I barely recognize. And now, finding out I have a sister I didn't know about? It means my short visit to Rockport just turned into something more permanent.

I stop in front of the old house, and time hasn't touched it. It's still as run down and forgotten as the day I left. Weeds crawl through the cracks in the sidewalk, dandelions scattered like an afterthought. It's eerie how every detail remains unchanged, yet the very soul of it feels alien to me.

I know why I'm here, or more accurately, who brought me here. *Blake.*

Motionless, I stare ahead. My hands fidget, fingers twisting together as if the movement might steady the uncertainty curling inside me. Part of me wants to bolt—vanish into the night, leaving everything and everyone behind. This wasn't the plan; I wasn't supposed to care. I was perfectly fine locking the door on this place and everyone in it. Or at least, I thought I was.

A new thought digs in—Blake deserves more than a half-present stranger orbiting her life. She deserves a sister who shows up, even if I'm still learning how.

The yard is still, the only sound is the soft rustle of leaves in the breeze. Every window in the house is dark, making me wonder if anyone's even awake. It's late. Too late for a reasonable visit. I should probably just come back in the morning. But my feet stay rooted in place, defying every instinct to turn and go. I can't walk away. Not yet. Not without trying.

"Um, do you need something?"

I spin around, heart lurching, and there she is—a girl no older than ten, standing on the sidewalk with a tiny dog at her feet. Her dark hair skims her shoulders, and her eyes—so vividly blue they steal the breath from my lungs—resemble a ghost of my own staring back at me. It's disorienting, like I've stumbled into a mirror where my younger self is staring back at me.

"I'm sorry," she stammers, shifting her weight from foot to foot. "I didn't mean to scare you. I was just walking my dog Zoey."

Her dog, some scruffy little thing with too much energy, tugs at the leash, and she tugs back absentmindedly.

"No, you didn't scare me." My pulse kicks up as I step forward, hands twitching like they don't know where they belong. The last thing I want is to spook her. "I didn't know anyone was out here. I was about to knock."

She glances down at her sneakers, scuffing one against the pavement before meeting my gaze again. There's caution in her eyes, but also a reluctant curiosity. "If you're here for my mom, she's not home."

"Oh." The word feels insignificant, weighted with too much expectation for something so small. I don't even know what I was hoping for, showing up like this. Of course she assumes I'm here for our mother. What kid wouldn't when a stranger shows up unannounced on their doorstep? A lump rises in my throat, my chest constricting until I have to force myself to breathe. Because that's all I am to her right now—a stranger on the sidewalk.

"And your name is?" I want to hear it, need to hear it—but the second it leaves my mouth, I regret it. She's going to think I'm some freak lurking outside her house, not someone grasping for proof that she's real.

Her lips press together, and I can tell she's debating whether she should answer. Then, finally, she says, "Blake."

Hearing it from her directly shatters whatever distance I'd tried to keep. Chloe's words felt like a rumor, something too big to grasp. But this? This makes it undeniable. I keep staring at this little girl like I'm willing her to recognize me, to say my name like it means something. Like I maybe mean something. But she doesn't.

"Do you know how to reach your mom?" My voice scrapes out rough and uneven. I'm not sure I even have the right to ask.

She's considering, her fingers curling around the leash of her tiny dog, eyes scanning me for something—danger, familiarity, a reason to bolt? I'm unsure. "Um, yeah. But she'll probably be back soon."

Soon. I nod, but the thought of standing here, waiting for my mother to just…appear, is too much right now.

I dig into my bag, pulling out a scrap of paper and a pen. The numbers come out in quick, harsh lines, my hand unsteady like my body's fighting against what I'm doing.

"Here." I hold it out. "Can you…have her call me when she gets home?"

Blake takes the note like it's made of glass, handling it with the kind of care reserved for fragile things. I nearly convince myself that she understands that this is more than just a scrap of paper. Maybe she knows exactly who I am and is too nervous to admit it.

I look back at the house, and it feels like I'm seeing it through two sets of eyes. The seventeen year old who used to live here and the uncomfortable stranger standing on the sidewalk now.

"It was nice meeting you." My words barely scratch the surface of what this moment is—of what it could change.

Blake's voice is soft as she agrees, and I force myself to turn away, my legs wobbling like the earth beneath me is about to crack.

My steps don't falter as I push everything down, but the moment she's no longer in view, the floodgates open, and all of it comes crashing down. A sister. A whole person I should've known, should've loved. How the hell do you make sense of something like that?

By the time I make it to town, I'm muttering a string of curses about Aaron ditching me without his rental car back at the high school. I can't fault him for it. Why wouldn't he? If there's one thing I've mastered, it's being the one left behind.

The streets are nearly deserted as I move through the old downtown neighborhood, the quiet broken only by the occasional passing car. I follow the same worn path I used to take years ago, past leaning fenced and rusted mailboxes that haven't changed. The first day I walked this route, I was trying to distance myself from that house. Now, I'm tracing the same steps, wishing I could just turn back. For her.

By the time I see Ruby's diner in the distance, my head is pounding, and my body feels like it's running on fumes. The neon sign flickers slightly, and for a moment, I consider walking past it. But my feet betray me, drawn toward the familiar red glow as if they know something I haven't figured out yet.

I stumble through the front door, my eyes darting for an empty table—anywhere to take a moment to breathe—but Ruby sees me first. She's behind the counter, mid-conversation with a customer, but the moment her gaze locks onto mine, her focus snaps to me instantly.

"Good lord, child. You look like you've seen a ghost!"

Ruby abandons her customer without a second thought, her hands already reaching for me as she steers me toward a booth. Her voice dips, wrapping around me like a worn quilt. "What happened?"

Collapsing into the seat, my limbs are useless. I press my hands against the cool table, like contact alone might pull the words from where they're stuck in my throat.

"I—" How am I supposed to explain everything that's happened tonight? How am I supposed to make sense of it when it still feels like it doesn't belong to me?

Ruby slips in beside me, her presence comforting. "Take your time." She leans in, close enough to remind me I don't have to say a damn thing until I'm ready. Maybe not even then. I try to shove the emotions back where they can't reach me—but they refuse. Ruby doesn't wait. She just pulls me in, arms holding me tightly, like she knows I'm coming apart at the seams.

And I let her.

I stay there, pressed against her, until the shaking stops and my breath comes easier. Until the tears finally loosen their grip.

When I was younger, working here was one of the few things that kept me afloat. Now, after all these years, walking in and breaking down feels like ripping open a wound I no longer have the right to bleed from.

When I finally pull away, Ruby studies me with a gaze so heavy it feels like it could press me straight through the worn vinyl seat.

"Did you know my mom had another daughter?"

Ruby doesn't answer right away. She doesn't need to. The slow drop of her shoulders, the downcast flick of her eyes—it's enough.

She knew. Of course, she knew. Everyone did.

"Yeah. It wasn't long after you left." I can tell she's trying to gauge how much of the truth I can handle. And I hate it.

"Dylan, when you left, your mom changed." A pause, as if she's bracing herself to continue. "She's sober now, sweetheart. Far as I can tell, completely sober. The way she treated you…it wasn't right, wasn't fair, and I knew it. Lord, did I know it. But I didn't know how to step in."

She exhales, her relief evident—like this truth has been sitting in her chest for too damn long. "But losing you after losing your brother? That was her reckoning, honey. It was like all the ghosts she'd been outrunning finally caught up."

I sit there, struggling to process what she just said. My mom? Sober? It lands like a foreign language, something I should understand but can't quite translate. The person Ruby's describing isn't the woman I knew.

Ruby doesn't slow down. "I don't know what you'll want to do with that, and I'm not implying you have to do anything. That choice is yours, always will be. But, sweetheart, Blake didn't ask for any of this. She's just a kid. So, whatever you do, don't let your mom's mistakes keep you from getting to know her."

I know Ruby's right. Blake didn't choose to be born into a story already stained with loss. And no matter how much anger curdles inside me, how much of it is aimed at the woman I ran away from, none of it belongs to Blake. Even if I can't forgive my mom, I owe it to my sister to try.

I glance at Ruby, and the tears I've been forcing down start to rise again. I hope she knows how much this means to me, her being here, even if I can't quite find the words to say it. She gives my hand a single, reassuring squeeze before drifting away, leaving a sense of comfort in her wake as she tends to another customer.

I sink into the booth, head tipping back against the faux leather, eyes tracing the ceiling like it might split open and hand me an answer. It doesn't. Just leaves me stewing in the mess of it all—Brooks, my mom, this town that clings to me like a second skin, thick with memories I've spent years trying to scrub off. I don't want to be here. Don't want to face any of it. But that past has teeth, and no matter how fast I run, it always knows how to bite back.

And now there's Blake.

The last few days feel like an eternity, and all I want is to hit pause. Or rewind. Just to escape for a little while. But that's not an option, not with my sister's name now stitched into my heart, tugging at my guilt, at the longing of what could have been if only I'd stayed.

Eventually, I drag in a breath, scrape together what's left of my resolve, and shove myself out the door before I'm pinned down for good.

The walk back to The Drift is a blur, my feet moving on autopilot while my mind thrashes against itself. By the time I shut the door behind me, the static in my head is so loud it feels like it might crack through my skull. I need to talk to Beckett. He's the only person I can call when everything feels too big to hold onto by myself.

I haven't touched a paintbrush since the accident. The thought alone feels like pressing my palm against an open wound. Photography was the only thing I could stomach, the only creative outlet that didn't tear me apart. But even that feels like a betrayal of who I was. It's tangled up in Brooks, in the way *he* saw the world…saw *me*. And hating myself for it almost burns worse than the memories themselves. Especially here, where every shadow feels like it still belongs to him.

Before doubt can sink in, I pull out my phone and press Beckett's name. The dial tone punches through my thoughts, calling attention to how desperately I need to hear his voice.

No ring. Just his dumbass joke, the one that fakes you out like he's actually picked up. One second. Two. Then his laugh—carefree, familiar, gut wrenching. *Leave a message*, he says, and then the beep cuts through me.

"Hey, KitKat, I miss you." The words slip out in a hush, like saying them too loudly might make it hurt more. My gaze skates over the room, but nothing sticks, like I'm floating outside my own body. "I went to the high school tonight. The reunion. Wish you were there. Wish everything didn't feel so—" I press my fingers to my forehead, like I can physically hold myself together. "It's just different without you here. Wrong."

I want to rip myself open, let everything spill out. But the words are knotted tight, strangled before they can escape.

"I found something out," I manage. Saying it feels like stepping into an alternative reality, one where the ground beneath me doesn't belong. "We have a sister, Becks. Her name's Blake."

There. It's real now. The truth, and with it, a slow, aching rip, fiber by fiber. The tears come, slow and unchecked. They're not from sadness exactly, but from the sheer meaning of it all—the shift, the rupture, the way I suddenly don't know what to do with my heart.

"She's beautiful. You'd love her. Those bright blue eyes, that wild curl to her hair—she looks exactly like us. *Like you*. And for a second, it stole the air from my lungs. I wanted to tell her. I should've told her who I am. But I looked at her and saw everything I'd lost—I just couldn't bring myself to say it. It felt wrong, like I'm trying to build something new with missing parts, like there's a piece of this that only you were meant to hold."

I pause, teeth sinking into the edge of my thumbnail until the sting cuts through the noise in my head—not enough to stop me, just enough to remind me I'm still here.

"And, uh…Mom's sober now." The words feel like they belong to someone else's life. I roll them around in my mouth, waiting for them to settle, but they don't. "It doesn't feel real. I don't know how to handle it, or if I even want to."

The dam breaks. Words tumble out faster now, like I've lost control of the floor. "I just—God, Becks, I miss you. I want to stop dragging all this shit around with me, but I don't know where to start. I'm scared. What happens when I finally move on? I'm scared that if I do…I'll start losing pieces of you, too."

The voicemail beeps, cutting me off and erasing the words I didn't have time to finish—just like it always does.

I sit there, stranded on the edge of this stiff hotel bed, fingers locked around my phone like it's some kind of lifeline. And if I hold on tight enough, I might pull him back through the static. Might hear his voice one more time, telling me what to do, how to make sense of all this. But the line is dead. And so is he. Waiting won't change a damn thing.

My breath rattles out, and my eyes drift to the nightstand. Three letters, stacked too neatly, were somehow placed there. Staring at me like they know I've run out of places to hide.

Reality tilts as I stare at them. I blink, half expecting the envelopes to vanish, like some cruel trick of the light. But they're still here, waiting. Then, it hits me—our letters from high school. The ones we wrote to our future selves, a lifetime ago. I'd forgotten they even existed.

My breath catches as I reach for them, fingers ghosting over the old ink and paper. My own scrawled mess of a signature. My brother's rushed, uneven print. And the last one—deliberate. My name etched onto the envelope in handwriting I'd know anywhere.

Brooks.

He must have put them in here. It's the only explanation that makes sense.

I swear I can hear Mr. Lyons' voice in my head. *Seniors, take this time to write to your future self. When your reunion comes, see if you recognize the person you've become.* It felt stupid back then. A waste of time. But now, I have the proof of who we were, pressed tightly between my fingers.

I don't stop to question it—curiosity sinks its claws in, dragging my hands to the paper's edge. The seal breaks. Instinct takes the reins..

And then, everything changes.

ON OFF
Fn
VIEW MODE

28

Brooks

"There must be some mistake." Fear distorts my mom's voice, strangled by panic as she and my dad tear into each other in the hallway. "He's young. He's a healthy kid," she insists, her desperation bleeding into every word. "We can get a third opinion. A fourth, a fifth! Whatever it takes!"

She doesn't realize the doctor and I can hear everything—the crack in her voice, the way she claws at denial like she can rip it open to find a different answer inside. My dad's voice is lower now, smothered, like he's trying to force the world back into something manageable. I can't catch the words, but they steady something in her—just barely. When they return, they move like paper dolls caught in a slow motion collapse, one breath away from breaking.

I can tell they're trying to hide it, but I know them too well. The way they move, the way they avoid looking directly at each other, it's all too obvious. They're not okay, and neither am I. A crushing pressure coils around my ribs, the cruel paradox of wanting to be unshakeable yet yearning to be someone else's responsibility, just for a moment.

My mom's fingers latch onto mine, ice cold and trembling. She squeezes, but it's desperate, grasping at straws hoping to trick ourselves into believing this is enough. Her hand is smaller than I remember— thin, breakable—like porcelain that's already been cracked once. And maybe I should be the one holding her up, telling her it's okay. But I can't. Not right now.

Someone's talking, but their words don't reach me. It's all just noise, like a TV turned up too loud in the background while my brain is stuck on repeat.

Cancer.

The word hits like shrapnel. It doesn't belong in my life, doesn't belong in this moment. It wedges itself into the cracks of my mind, refusing to make sense. Just weeks ago, I had direction—I was supposed to be there for Dylan, the boyfriend who held her up after losing her twin. But now? Now, I'm the one slipping, drowning in something I can't even fathom, let alone survive.

The day after the accident, my legs just gave out. I told myself it was exhaustion, that my body was just catching up to the grief. My parents chalked it up to shock, but deep down, I knew better. Dr. Abrams had brushed it off previously as severe anemia. I wanted to believe him. I wanted it to be simple—just a bag of iron dripping into my veins, a few pills, and I'd be fine. Patch me up, send me on my way, no questions asked. But bodies don't work like that. Mine doesn't, anyway.

This time…they ran more tests, and found *it*. Cancer. I swear I felt the axis of my world tilt. The idea that my own body had betrayed me, that something was rotting inside me—I couldn't make it make sense. I'd been ripped out of my own life and shoved into someone else's nightmare.

And even now, with it staring me in the face, I can't make it real. It doesn't belong. How the hell is this my life? How is this the next chapter? I cling to who I was before, but it's already slipping, leaving me staring at a version of myself I don't recognize—one I never thought I'd be.

Here we are again—another sterile room, another stranger with a clipboard, ready to carve my world into something unrecognizable. The whole goddamn room feels like it's closing in, the ground beneath me itching to drop out and send me into whatever hell this is meant to be.

Dr. Hawkins' eyes are too damn knowing, like he's rehearsed this exact conversation a hundred times before. It pisses me off. My hands twitch, restless for something to hit. His words take a second to land, like they have to beat their way through the fog in my brain before they mean anything at all. *Chronic Lymphocytic Leukemia.* I think I'm supposed to understand what it means, but it feels like a misfired bullet—meant for someone older, someone else. Not me.

"It's rare in someone your age, but the tests unfortunately confirm it. I know this is a lot to process, but we need to discuss next steps."

I vaguely hear him explaining the disease, how it progresses, the treatment options available, but it's all blending together. It's like his voice is muffled behind the pounding in my ears. I try to focus, but I can't. My mind keeps drifting, trying to catch up with the fact that my body is betraying me in ways I didn't even know were possible.

There's a part of me that just wants to jump out of my own skin, to escape all of this. But I know I can't. I know I have to listen, to prepare for what's coming. But right now, the only thing I'm certain of is that nothing feels like it's mine anymore.

The other part is still clinging to the idea that any second now, I'll wake up, and this whole thing will turn out to be some kind of fevered nightmare. But with every passing second, it starts to feel more and more like this is my reality, and there's nothing I can do to change it. It's shackled to my body, and apparently I can't fucking cut it out.

I keep thinking about Dylan. About how I fucked it all up. I told myself I was doing the right thing, that shoving her away was some noble sacrifice instead of straight up cowardice. But the second I saw the betrayal in her eyes? Every bullshit excuse I clung to turned to dust. I couldn't even give her the truth after what she's been through. Her twin is dead, the other half of her soul, and I decided for her that she didn't need to grieve me too—like I had the fucking right. Like I wasn't just taking the easy way out.

Maybe if we could just escape—take that trip to Paris she always dreamed of—I could tell her the truth. Why I ended things the way I did, why I couldn't face her. We could spend the time I have left just being together, no doctors, no treatments. Just us, for however long we have. Why would I waste that precious time on something that might not even work, when I could be with her, even if it's just for a little while?

The doctor's words slip past me like water down a drain, gone before I can grab onto them. By the time I snap back, it's too late. I've lost too much.

"Do you have any questions?"

It takes a second to find my way back to the moment, to remember where the hell we are and why. "How long would I have if I don't do the treatments?"

My parents' eyes burn into me, my mom's protest practically vibrating before she even speaks. "Honey, no, you're doing the treatments. It's your best chance—."

I barely acknowledge her, keeping my eyes on Dr. Hawkins. "What are the odds? Fifty percent? Thirty?"

Dr. Hawkins clears his throat, the sound splintering through the room like a bone snapping out of place.

"Given how aggressive your case is, treatment is strongly recommended. Without it…" His pause says everything. "Your prognosis would be grim."

I hear the words, but they don't really feel like they're meant for me. They're just facts. Nothing more. The kind of cold, indifferent truth a doctor has to give, no emotion behind it.

"There's still a chance I'd die anyway, right?"

My dad's voice lashes out, like he's gripping onto the last of his hope with bloody fists. "Brooks, don't talk like that. You *will* be fine. You have to believe that. We all do."

I meet his gaze, and see it—that irrefutable conviction, the kind of belief that makes everything seem like it might just work out. But it's suffocating, tightening every time I try to pull away. Now…I let it pull me under, I'm too drained to fight, and too broken to reach for the surface.

A resigned exhale slips past my lips as I sag into the chair, my voice fading as my words wither into nothing.

"No more questions."

"She's not here."

Dylan's mother, Denise, stands in the doorway, stitched together by exhaustion, barely holding her shape. Her fingers worry at the raw skin around her nails, tearing at herself in slow absentminded destruction. She doesn't look like the woman I remember—she looks caved in, someone gutted by the absence of her children. The house reflects it, scrubbed clean, too neat in a way that feels unnatural for her. Like someone tried to bleach the grief out of it but only succeeded in making the emptiness louder.

"I'm sorry, Ms. Rivers," I force out, the words stiff. I shove the guilt aside, let it fester in the background, and force my words to come out smooth.

"Do you have any idea where she might've gone?"

She sighs, and it's not just a sigh—it's something breaking. Her eyes glimmer, swollen with tears that haven't yet fallen. "She left in the middle of the night a few days ago. Didn't leave a note. Nothing." Her voice splinters, and her hands tremble, continuing to pick the skin around her nails. "I've called everyone I can think of back in Wyoming.

Nobody knows anything."

I just stand there, throat thick, lungs tight, but she keeps going—because stopping would mean sitting in silence, and I think it might crush her.

"I know I was hard on her—too damn hard. Especially after Beckett. She didn't deserve it." Her voice cracks like she's holding herself together with nothing but spit and regret. "I needed somewhere to put it. All that anger. And she was right there."

She won't look at me. Just stares past, like eye contact might shatter whatever fragile grip she has left.

The remorse isn't just on her face—it's in the slump of her shoulders, the way her hands twitch like they want to turn back time.

"I made her my scapegoat, let my grief chew her up because I was too much of a coward to face it myself. She was already drowning, and instead of pulling her out, I left her there. She never stood a chance."

I clamp my lips shut and give a single nod. What the hell else is there to do? She's right. And we both know it.

"I see too much of myself in her. That fire. That sharp, stubborn edge. And it fucking terrified me. I didn't know how to love her without trying to snuff it out first." She swipes at a tear like it's an inconvenience, but they just keep coming. "She needed more from me. She deserved more. How was I ever supposed to give her something I never even got a taste of? Love isn't instinct when you've spent your whole life starving for it."

She takes a breath, but it doesn't help her. The words keep spilling. "And the drinking, God. I thought it was numbing me, thought it was helping. But it just turned me into something uglier. Bitter. It poisoned every inch of me until there was nothing left to give her but the worst parts of myself."

Her throat bobs as she swallows hard, and for the first time, she looks small. Hollowed out. Like she's been burned down to nothing but embers. "I've quit…drinking. Since she left. I dragged myself out of that hell, fought like a rabid dog to stay sober these past few weeks—so if she ever comes back, if she ever lets me in again, I can finally be the mom she should've had all along."

None of this erases what Dylan's been through, but it's not my place to say that.

"Do you think she'll come back?" I ask instead, the question feels useless, but it's all I have.

Denise looks at me, eyes bloodshot. "God, I hope so. I beg for it. Every damn day. But if she doesn't…" Her breath shudders, and she grips her shaking hands like they might hold her together. "I wouldn't blame her."

Her gaze drops, shoulders curling inward like she's trying to disappear. "I just— I want her to know I love her. That I'm sorry. That I never meant to make her feel like she was a burden, even though I know I did. I said things I can't take back. Made her feel like she had to earn a love that should've been hers without question." She shakes her head, letting out a choked sob. "If she can't forgive me, I'll understand. But she's my baby. My only baby now."

She looks like a structure caving in, one cracked beam away from collapse. Like if she moves too fast, breathes too deep, she'll scatter into pieces too small to put back together.

It does something ugly to my stomach—sits there like rusted metal, heavy enough to sink me. "I'll find her," I say, and I mean it. I mean it with everything in me.

She nods, but it's absent, like she's here but only because her body hasn't figured out how to quit yet. I start to turn away, but something drags me back.

"I never said it," I start, voice rough. "But I'm sorry about Beckett. He was solid. Loyal. A better friend than most people deserved. He shouldn't have—" My throat locks up, and I force myself to finish. "None of it should've happened."

Denise blinks like she wasn't expecting it, like she forgot how to hear kindness. Tears spill over, running unchecked down her face. And for the first time, she really looks at me—like I'm not just a reminder of what she lost, but someone real.

"Thank you," she whispers. And then she's gone, retreating into the ruin of her grief. And I? I walk out into the night, carrying a piece of it with me.

***

I hunch forward in the front pew, elbows digging into my knees, eyes fixed on the emptiness of the old church. Light filters through the shattered windows, catching dust in its grasp, twisting it into something ethereal before letting it fall. The floorboards are tired, worn thin from time and ghosts of footsteps long gone. It's so quiet that the sound of my breathing feels louder than it should, uneven, like I've been holding it in too long.

This place is nothing special, but it mattered to Dylan. Maybe it still does. That's why I'm here, gripping this envelope like it's the only thing still connecting me to her. Her name is desperately sprawled across the front in my own uneven handwriting like it might bridge the distance between us.

I flip the envelope over in my hands again, running my thumb along the edge, worn soft from all the times I've held it. Months have passed, and she's still nowhere. No social media posts. No updates. Just silence. Like she's been swallowed by the earth itself. I keep dialing the number etched into my memory, knowing it won't ring, knowing no one's on the other end—but I do it anyway, like repetition might rewrite reality.

Graduation came and went, and I stood there like an idiot, cap in hand, scanning the crowd for a face I knew wouldn't be there. But she was gone, and I was just another name on a list, another body in a sea of futures that didn't include her. Still, I waited, long after the last speech, after the chairs emptied, and the sun dipped low. Like maybe, somehow, she'd change her mind and I hadn't given her every reason to disappear.

I drag a hand down my face, the chemo buzzing under my skin, a restless, electric sickness that won't settle no matter how still I sit. The doctors say it's working—great, good, whatever—but all I can think about is how I destroyed the one thing that mattered. How I let fear worm its way into my head and take the wheel. I didn't want Dylan to see me like this, didn't want her looking at me like I was already one foot in the grave. So, I shoved her away, convinced myself I was saving her from loss. But let's be real—I wasn't some noble martyr. I was a goddamn coward.

Mr. Lyons said if I got him a new letter in time, he'd sneak it in with the rest from our class. It's a long shot, a desperate swing in the dark, but I have to try. One last attempt to tell her the truth, to let Dylan see the things I was too much of a fool to say when it mattered.

I let my gaze drift to the mural on the far wall, a riot of color sealed in time. She poured herself into it, brushstroke by brushstroke. The walls may be cracked and the wood faded, but her colors refuse to dull, defying time. It's a relic of her, a pulse of life she left behind, preserved by the elements, untouched by loss. Somehow, that's enough to trick my brain into thinking she's still with me—beyond the paint.

I stare at the envelope like it might burn a hole through my fingers. Then, with a sharp exhale, I fold it and tuck it into my back pocket. I tell myself it's just paper, but it feels like a confession, a reckoning, a hopeless attempt to reach her across the distance I built between us. If she ever reads it, I hope she understands. If I don't make it another ten years—hell, another month—at least she'll have this. At least she'll know.

My fingers press into the worn edge of the pew, splinters biting into my skin. I close my eyes and breathe through the nausea curling low in my stomach. I don't pray. Never have. But I do now. Not for me—for her. That wherever she is, she's not curled up on some lumpy motel mattress, staring at a ceiling stained with water damage, counting cracks like they hold all the answers. That she's not drifting from place to place, running on fumes, feeling like she has nowhere to land. That she's not out there believing—even for a second—that she was too much or not enough. That she knows—God, please, let her know— that she was the best thing that ever happened to me, and I was the dumbass who let her slip through my shaking, unworthy hands.

Brooks Letter

Dear Dylan,

I've tried to write this a hundred times, but the words never came out right. Maybe because there aren't words strong enough to hold everything I should have said. Everything I should have done. I let you go. I let you think you were easier to lose than to fight for, and I hate myself for it.

I don't know where you'll be in ten years, if you ever made it to Paris or if life kept you stuck somewhere, the way it did me. I don't know if you're happy. If someone else gets to love you now. But God, I hope so. I hope you're somewhere safe, where the walls are covered in art that speaks to you, where every brushstroke reminds you that you were always enough.

If I could erase every moment I made you question it, I would. But I can't. All I have left is the ink on this page and a hope so violent it rattles in my bones.

I'm not sure how to start this, and that's honestly fitting—there was never a right way to leave you either. I'm sorry. God, Dylan, I'm so fucking sorry. For walking away. For tearing us apart when you had already lost so much. For every second after Beckett died that I didn't tell you the truth.

You might tear this to shreds. I wouldn't blame you if you did. Hell, I deserve worse. But if these are the last words you ever get from me, then you need to understand why I turned my back—why I let you go, even though it felt like ripping out the only pieces of my heart that still knew how to beat.

I have cancer. A rare kind. One that doesn't offer mercy, only maybes. Maybe treatments will work. Maybe they won't. Maybe I'll still be here when you find this, or maybe I'll just be a ghost—a name you haven't said out loud in years.

Turns out, it was there before Beckett died. Lurking. Waiting. Hiding behind every dizzy spell, every misdiagnosis the doctors gave me. And I believed them—just like I once believed in forever, in us, in the foolish idea that life moved forward like it's supposed to. But it doesn't. It stops when you least expect it, and there's nothing anyone can do about it.

I didn't know how to tell you, Dylan. How the fuck was I supposed to hand you *more* grief when you were already drowning in it?

So, I fed myself a pretty lie, let it take root in my mind—a parasite gorging itself on every doubt until I mistook it for certainty. *That hating me would be easier than mourning me too.* That if I burned every bridge between us, made you despise me enough, it would cauterize the wound before it could bleed.

It would hurt less when I was gone.

I let it fester until it felt like the only way forward, because if someone had to swing the scythe, it was damn well going to be me.

But every day since, I've been eaten alive by the regret of how I let it all fall apart. I should've torn myself open, bled the truth into your hands, and let you decide whether to hold on or walk away. But I was terrified of how saying it out loud would make it real, turning my worst fear into something I couldn't take back.

And yet, I'm still here. Barely. Some days, it feels like my body is more poison than blood. Chemo is war—one I'm not sure I'm winning. Some nights, I swear I can feel myself dissolving. But when it gets bad, when I'm too sick to move, too weak to fight, there's one thing that keeps me breathing.

You.

The first night I met you, something in my chest came unstitched. I'd spent my entire life moving through the world in grayscale, and then there you were—color, brightening everything I thought I knew. I didn't just see you. I recognized you, like some part of me had been *waiting* for the moment our worlds would collide.

You were the best thing this life ever gave me. You still are. Always will be. If I leave this world, I need you to know—I didn't just love you. I was created for you. Every breath, every beat of my heart, is yours in a way that defies choice or reason. And if there's anything after this, beyond the pain, I'll tear through eternity to find you until forever is ours again.

I swore on everything I had that I wouldn't leave you alone. And then, when it mattered most, I did exactly that. A betrayal disguised as love. And now, I can't unmake the empty space I left behind. But God, Dylan, I would carve out my own ribs to go back and keep that promise.

Still, I hope you remember the good. Even if it's tangled up in everything I ruined. The way we laughed until we couldn't breathe, the late night drives with the whole world rushing past us, like we could outrun everything waiting for us back home. The outdoors you swore you'd never love, and yet—somehow, you did. You painted it, breathed life into it, poured pieces of yourself into every canvas until the world made sense through your hands.

Time can fade pigment, crack edges, turn masterpieces to dust, but it will never erase you.

And I wouldn't trade that for second. Not for time, not for a cure, not for salvation itself. Because you gave me something no one else ever has. A reason to stay, to fight, to love. *A reason to live.* Even when it meant losing.

By the time you read this, it could be too late. But I want you to know—I'm fighting. Every second of every day, I'm clawing against the inevitable because I believe in what we were. In you.

So live, Dylan. Live the life you deserve. Make it everything you ever wanted, and if my name ever crosses your mind, let it be a memory that doesn't hurt anymore. Because for all my mistakes, for all the ways I let you down, loving you was the one thing I got right.

I will continue to love you beyond what is possible, until forever itself ceases to exist. Until forever falls.

Brooks

29

Dylan

Now

My fingers hover over the words as if touching them might burn me. My eyes rake over the sentences again, again, again—frantic, starving for a different version, some loophole that makes this easier to wrap my head around. But the ink doesn't shift. The truth doesn't change. It just sits there mercilessly, the one question I never stopped asking, finally screaming back at me.

With every reread, the anger spreads like oil in water, impossible to contain. A decade I spent gripping a lie so tightly it became part of me. Even then, in that cold parking lot, I knew he was holding something back. I stood there begging, my heart in my hands, and he didn't even reach for it.

So I left. Tore myself from Rockport's grip, convinced I was alone.

Trust was a currency I'd never afford again. Because the one time I spent it, it bled me dry.

It's funny, in a messed-up kind of way, how that betrayal didn't just wound me—it rewired me. It left me cold, guarded, terrified of letting anyone too close. For years, the thought of tearing down those walls felt impossible.

And now? Now I find out it was all based on a lie. Not a cruel, vindictive one. A scared, messy, human lie. It's almost worse, because there's no easy way out now. I can't just turn my back on him and be done. Instead, I'm buried under a heap of contradictions, stuck between what I should do and what I can't seem to let go of.

I used to think I was reckless, letting myself fall so fast, so completely—for someone who abandoned me when I was at my lowest. I've replayed that story a thousand times, convinced my mistake was loving him at all. But now I see the real failure wasn't in loving him. It was in believing he didn't love me, in never demanding the truth, in running away without a fight.

Now I see it. I've spent a decade resenting him for a choice he made out of fear, believing it was the only way to protect me. He was terrified, convinced he wouldn't make it, and he carried that burden alone. I'm furious—not just at him, but at myself—for never stopping to consider there was more to the story.

I was held hostage by my own grief, so ensnared by it that I never noticed he was breaking too. Bitterness became my armor, easier to cling to than the truth. That I wasn't the only one hurting. That maybe Brooks wasn't the villain I painted him as, just the easiest one to blame.

The realization slams into me—*I'm my mother.* Not with a bottle in my grip, but in every way that truly matters. I let affliction fester, let it burrow into me the way she let the liquor seep into her veins. Her addiction was alcohol; mine is this relentless, all consuming resentment. And just like her, I've let it incinerate everything good before I even realized I was holding the match.

I feel disgusted. I swore I'd never turn into her, yet I've let my own pain become the thing I lean on the most. I was too lost inside it to see how it was carving me into a reflection I couldn't stand.

My phone is a live wire against my palm, radiating heat like it knows the war raging inside me. Brooks' name stares back at me, a taunt, a challenge, a door I keep pacing in front of but never open. My heart pounds as I force my thumb down before fear can pull me back.

One ring. Two. Then his voice. "Dylan?"

"Hey," I say, though the word fractures on its way out.

"I read the letter. Can you meet me? I know it's late, but I think we should talk."

Silence.

It stretches, pulls, swells into something unbearable. The longer it lasts, the more convinced I am that calling was a mistake—another entry on my growing list of things I should've left alone.

Then finally, "I'll be there in ten."

"Okay." The word barely leaves my lips before I end the call, cutting off any chance for hesitation—his or mine. If I stay on the line I could second guess this entirely. And I can't afford that. Not after learning the truth.

The dress I was wearing at the reunion felt like a costume—too delicate, too much like someone I was *supposed* to be. So, I stripped it off the second I could, swapping it for worn jeans and an oversized sweater that hangs loosely around me. The sleeves slip past my wrists, my fingers disappearing into the fabric as I flex my hands, grasping for something solid.

The low rumble of Brooks' truck pulling into the lot startles me out of the endless loop I've been tracing in the damp grass. My footsteps have carved a restless path in front of the hotel, the salty air clinging to my cheeks, the briny bite of seaweed permeating the air. I didn't realize how much I needed the aroma of it, something tangible to cling to while my mind spun itself in circles.

His truck door slams shut, but he's already moving before the sound fades. There's an ease to the way he crosses the lot, like he's been waiting for this moment.

Stopping just short of me, he shoves his hands into his jacket pockets. "You okay?"

His words carry more than just concern, but I'm not ready to dissect what's hidden beneath them. Not here.

Instead, I lift a shoulder, keeping my voice from cracking. "Can we walk?"

Brooks doesn't ask where—we just move, my steps falling into rhythm with his like they always have. He steers us toward the beach, where the tide restlessly gnaws at the shore. The silence between us isn't awkward, just tense with all the words we haven't figured out how to say out loud yet. It lingers, pressing in around us, as if the night itself is holding its breath, waiting to see who will break first.

The sand shifts beneath me as we near the water. Each step buries me for a second before letting go. I stop just short of the tide, watching the waves roll in, as if they might tell me where to begin.

"I don't really know where to start." It's an admission I didn't mean to voice, but I know he hears it. I feel it in the way he shifts, like he's steadying himself for whatever comes next.

"It's like I've been dragging these heavy suitcases around for years, convinced they were packed with betrayal. And now you're telling me they're empty. That I've essentially been breaking myself under a weight that was never even there."

"I wanted to tell you the truth. Even tonight, I wanted to say it." His tongue swipes over his bottom lip, deliberating. "But every time I tried, it felt like prying open a door that wasn't mine to unlock. So I left the letter in your room instead, hoping it could break through to you where I couldn't."

The sincerity in his voice cuts through me. It's not grand, not laced with theatrics, but it's real. And that's all I've ever needed.

I tear my focus away from him, locking onto the horizon where the sea and the sky blur into something infinite. My fingers fidget, skimming over one another in frantic, meaningless movements. He's given me honesty—I owe him the same. But the waves are louder now, their crash and retreat pressing in, like they can sense the fractures beneath my skin.

"I couldn't afford both," I say after a long moment.

"What? What do you mean?"

"When I left, I had just enough money to keep one phone active. I made a choice. I shut mine off and kept Beckett's. That's why no one could reach me." I press my tongue to the roof of my mouth, attempting to sort through everything in my mind that wants to break free. "I needed his voicemail. I needed to hear his voice even if it was just a recording. It was the only piece of him I had left. I couldn't risk losing it."

The confession shakes something loose in me, but I press on, even as my voice wavers. "I got a new phone eventually, when I could afford it, but the number changed. I assumed my absence was just another thing people would adjust to without any effort. So, reaching back out was never something I considered. I wasn't intentionally hiding from you, Brooks. I was just trying to survive."

"You were surviving, I get that. But damn, I would've given anything to know you were out there, still breathing."

"I convinced myself no one cared," I murmur, exhaling like it might lighten the weight in my chest. "Until now." I force myself to meet his eyes, to let him *see* everything I never had the chance to say, because this next part is what really matters. "But you know what hurts the most?"

He shifts slightly, tilting his head just enough to catch the moonlight, his short chestnut brown hair tousled in a way that makes something ache deep inside me. I used to tease him about the way it always fell into his eyes—now, I almost miss it. He watches me, waiting, like he's searching for this moment when everything will finally make sense.

"I would have stayed," I admit, a confession years too late. "Even when my entire world was caving in, even when I felt like I was nothing but broken pieces, you were always worth risking more pain for."

"Would you still?"

His question is a scalpel, cutting clean through my defenses. Would I stay? Now? I barely know what that means anymore. I mean, New York was never really home, just a place I existed. And even if I wanted to return, what would be the point? The city wouldn't notice my absence, my nearly empty apartment wouldn't miss me, and Aaron. He was always meant for more than I could ever give him. We both know that now.

"I would." The conviction in my voice seals off any room for doubt and I scrape my thumbnail against my knuckle, needing the sensation to remind me this is real. "For Blake. I can't pretend like she doesn't change everything. I've spent so long convincing myself that my choice to leave made sense, that I was exactly where I was supposed to be. Gone."

I let out a breath that feels stolen from a version of me who never thought she'd say this. "But I wasn't. I was lost, I just didn't realize it until tonight. Knowing Blake's been here all this time—that I've missed so much of her life—made it impossible to keep lying to myself."

"So what happens next? What about your life in New York?"

I touch my necklace absently, a habit born from needing something to hold on to. "The life I built there wasn't real, Brooks. It was a placeholder, something to keep me moving so I wouldn't have to face the wounds I never let heal. Blake is proof that not everything in this town is stained with the memory of what I lost. Beckett. *You.*" My gaze drops to his hands, to the space between us, to the past and future colliding.

"My time in Rockport was brief, but it was real, and somehow it became the only place I ever felt at home. Staying feels like the first step to finding my way back to that."

"So stay, Dylan. Not because of Blake. Or me. Stay because this is where you finally let yourself belong." I take him in—the slight furrow between his brows, the worry settling in the creases at the corners of his eyes. And just like that, I know. He's never been anything less than everything. My heart has belonged to him since that first bonfire, since the flames cast their glow across his face and made me believe, if only for a moment, that some things are meant to burn forever. Maybe not as we once did, but as something that still matters.

"After I read your letter, I realized I've spent the last decade treating my grief like a place to live. I barricaded myself in it, let it decide who I was allowed to be. I built a life so small it couldn't hurt me, one without color, without anything real enough to lose."

My breath hitches as I press my fingers into my collarbone and force myself to keep going. "Because of that, I haven't touched a paintbrush since I left. The idea of it made me sick. Because Beckett was in everything I tried to create. So I didn't. I refused. I lost the one outlet that helped me make sense of the world."

I roll my shoulders back, forcing myself to stand in the moment instead of running from it. "But you…and Blake have opened my eyes again. I have to stop living like a shadow of someone I don't recognize anymore. Staying would be for me, but it's because of the two of you that I can finally see *why* it matters. I may never be who I was before, but if it leads me to something worth holding onto again, then maybe that's enough."

The wind picks up, threading through pine trees that line the beach, their branches shifting like restless hands against the sky. "You don't owe anyone the person you used to be," he says, his voice carrying through the breeze with a quiet certainty. "I just want you here, and I'm sure Blake will too. Take it slow, see where things fall. We're not demanding anything."

A restless gust catches my curls, blowing them across my face. I brush them back but the moment stills—something shifting within me, a question that's been pressing against my chest, demanding its turn since I called him.

"I don't want to cross any lines, Brooks, but…" I pause, gathering my thoughts carefully. "Can you tell me about your cancer? If you don't want to share, that's okay. Are you still fighting it?"

His shoulders tighten, and he tugs at his jacket, vibrant green eyes flicking to the side as if searching for an escape before returning back to meet mine.

"I'm not trying to cross any boundaries," I say gently.

The truth is already there between us, waiting to be acknowledged. He simply gives it shape. "You're not crossing a boundary. It's just…it's been a while since I've let myself put it all into words. But no, I'm not."

I stay still, letting the conversation breathe, making sure he knows the choice to continue is his.

"Um." His voice bends, as if carrying too much for one breath to hold. "The first few months, I was convinced I'd die anyway, so nothing felt like it mattered. But eventually, I told myself that if I just kept going—if I refused to acknowledge death—I could beat it. The doctors, the treatments, the way my parents looked at me like I was already gone. I shoved it all down and acted like it couldn't touch me." He stares at a fixed point in the distance, as if the horizon might hold the words he's struggling to find.

"Chemo hit me like a wrecking ball, leaving nothing untouched. I lost weight, lost my hair, lost the ability to feel like myself in the mirror. I spent so much time throwing up that I forgot what it felt like to be hungry." His words thin out. "My body didn't belong to me anymore—it belonged to the disease, to the medicine trying to kill it, to the doctors deciding how much poison I could take before I broke." He presses his thumb against the inside of his wrist, like he's checking to see if he's still here.

"And I did break. Over and over again. But I kept going, because what the hell else was I supposed to do? There were days I swore I wasn't going to make it, nights I laid awake wondering if my heart would just stop in my sleep. Sometimes I thought that would have been easier." He laughs, but there's nothing light in it—just depletion.

"The worst part? It wasn't the pain. It was waiting." He presses the tip of his shoe into the sand, twisting it back and forth, burying it deeper. "The scans, the tests, the people who looked at me like a fucking puzzle missing half its pieces. The 'maybes', the 'we'll sees', the 'let's hope for the best.'" He shakes his head. "That's what no one tells you—it's not just a fight. It's a waiting game. Every test result a coin flip, and you're the one waiting to see if it lands heads or tails." Pulling his foot back, he kicks up a soft cloud of sand that scatters in the wind, disappearing too easily—too much like everything he's lost.

"The years passed, and somehow, I was still here. But surviving isn't the same as living, Dylan. And I didn't live—I just existed for a long time."

His words land with a nerve deep burn that doesn't ask for permission. They don't demand, or twist the knife—just settle, heavier than I expect. I sit with them, he's choosing to share this with me, despite everything we've been through. A piece of me grips onto the anger, the betrayal. It's familiar, easier to carry. But beneath it, something quieter stirs, something that has nothing to do with rage. Sorrow. Not just for what we both lost, but for the version of us that never had the chance to exist, for the story that faded before it could be written.

"I didn't see it back then," I confess, taking a deep breath. "But now, I get it. Why you made the choices you did, and I can't hold that against you, B."

It's not about changing the past or wishing for another chance. It's about accepting what happened, and finding a way to move forward, unburdened by it.

"When the doctors said I was in remission, I thought there'd be this…release. Like I'd finally gotten my life back. But I didn't feel that way. Instead, I felt more disconnected than ever. I was still searching for something, but I didn't know what."

The despair in his voice is palpable, and I can nearly picture the version of him that never got the chance to find peace, the person lost to that struggle.

"So, I did the thing I promised myself I'd never do," he admits, his tone laced in contempt. "I put my camera away, went to work for my dad, and buried myself in routine. At the time, I thought it was what I needed—something safe, predictable. Like I said, I was existing, merely drifting through my own life. And then one day, I passed the old church." His attention drifts down, colliding with mine in a way that steals my breath. "Something pulled me in. And when I stepped inside, it felt like it was begging to be revived, waiting for me to breathe life back into it. In its own way, it did the exact same thing for me."

"That's when you decided to open The Drift?"

He dips his head in agreement. "It gave me a reason to look *forward* again. It wasn't about making up for the past, or trying to prove something to anyone. It was about creating something meaningful. Something that could stand, no matter what else fell apart."

The steady conviction in his voice pulls at me, as if he's taken everything life has thrown at him and chose resilience over surrender. The Brooks I thought had faded into memory is still here—changed, tempered by time, but unmistakably the same. It's unsettling and steadying all at once, something that echoes the fight still burning in me. It's a collision of our past and present, a strange reassurance that even though we've been running parallel for years, we've finally found our way back.

Wordlessly, my fingers slip into his, the pulse beneath his skin proof that despite whatever was broken between us, we're still here. Simply beginning a new chapter.

A barely-there kiss lingers on my temple, as I return to my room, the distant rush of the ocean fading behind me. Leaving only the quiet and the remaining letters on my nightstand. I pick up mine first, fingers gently tracing the seal. The fear of what's inside has dulled—replaced with something closer to understanding. Or perhaps I've learned that courage doesn't come from having all the answers, but from daring to face the questions.

Dylans Letter

Dylan,

First off—holy crap, we actually made it. High school. Done! Wild, right?

I don't know where you're reading this, but I hope it's somewhere good. A place that feels like yours. Because if you're anything like me right now, you need it.

I won't lie. I wasn't exactly excited to write this. The whole *letter to your future self* thing felt weird, but maybe one day it'll mean something? Hopefully, it'll at least remind you how far we've come, and that we've survived.

Do you remember all those nights before moving to Rockport when we couldn't sleep? How we'd lie there, staring at the ceiling, planning our escape like it was the only way we'd ever really start living?

It felt like our only choice back then. Like if we didn't run, we'd get stuck watching mom drown herself in everything she could get her hands on, and probably end up just like her. Miserable. But somehow, we landed in Rockport, and to be honest, it doesn't feel as temporary as I thought it would.

Of course, there's Brooks. Yeah, yeah, I hate to say it, but he's probably the biggest reason. He talks about working for his dad's construction company like it's set in stone. His whole life has already been laid out for him. But I can see it—the part of him that wants something else but won't say it out loud. That's what finally made me stop and ask myself what I really want. Maybe art isn't just a hobby. Maybe I don't have to put miles between me and Mom to figure out who I am.

And Beckett. God, Becks. He's actually happy here, like really happy. For so long, it felt like it was just us against the world, always waiting for the next disaster. But now? He's found his people—not just teammates he shares the field with, but *real* friends who get him. A life outside all the crap we went through. A future.

But here's the thing. Becks still thinks the plan is to leave this place, leave mom behind after graduation, like we always talked about. But the more I see him here, the more I think maybe he doesn't need to go. Maybe this is what we've been looking for all along. I just need to figure out how to bring it up without totally blindsiding him.

And maybe I'm starting to see things differently for myself, too. I get it—we've always kept our walls up. It felt safer that way, like if no one could see the mess, then no one could hurt us. But not everyone's out to tear us down. Some people actually show up for you, and they prove they're worth the risk.

So, listen—don't forget about yourself is all I'm saying. I know we've spent so much time worrying about Beckett and Mom, but we matter, too. You matter. Your dreams? They're worth something. I hope you travel, paint the world, and do whatever you want ten years from now too. Stop waiting for some perfect moment to start living your life. Just go for it. Whatever's next, you'll figure it out.

So…did we do it? Did we finally get to Paris?

Are we still in Rockport, or did we end up somewhere else?

What about Becks? Did he stick around, or did he chase something bigger?

Did Mom ever get better?

And Brooks…is he still in our life? I hope he's happy. And if he's not, I hope at least we are.

Love, Dylan

30

Brooks

Now

Dylan's fingers pass over mine, a brief, unsteady brush, like the wind pulling at the edges of a torn flag. It doesn't tie us together. But it doesn't let us go either.

The night didn't originally go as planned. It cracked me open in that parking lot, scraped at old wounds, and still, I can't call it anything but right. We let the past sit between us on that beach, let it have its say, and in the end, we were still standing. She's staying. Maybe not for me, but for Blake.

And yet, it still feels like a prayer answered, like something in the universe finally shifted in my favor, just a little.

Because Blake—God, she's so much like them. I've kept up with her over the years, always felt like she was family, even when Dylan wasn't around. She has Dylan's drive, that all-consuming need to create, to throw herself into something bigger than her. And Becks… she's got his heart. His optimism. That belief that things will work out, that love is worth the risk.

I don't know when Dylan will meet her. If she's even ready to. But I know, when she does, she's going to love Blake the way she loves Beckett, the way she loves anyone that truly matters. Because that's just who she is.

The morning is creeping in, stretching long shadows across the pavement as I sit behind the wheel. I kissed the side of her head before I left, a restrained goodbye when everything in me wanted to never leave. Walking away felt wrong. But driving away? That feels worse.

I tip my head back against the seat and stare up at the headliner, like it might have the answer. What I'd give to stay a little longer. To walk right back into the hotel, and go straight to her room. To finally show her what I've been holding inside all these years. An unsettling thrum builds in my chest and I flip the sun visor down, a worn photograph slipping free, landing face up in my lap. The edges are curled, the colors faded, but I don't need clarity to know what it is.

Her. Framed by stained glass, brush in hand, coaxing butterflies from her soul. She never knew I took the picture—too deep in the trance of creation, breathing color into her trauma. Healing.

I turn my gaze toward the entrance of The Drift, the place that's been my everything—my home, my work, my safety. But now, with her here, it's complete in a way I didn't know it could be. I've gone through the motions, tried to let other people in, but no one has ever quite fit like she did.

I place the photo back where it belongs and push the visor up. The truck idles beneath me for a moment before I shift into gear, rolling through town slower than I need to. There's a lightness in my chest where the secret used to sit—a looseness I didn't have yesterday.

I roll into my driveway, gravel shifting under my boots as I climb out of the truck. I shut the door, harder than I need to, and head inside.

The house is dark except for the glow of the microwave clock. I toe off my boots by the door, leaving them in a heap before making my way to the kitchen. Water. Food. Something to do with my hands. I yank open the fridge, stare at the half shelves like an answer might be tucked between a beer and last weekend's produce.

My whole body feels wired, like I've got nowhere to put all this… whatever this is. Restlessness. Hope?

I glance at my phone, half expecting a message, half knowing it won't be there. I should sleep. Instead, I grab a glass, fill it at the sink, and lean against the counter. I take a long sip of water, the cold biting at my throat, but it does nothing to settle me. The house feels too still. Or maybe I am. Either way, standing here is not helping.

I set the glass in the sink and push off the counter, rubbing a hand over my face as I head for the bedroom. My body knows I need to rest, even if my mind isn't on board. I pull my shirt over my head, toss it toward the chair in the corner, and drop onto the bed, the mattress dipping under my weight.

Lying down makes it worse. The second my head hits the pillow, my thoughts start spinning again. I flip onto my side. Then onto my back. Exhale hard and shove my arm under the pillow. Sleep isn't coming easy, but I close my eyes anyway, forcing myself to at least try.

Morning drags its way in, slipping through the gaps in the curtains, indifferent to whether I'm ready for it or not. Sunday means breakfast with my Dad at Ruby's—a routine we fell into over the last couple of years.

I rub the back of my neck, working out the stiffness from a night that barely counted as sleep. However much I did manage wasn't enough, but there's no point in dwelling on it. In the bathroom, I brush my teeth, the cold water cutting through some of the grogginess. I pull on a henley and a pair of jeans, rolling my shoulders to shake off whatever's left of sleep before shoving my feet into my boots. Fingers comb through my hair, I grab my keys and step outside, letting the cool air do what coffee hasn't yet—wake me up.

Ruby's is alive with the kind of morning rush that never changes—orders being shouted, plates sliding onto tables, coffee pots making the rounds. The scent of maple syrup and frying bacon clings to the air. My dad's tucked into our usual booth, already deep in his first cup of joe, and in front of my seat, a hot plate of untouched pancakes sits, waiting.

I settle in across from him, and neither of us rushes to speak. There's no need. We've spent years rebuilding this, chipping away at the mistakes, until we finally landed here—two men who finally learned how to meet each other halfway.

Scott Holland, the man who once measured my worth in expectations and sacrifices, isn't the same. I spent years resenting the pressure, the feeling that I was always falling short. But now, I understand it for what it was—his way of protecting me from failure.

"Figured you'd sleep in today."

I know what he's really asking—how'd it go with Dylan?

I push the pancakes around on my plate, not quite ready to lay it all out. It's still too raw. But it's my dad, and there's a certain kind of honesty between us now that wasn't always there. It makes me feel like I can say it.

"I talked to her last night. After the reunion." The confession settles between us, thick as the syrup on my plate. "She knows. Everything's out in the open now."

Dad doesn't press, but he doesn't look away either. He just sits with it, with me, waiting. He saw me tear myself apart over her once. He watched me rebuild, piece by piece over the years. And now, with her back, I think we're both trying to figure out if I'll have to start over again.

"She's staying." I say it like I need to hear it aloud to believe it. I lean back, running a hand along the back of my neck. "For Blake. Because she wants to be a part of her life." I exhale slowly. "I get it. I do. It isn't about me. But…I can't screw this up again. Not when I've been given another chance."

"Then don't." He sets his cup down, leveling me with a look. "You don't have to be perfect, son. You've learned. You've already faced the worst and come out on the other side. Don't stop fighting now."

"I know. It just feels like there's already so much time we can't get back."

"Then don't waste the time you have now. Just let it happen."

"Yeah, I know. I'm just trying to be patient."

My dad smirks, lifting his coffee. "Well, who knows? Maybe one day, you'll finally get around to that Paris trip you used to go on about."

I huff out something close to a laugh, but then Ruby's there, coffee pot at the ready, as if she's mastered the art of showing up right when someone needs an escape.

"Well, well, look who finally decided to show up. Hope I'm not interrupting anything too serious. Should I be topping off the coffee or the advice?"

My dad chuckles, leaning back in his seat. "I've been trying to get him to stop worrying himself in circles, but you know how that goes."

Ruby arches a brow, refilling his cup before glancing at me. "What's got you in a twist?" She nudges the coffee pot toward me. "You need this more than anyone."

I let out a breath, wrapping my hands around the warm mug. "I just don't want to mess things up with Dylan."

Ruby's gaze softens and she places her free hand over mine. "Then don't. You're complicating something simple—she loves you. She always has." Her fingers squeeze mine before she steps back, then offers the simplest, most frustrating answer. "You want her to stay? Give her a reason that has nothing to do with the past."

My dad shifts, one elbow on the table, his gaze still on me. Then, with a measured breath, he moves us along, giving me room to breathe.

"Did Colt show up?"

"Yeah," I mutter, dragging my fork through the syrup. "Didn't take much to see that Dylan being there rattled him. Looked like he wanted to be anywhere but there. Then suddenly he's got to rush back to the ER. Could've been legit. Could've been convenient. Either way, he didn't stay long."

"He still hasn't made peace with what happened with Beckett?"

I take a slow sip of my coffee, letting it run down my throat before I answer. "I don't think he ever will. Not completely."

"Guilt's a heavy thing," my dad says, his voice edged with knowing. "But until he stops carrying it like a cross on his back, it'll own him. He wasn't at fault that night, but in his head? He's still the one holding the wheel."

I push my plate away, appetite gone. "Yeah, well, tell that to Colt. He's been living like he's got a debt to pay ever since. Became a whole doctor just trying to balance the scales."

I let out a frustrated breath. How do you get someone to see they're not responsible for a tragedy they couldn't have stopped? It's like trying to talk someone out of drowning when they're convinced the water's their fault. How do you bring someone back to shore when they're certain they belong in the depths, convinced the waves are some kind of penance they have to pay.

I've seen it for years—the way Colt carries himself, like he's not even allowed to breathe. It's like he's convinced that forgiveness is something he'll never deserve, even though deep down, he's desperate to believe otherwise.

I drain the last of my coffee, absently tracing the rim as my dad finishes eating. When I was fighting for my life, Colt never let me do it alone. When everyone else left, he showed up, no matter how exhausted he was, or how much else was on his plate. He'd watch mindless TV with me for hours, crack the worst jokes just to get me to laugh—because that was his way of telling me I was still here, still me.

I push back from the booth and stand, tossing a few bills on the table. Outside, the weight of an oncoming storm is pressing down. I have things to do, work to keep me busy. But even as I walk out of the diner, my mind isn't on any of it. It's still stuck on her.

Dylan's here. In the same town. Breathing the same air. And she's *staying*. That simple truth makes me believe, with a surge of cautious optimism, that Colt can finally shatter the illusion of culpability he's carried with him for so long. He just has to take the first step.

31

Dylan

Now

My phone stays silent, an empty screen staring back at me, erasing any trace that the fight with Aaron ever happened. Maybe that's for the best. As awful as it sounds, I'm relieved. Constantly holding everything in felt like standing on the edge of a cliff, waiting to fall. But now, being here, talking to Brooks, I finally feel like I'm on solid ground.

The salty harbor air caresses against my skin, lifting along my neck, weaving through my hair. I press my shoulders back, push my hands deeper into my pockets, and clench my fingers against the fabric. A useless attempt to keep my hands from shaking. Any minute now, my mother will show up—with Blake. I shift my weight from one foot to the other, restless, my pulse stuttering between panic and excitement.

I'm officially meeting my little sister. Only the second time I'll be seeing her, and yet it feels like I've been waiting for this moment forever.

I'm surprised my mother didn't put up a fight when I asked to see her alone today. No prying, no guilt, just a simple yes. It's a rare thing, and I'm letting myself appreciate it. This morning, I found myself back in front of the house, like muscle memory had pulled me back there. Blake wasn't home. She had dance class. Maybe that was for the best—I wasn't ready to step inside yet. So, I picked somewhere else to meet, somewhere that didn't come with memories tucked into every corner. I may not know how to hold all this at once, but I do know one thing—right now, Blake is what matters.

A small, nondescript sedan rolls to a stop, its faded blue paint catching the afternoon light. It's the kind of car you buy when reliability matters more than sentiment. I'd recognize that grip on the steering wheel anywhere—firm, precise, hands at ten and two. Unmistakable. My mother. Even before she steps out, before she moves to help Blake from the back seat, I know. It's her.

Blake barely pauses before closing the door, and when her gaze lifts, it snags on mine. The resemblance to Beckett is undeniable—like someone copied and pasted his features onto a smaller frame, dark hair just as unruly, storm-colored eyes just as wide and sharp. It's like looking at a crossroads between timelines, and I'm not sure which one she belongs to.

Mom's fingers press lightly against the top of Blake's shoulders, but she doesn't react. Her focus is on me, her steps confident with an energy that's almost electric. The anger towards my mother, the resentment—all the things I worried would take up space in this moment—shrink down to nothing. None of it matters. Not right now. Blake is a bridge between what I lost and what I still have, and I want to meet her in the middle.

"Hi, Blake," I say, the words careful, like setting down something fragile.

The corners of her mouth lift, just barely, like she isn't sure whether she's allowed to let her excitement show. She exhales, shifting slightly, her gaze skimming the ground before meeting mine. "Hi, Dylan." She blurts, as if she's been holding it in for hours. "I knew who you were the other day when you came by the house." A pause, then another breath. "I was too nervous to say anything."

"You did?" I ask, though I'd already guessed as much from what Chloe told me.

She squints up at me, her curls brushing her cheeks. "I've seen pictures," she begins, like she's just let me in on the best secret in the world. "Of you and Beckett. There's a whole box of them in the closet. Some are kind of old and crinkly, but I liked looking at them. Mom told me about you, too." She nudges a pebble with her toe as she speaks, like the ground is part of the conversation. "I used to pretend when I was younger I had a big sister. Like, if I wished hard enough, maybe you'd just show up one day. And now you're here." She pauses, glancing up at me again. "It worked!"

Her words land somewhere deep, in a place I didn't realize was still tender. I sink to one knee, meeting her eyes, hoping she can see everything I don't know how to say yet. "Would a hug be okay?"

Her answer is immediate—she steps forward, arms looping around me like she's done it a thousand times before and this isn't only our second meeting, but it's something we've always known how to do. She holds on tighter than I expect, her small fingers clutching the back of my shirt. I close my eyes, letting the moment settle, letting it stitch up something I thought would always stay broken. Tears gather at the edges of my vision, but they're not from loss. They're from the hope that maybe life isn't too far gone to find my way back.

Blake and I spent the whole day together. We wandered, letting conversations take us wherever they wanted. Mini-golf was ridiculous. I was even worse than I thought, but Blake hyped me up like I was some kind of olympian.

It was a chaotic mess of me losing every ball and her laughing so hard she had to clutch her stomach. I let myself enjoy it. And honestly? It might have been the best game I ever played. There were moments I could almost pretend Beckett was right there, that I could turn my head and see him beside me. It's strange, the way grief begins to shift without warning. I've been carrying it around like a heavy coat, something I can't take off. But as I listen to her talk—about dancing, her friends, the future that stretches out ahead of her like an open road—it occurs to me that Beckett never really left. He's still here, in her, in me, in all the places I forgot to look.

Every little thing she shares, things she might not think twice about, feels like something I've been waiting to hear. I don't care if it's mundane, if it's about the way she hates tomatoes or how she always loses her socks. It all matters. She matters. And with her here, things don't feel so empty anymore.

Before she left, she held on a little longer than I expected, like she was afraid we'd slip away from each other the second she let go. I didn't want the day to be over. Or let go of this feeling that things might be okay. I considered talking to Mom, but when the moment arrived, I let silence win. Maybe tomorrow. Maybe never. I don't know.

She let it be, and I held onto it like a fragile truce. I'll always remember what happened, but some conversations don't need an audience. She seems changed—I hope it's real. Blake doesn't need to carry what I did. She gets to have the mom who tries, and I'm still figuring out how to make peace with that.

The cab eases to a stop outside The Drift, and I tell the driver to keep the meter running. My steps quicken as I head inside, straight to my room. The letter is right where I left it, waiting. As soon as my fingers graze the envelope, my ribs tense, like a violin string drawn too tight. I let out a slow breath.

It's time.

The cemetery gates blur past the windows, and before I know it, the drive is over before I have time to prepare. The driver eases the car to the side of the road without needing instruction. I pay him without looking back and step onto the grass. The sun is slanting low behind me, gilding the headstones with its final light. When I kneel beside Beckett's name, I trace the ridges of the letters, as if the touch alone could bridge the space between us now. He's not here, not really. But

I can still feel him.

I used to think I had all the time in the world to say what mattered. But time is ruthless, slipping through cracks and closing doors before you even realize it's happening. Now, all I have is this letter, Beckett's words frozen in ink from a life that should have stretched so much further.

"Hey KitKat," I murmur, my heart heavy as I speak. "I don't know where you are, if you're watching, if you even care. But I miss you. That much, I know." I press my palm against the cool stone, my throat tightening. "You'd be rolling your eyes at me right now, telling me I should've come sooner. And yeah, you'd be right. I should have. But I wasn't ready." I swallow hard, staring down at the letter. "I think I am now. Or at least, I want to be. But before I can move forward, there's something I have to say."

The pressure behind my eyes builds, but I refuse to let it take over. "I'm sorry." The words are bitter in my mouth, too little, too late. "I should have told you when it mattered, when you were standing right in front of me instead of buried under six feet of dirt. But I didn't, and I hate myself for it." My breath shudders. "You were brilliant, Beckett. You were everything. And I wasted time being angry when I should've just said I was proud of you. I'm still proud of you."

I slam my eyes shut, but it does nothing to hold back the flood. The grief boils over, the self loathing twists deep, and then—then I'm crumbling, shaking, the tears tearing their way free.

"You were fearless. Or at least, that's what it looked like from where I was standing. Every dream you had, you just reached for it and somehow, the universe made room for you. But me? I spent my whole life feeling like I had to ask permission just to exist. But when I found out you kept your scholarship from me, it was more than just a secret. It was proof that you saw it too—the gap between us, the way my world was so much smaller than yours." Tilting my head back, I blink hard, willing the tears to ease. "That crushed me more than the secret ever could. You never really knew how much I wanted the world for you."

Wind stirs the grass around me, dragging against the earth in a way that feels almost impatient. The sky bruises with the retreating sun, streaks of deep purple and orange stretching wide, the world feels too open, like it's waiting for me to finish.

"I should have been there that night. I told myself I needed space, that there'd be time to fix things—but there wasn't. Tomorrow never came for you." I press my palm to my sternum, like I can keep my insides from spilling out. "And now, I'd give anything to go back, to find you by the fire, and tell you what mattered most." My throat cinches around the words I'd give anything for him to actually hear. "I love you, Beckett."

My lips press together as I smooth out his letter, the words settling into the space grief carved out a long time ago. For a second, he's here—not in body, not even in voice, but in the rhythm of his handwriting. Each sentence sinks deeper than the last, pressing into me like footprints left in wet cement.

When I reach the end, my eyes catch on his signature. My thumb dragging over the slant of each letter, half expecting it to smear beneath my touch, to react in some way—to acknowledge me. But the ink stays. The silence stays. And for the first time, I let myself stay with it.

Becketts Letter

It feels strange addressing this to myself, so we're just gonna skip that part…but dude, we did it! Western Oregon University! I still can't believe it. I mean, who would've thought this clumsy freaking kid from Wyoming would actually end up playing college football?

Not me, that's for damn sure. But here we are. Well, at least I am. You're probably living it up by now.

Alright, alright, I'll stop bragging. But come on, this is insane! For once, it feels like things are actually working out. I can't stop thinking about it—college ball, dude!

A scholarship, man. Actual stadiums and crowds yelling for *us*. I've been dreaming about this forever, but now that it's happening, it's kinda insane. Scary, but in the best way.

Dylan's probably gonna say she's proud or whatever, but I can't stop feeling like I'm letting her down. It sucks. We've had this plan forever—graduate, ditch our lives, head back to Colorado. Now I'm doing this, and school's never been her thing. I know I'm messing up what we've always talked about, and I feel guilty as hell.

I know she's been through some real stuff—way beyond just surviving Mom's fucking circus. But there's other shit, things she doesn't share. I get it, though. She's always had her own way of dealing. Honestly, I never blamed her for not wanting to make friends or anything. She had me, right? (Yeah, okay, not the same.)

She's been so different since we moved to Oregon. Like, actually different. In a good way. It's like she's finally letting people in. And yeah, let's give credit where it's due—Brooks. Dude's got her smiling and talking, like it's easy or something. No clue how he does it, but it's working, so I'm not about to question it.

I've seen her laugh, actually laugh, not that weird fake thing she used to do when we were kids to blend in. I don't think she even hates the world as much anymore. She's…happier? Honestly, it's kinda cool to see.

Shit man, I don't want her to think I'm bailing. She's my freaking twin, my best friend honestly. Really the only person I've ever trusted to have my back, no matter what. And now, here I am, chasing this football dream and I feel like I'm leaving her behind to figure things out.

She's my little sister. Two minutes younger, but still. She's tougher than most people I know, and I hope you've told her that by now because I know I haven't done it enough.

Just don't get all weird about it. Keep it cool. You know she hates the mushy stuff.

You better have figured out how to balance everything, future me. If you're living the dream out there on the field, I hope you didn't leave her behind. Take care of her, because if you're reading this and everything's gone to shit between us, then you're an idiot, and you better fix it.

Alright, let's be real for a second—I didn't think moving to Rockport was gonna be any good. Like, at all. I thought we were just gonna be stuck in another small town with nothing to do but wait for graduation. But, I'll admit it, I was way wrong.

Turns out, Rockport's kinda cool. I mean, who knew? Colt and Miles? Dude, those guys have turned out to be some of the best friends I've ever had. I didn't think I'd click with anyone after leaving the old place, but they've got my back like no one ever has. Whether we're messing around on the field, grabbing burgers, or just talking trash, it's been a hell of a good time.

Honestly, I don't think I would've made it through half of this year without them. At this point, they feel more like brothers than anything else—not that I'm exactly in the market for more siblings. One Dylan is plenty, thanks. But coming here, that's probably the one good thing my mom's ever done. I can at least thank her for that.

Anyway, I'll stop getting all serious now. Go Wolves!!

KitKat

Dylan

Now

A splash of purple catches on my skin as I continue to put the finishing touches on the canvas, and a familiar throbbing in my head reminds me how long today's been. The sound of *Chasing Shadows* by Alex Warren fills the air as I move to the stereo, my fingers brushing the dial to turn up the music. With a fluid motion, I return to blending the brush into the dark paint, adding another layer of depth to the scene. I take a step back, a faint smile tugging at my lips as I look over the piece. It's nowhere near finished, but the foundation is there, and that's enough to spark a sense of pride.

My brush makes a soft clink as it dips into the water, but my gaze never leaves the canvas. That spark of creativity within me ignites, coaxing me to layer more, to add just one more stroke. It's been too long since I felt this buzz—the satisfaction of transforming emptiness into meaning, of filling the void with something that speaks.

I found myself wandering into a quiet art store downtown after visiting Beckett's grave. What began as a single glass of wine soon became several, and now midnight is creeping up on me.

A sudden flicker of light dances across the room, followed by the unmistakable hum of electricity, before the room plunges into darkness. "Great," I mutter, rubbing my eyes as they struggle to adjust.

I move slowly through the shadows, my fingers brushing the dresser before my body jolts from hitting a chair. "Seriously?" I breathe through gritted teeth, stumbling back. The windows tremble with the wind outside, and briefly, I question if I should have just turned in earlier. But the painting…it was like it was waiting for me.

I stumble toward the nightstand, my hands skimming along the bed for stability. When my leg hits the side, I almost lose my footing. Just as I grab my phone, it vibrates in my hand. I let out a sigh of relief—it's not dead. I swipe at the screen, squinting at the name of the person texting me so late.

Brooks: Hey, just wanted to warn you, there's a pretty bad storm coming in.

Dylan: Yeah, I noticed. The power just went out here.

Brooks: At The Drift? When?

Dylan: No…at my place in New York lol

Dylan: Jk. Yeah & only a few minutes ago.

Brooks: Strange. The backup generator should've kicked on by now. You good?

Dylan: Yeah. Just painting actually. But I think I'll call it a night, nbd.

Brooks: You were painting?

Brooks: I'll head over and check it out.

Dylan: No, don't. I can just go to bed. It's fine.

Brooks: Nah, I'm coming. Be there in ten.

Dylan: You're impossible.

Brooks: You love it. See you soon.

I let out a soft, almost bubbly laugh, the alcohol blurring the edges of my thoughts. His message is still on my screen, teasing me, and I can't help the smile that creeps up. I nibble on my nail absentmindedly, my mind swirling with thoughts of him and this sudden arrival.

Then, it hits me—the excitement building in my chest.

Wait. What the hell? Am I…giddy?

I need to distract myself.

My hand fumbles for the lamp, but the room stays inky black. Duh, no power. I slip off the bed, switching on the flashlight from my phone. The narrow glow cuts a path through the dark, guiding me back to the canvas. The faint light stretches over the painting, casting odd shadows, but there's a strange power to it now.

Typically the paint tends to settle, its boldness fading as it dries, but tonight it holds. It feels almost alive, breathing with energy, or maybe it's just the play of light, but it's magnetic.

Time slips away unnoticed as I stand there, until a knock stirs me. It's light, but thoughtful, like he's unsure whether to disturb the quiet. As I open the door, Brooks steps inside, shifting the weight of a large cardboard box in his arms. I flick the flashlight off in a rush, realizing too late that I'd been unintentionally spotlighting him like a deer caught in headlights.

"You finally picked up a brush again," Brooks says, his smirk widening as he steps inside. "No way I'm letting a blackout ruin that. I brought reinforcements."

"It's just paint, Brooks." A breath of amusement escapes me as I tilt my head. "I'm not sure it's worth all this."

"Some things are worth any excuse to show up. You're one of them." He bypasses me, his shoulder brushing mine, and places the box on the table with practiced ease. "Generators aren't cooperating though," he continues, glancing at me over his shoulder. "But candles? Candles I can do."

It's ridiculous—I forget to move, my focus caught on the way his dimples threaten at the edges of a grin as he rummages through the box. The candlelight carves shadows along the sharp lines of his jaw, flickering over the faint scar above his brow—the one I always forget about until I'm close enough for it to matter.

"Pretty sure this violates at least three safety codes," I mutter, mostly to myself. He doesn't acknowledge it, just keeps arranging candles, each flame dancing to life under his careful hands. The light spills outward, creeping into the corners, casting restless shapes along the walls.

"You focus on painting—I'll handle the potential fire hazards." Brooks says, smirking.

"Oh, so you're a firefighter now?" I cross my arms, watching as he flicks the lighter again, another candle catching.

"I contain emergencies of all kinds," he says, straight faced. "Structural, emotional, mildly inconvenient power outages." He gestures toward the room like he's unveiling a masterpiece. "See? Crisis averted." The final wick catches just as Brooks' gaze finds mine—and in an instant, the room feels smaller.

Rain lashes against the glass, a steady drumbeat against the windows. Brooks moves toward me, about to speak, but then his attention veers. His gaze drawn toward my painting as if it pulled him in without permission.

A strange vulnerability settles over me, as if I've poured too much of myself into the image without meaning to. The storm rages on, but it feels miles away, drowned out by the way Brooks takes in every detail—each line, each shade—as if deciphering a language I thought only I understood.

Swirls of violet and obsidian paint bleed into one another forming a horizon that blurs like a dream slipping away. In the heart of it all, a woman stands on the precipice of a jagged cliff, her figure caught between the wild sea and the unruly sky. Clouds coil and rage above as tendrils of the girl's hair dissolve into slivers of molten light, fracturing the shadows that cling to her.

His fingers flex once before stilling, a muscle in his jaw tightens. He doesn't have to say a word—I know when something hits him. And this? This has landed square in his chest. He leans in slightly, drawn to the rocky foundation she stands on. There's something almost reverent in the way his eyes move over it. I can nearly see the realization settle in. She isn't bracing for impact. She's holding firm. Resilient.

"You didn't just paint this on a whim. You said you haven't touched a paintbrush since you left. Something broke through—what was it?"

The name sticks to my tongue like glue, but I push it out anyway. "Beckett." My heart pounds furiously, and there's a weight lifting with every beat, a rhythm I haven't felt in years settling into place.

"I've seen you in a lot of ways, but I think this is the closest I've ever been to seeing you completely," he murmurs, taking a slow step closer. "Dylan, you…"

His sentence dissolves, his eyes catching on mine. His focus dips to my mouth, and instinctively, my tongue darts out, a motion I don't even register until it's done. Maybe it's the way the storm sings against the walls, the cabernet blurring the sharpness of my thoughts, or the way this painting is spilling my secrets. But the way my body responds to him, the way he shifts something inside me—none of that can be blamed on the weather or the wine.

The distance between us fades so naturally I don't decide to touch him—I just do. My fingertips skim over his stubbled jaw, following the slope until they reach his lips. His lips part beneath my touch, and I take my time tracing their shape, like I'm etching this moment into memory.

Brooks takes my hand, his touch light as he tilts his head, finding my palm in a kiss that feels more like a confession than a touch. The heat of it seeps through my skin, curling through me so slowly I forget to breathe.

My body molds to his as if it was always meant to and his free hand finds my back, holding me there, like I might slip away if he doesn't keep me close. *This isn't a dream.*

His touch ignites something deep inside me, every inch of my skin hypersensitive. His lips brush mine, featherlight, but then he stops—hovering in the space between caution and surrender.

I see it now, plain as day—he's fucking starving for this, and I'm the feast he's been denying himself. His grip isn't careful, it's possessive, like letting go would break him in half.

Ten years ago, I left. I thought I could sever this connection between us, but the way he touches me now, makes it clear I never really let him go. His hands on me rewrite the past, erase every year I spent pretending this wasn't inevitable. I am his, always have been, and I don't have it in me to fight it anymore.

"Dylan, if this isn't what you want, you need to tell me now." He growls the words against my lips, a plea wrapped in a command, as if the effort to hold himself back is killing him.

My fingers push beneath his shirt, greedily mapping the hard planes of his stomach. His breath stutters, hot against my skin, and it's a goddamn miracle I can still speak. "I fucking need this."

"God, Dylan." His voice drips with sin, a languid, tantalizing game as his fingers skim the edge of my satin shorts. When our lips finally meet, it's an unrelenting collision, the kind that demands to be felt in every cell.

I ease back, and his eyes—green, endless, impossible—snare me. They glow in the dim light, something eternal, something I'll forever know in my bones.

His pupils go dark, blown wide as he drags both my shorts and underwear lower, fingers skimming over the lace that's already ruined for him. "Fuck," he rasps, his voice vibrating with need. "You have no idea how many times I've dreamed of this. Of you."

I fumble with his belt, my hands clumsy with urgency. His hips shift, pressing into me, and I swear I nearly whimper at the contact. He chuckles, the sound rich and infuriating, but when his hands move to help, I don't push them away.

His breath is uneven as I slide down the last barrier between us, releasing him. A hand in my hair, a sharp tug at my scalp, and suddenly I'm turned, his body caging mine against the slow burn of the room. His fingers splay over my neck, the inked branches on his wrist stark against my skin, my pulse hammering beneath his grip.

He takes a step forward, silently urging me to match his movement, and I blink, suddenly aware of the mattress's edge grazing my knees. My pelvis clenches as his length swells behind me, and I rock against him eagerly, gasping at the feel. Instinct takes over, my hand grasping his wrist where it's wrapped around my throat, wanting nothing more than to feel him even closer.

His stubbled jaw grazes my shoulder, teeth scraping lightly over my skin. He tastes me with the hunger of someone who's waited too long, and I want to lose myself in it. His mouth finds my ear, breath scorching as he whispers something that has my nails digging into his skin like I might never let go.

"Every. Damn. Dream. And now, I'm *not* wasting another second."

With a guttural growl, his grip finally releases, and in one smooth, calculated motion, he bends me over the bed—like I was always meant to be here. With him.

33

Dylan

Now

A broken gasp tumbles from my lips as Brooks' fingers slide along my skin, one hand pressing firmly into my lower back, securing me against the bed. The other trails slowly up the inside of my thigh, a taunting path that makes my legs part instinctively. I forget to breathe as his lips leave a trail of heated, wet kisses down my spine, and my back arches eagerly.

Every kiss, every movement, sets my body alight. The world seems to fall away, leaving only him. I try to focus, but my brain feels like mush. It's maddening. The intensity between us flares with every shift, every inch of contact, as if he's drawing out tension in me I didn't even know existed. I can't think straight. I can't even catch my breath.

Lips press gently against the back of my thighs, and a shudder runs through me like an electric jolt. I want more, need more, but I can't move, can't force myself to reach for it. His teeth graze over my sensitive skin, and a soft gasp that escapes me without my control.

I shift, just enough to glance back at him, but his deep green eyes catch mine. For one heart-stopping second, everything stills. He looks at me like he's memorizing every detail, then his gaze drops lower, roaming over my exposed flesh. It's methodical, as though he's studying every inch of me. I can't help but ache for whatever comes next.

"The last thing I want to do is rush this."

Sliding from my lower back to my hip, his hand tightens, shaping crescent-shaped imprints on my skin. He pauses, letting my anticipation build, his breath feathering against me. "You move," he warns, his tongue darting out just enough to send a wave of desire through me. "I pull away. So be good for me—just this once."

The wait is agonizing, the suspense coiling inside me like a spring wound too tight. I've been nothing but broken pieces for years, but with him, it's like I've got a shot at being whole again.

A moment passes, and when I feel his lips return, my body responds with a deep pulsing, hungry for his touch. I remain perfectly still, holding my breath until finally, *finally* the soft, silky sensation of his tongue sweeps up the length of my center.

Ecstasy floods my veins as his fingers follow, sinking into me with expert, intoxicating precision. He curls them, pressing deep, tracing patterns with an almost devastating finesse that leaves my hands clutching the bedsheets. My body is a bowstring, pulled past its limit, quivering with the need to let go.

A strangled moan catches in my throat as his teeth nip lightly at my clit. My thighs tremble, a violent shudder tearing through me as the pleasure builds, overwhelming, impossible to contain. Against my own protests, my hips buck back into him, begging, searching, *pleading* for the release I'm suddenly craving.

I'm insatiable, reveling in the feeling like I'll never get enough. Every stolen year, every unspoken truth we buried, feeds the hunger thrumming beneath my skin.

It's primal, urgent—years of pain crumbling in an instant. I need this. I need *him*.

He clicks his tongue. "Greedy little thing," he muses, withdrawing his touch just as I start to chase it. "I give you one simple instruction, and here you are, squirming for more." I shift, trying to steal another glance at him, but the candle's glow betrays me, showing only the movement of his silhouette.

"Stand up," he orders. It's not harsh, but it's an unmistakable command. I push myself up, gradually turning to face him. The fabric of my cami slides against my skin as I tease it up over my body, tossing it aside with a tantalizing movement. I roll my shoulders back slightly, watching him, waiting to see if he breaks.

"You're intoxicating," he groans, stepping closer, drawing me tighter into the blaze of his body. His fingers slide over my jaw, tracing, testing, learning, before dipping lower, following the curve of my chest until he finds the soft swell of my breast.

He toys with my nipple, rolling it between his fingers, pulling a sharp whine from my throat. His lips crash into mine, the kiss all consuming as his fingers skim lower, mapping the ridges of my abdomen before returning to stimulate the heat between my legs.

A startled breath escapes me as he hoists me against him, my body molding to his, the rigid length of him pressing exactly where I need it most.

"You don't even realize what you do to me," he growls against my mouth. A heartbeat later, my back meets the mattress, and before I can catch my breath, he's pulling away, a rush of cool air chasing his absence.

The shadows shift, and then the bed dips beneath me as he returns. My hands stretch toward him, but he catches my wrists, pinning them above me as he hovers. A slow glide of leather, a gentle but firm pull. Then the snap of a clasp, *his belt*. I shift, a reflex, but he's faster, his body covering mine, pressing me deeper into the sheets.

"I want to watch you fall apart," he whispers, his fingers pressing into my thighs. "Now be good, spread them wide, and don't you dare finish before I let you."

This *fucking* man.

The intensity of his stare pins me in place, his pupils absorbing every last shade of green. I want to be the reason his self control snaps, the reason he loses himself completely. He doesn't even have to ask. I'm his. I've always been his.

"You gonna listen?" He trails his thumb over my lower lip with a featherlight drag. My mouth parts, tongue flicking out to taste the salt of his skin. The muscles in my thighs loosen, legs widening as if pulled by invisible strings, my head tilting in a slow, deliberate nod.

His thumb glides down the side of my throat, leaving a slow trail of heat and dampness that lingers at my collarbone. "Good girl." His mouth follows, finding the ink first—lips pressing to the B, a kiss that lands too close to grief. "I left when you needed me most. I have to live with that. But Dylan, I swear on everything—I'm here now."

I try to form a single thought, a single sound, but he devours it before I can, leaving no room for doubt.

Torturous pleasure spreads through me as he hooks two fingers inside, summoning an exquisite ache that sends fire licking up my spine. A tremor rattles through my body, toes curling into the sheets as a plea catches in my throat. He keeps me right where he wants me, building the pressure with maddening precision, every pulse of sensation tightening the hold he has over me. My body writhes, but he refuses to relent. "Patience."

If patience were a virtue, I've long since lost it. Ten fucking years spent without him. Just days ago, the thought of this was a fantasy I wouldn't even let myself entertain. But now? Now, he's here, and patience isn't just out of reach—it's a cruel joke, a test I'm doomed to fail.

White musk and amber lace the air, the scent of him settling into my lungs like a brand. I focus on it—on anything other than how he feels against me, on the ache demanding I move. In the next breath, he trades touch for something far more devastating, the blunt head of his cock pushing against my entrance, his chest vibrating with a deep, primal sound.

His pace is merciless in its control, every thrust a promise, a warning, a tease. My vision blurs, my body caught in the sweet agony of pleasure stretched to its very limits.

"Don't you dare," he rasps against my temple. My spine locks, fingers curling so tightly around the belt binding my hands that my knuckles ache, every nerve screaming for release.

He angles my disheveled face toward him just enough to trap me in his stare. "That's my girl." Then he moves, an intentional roll of his body against mine that steals every last thought from my head.

His mouth finds the swell of my breast, every exhale searing against my skin as he buries himself inside me. The stretch, the fullness, the sheer intensity of him is dizzying. I clench around him, lost in the sensation of being so completely filled. The sound I make is pure surrender, my moan echoing between us like a confession.

Brooks stills, and the loss of movement is agonizing. A frustrated cry rips from my lips as I arch into him, seeking friction, seeking anything to pull me from the edge of madness.

"Now, Rivers. Fall apart for me," he commands, his pace never faltering, the sheer authority in his voice sending me spiraling into oblivion. Pleasure crashes over me, consuming me completely, and he's right behind me, his movements turning reckless before he spills inside me.

With deliberate care, he loosens the restraint, the leather slipping away from my skin before he discards it. His gaze flickers down to where our bodies meet, watching himself pull out of me slowly, taking in the mess he's made. The sight seems to draw a primal satisfaction from him, his breath hitching as he watches, absorbed by the visual.

I should feel exposed…maybe even embarrassed, but instead, I feel a strange kind of power in it. The vulnerability of what we've shared, of what he's made me feel. I've never felt more connected to him.

"You should stay." I breathe, searching his face for an answer before he even speaks.

A surge of panic rises within me as I ready myself for his rejection—but it never comes. Instead, his arms envelop me, mending the cracks in the fragile hope I had been holding onto. He exhales against my shoulder, his grip anchoring me to him, like he's afraid I might slip through his fingers.

Beyond us, the night is wild—wind tearing at the eaves, rain hammering in relentless sheets—but under these covers, my body melts into his. I bury my face in the crook of his neck, his hold on me a solid comfort against the storm outside. Exhaustion pulls at me, and sleep becomes impossible to resist.

"Did something happen?"

Brooks' voice presses in, shaking me loose from sleep, my eyes fluttering open. "What?"

The bed shifts as he moves behind me. "You said Beckett got you painting again?"

I track the flickering light from the candles, their glow stretching thin across the room. I chase after my own thoughts, trying to gather them into something coherent.

"Oh. Yeah…I finally went to see him. Spent time with Blake too. My time here has been…messy. But for the first time since he died, I don't feel like I'll break by just being here." I pause, my foot nudging against the edge of the blanket.

"I spent so long outrunning this place, convinced that if I never looked back, it didn't exist. If I stayed far enough ahead, I wouldn't have to feel. Grieving, remembering, even saying his name—I treated it like an open flame, terrified to get too close. But I can't keep living like that, carrying ghosts, choking on everything I never let myself say. And Blake, she just—" I bite my lip, feeling Brooks' fingers comb through my hair, lightly tracing a curl. The subtle gesture, makes it harder to keep my walls up, draws me closer into him.

"Blake is everything I forgot how to be—reckless in her joy, fearless in her love, alive in a way I've spent years trying not to be. Beside her, I felt it—how much of myself I've lost in the name of self preservation."

Brooks doesn't say anything at first. When I finally glance over, his expression is so open, so raw, it makes me want to fall apart and sink into him all at once.

"I wish you could see yourself the way I see you. If you did, you wouldn't just see grief—you'd see strength. The power in the way you're choosing to stay, to feel, to be something more than what you left behind. If you ask me, that's the bravest thing you've ever done."

His words don't rescue me; they don't need to. They just remind me I'm still here. That I never stopped being here, no matter how fast or far I ran. This place, these people—they've lived inside me all along, waiting for me to stop holding my breath.

It starts as the softest nudge, his foot brushing against mine beneath the sheets, a hesitant kind of reach, pulling me in closer. "I'm sorry," he murmurs, slipping his fingers into the spaces between mine.

I frown, confused. "For what?"

"I'm sorry I walked away, Dylan. I know I said that, but seeing you in Maine—after I'd stopped searching for signs, stopped hoping for second chances—felt like the universe had been listening the whole time. Over the years, I stood in rooms full of people, held hands that weren't yours, told myself I was moving on. But nothing ever settled. Every smile felt borrowed, every love story belonged to someone else."

It's not just what he says—it's how he says it, as though fate has already decided this for us.

"I let you go once because I thought it was the right thing. Because I was afraid. But I never stopped loving you, not for a second." His brows knit together, his eyes glossy as he holds back years of emotion before continuing. "And this time, I'll fight. I'll stay. I'll be whatever you need, for as long as you'll have me."

Brooks' heartbeat knocks against mine, steady where mine stumbles. And instead of retreating into doubt, into the past, I do something terrifying—I trust him. I trust that his love never left, only waited. That even in our years apart, his heart still beat in time with mine. A pause isn't an ending, and love isn't something that time can steal.

"The second I walked into The Drift, it hit me—even if I hadn't realized it right away—that I'd spent so long running from the one thing I should've held onto." I give in to the truth, my eyes skimming over him, drawn to the way it settles in his posture. "You. And if I could go back, I'd do everything differently. I love you. You are my home. And I should have understood that wasn't something I could leave behind."

The second his lips touch mine, the world reorders itself, like an artist dragging fresh color over a faded canvas, brightening the lines of my existence. I grip his shoulder, anchoring myself in his solid presence, desperate for proof that this isn't some fleeting dream.

In the moment that follows, we find each other again. We fall back into each other like we were always meant to. The storm outside continues its fury, but here, with him, we make promises to one another. That we'll never be apart again. That nothing will ever tear us from this. We're safe in the certainty of us.

His hands frame my face, thumbs brushing over my cheekbones as he exhales against my lips. "Paris," he whispers, drawing it out like a promise he didn't forget. "If you never made it there, then I think it's about time we change that. If this life has shown me anything, it's that tomorrow isn't guaranteed. I've spent enough of my life waiting. That ends now."

Love has never arrived gently for me. It always came with conditions, with rules or an escape plan. But his voice holds no expiration date, only permanence. He's right, I never made it to Paris. But I'm done holding back. I'm done keeping life at arm's length, afraid to feel too deeply. I'm stepping into it now—into all of it. The dreams I tucked away, the love I told myself I didn't need, the messy, beautiful reality of being alive. I want to feel it crash over me and turn every locked door into an open invitation to the unknown. I want to live like I was always meant to—without fear, without apology. Fully. Freely. *Finally.*

"I never made it. So let's go—no more waiting, no more what-ifs. I want to see the world, chase the dreams I left behind. And I want to do it all with you."

"Alright, then." His wink is quick, almost imperceptible, but I catch it. Just as the edge of his mouth tilts up, the kind of trouble that doesn't ask permission before it takes over. "Let's go...explore."

No more questioning if I'm enough, if I deserve this, if love is something meant for me. I spent years convincing myself that healing was out of reach, that some cracks could never be filled. But here, with him, I don't feel broken. I feel whole in a way that has nothing to do with being fixed and everything to do with choosing to move forward.

Brooks loves me. That love isn't a battlefield littered with losses, nor a coin flipped in the dark. It's a certainty, as natural and infinite as the tide meeting the shore.

I feel like I'm stepping into a life I get to build. A love I get to choose, again and again.

I am not the same person who ran away, who let fear dictate her future. I am here, fully, without reservation. Not because I've outrun the past, but because I've finally stopped letting it define me.

This time, I'm not bracing for the fall.

I'm ready.

"Oh? Stealing me away already? I must be special."

Epilogue

Dylan

One Year Later

H*i KitKat,*

I know it's been a year, and for the first time, I'm actually not calling because I miss you—I mean, I do, I always will—but because I want to tell you I'm okay. I made it. I'm living again.

I thought I had to keep calling, as if holding onto your voice would keep you here. But I know now—I don't need to say your name into the static to know you're listening. You're everywhere. In every sunrise, every song, every ridiculous inside joke that still makes me laugh. You never left me. And because of that… this is my last call.

I think you'd like who I'm becoming. I think I like her too. Maybe that's what healing really is—not about forgetting or replacing, but making space for joy alongside the sorrow.

So, guess what?

I'm a teacher now. Can you believe it? An art teacher, of all things. Rockport High needed someone after Mr. Lyons retired, and somehow, that someone ended up being me. Wild, right? But the real surprise? I love it. Every day, I stand in the middle of a whirlwind of color and possibility, watching kids pour themselves into their ideas. I never imagined I'd be the one nudging hands toward creation, but here I am. It's not just a job. It's a privilege. One I never expected, never even considered. But now that I have it, I'll fight like hell to keep it.

You probably wouldn't believe it if I told you, but a few months ago, Brooks and I went to Paris. I still can't say it without feeling like I'm dreaming. I don't know if it was the city itself or the way the two of us fit into it, but something about being there felt like proof that no matter how much time has passed, some people are meant to find their way back to each other.

I saw the Louvre, Beckett. It was overwhelming, but in the absolute best way. I stood in front of The Winged Victory of Samothrace for what felt like hours, tracing the arc of her missing arms in my mind, wondering if she felt incomplete or if she had transcended the need for wholeness.

At the Musée de l'Orangerie, I sat in front of Monet's Water Lilies, letting the ethereal blues, moody purples, and lush greens consume me. The brushstrokes weren't perfect up close—messy, layered, chaotic—but when I stepped back, the image softened into something infinite. It made me see my own life as a series of jagged strokes on a canvas—chaotic up close, but maybe, from a different angle, something beautiful could take shape.

Oh! I also got Brooks a vase. Not because I'm sentimental, but because I owed him one. The Drift's lobby used to have a perfectly nice one—until it met an unfortunate, tequila-induced demise at my hands, or more accurately, my stomach. So, in the spirit of redemption, I scoured Paris for a worthy replacement, set it in the lobby when we got back, and watched as Brooks' expression flickered from irritation to reluctant amusement. I think we're even now.

Now, we're sort of living together. And honestly, KitKat? It feels unbelievably right. I left my apartment in New York without a second thought. For a while, I stayed at the hotel, giving Brooks and me time to relearn each other. Not that we ever really changed.

Then, one night, one conversation, and suddenly, I was moving in. I teased him that he just wanted to make more money off the room he was practically giving me, but we both knew better. It wasn't about money or convenience. It was about us. Reclaiming something we lost and making it ours again.

Now, here we are. The way everything has fallen into place—it's almost eerie. I can't remember the last time I felt this secure, this sure of where I'm supposed to be. Probably not since you were here. I don't know. My life, my choices—even my heart—are mine again, no longer claimed by grief.

I see Blake a few times a week, and every time, she's grown—not just in inches but in confidence. She talks more, laughs louder, and when she dances, she lights up in a way that makes my heart explode. She lives for it, and I never miss a chance to take her, to sit and watch as she moves like the music is part of her. She commands the studio with the same ease you had on the field. And though I miss those bleacher seats, I wouldn't trade this view for anything.

I'm not chasing some perfect version of happiness anymore. I'm just here, now, letting life happen instead of bracing for the worst. It's freeing, terrifying, and completely necessary.

Mom's still sober, every day she chooses that fight, and I'm trying to meet her where she is. I don't know what our relationship will look like in the end, but I know this—she's trying. And that's something.

After today, your number won't ring. Your voicemail won't catch my words—but I'll never stop talking to you. Your heartbeat shaped me before I even opened my eyes. I'll love you past forever, Beckett—even when time forgets us.

Death can't rewrite that.

Acknowledgements

Y'all…I wrote a book. I *wrote* a book! It still doesn't feel real. Writing has always been a part of me, but it's never been a constant. It came and went throughout my life, like a friend I'd see when I needed them most. But I never truly took it seriously—not in a way that made me believe I could one day write something like this. Now, here I am, with a dream I never fully dared to chase, turned into something real.

Until Forever Falls wouldn't exist without a handful of extraordinary human beings who keep me upright when I'm spiraling, remind me to eat when I forget time exists, and somehow never block my number despite the amount of unhinged text messages I send.

They've all shown up in ways big and small—sometimes with advice, sometimes with snacks, and sometimes just to listen. I don't know what I did to deserve it, but I do know I'd be lost without them. From the bottom of my chaotic, over-caffeinated heart—THANK YOU!

First and foremost, to **Brittney, a.k.a Bitty Pie**—my partner in literary crime. I can't thank you enough for your friendship. From the very first draft to the last soul-crushing round of edits, you've been there—cheering, scolding, dragging me through the creative trenches, and, most importantly, never letting me wallow in self doubt.

Without you, this book would still be a collection of half formed ideas. Instead, it's real, and that's largely because you *never* let me quit. So, from the deepest part of my soul: THANK YOU!! I owe you the world. Or at least an ungodly amount of pickles, brownies, and ice cream—because I know asking you to choose just one would be a crime against your indecisive soul. I love you!

Kali—Bestie, listen—I don't care where life drags us, you're stuck with me forever. We could be on opposite sides of the world, living completely different lives, and you'd still be the yin to my yang. Just knowing you're out there, cheering me on, makes me feel unstoppable. You're family, no matter what, and I adore you endlessly.

I want to take a moment to honor your brother, Tyler—a soul I never had the privilege of knowing. Some people leave such an imprint on this world that even those who never met them can feel their presence. Tyler is one of those people. Through you, I've come to understand just how deeply he is loved, missed, and forever part of your heart. I've watched you navigate the waves of grief, seen the quiet moments of ache and the incredible strength it takes to keep going. I hope Beckett and Dylan's relationship spoke to you, because in so many ways, you and Tyler are written into their story. I love you, always.

R.I.P. Tyler Sapp Dec 28th, 1991 - July 10th, 2016

Mallory, a.k.a Mally Mouse—My Taurus queen! Back in August 2024, you quite literally lit a fire under me, dragging me out of my procrastination pit and shoving me toward greatness (or at least toward getting my act together). We bonded over Love Island—because obvi, PPG—but more importantly, I gained a fierce no-nonsense tell-it-like-it-is friend who keeps me accountable. Your honesty is a gift, and I will forever treasure having you in my corner. ILY!!

Janine—You stepped into my life with the heart of someone who's always been there, and I'm in awe of how you go above and beyond for me—someone you crossed paths with only once in Vegas. It's a rare, extraordinary thing to find people with such pure selflessness, willing to drop everything and help without a second thought. From the deepest part of my heart, thank you. You are an absolute miracle in human form.

Katy—Oh how I adore you! Seriously, you were one of the first people to read my manuscript, and I still can't believe you took the time out of your crazy busy life to help me out. Between being an amazing mom and working nonstop, you somehow found a way to fit me into your schedule. You're the definition of a friend who shows up, and I can't thank you enough! Love you, Katy Bug!

Camie—You are the absolute sweetest! The way you hyped me up, loved these characters like they were your own fictional children, and blessed me with A+ text messages? *Unmatched.* Thank you! I owe you my sanity (what's left of it, anyway).

KamBria—Thank you for always being a voice of encouragement, for believing in me, and for pushing me to chase my dreams. Honestly, I don't think I deserve a sister like you. No matter what life throws my way, you've been there for every major moment—despite not growing up together. You're a treasure, and I'm SO incredibly grateful for you. I love you so much!

Chelsea—Thank you for being my compass in the wild world of becoming an author. Your general brilliance has saved me more times than I can count. I'm so grateful for your friendship and your willingness to guide me through every ridiculous question I've thrown your way. You're an inspiration!

Mackenzie—I know life can be an absolute whirlwind, so the fact you took the time to dive in and beta read my book is incredible. Your comments were seriously invaluable, and I'll never forget the effort you put into it! I appreciate you!

Jenn—Thank you for making time in your busy schedule to help me wrangle this messy manuscript into something readable. Your patience, insight, and keen eye made all the difference. I'm endlessly grateful!

Kate—Thank you for bringing Brooks and Dylan's story to life with this cover! Your talent captured their world in a way I never could have imagined! Thank you!

A huge shoutout to **Ember Literary PR** and **Grey's Promotions** for your support and guidance in helping me navigate releasing my debut novel—I couldn't have done it without you! Thank you SO much!

Readers who take a chance on this story—thank you, thank you, THANK YOU! You have my deepest gratitude. This book has been a dream of mine for as long as I can remember, one that always felt just out of reach...until now. The fact you're here, reading these words, breathing life into this story? It's something I'll cherish forever!

For so long, books were my safe haven, my way of making sense of the world. Now, to be the one creating stories that might offer you that same refuge? It's nothing short of surreal. It's everything I've ever hoped for and more.

Whether you're here for the romance, the angst, or just a moment of escape, the fact that you chose to spend your time with Brooks and Dylan means everything. Thank you for taking this journey with them—and with me.

Saving a few of the best for last—my husband, our four wonderful boys, and my dad—where do I even begin? **Garrick**, thank you for being my rock, my safe place, and the person who never questions why I talk about fictional people like they're real. Your love and support are my lifeline, especially when I'm spiraling into the abyss of my own mind. You are the reason I don't completely lose it. **My boys**, you are my greatest adventure. Life with you is chaotic, loud, and absolutely perfect. Thank you for making me laugh when I need it most, and inspiring me every single day. I hope you always chase your dreams the way you've watched me chase mine. **Dad**—thank you for believing in me even when I didn't believe in myself. Your support has been constant, even when I had no idea what I was doing. Thank you for always being there.

I love you all, infinity.

There are certainly people I've likely missed in this list, but please know that your encouragement is the fuel that keeps my fire burning. Whether you've been with me from the start or cheered me on along the way, I am immensely grateful to each and every one of you. Thank you for being part of this story, and for helping make this dream a reality!

About the Author

Micah Riley, a former photographer who once captured love stories through her lens, has traded her camera for a pen—or more accurately, a keyboard. Now, she brings small town romances to life, creating characters you can't help but root for as they navigate life's twists and turns, only to discover love when they least expect it.

A self proclaimed coffee addict and daydreamer, Micah has found her passion in writing stories that remind readers of one simple truth. Sometimes, love really is a little magical.

Trigger Warnings

I believe in creating a safe space for all readers, and I encourage you to read with care, knowing that you have the power to step away if anything feels overwhelming.

<u>You are not alone.</u>

Intimate Scenes & Sexual Content

Parental Alcoholism

Emotional Neglect & Familial Struggles

Childhood SA (Referenced, Not Detailed)

Grief & Loss (Off-Page Death)

Cancer Diagnosis & Illness